MORRIS AUTOMATED INFORMATION NETWORK
0 1029 04715
P9-CLE-831

In the Name of Friendship

Other Books by Marilyn French

Fiction

The Women's Room (1977)

The Bleeding Heart (1980)

Her Mother's Daughter (1987)

Our Father (1994)

My Summer with George (1996)

Nonfiction

Beyond Power. On Women, Men and Morals (1988)

Women in India (1990)

The War Against Women (1992)

A Season in Hell. A Memoir (1998)

From Eve to Dawn. A History of Women. Volumes 1–3 (2002, 2003)

In the Name of Friendship

Marilyn French

With an Afterword and Bibliography
of Marilyn French by Stephanie Genty

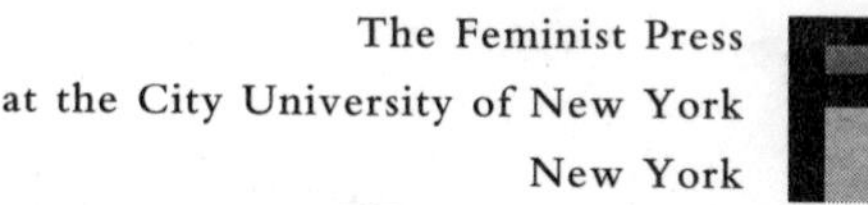
The Feminist Press
at the City University of New York
New York

Published in 2006 by the Feminist Press at the City University of New York
The Graduate Center
365 Fifth Avenue
New York, NY 10016
www.feministpress.org

Library of Congress Cataloging-in-Publication Data
French, Marilyn, 1929-
In the name of friendship : a novel / by Marilyn French.
p. cm. — (Classic feminist writers)
ISBN-13: 978-1-55861-520-5
ISBN-10: 1-55861-520-2
ISBN-13: 978-1-55861-521-2 (pbk.)
ISBN-10: 1-55861-521-0 (pbk.)
I. Title. II. Series.
PS3556.R42I6 2006
813'.54—dc22

2005032142

Acknowledgments:
The author is indebted to the following for permission to reprint excerpts:

"The String of Pearls," by Jerry Gray, copyright ©1941, 1942 Mutual Music Society, Inc. Renewed and Assigned to Chapell & Co and Scarsdale Music Corp. All rights reserved. Used by permission.

"April in Paris" by E.Y. "Yip" Harburg and Vernon Duke, Published by Glocka Morra Music (ASCAP), Administered by Next Decade Entertainment Inc. All rights reserved. Used by permission.

This publication was made possible, in part, through the support of Johnnetta B. Cole, Jan F. Constantine, and The Laurence W. Levine Foundation, Inc.

Text and cover design by Lisa Force.
Printed in Canada

13 12 10 09 08 07 06 5 4 3 2 1

Contents

Chapter 1 1

Chapter 2 14

Chapter 3 29

Chapter 4 39

Chapter 5 55

Chapter 6 69

Chapter 7 84

Chapter 8 101

Chapter 9 119

Chapter 10 136

Chapter 11	150
Chapter 12	166
Chapter 13	184
Chapter 14	198
Chapter 15	211
Chapter 16	224
Chapter 17	243
Chapter 18	258
Chapter 19	275
Chapter 20	294
Chapter 21	309
Chapter 22	326
Chapter 23	340
Chapter 24	354
Chapter 25	368
Afterword: The Writer As Thinker	383
Bibliography of Marilyn French	404

1

"Things are entirely different for women today," Maddy said. She twisted in her seat, a tall large-bodied woman of seventy-six with short brown hair cut smartly to frame her long face.

"Yes," Alicia agreed. "They're lucky." Alicia was fifty, with pale skin, a delicate face, and a halo of curly black hair.

"Not they, you!" Maddy protested. "Your generation was the one that fought for liberation! What were you—eighteen?—in 1968? You were part of the Vietnam generation, one of the love children, the pioneers. The ones who started the second wave. I remember it! I already had teenaged children by then."

"Well, but I was a good little Jewish girl," Alicia said with chagrin, "and I knew nothing about what was going on. I was much too afraid to experiment sexually. Jenny is the only one of us who grew up sexually free."

The women were sitting on Jenny's porch, comfortable in wicker chairs piled with cushions. The electric heater that edged the floor sent out warmth that condensed on the windows walling the room, fogging their view of the mountain. The trees were bare, their branches gray brown, without foliage, so the waterfall showed, white ruching on a wall of rock.

"It's true," said Jenny, a short blond woman of thirty. "I never felt sexual constraint. We did what we wanted, me and my friends. Or what we thought we wanted. But you know, everything has a cost. There was a lot of pressure on kids to have sex, boys and girls. And some of us were too young for it, and it made us miserable. My boyfriends of those days . . . it doesn't feel right to call them lovers—my early . . . experiences . . . were sort of unpleasant—you know, crude, quick, almost furtive. Abortive. Boys are so hot with lust but also so guilt-ridden! There's something wrong with the way boys mature. For all their sweetness, there's something furtive, dirty, in their way of seeing sex. And of course they were inept."

"I think so too," Emily put in. "Nobody prepares them for sex. All of a sudden their bodies betray them—well, the way ours do too when we start to menstruate—but at least we're prepared for that. And people, someone in our lives, tell us it's normal. Whereas boys suddenly find this organ that hangs on the front of them has a will of its own and, at night sometimes, embarrasses them to death by wetting the bed. And no one knows it's happening to them, and no one tells them it's normal and doesn't mean they're monsters."

"Even if someone does," Maddy sighed, "they probably still feel bestial. They already know control is the name of the game, and they don't have it. So they blame girls for what happens to their bodies: Girls control it, they don't.

"Still, Jenny's generation was better off than ours. At least they learned. My generation was told that sex was something that came naturally, that you didn't need information about. Good grief, information about it was taboo! Well, desire may come naturally, but technique doesn't. You need to learn, and we didn't, not even the men. So even when we could have sex, after we got married, we didn't know what we were doing. A little experimentation would have helped. Of course, a few people experimented: like Emily." Maddy turned to her with an evil smile.

The other two turned, smiling, to the woman in question, a slender pale woman of seventy with light brown hair worn in a bun.

"Emily? Really?"

Emily laughed. "You see?" she said to Maddy. "I have such a schoolmarm image, they don't believe you!"

"What is this!" They grinned accusingly. "Emily with a secret past?"

Emily and Maddy laughed. "She was a sexually liberated woman back in the fifties, the dark ages!" Maddy proclaimed.

Alicia and Jenny crowed, "Congratulations!" But puzzled, they waited. Emily, the introverted artist, the one who lived alone, who had never, as far as they knew, had a partner, the one people considered a dowdy spinster? That Emily?

She laughed ruefully. "I was far enough away from home that I could dare to be free. But you know, the fifties were the dark ages, no matter where you were. I had sexual encounters, which is more than most women had then, but I can't say I experimented sexually, because after all, I was screwing the boys of my generation—who were as uptight as we girls were. They thought the expression 'Bim, bam, thank you, ma'am,' was hilarious, and that's how they fucked. Really. Oh, lots of girls slept with someone they loved, got pregnant, and married in humiliation, beggars with babies in their arms.

"No difference really from ages before—just like all those girls in fourteenth-century English and Scottish ballads, girls standing in the cold outside the castle with babies in their arms, weeping, begging, and cruelly sent away. One day pretty soon nobody will understand those poems. It'll be like reading a foreign language. That wouldn't be the worst thing in the world, I guess. I mean, it would be good if that never happened again. But it would be sad to lose the ballads; they're really moving. Anyway, that didn't happen to me. I had a diaphragm and used it. But men were so . . . full of guilt and fear that they made love fast, desperately, really. They didn't seem to know that they could make it pleasant for their partner. They saw women so narrowly . . . they never quite lost their sense that a woman they could screw without marrying was cheap, a whore, or that a woman they married felt sexual desire. Whatever they said, they really believed that good women stayed virgins until marriage. I'd bet anything that in the end the men I lived with married virgins."

"But you had adventures!" Alicia exclaimed greedily.

"I lived with a few guys. Duncan in Philadelphia and, later, in Rome; Douglas, and later Phil, in Boston. I was with Duncan for four years, Douglas for two, Phil for a year or so. Funny thing is, they're all famous now. Duncan Scott is a famous pianist; Douglas McHaig is a famous oboist, probably the top oboist in the world, although most people don't know the names of oboists. Funny, two Scots. And Phil Ferrutti is a conductor, he's well known, he's in Pittsburgh now. Three lovers, that's all. Three lovers is hardly anything nowadays, when girls think nothing of having fifty, sixty . . . They don't even bother to count.

"None of them ever wanted to do anything kinky, none of them seemed to imagine anything but the ministerial position, and all of them really, really wanted head. They really preferred not to enter the vagina, and when they did, they all had orgasms almost on contact! They didn't seem even to know that I wanted one too. If truth be told, I was always my own best lover."

The women howled.

"Probably true of lots of us," Alicia agreed sadly.

"Not me. I never could manage it," Maddy said. "Couldn't figure out how to do it. Emily told me what to do, but it just didn't work for me."

"Jesus, Maddy! Another deprivation!" Emily cried, and the women laughed again.

•

It was a Saturday in March and the women were having lunch at Jenny's house. They were friends and got together regularly. They were more than friends: They needed each other. Alicia declared that her friends kept her sane. Jenny said they were the only people in the world who made her feel like a grown-up. Maddy, a plainspoken woman who nevertheless expressed feelings obliquely, did not discuss her friends, but uttered the phrase "my women" as if it were a sacred term. Emily one day realized with some wonder that the voices of her friends were the only human voices she could really hear, those of other peoples touching her ears with the ring of tin or copper, sounds she sometimes grabbed at trying to catch the brass ring before it disappeared, but of no more importance than the stuffed animal that was the prize. In Emily's sound world, most voices were no more important than wind, branch, cow bellow, goose chatter, church bell, or the insistent cry of a bird at sundown like a rusty hinge on a screen door screaming E-sharp–B-flat.

Jenny's house was modern, which was unusual in Steventon, a New England town settled in the seventeenth century and dotted with colonial and Victorian houses. Jenny's husband, the artist Tim Halliday, had designed the house himself and was proud of it. The living room had a soaring ceiling and glass walls; dramatic sculptures from Botswana and Mali and Côte d'Ivoire stood in silent sunlit spaces on the parquet floors of rooms large enough to skate in. Tim had planned the steeply slanted roof; the twenty-foot-high glass walls in the living and dining rooms; and the balcony, cantilevered over them, holding the huge master bedroom and bath, with a Jacuzzi and whirlpool bath. He had designed the two studios, a large one for him in an old barn on the property, a smaller one for Jenny, connected to the house. He'd laid out the house with an eye to the placement of each piece in his collection of paintings and sculpture, garnered over thirty years. The furniture was spare and austere, with beautiful lines. Overall, Maddy (the expert on houses) thought, the house lent itself more to aesthetic considerations than human ones: It was beautiful but uncomfortable. But that was true of all really modern houses, high-design houses. Give her a nineteenth-century house anytime, for comfort, for livability. But she did not say this to Jenny.

Actually Jenny thought the same thing, but the house was not hers; it was Tim's, and she sensed that Tim would be humiliated at living in anything less than a cutting-edge house. In the city, they had lived in a loft with a fanciful wrought-iron circular staircase leading to a sleeping platform, a staircase so treacherous that when Jenny moved in, she complained until he installed a railing. He didn't want to do it: He said it would ruin the lines. But she would not mount the staircase without a rail, and he very much wanted her to mount the staircase. Jenny knew Tim had a horror of being bourgeois, but having been born in the sixties, she wasn't sure what bourgeois meant. She tried to analyze the living spaces of people he or his friends sneered at as bourgeois. For a while, she thought it might mean having a decent kitchen, but Tim, who liked to cook and did it well, had a large, well-equipped, convenient kitchen in his loft, and included one in the new house. Later, she decided that *bourgeois* meant "comfortable." But she enjoyed comfort herself, and she tried to find it around the edges of his designs, in the interstices, in hidden corners.

His cry of pain when, during the planning of the house, she asked for a screened porch, informed her that bourgeois definitely meant having a screened porch. It would ruin the line, he cried, it was old-fashioned, a vestige of the past that would mar his masterpiece. It was, he almost wept, bourgeois. This house, he argued, was a twenty-first-century house. No, no, absolutely no. It almost wrecked their marriage, Jenny told her friends, laughing. In the end, she got her porch, tacked on to the same side of the house as her studio, so it didn't show from the front. Tim had built these rooms on the outside of the house so they could be removed without ruining the stone and redwood exterior. He told Jenny he had done this to increase the salability of the house, should he ever want to sell it. The back of the house was omitted when it was featured in *Architectural Design*.

But he did build her porch for her, one with a gorgeous view of the waterfall behind the house and with electric heating and glass panels. And he let her furnish it herself—for which she was grateful. She bought cushioned wicker armchairs, good reading lamps, a sofa bed, a glass table, and even a footstool. Talk about bourgeois! She lived on the porch, except in deepest winter, and it was on the porch that she entertained her friends, turning on the electric heat to fight the March chill or basking in the perfumed air when warm weather came and the glass panels were removed and she could smell the flowers that grew all around it and hear the waterfall (an amazing roar from such a narrow cascade) and the birds and the wind through the leaves and watch the hummingbirds flit in the bee balm.

•

"It's so beautiful here," Emily said. They all agreed, as women often do, in little sighs and cries, faintly uttered yesses, contented smiles, creating a music of acceptance. The room was warm, even in the cold New England March, and they leaned back in their cushioned chairs, replete with food and drink, warm, feeling wanted, accepted. They shared without speaking a sense of companionable well-being.

Their meetings were not formal, they were not a club. They called their group "the women," as if it constituted the entire female sex. And the truth was, they felt something like that; pressed, they might declare that their friends were genus *Woman* at its most intense and real and interesting, what all women would be in an ideal world.

They had met today to celebrate Lady Day, March 25, for centuries the first day of the year. Emily knew this from her work with Renaissance music; music for Lady Day was devoted to the Virgin. They liked the idea of a day named for a woman, even a symbolic one. It had become one of their private holidays, their New Year's Day. They had other holidays: They celebrated the birthdays of Emily Dickinson (December 10) and Emma Goldman (June 27). Maddy, the only one of them who was church-going, had suggested Lady Day after she learned of it from Emily. Emily, who since her youth had admired her namesake, whom she considered America's greatest poet, urged the women to celebrate Dickinson's birthday as the day of magical sound, word and note. Alicia wanted to honor her heroine from college days, Emma Goldman, so they celebrated Goldman's birthday as Revolution Day, a day for dancing. When Jenny joined them, she wanted a heroine too. She had become interested in Eleanor of Aquitaine while watching *The Lion in Winter* on television one late night. She began reading about Eleanor and was awed by the woman's powers, her daring and courage, her sexual freedom, her stubborn willfulness, her endurance. She offered Eleanor as her celebrant, but no one knew when she was born, not even the year, only guessing at 1122. Alicia suggested they use a date in September (since they had no holidays then); September 12 was Jenny's birthday so they chose that date. Their holidays were roughly coincident with the solstices and equinoxes, which pleased them. And this March, they were celebrating not only the start of the year 2000, but also Jenny's sale of a painting, her first to a major collector.

Instead of sipping tea, their usual drink, they were toasting Jenny with champagne. They clinked glasses, hailed her work, told her she was great. She knew they really liked her work, and she was pink with pleasure. Of course, she knew that Maddy knew little about art, and that Alicia and Emily could not be regarded as experts. But their love of her paintings was not feigned, and that, after all, was all she wanted from life: that people get pleasure from her work, that they find it beautiful. She did not want to be a revolutionary force in art, just someone who made beautiful things, things to be loved.

All the women admired Jenny. Maddy thought her life ideal—here she was, married to a handsome man with money, who supported her, and did the cooking to boot! She could paint all day if she chose. And now she was successful! And besides this, she was pretty and young. What more could anyone ask?

Alicia was especially pleased at Jenny's sale, feeling that Jenny must succeed if she were to hold her own in her marriage. To Alicia, it seemed that Tim's fame hung over his and Jenny's marriage like a canopy, casting Jenny in shadow, just as Steven's intellect shadowed Alicia. She saw Jenny as a little furtive, glancing behind her at every step. She wondered if, if Jenny had a child she would gain power in the marriage. But after thinking about it, she decided that the economic dependency children generate for women was men's strongest hold over them.

Emily did not think about Jenny's life beyond the fact that she painted. For Emily, to have the right and the power to dedicate oneself to one's art was the central, if not the only, desideration in life. Jenny had it, ergo Jenny was happy. And Emily liked Jenny's work. This was deeply satisfying to both Emily and Jenny. So hard to be friends with an artist whose work you didn't like, Emily thought.

Jenny herself liked that Tim was famous and rich and not jealous, a trait some former boyfriends had unpleasantly displayed. She did not think about costs; she had been raised, as girls still are, to believe that she could find Prince Charming, marry, and live happily ever after, and that was what she was doing. She did not understand the sense of dread she was increasingly carrying with her—not where it came from or why it stayed. There was no reason for it, she told herself: Her life was perfect.

•

The conversation moved from Jenny to art to Jenny's house to houses generally, a popular subject in the Berkshires.

"Whatever happened to the deMarco house?" Alicia asked Maddy. "Did that rock star buy it?"

"No," Maddy said. "He wanted more privacy. More land. They're looking east of here, in South Mill and Trent. But a nice couple of bankers bought it, two women. For weekends. They're music lovers," she explained.

Emily perked up. "Really?"

"Oh, not your sort, Emily. They like Tanglewood, they like the Berkshire Chorus, but you might find them musically illiterate . . ."

"Oh," Emily replied, subsiding.

"Well, Steven enjoys Tanglewood," Alicia put in, speaking to the crestfallen Emily, "and you know what a music snob he is," she smiled.

Emily sent a wicked smile in Alicia's direction, tacitly acknowledging a liberation in her friend, who could not have said that about her husband ten years earlier. "Well, why not? They do some wonderful things there," she admitted, then paused. "Chamber music," she announced after a moment.

Maddy listened skeptically. She had been burned many times by assuming someone was on Emily's musical level, and she was wary of her friend's unpredictability on this subject. "Well, I guess Emily's a musical snob too," she said amiably.

They all laughed, including Emily.

"Yes. When Steven and Emily are together, Steven's the one who can't keep up."

Jenny whooped. "Steven? Bettered? I don't believe it!"

Alicia's face developed a strange expression.

"What's wrong?" Emily said.

"Oh! Nothing. Jenny said 'Steven bettered,' and my mind just went off . . ."

"To? . . ." asked Jenny.

"Stevie's coming up this weekend. With Neil."

The room hushed.

"That's good!" Maddy declared. "Good."

"Yes," Alicia agreed reluctantly. "I guess . . ."

"How long since he's been up to see you?"

"Three years. I see him in New York, whenever I go down. Trouble is, I don't go down much anymore these years. Since I moved up here full time. Before, when I was in the city during the week, Stevie and I often had lunch, and once, when Steven was in Atlanta at a conference, he and Neil and I had dinner. But Steven hasn't seen Stevie in three years."

"How is it that he's coming?"

"I invited him. With Neil. I told Steven I was going to do it, and I did it. I told him, It's been too long. He didn't say anything."

"And what do you think?"

"I don't know. I hope it will be all right. I pray it is. But I can't be sure. I don't want them embarrassed. Steven can . . . you know . . . he could humiliate Neil easily. It's so easy for him to be difficult. Supercilious," she added, with a little extra energy.

They refrained from comment. Into the silence Emily offered, "Why do people feel that way, do you know? I mean, about gayness. I think about my parents; they would have been horrified to learn about my life, but they would have died of mortification if someone had said my father's cousin Agnes was homosexual. They would have denied it absolutely. It was a category outside their experience. They took it for granted that she lived with another woman only because she couldn't find a man to love her. It was acceptable for two women to go on trips together, to go to the movies together. But it never occurred to them to invite Millie to holiday dinners, and Agnes never demanded it. Of course, Millie had a family of her own."

"In my family too," Maddy said. "My mother's cousin Sarah climbed mountains."

"She did?" The women laughed triumphantly.

"That's what she liked to do. All year long, she worked for the board of education in New York City, and summers she went mountain climbing. She climbed in the Alps, mainly, but she also went to Alaska and the Himalayas. She lived with another woman, for most of her life. My family always spoke about her with pity as a spinsterlady, without a sexual life."

"Yes, in that generation it was easier for gay women to be accepted," Alicia agreed, "if not men. Now, people demand acceptance . . . Stevie wouldn't be willing to pretend he was just a single man. He wants to be recognized as living with his lover."

"So many people have problems with that," Maddy said. With eight siblings of her own, and her husband's four, almost all of them close, she had a village of relatives as examples. "When Dickie Lapp—Charley's sister's son—came out, in the eighties, the family went into a state of shock. They haven't spoken to him since. He doesn't exist for them."

Alicia's eyes filled with tears. "Oh!" she cried.

"Yes. It's particularly sad now because Dickie has AIDS. Not one of them will speak to him. Charley and I invited him and his friend up for a weekend, and I invited his whole family. Not one of them showed up. Luckily my family is big enough that the void wasn't glaring. Except to him, of course . . ."

"How cruel! How sad! I won't let that happen! I'm going to make Steven accept Stevie!" Alicia said fiercely.

"How can you do that?" Jenny wondered.

"I don't know, but I will. I have to find out the root cause, you know? I mean, what could be strong enough to make you reject your child, your baby, the child you love? It has to be something profound and, maybe, unrecognized."

"But Steven's a shrink. Don't you think he'd know what's going on in his unconscious?"

"Oh, psychiatrist or not, Steven knows nothing about himself!" she said sharply—then heard herself and added, in a softer voice, "Not about this, anyway."

"Is there anything we can do to help?" Emily asked.

"If there is, I'll ask for it."

"Listen, if he's in a bad mood this weekend, you call us. We'll come over and jolly him up! You know I can always jolly Steven up," Jenny laughed.

"You do!" Alicia laughed too. "He loves you! I'll call all of you to come and wave your magic wands. Turn him into a benevolent familiar."

"We'll sing," Emily said. "Enchant him. I have just the song! I wrote it for my *Hansel and Gretel.*"

"I'll dance," said the ungainly Maddy. "My special fairy dance." She stood up and demonstrated, first waltzing while humming the *Blue Danube* then moving into the flamenco.

The women howled.

As their laughter waned, they wiped their eyes.

•

"The new year begins," Maddy said softly in the silence. "Now." She pointed to the maple trees behind the house. "You see that reddish tinge in the tree bark? That always appears in the spring in maple trees. I think of it as blood returning to the tree's veins in preparation for spring. It makes me understand tree worshippers: The trees really are living beings." The sky was a very pale blue, almost white, broken by puffball clouds, and they gazed out at the distant mountain and the many shades of purple and beige in the tree trunks; the disparate greens of pine and fir needles; the bare branches of apple, oak, chestnut. They were only asleep, Maddy thought. It was a day of peace in nature; the women could feel it sigh as it turned over for another month of sleep.

The women sighed, and turned over in their minds. They looked around the room as if newly awakened, and reached out for handbags, shawls, eyeglasses. They prepared to leave. As she rose, Emily mentioned she was giving a concert at the college in May, and the women pulled out their pocket calendars to record the date. Alicia offered to hold a party afterward, to celebrate the occasion.

"We'll have—well, all of us, of course, and the men, and Clea—if—will Clea come in for it, Em?"

"Oh. I don't know."

"Get her to come," Alicia said energetically, then continued with her list, "And the dean, and the head of the music department, and whoever else you want. You make up the list from the school and any music people in the area. Everyone's welcome to invite someone. It'll be a buffet, so we can have as many as we want. You don't eat before a concert, do you, Em? No, of course not. I'll have finger food, and sushi and tacos and lasagna and stuffed grape leaves. Stuff like that."

"Wonderful!" "Terrific!" "Great!" the women cried as they prepared to leave. They stretched out the leaving process, embracing and chatting one-on-one for some time before they got their bodies out the door. When they were gone, Jenny leaned back against the door, a blissful smile on her face.

2

Jenny waved to Alicia until her car disappeared around the curve, then stood a moment longer in the driveway. Her smile lingered on her face as she reentered the kitchen. Debby Dew looked up and saw it and smiled back, thinking, What a nice woman she is. Jenny smiled more broadly at Debby, not realizing that Debby's smile was inspired by her own. She felt warm, embraced by Debby as well as her friends.

She leaned against the counter. "The lunch was delicious, Debby. You did a beautiful job."

Debby grinned. "I'm glad. I'm just sorry I didn't know how to do the cream for ya. But I watched ya. I'll do it the next time."

"Sorry to be so fussy, but it makes a difference."

"I know! I tasted it. It's amazing, the same cream, just whipped with a different tool and it tastes different. I never knew that."

"I didn't either until I met Tim. You know he's pretty fussy about food," she laughed, and Debby laughed and rolled her eyes. That was all right, Jenny knew: It wasn't serious criticism. Men were allowed to be fussy about things.

"Yeah, I'll never forget him teachin' ya to make that sauce for your company the first time I cooked for ya. Hours it took ya. I cooked the whole rest the dinner and you was still makin' the sauce."

They both laughed.

"What was it called again?"

"A reduction."

"A reduction," she repeated uneasily. "I never seen a thing like that beater you used on the cream . . . what do you call it? A whip?"

"Wire whip."

"Well, it just whipped it right up, didn't it?"

"Maddy taught me how to do it. I was too embarrassed to ask Tim to teach me. He always whips the cream when we have it."

"Yeah, Maddy, she's a great housekeeper. She's famous for it. But I'm a better cook," Debby said forcefully.

"You're a great cook. Listen, Deb, don't worry about whipping cream," Jenny smiled. "I don't mind doing it."

"Well, it sure takes a while."

"It does," Jenny said ruefully. "Deb, I'm going to work. I'm leaving your money here on the counter," she said, pulling some bills from her purse.

"Thanks, Jenny. I'm just about finished here. Everything put away except the silverware. I'm still countin' it. You be needin' me again this week?"

"Saturday. Tim's invited some people from New York."

"What time? The usual, around five?"

"That should be good. Dinner's at eight. If Tim thinks we need you earlier, I'll call you."

Jenny went into her studio. Tim's studio, a former barn that had stood on the property for years, had a soaring ceiling, high glass walls and a shining wood floor. Jenny's studio was smaller. (He had explained that this was because he did big paintings, eight or ten by four or five feet, or more. They did not fit into most living rooms; he had to sell mainly to museums, which was okay because museums always wanted to buy them. Jenny's canvases, on the other hand, were two by three or even smaller, and she had sold her first one only last week.) But he had put a glass wall and shining wood floors in hers too.

Galvanized by her friends' acceptance, Jenny was eager to start a new painting. She painted representationally—fruit, houses, vegetables, interiors. What she cared most about was light, color, and solidity. But today she had a desire to paint her friends, four women's figures together, sitting, standing, or dancing, she wasn't sure. She sat on a bench and stared at the wall. Maybe they should all touch each other, make a daisy chain, a circle of life. Maybe they should form a circle of dancing women, like the Graces. But people might think she was copying Picasso, doing an homage of *Les demoiselles d'Avignon*, or imitating Matisse. She'd get killed for that. People would say, How dare she? A mere woman. And indeed, she felt that herself—how dare she compare herself to Picasso or Matisse? Anyway, that wasn't the feeling she wanted: Her women weren't like Picasso's, sexual with a fierce galvanizing power. Nor were they like Matisse's women, Graces, the music of life. Her women were life's solid essence, what made the world keep going eon after eon. They would have opaque faces, and their bodies would be squarish shapes lighted from the left, giving shape to the world. Maybe they should all stand. Or all sit. Maybe Emily and Alicia should sit, and Jenny lie in front of them on the floor. Maybe only Maddy should stand. Maybe she should be behind them, to the left, like a guard. Guardian. Old guard. They would get successively younger. Jenny would be like a baby. Yes. She liked that idea.

She slipped on the old shirt of Tim's that she wore to paint in and began to nail stretcher slats together, musing about size. Bigger than usual, she thought, not as big as Tim's, of course, but bigger than usual for her. Maybe five by three and a half. Or four by four.

Tim might think she was imitating him if she started painting bigger.

She paused. Tim's face when she told him that Harold Rothschild had bought her painting.

Tiredness hit her in a wave, overwhelming her. Shrugging, she tried to shake it off.

Rectangle or square? Should the women make a wreathe within a square?

No. That would turn them into ornaments. Four important figures. Each important in itself, but also constituting a group. A group of pillars. Four by four. Yes.

She stood there, swaying a little, then let herself down into a rocker and sat rocking back and forth, her arms folded across her chest, holding it tightly.

Why am I so tired? I did hardly anything—just ran to the market in the morning for the fish so it would be fresh. And bought flowers for the table . . . nothing in the cutting garden this time of year. Debby made the pastry, the sauce, cleaned the strawberries, made the salad. I set the table and whipped the cream . . .

She stopped trying to figure out why she was tired and let herself feel it. She had felt such energy a few minutes ago. Where did it go? Why did it dissipate like that? She pictured the women laughing in the doorway and smiled. Maddy was so . . . calming. Like she'd been through everything. She must have been a wonderful mother. Jenny wished again she'd had a mother like Maddy. She wished she'd had a mother at all. Her mother was a faint scent of powder, a flash of turquoise silk. How I cried when I unearthed that turquoise housecoat from the old trunk when we were packing to move to Darien. Dad wanted to toss everything. I must have loved her, to cry like that. I must have missed her. I must have cried a lot after that for years. In high school, Mr. Blazej asking me why I was always crying. Not unkind. I tried to stop, I never cried in school again. It was hard, pressing my lips together. Always frightened, always losing things, never knowing where I was supposed to be. A ditz, really. I'm still a ditz. I hide it but Tim probably knows. Can't hide things from the person you live with. But he loves me anyway.

She let herself down onto her studio daybed.

Maybe because I'm not all that bright. I don't understand why I did so well in school. Maybe the teachers felt sorry for me. They knew Dad was never home: Our house was so quiet. Dad never spoke to me. No sounds in the house at all except the TV. Even after Cheryl moved in. She didn't like me at all. Oh, who knows if she liked me or not. I didn't like her. I never gave her a chance. But I was thirteen then, and they'd forced me to go to Darien. I hated Darien. I still hate Darien. Still, my adult life began there. If what I've lived is my own life. Maddy says she lived someone else's life until she was fifty. But whether my life was really my life or not, it was what I had, wasn't it? I became popular. Always out. Silent house. Two can play at that game, Father. Silent days, silent nights.

It wasn't bad, compared to some childhoods I've heard about. Some people go through horrors as children. Incredible how some people treat their children. Jillian Rose's mother abandoning her, Dave MacAllister's drunken angry father hitting him with a belt all the time, Lily Bergreen's mother tying her wrists to her crib slats . . . What stories! So common they've become clichés: Horror mothers, horror fathers are the rule. Yet they survived, Jillian, Dave, Lily. Compared to them, I had nothing much to complain about, except I still feel so . . . I just felt alone. Unloved. It can't have harmed me much, though. You get over it, grow up. When do people grow up? I'm still a baby, I just pretend to be grown up . . . I don't know anything. When will I? If I ever had a child, how could I love it? Would I love it?

Overcome with weariness, she let her head fall back against the pillow. Oh, okay, she thought, I'll nap for twenty minutes.

She had been looking forward to painting all day . . .

She reached for the afghan at the end of the daybed, pulled it over her body, and fell instantly into a deep sleep.

•

The four women could not articulate what brought them together. They were of different ages and backgrounds; the only things they seemed to share were being female and living in Steventon, in the Berkshire Mountains of Massachusetts. Only Maddy ever went to church, and she didn't seem to care which church she went to—the Lutheran or any other Protestant sect. Emily and Alicia were political progressives—Emily claimed to be an anarchist. Maddy and Emily had been born in the area; Maddy had lived there all her life. Emily had grown up there, left at eighteen, then returned at forty. Alicia had grown up in New York City; she had arrived twenty years ago, in 1980, as a summer resident.

Yet after only three years, Jenny felt she knew them better than anyone in the world. Maddy Gold, the oldest, was seventy-six. She came from an old New England family, the Thaddeuses, and was the oldest girl in a family of nine children. She had attended local schools back in the days before Berkshire parents sent their sons to college, much less daughters. She loved to read and was the best student in her class of four in the local school—her main claim to distinction, she was fond of saying. She had read every novel in the local library by the time she was fourteen and was given permission to use the library in Winchester. Berkshire high school graduates went to work after school—boys on the family farm, in a mill, in the gravel pit, or on a delivery truck (most still pulled by horses then), girls in the Steventon Dairy or at an inn in South Mill or Trent, as maids or waitresses. But Maddy was an outstanding student, and when she was graduated in 1941, she took the tram (long since defunct) to Winchester to a job as a secretary in the town's sole law office, Willis and Gold.

She took her job seriously, but had no training for work in a law office. In those days, out in the country, legal secretaries were unheard of, and Maddy had to become one without tutelage. She learned some law, but mainly she learned to be efficient. She soon perceived that practicing law requires strict adherence to a calendar of dates for filing papers and making court appearances and became invaluable to her firm by keeping scrupulously clean calendars and sweetly but insistently nagging the men to their duties. She was in the peculiar position of a slave holding a whip over whimpering overseers who made four or five or even six times her salary of ten dollars a week.

Lister Gold's son Charley was studying law in Boston when the war broke out in 1941. He immediately enlisted in the air force, and was sent to Officer Candidate School. He was trained in bases all over the States and in 1943 was sent to England to make bombing raids over Germany. He was a hero, an ace, but he hated the war and buried it deep in his memory when it was over. By the time Charley was mustered out, finished his last year at the law school, and joined his father's firm, Maddy was the office crackerjack. Charley, whose powerful mother had rendered him a little passive, was new to law practice, and he found himself depending on Maddy's knowledge of procedure. He leaned back and easily relaxed into her strong embrace. They married when Maddy was twenty-two, in 1946.

In the next years, the Golds had three children: Thomas, Lily, and Parrish. Maddy devoted herself to them and to Charley, maintaining an immaculate house and a huge vegetable garden. She shared its bounty with her friends and put up the surplus, as countrywomen did in those days. She made all the curtains, bedspreads, and slipcovers for her house, and most of the children's clothes. She was famous in the area as an exemplary housewife.

Her last child, Benjamin, was not born until 1967, when Maddy was forty-two. Once he was a teenager, Maddy began to sell real estate. She studied for a license, opened her own agency, and was now the top real estate salesperson in the area, and a rich woman. Charley retired in 1985, but Maddy, full of energy and strength, still ran her agency with an easy command. The Berkshires, once known for beauty and remoteness, had developed into a center of culture and was considered a highly desirable area by people in New York and Connecticut seeking a second home. In that arena, Maddy Gold was central, the one who knew everything and everyone.

Jenny adored Maddy. Maddy was the mother—or grandmother—she'd lost, the mother par excellence, Jenny thought. Maddy had been involved in the raising not only of her own four children, but also of innumerable nephews and nieces. Jenny wished Maddy had been her mother. You could ask Maddy anything. Not only did she always answer, but she always answered honestly. Straight-speaking, no-nonsense, direct, Maddy was a breath of fresh air, Jenny told Tim.

•

Emily Oldfield, of the Oldfields who had built Steventon, was born in the house she lived in still, built in 1792. Maddy and Emily had known each other when they went to the Morton Street School, in 1935 a two-room schoolhouse for grades 1–12 (total student body, thirty-six). Emily, six years younger than Maddy, entered first grade as Maddy started sixth. The eleven-year-old was taken with the intense little girl. Emily was a serious child who seemed attuned more to her own thoughts than to the world. Maddy, the oldest girl in a family of nine, had resentfully tended, one after another, her younger siblings, and she had no interest in caring for another child.

Emily appealed to Maddy in some deep way, perhaps because she seemed self-sufficient. She did not need tending; in some odd way, she tended Maddy.

Maddy, dark haired, with skin as white as paper except for a rose blush in her cheeks, was physically vivid, whereas Emily was "tan." Years later, Maddy tried to explain her impression of Emily's "tanness" to Emily, who said sarcastically, "You mean I'm a beige person." "No," Maddy insisted, "tan. Gold, really, but not shiny. A dull gold I call tan. That kind of beige." Emily's skin was beige, her hair was a paler beige like gold, her eyes a tan like maple syrup; she was a monochrome vision, tall and bronze, like an ancient statue of a goddess.

They were always together, best friends, these ill-matched girls, one tall and sturdy and forthright and outgoing, the other less tall and with delicate slender bones, shy and silent. When Emily wasn't practicing the piano (which she did for an hour a day even at age six), they took long walks with Maddy's dog, Panther, on the mountain trails nearby. When Emily got older, they spent afternoons at the library in Winchester, avidly reading eighteenth- and nineteenth-century novels, and any modern ones the library had, and on Saturday afternoons they went to the movies.

When at twenty-one, Maddy got engaged to Charley Gold, fifteen-year-old Emily pouted, claiming that Maddy was abandoning her—it was true that Maddy was spending less time with her. Maddy promised she would never leave Emily, no matter what. They would always be best friends, she vowed. And in the end, it was Emily who abandoned Maddy. When Emily was seventeen, her father came out of a long stupor to announce that he wanted her to study further, that he believed in her talent. He had heard of a school in Philadelphia, Curtis Institute, that he wanted her to attend. She was eager to go, and in 1947, after being graduated from high school, left for Philadelphia. Maddy saw her when she came back during the holidays in 1947 and 1948, and in June 1948, when Maddy married Charley Gold, Emily, in pale blue satin, walked down the aisle with her as maid of honor.

But then she won some prize and went to Rome in 1949. She wrote Maddy occasionally; Maddy knew she'd returned from Europe in 1953. But she did not come back to Steventon; she stayed in

Boston, teaching at a conservatory there. Letters were rare, and Maddy felt that Emily was gone from her life forever.

In 1967, Emily's father died and Emily came back for the funeral; afterward, she returned for good. Maddy told Jenny that Emily's return was for her a blessed event, a miracle. Jenny thought this must be because of the loneliness of a place like Steventon, remembering how alone she'd felt when they first arrived there.

Emily was unusual among Steventonians because she had lived in Europe, but since she rarely spoke of her past, or her time away, people forgot her sojourn abroad. She was the same as ever, people said complacently. She seemed comfortably settled in her time and place. Even with Maddy, who almost immediately returned to her position as intimate friend, Emily rarely spoke of the past.

Emily taught at the Browning School, a college in nearby South Hills. She taught piano, cello, and flute; harmony and theory; and orchestration. She gave concerts at the college a few times a year to raise money for the music department. No one reviewed her concerts, and her reputation grew only locally; but because of Tanglewood, the area drew musicians, and she developed a small devoted following. It was vaguely known that she composed, but she was such a lady that people assumed her work must be ladylike—that is, sentimental—and automatically dismissed it.

In 1980, Emily's youngest brother, Martin, and his wife, both doctors in California, were killed in a plane crash. Their thirteen-year-old daughter, Clea, came to live with Emily, bringing conflict and new ideas into the older woman's life, animating and grieving her. Clea had remained for a few years, then went to boarding school, then college. She was grown now, a woman on her own, and, for mysterious reasons, estranged from Emily. This was a tragedy for Emily, Jenny sensed. But she wondered how a girl of thirteen, who'd lived with Emily for only a few years, had become so important to her. Jenny didn't think much about it because Emily never spoke of it. It was the others, Maddy and Alicia, who would refer to it sotto voce, out of Emily's hearing or presence. For Jenny, Emily was miraculous: Her compositions were wonderful, her playing brilliant, and her occasional sarcastic remarks stimulating. Emily looked at things with an odd slant, like no one else, and she said things no one else would say. She was always a surprise. Jenny cherished her.

•

The first time Jenny saw Alicia was after a concert, when Jenny had lined up to congratulate the pianist, Emily Oldfield. A woman ahead of her on line embraced Emily upon reaching her, catching Jenny's attention. She was fortyish, with smooth olive skin, and was wearing a good wool jacket and skirt, a cashmere sweater, and pearls, all in browns and beiges. A beige cloche covered her head, except for some smooth, dark hair at the sides. The woman's exotic looks contrasted with these clothes, which Jenny associated with Darien WASPs. And the next time Jenny met her, at Emily's tea, Alicia's hair was wild and curly, haloing her head. The lively hair brought out a brilliance in the eyes, a kind of awareness or eagerness that contradicted the WASP style of dress and manner. This contradiction continued to characterize Alicia for Jenny—a quiet, understated manner, soft voice, and polite smile, under which lay a vivid driving force.

Of all her new friends, Alicia was the one Jenny was closest to. Alicia, who was fifty now, really could have been Jenny's mother.

Alicia Gilson was one of the many city people who had discovered the Berkshires in the affluent eighties. When she was thirty, she suggested that her husband, Steven; their two children, and she go to hear music at Tanglewood. Steven frowned. The mere thought of schlepping a picnic lunch, chairs, a blanket, and toys through muddy fields injured his dignity. And then sitting among a huge crowd of the great unwashed, who would leave chip bags and empty bottles cluttering the lawn, and who would no doubt clap after the first movement, would compound his humiliation. Beyond that, the place featured symphony—not his favorite musical form. Alicia remarked mildly that it also offered chamber music (albeit on a different evening), but her main argument was that it would be an easy way to expose the children to serious music. Steven cared about his children's cultural development. So in August 1973, they went to Tanglewood en famille.

Since Steven regarded as frivolous all music after Brahms but before Ives, all French and all Russian music except Prokofiev and Shostakovich, the Sunday-afternoon concert was a trial for him. They heard a Tchaikowsky symphony (treacle); Berlioz's *Symphonie fantastique* (undisciplined romanticism); and a Beethoven piano concerto played by the latest winner of the Tchaikowsky Prize, a young virtuoso (all technique, no soul). Still, whatever he thought of the program, Steven appreciated that the afternoon had in fact been pleasant, that the chamber music on Wednesday evening had been brilliant (the Tokyo quartet had played Schubert, Haydn, and Mozart, his composers), and the children well behaved. Their Sunday-afternoon picnic of salade Niçoise (purchased at a local emporium) was elegant and delicious. His fear that schlepping stuff would make him feel like a peasant became moot as he found himself among so many men who looked like professionals but were also carrying coolers, chairs, umbrellas, and even tables, which were later set up with lace cloths and candles. The children were adorably eager to carry what they could and seemed to enjoy the music and the day. He thought he saw on their fresh dewy faces the glow attendant on exposure to great art. He announced that it was fun, a rare word in his mouth.

After this success, Alicia was able to persuade him to go up again. It was closer than the Cape, less crowded than the Hamptons. He began to think it might be a good place to spend August, his month off, and they idly gazed about for a place to rent. He was even willing to drive aimlessly around the countryside, past farms, forests, and mansions hidden behind greenery—the landscape enchanted them all. The kids would cry out, spotting some splendid house that suddenly soared into view at the top of a hill. Delighted to be with the father they so rarely saw, they were well behaved even at the Clark Art Museum in Williamstown and at a dance recital at Jacob's Pillow. Together, the family walked in Winchester and fell in love with the town.

So it was not Alicia's doing that they happened to be driving down that country lane and admiring that house, which, startlingly, had a *FOR SALE* sign. It was not at her behest that they stumbled in and bought it as if it had been waiting for them. They would spend weekends in it, they said, all of them high with excitement about the beauty and quiet, its difference from the Upper West Side of Manhattan.

Alicia had been born and brought up in New York City, first in the Bronx, later in Manhattan. A child of immigrants fleeing European horrors, she did not remember her father, who died when she was three. Her mother later remarried a prosperous man with his own business, who moved them to an apartment on Riverside Drive. He agreed to send Alicia to college, to Hunter, where she majored in history, planning to teach. But at a family party, she met Steven Gilson, a psychiatrist eight years her senior, and was impressed by this brilliant, sophisticated, elegant man. They married on her graduation, and she thereafter at his wish devoted herself to him and their apartment, also on Riverside Drive.

They bought the house in Steventon in 1980. Alicia explored the area, filled with buildings as historic as any in the United States, and found in herself a powerful hunger. She wanted to know everything about the Berkshires; she wanted to possess the history as if it were her own. She wanted it to be her own. After their first summer, she decided to write a history of the area. Terrified at her own presumption, she interviewed everyone she could find who was a descendant of the original settlers. In the process, she met Emily Oldfield.

Emily and Alicia drank iced tea together one afternoon. Alicia was profoundly impressed by Emily, the "real thing," she thought with awe, a woman whose forebears went back to the seventeenth century. And Emily was talented and smart and utterly unimpressed by her own background. "My ancestors were dirt farmers, Alicia. They grew what they could in this rocky land, and they stayed thin. Mainly they raised cows. Nothing to brag about." And mine? Alicia thought, saying nothing. You have a past. You know the story. You even have a list of ancestors—a genealogy! Her quiet admiration reached Emily, who didn't understand it, but seeing something deep in Alicia, welcomed her into her silent spaces. They became friends.

When Emily introduced Alicia to Maddy, Alicia saw Maddy as Emily's twin, her fellow native in this beautiful land, another woman with roots and a history. And Maddy too was seduced by Alicia's veneration. Now, Alicia loved them both deeply. They were the women for each other, and for Jenny, too, later.

•

Jenny slept for more than an hour, too long. She woke feeling logy, hot-faced and upset from the nightmare that had mauled her rest. She was a spy, constantly afraid, under constant surveillance, living in a mansion somewhere, yes, Uncle Linney's house. She moved nervously down the curving staircase, but she didn't belong there, she was subversive. Someone was waiting for her at the foot of the stairs, someone who knew . . .

She threw water on her face, then took big strides around the room. After a few minutes, she felt her blood moving again and calmly picked up her materials to build her stretcher. She lay the slats on the floor to measure them, then measured the canvas and carefully took a box cutter to the roll. Four by four, she was sure now, had become sure in her sleep, funny how sleep could do that, you would wake up sure of what you had been questioning before. Slowly, the dream faded; by the time she was hammering the stretcher together, all trace of its mood had vanished.

Funny, Tim hadn't come in today. Most days he came into the house for something to eat or to replenish his coffee jug. Of course, he knew the women would be there today. It was considerate of him, giving her privacy with her friends. He would go out to his studio early, around ten, with his thermos of coffee and some fruit. He usually came back around two for lunch, but maybe today he'd taken his lunch out with him. He had a little fridge out there. Most days he worked until afternoon, then drove into town, did errands at the hardware store or the post office or just meandered around, looking at junk in antique shops, picking things up and laying them down again. Some days he didn't paint at all, but drove down to the city to see his dealer or have drinks with a friend. He was self-sufficient.

She hit her finger with the hammer. Damn damn damn. She jumped around the room a bit, waving her finger in the air, tears in her eyes. She darted into the bathroom and held her finger under cold water. The pain lessened, and she went into the kitchen and in the freezer found a small ice pack, wrapped it in a towel, and laid it on her finger. It was hard to hold there, though. She thought of quitting, just going out to the porch and reading. She had a stack of new books.

At least you ought to get the canvas gessoed, Jenny, she scolded herself, you've done absolutely nothing today.

So she went back into the studio, ignoring the finger, and finished the stretcher. She didn't hear Tim come in and was surprised, when she went back into the kitchen, to find him at the sink, washing shrimp, scallops, and mussels.

"You're here!" she cried. "I didn't hear you come in."

"Yeah. I finished a couple of hours ago. All I could do today. Canvas too wet. I went into town to get stuff for dinner. Saw these pastry shells sitting on the counter, so I thought we'd have seafood en croûte—okay with you?"

She looked at him wryly. "The pastry shells were there because they were leftover from lunch, Tim . . ."

He turned to face her. "You had seafood en croûte for lunch?" He laughed. "So that's where I got the idea!"

"Yes. You asked me this morning . . ."

"And you told me." He gave a low laugh. "What an ass I am."

I would have remembered, if it were you, she thought. How could you forget?

He glanced up at her as if he had heard her thoughts. "It just went right out of my mind."

"No matter," she said lightly.

"I must have been jealous. I love seafood en croûte. Do you mind having the same dish again?"

"It's too rich to have twice in a day. All I want is a salad."

"You sure? I'm sorry. I could make pasta with seafood instead. . ."

"No. It's just as rich. Seafood and cream. Make what you want to eat. I wouldn't have wanted more than a salad anyway. You'll have one with me, won't you?"

"I will." He had put the Brahms clarinet quintet on the CD player and switched on the speaker in the kitchen. Jenny fished in the refrigerator for vegetables, laying them on the counter.

"What are you going to put in it?" Tim asked.

"Oh, I don't know . . . mesclun, red onion, avocado . . ."

"Don't put avocado in mine, okay?"

"I thought you liked avocado."

"I do. But I have to start watching my waistline." He pulled at his pants waist. "Tight. And avocados are pure fat."

"You're dieting and you're having seafood en croûte?" Jenny shook her head wonderingly.

"It doesn't have much cream," he said.

She looked at him. He was studying the shrimp he was peeling. She turned and began to wash vegetables at the other sink.

"What else are you putting in?"

"I'm having fruit—pineapple, pears, and grapes. What do you want?" Her voice had an edge.

He glanced over at her pile. "Uh, asparagus. Tomato, endive. And put some cannellini beans on mine, will you?"

She stopped again and stared at him. He was looking intently at the mussel in his hand. She shook her head, then returned to work on the salad. No avocado, but cannellini beans. Who could understand him?

3

Maddy had picked up Emily and driven her to Jenny's; now, she was driving her home. She didn't like Emily to drive and wished there were some way she could prevent it—she frequently offered to pick up groceries for her or to take her to the market. She thought Emily was a danger to herself and others on the road. Once she told Emily she was always in the clouds and Emily said, "Not in the clouds, no, but maybe in Paradise with Mr. Blake." That was just the kind of thing Emily would say, why some people thought she was crazy. Maddy knew that "in Paradise with Mr. Blake" had to have some abstruse meaning but she refused to show her ignorance by asking.

"What are your plans for this week?" Maddy asked.

"The usual," Emily said. "Lessons, my counterpoint course. It's really fun this semester—great students. The four of them are writing a great joint fugue, for six instruments. What a lark! And I'm practicing for my concert in May, and arranging a student concert at the end of the semester. And lot of the kind of work I hate—administrative work," she concluded. "What about you?"

"I have to usher around some bigwig from Philadelphia, a billionaire businessman. He insists on looking in Steventon, even though I told him he won't want to live here. Not fancy enough. He'll end up in Trent or South Hills, I imagine. But that's the way rich people are. They have to reject something before they can accept something."

"Poor Maddy." Emily smiled, knowing pity would make Maddy respond with spirit.

"Oh, I don't mind, really. I enjoy showing houses, you know that. I'll tell him he won't want the houses I show him, which will make him trust me. Then he'll insist on going to the richer towns. He won't leave me and go to Stella Palmer in South Hills. And I'll sell a house in her territory! Hah!" Maddy exulted. "And if he gets too difficult, I can always tell him to get lost. I love being my own boss. That's the good part, responsibility though it is."

"Yes. At our age, it's kind of a necessity, don't you think? To have some autonomy in work? I'm pretty free too; I do mainly what I want. My department head never tries to boss me around . . ."

"Well, I should hope *not*! He's just a pipsqueak and you have thirty-five years of experience and your concerts that keep the music department in velvet."

"I wouldn't call it velvet exactly." Emily smiled faintly. "More like sheet music."

Maddy laughed. "So, do you want to catch a movie some night?"

Maddy loved movies; Charley did not. So Emily and Maddy had gone together to the movies every week for years. When Winchester's one house ran the same film for months at a time, they would drive an hour to East Hollis; nothing stopped them, not even icy winters. Now there was a multiplex in Winchester, so they had a wider choice. Still, it was sometimes hard to find a movie they wanted to see.

"Sure. What's playing?"

"I don't know. We'll find something."

"Okay. Thursday night?"

"Good." Maddy had driven up the long driveway to the front

door of the Oldfield house and Emily kissed Maddy good-bye and stepped out of the car.

Emily pushed open her front door, which was never locked, had never been locked in its life. Heading straight for the kitchen, she kicked off her shoes, poured a glass of tap water that came straight from her well, and carried it back to her studio.

Her studio was in a wing of the house added by her grandfather, whose household when he was forty consisted of his parents, one grandparent, one uncle, two aunts, and five children. The addition, on the first floor, contained three small bedrooms and a bathroom for the children. When she inherited the house, Emily broke through the walls of those rooms to create one large space with several large windows facing the mountain to the south; she left as they were the two polite windows that matched the windows on the other side of the front door. This room held her piano, flute, and cello, as well as her CD player, her old phonograph and thousands of LPs she still occasionally played and the CDs she'd been gradually accumulating. A computer stood on the desk, but Emily usually worked sitting in a comfortable upholstered armchair next to a standing lamp, with a lapboard over her legs.

Clipped to the lapboard was a pad of staff paper. The top sheet had notes drawn on the first two lines. She sat down and put the board on her lap, then picked up the pencil and began instantly to jot notes on the staves, as if they had been lying in her head waiting to explode out of it, as if she had been thinking about it all afternoon and was getting it down as fast as she could now that she finally had the chance.

As indeed was the case. A musical idea had come to her when Jenny was talking about Tim's cooking, and got a strange tone in her voice, which triggered in Emily an understanding of a problem between Jenny and Tim, which she instantly realized was the problem with her scene. She was writing an opera. In the final scene, a young man is trying to tell a young woman that he loves her, while she tries to tell him what she wants in life. She can't hear him and he won't listen to her. What Emily heard Jenny do was sing in a different key from Tim. The insight flickered in her mind: The singers should sing in two different keys. Now she was rewriting the character Sylvia's song in G major modulating into D minor. She sings that she has a great need to use herself; she feels she has a talent she can use in the world. But Ted, the young man, bursting with love, wants to shower her, overpower her, with passion. He has the idea that passion is all she needs and that he can satisfy her completely (he *knows* he can satisfy himself completely). He wants his passion to incinerate them both, fusing them together forever. He is so taken with this drama that he overrides her voice, singing louder than she does in F-sharp major, which clashes horribly with her key. The dissonance, the overriding—his voice is stronger than hers—makes Sylvia gradually subside. She lets his voice triumph and eventually falls silent.

Emily scrawled the notes hastily; they poured from her pen. She imagined Ted, craving a response from Sylvia but getting nothing, hurt and angry. He thinks, because he has been telling her of his passion for her, that he has been singing about *her*. He laments that he thinks only of her, but she turns her back on him. He says she is cold by nature. She shrugs and walks away. She addresses her dead mother in a prayer, saying that Ted sings about himself alone, that he isn't interested in her except for sex. She desires him but she has a dream of living a shared life, a shared mission. She wanders off from him to stand somewhat listlessly at the edge of the stage. Then, with her back turned to him, she again addresses her dead mother, gradually picking up her theme, singing softly to herself, trying to articulate her vision of life. Ted has fallen silent and now listens halfheartedly, then with growing interest. As his comprehension grows so does her volume, and when she is singing at full voice, he begins to sing with her, *his* theme but in her key. His voice winds around hers as he articulates his vision of *his* life, as he suddenly realizes that his passion for her is part of a larger picture of himself. He tries to make their two visions mesh, and eventually Sylvia turns to him and they fuse in a duet as subtle and delicate as lace, and as powerful as trumpets, winding their voices together, singing two different songs in the same key. Even the dissonances harmonize. It is paradise! This would be the conclusion of the opera. She would finish it this week. She had it in her head. She wrote with fierce concentration.

•

Maddy drove home and parked in the yard near the garage. She went into her house through the back door, to the kitchen. Charley was on the phone in the front hall. After retiring from his law practice, Charley had started a mail-order business, selling tools of various sorts. He ran it from the garage, a converted barn that could hold six cars. Part of his pleasure in starting the business came from working with his hands, which he had always loved doing, when he had partitioned off a section of the garage to make an office. He had a window, a desk, a chair that reclined all the way back, and a storage room heated by an electric bar and lined with walls of shelves piled with his wares. It was his secret delight because he could smoke out there—although he smoked only ten cigarettes a day. He'd go out early in the morning with a thermos of coffee or water or iced tea, depending on his mood and the weather. He kept his office as shipshape as a naval officer's cabin, and the fact that he lacked a single object that Maddy would consider beautiful was restful to his eyes. He had no telephone, which he also found restful. He took so much pleasure in his office that he spent most of the day there, reading two local papers and the penny saver (where he advertised).

The business required little time and brought in small rewards, but he wasn't doing it for the money: After forty-four years of practicing law, he had a full portfolio of investments and an income ample for his needs. Maddy earned a high income, and they both now had Social Security. But he had felt he needed something of his own. The house was his, had been passed down in his family for generations, but it didn't feel like his. It felt like Maddy's house because she took care of it: For years she had cleaned it or supervised Mrs. Clements's cleaning of it; she decorated it, repaired it, thought about it. It was her turf, whatever the deed said. There was a Faulkner story, "The Bear," he'd read in college, that said the land belongs to the one who works it. He had found that true. His office was his.

He was as delighted with each car scrub brush, flashlight, and bucket he sold as if he'd bartered them for a ham or some eggs or a basket of spinach. He preferred barter to money exchange. When he'd first practiced law in Steventon, it wasn't unusual for a farmer to trade him a ham or a lamb half for legal services. Such things felt real in a way that money never did. Most days he went early to the post office for the mail, then sat in his office writing up the orders he'd received—if there were any. He'd pack the boxes for delivery neatly in heavy brown paper and strong tape and carry them to the post office, stopping at the bank to deposit any checks he'd received. He'd return home pink with pride. He'd come into the kitchen through the back door and announce the new sales figures: "Five more this week, Mad!" he'd crow. "That's eighty-five all told so far this month. Eight hundred and fifty dollars pure profit!"

She'd smile at him and say, "That's wonderful, Charley," and he would be satisfied.

Maddy would think, How easy he is to please. Simple things made him happy. She loved that about him. But she wondered if he imagined that he could live on eight-fifty a month nowadays. Once upon a time, of course, one could—up here at least. In the fifties and sixties, that would have been a luxurious income. And maybe even now one could get by on eight-fifty, if you also had Social Security and a pension. But these days, without her income, he'd lose this house, the house of his parents, his grandparents, his great-grandparents and great-great-grandparents. He probably didn't realize that. Maddy, who paid the bills (always had), knew how things were. Taxes had gone up, repairs cost a fortune, and an old house required constant repairs. And there was the gardener and the pool man and the maid and the handyman, not to mention the oil heat . . .

•

"Have a good lunch?"

"Wonderful."

"How's old Emily?"

"Good. She's giving a concert in May."

"Well, that's fine. And Alicia?"

"She's good. Stevie's coming up this weekend. And Jenny was all excited at selling that painting."

"Well, that's fine. Fine women all. Fine women." Charley nodded and wandered back out. Maddy heard the side door close and knew he was going out to his garage office to smoke. He was happy there. He loved his little business. He'd never been an entrepreneur, and it suited him. Maybe that's what he should have been instead of a lawyer, had a hardware store in Winchester, maybe. He'd never much liked practicing law. Maybe he'd lived the wrong life too. But with his father, he'd had no choice. Charley never seemed unhappy, though. He accepted his duty, seemed to think that was what a man had to do. His definition of manliness. She would tell Emily this new thought: How society keeps men quiet. Define manliness as being part of the system, so they have no choice but to join it. Still, Charley had always maintained an even temper, a quiet cheerfulness that made him easy to live with.

She headed for the room she called her office. She had brought home the keys to the houses she planned to show Mr. Harris to save herself a trip to the Winchester office tomorrow. She picked up the list of houses and ran her eye down it. Five houses, none of them right. Not big or important enough. He needed a house like this one, as big as hers. But she wasn't ready to sell. Yet. Although, if she could get the right price . . . But her house wasn't grand enough for him.

She settled in the chair facing her desk and swung around to face the side yard. It was broad; the lawn reached all the way back to the mountain, lined with trees. The children used to play on that lawn. She would sit here and keep an eye on them. It was a sewing room in those days. She no longer needed a sewing room.

She didn't want to leave her house. She loved it, even if it was too big for them now. Seven bedrooms, three sitting rooms, a huge dining room, huge kitchen, porches, pantries, and closets, her office. Mr. Harris could turn one of the sitting rooms into the billiard room he wanted. By today's standards, the house was a little short of bathrooms; there were only two and a half—but he could add more. The Gold house was nearly as old as the Oldfield house, probably built in the 1790s and added onto over the years. It was huge now. Much bigger than Emily's. And while most of its farmland had been sold, it still had fifty acres. All the large old holdings had dwindled. Emily had only about ten acres left.

The house wouldn't be passed on to their kids. In the first place, all the children lived far away. Was that a comment on her? She brushed the thought away. None of them had big families, and none of them wanted to live in an out-of-the-way place like the Berkshires. It upset Charley when she said the kids wouldn't want the house. He hadn't said anything, just frowned and gone out to his office to smoke, but he'd been subdued all night. He hadn't thought about it before, had probably just been assuming that it would be passed on to Thomas as it had been passed on to him. He didn't have any idea that it was too expensive now for anyone but a millionaire to keep up. Of course, Thomas was rich; Lily was too, as was her husband, Parsons. But they didn't want to live up here. To think, generations of Golds had lived in this house, ordinary farmers who never imagined they were living in luxury. They worked very hard and just lived like most folks in those days. Of course, in those days, most folks weren't in the middle class, the way they were now. In Steventon.

Things had changed.

It grieved Maddy that her children lived so far away, Thomas in Los Angeles, Lily in New York, Benjamin in Arizona. Only Parrish had stayed close to home. It had saddened Charley more than he let on when Thomas chose to practice law but not in Charley's practice; Thomas said he liked entertainment law, and for that you had to be in either New York or L.A. He decided on the latter: He loved the climate out there. You couldn't make real money in Steventon, he had said. After all the long cold winters Maddy had gone through up there, she could understand his not loving the climate, but she had trouble comprehending why he needed so much money. Charley had always made a decent living for them in Steventon. And Lily was in advertising, she developed campaigns for companies, for television, magazines, newspapers, radio. She made a lot of money. Maybe *she* was even a millionaire. This thought stopped Maddy cold. Could that be? . . . her *daughter*? It had never occurred to her before, although she knew that Lily's husband, a partner in an investment house, made a lot of money.

They lived in a townhouse in Manhattan's East Sixties. Maddy had only been in the house a few times; she remembered it as very fancy. She hadn't felt comfortable there. And she'd gone out west to visit the boys once, twisting Charley's arm to make him go with her.

They took the train—Charley hated flying. Never got over the war, never got over bombing people's houses. It didn't matter to him that they were German. He felt it was a sin to bomb houses. Maddy's eyes misted. He was a good man. Thomas's house in L.A. was very grand too, swimming pool and tennis courts. He said everybody had swimming pools, but still . . . And Benjamin's ranch in Arizona, where they stopped on the way back from California, was even grander. Sprawled across the land, all stone and glass, rooms two stories high . . . Her children had done well; unlike most of their cousins, they were part of this new moneyed world.

Well, in truth, so was she!

She didn't like thinking about that. She was grateful that Parrish lived nearby. He taught at the local high school and he and Jean came over at least once a month, for Sunday dinner, and invited Maddy and Charley just as often. Maddy also stayed close to Charles, Parrish's son by his first wife, Susan, and to Susan, too, for that matter. God knows it wasn't Susan's fault that the marriage broke up. Charles was a grown man now, of course, almost thirty years old. He was a little bit sad, kind of beaten down, Maddy felt. Parrish had been terribly hard on him. Hated himself, took it out on Charles. Poor child. Her heart curled around him as if he were her son, not her grandson. In her will, she wanted to leave him a little more than the other grandchildren, but Charley said that this was not a good idea, it would provoke jealousy. Still, she was intent on doing something. What she was thinking about now—she'd been talking to Emily about it—was giving him some stocks right away, secretly, so the others wouldn't know. She wanted to make him feel special. Loved. Money was love. Alicia told her that Freud said money was shit, but he was wrong.

But if most of Maddy's children lived at a distance, she did not lack for family. Her eight siblings had produced forty-five children, many of whom lived nearby. And as the oldest sister, a surrogate parent to her siblings, she had become surrogate grandparent to their children. She'd helped raise more of them than she could count. She'd tended them through measles, mumps, scarlet fever, pneumonia, infections, broken limbs, broken hearts, being left back, automobile and motorcycle accidents, even cancer and MS, not to speak of fights with their parents and each other, dropping out of school, getting in trouble with the police, getting into drugs, having to go to shrinks. Amy was almost a daughter to her; Matthew was almost a son. As were Mitchell, Fleur, and Toni.

So many years of parenting had made her tired. In fact, she felt tired right now. She'd like to lie down now, but she had to bake a couple of pies. Amy and Don and Mitchell and Lou and their three kids were coming tonight; she had a big dinner planned, and she needed to make some dessert. She bustled into the kitchen and put on her apron, a huge wraparound garment that covered her sweater and skirt. She went downstairs to the cold cellar and gathered up some apples, then dug in the cellar freezer for the blueberries she'd frozen last fall. She pulled out butter, flour, and sugar and began to make the dough for pies. She turned on the radio, which was permanently set to the classical music station in Poughkeepsie. She hummed along with the music—it was Mozart—as she kneaded the dough, then rolled it, and laid it in a buttered pan. She put the two pie plates in the oven and began to peel apples. She could make a pie in her sleep; she knew exactly what she was doing and found pleasure in it. Thank heavens. Her poor mother had had to cook for ten people every day and night and hated it. Like poor Charley, having to practice law every day of his life for forty years. Thank heavens the world had changed and people could choose their own lives. Imagine that! A revolutionary concept! Choosing your own life!

4

Parking her car in the driveway, as she always did, Alicia realized that she no longer felt the least twinge of guilt about it. Everybody left cars in driveways nowadays. Steven, of course, always confined his safely in the garage, but he'd finally given up nagging her. Entering through a door in the garage that led to the laundry room and kitchen, she felt a rush of pleasure at the house. She paused and closed her eyes to let herself feel a moment of gratitude to the fates for letting her have such a lovely life.

"Steven? Hi," she called.

His voice came from the study. "Home, dear? How was your luncheon?"

She walked to the study door. He was listening to music, following the score—the Brahms Alto Rhapsody, Marion Anderson singing.

"Lovely. Did you play tennis? Or was it too cold?"

"No. It was cold, but once you get running around . . . I beat Tom," he gloated. "Twice."

"Good! That must be worth a dinner at the Harvard Club."

"Exactly," he smiled, pleased with himself.

She went over and hugged him, then walked to the hall leading to the bedrooms, stopping at the closet that held her gardening clothes. For a week she had been itching to clean up the herb bed behind the house. It was filled with debris from the winter, and she wanted to plant it as soon as the threat of frost had passed. Today was the perfect day—not too cold, some sun. The day was half over, and she in no mood to study; gardening was the answer. As she walked into her bedroom she began removing her silk shirt and pants. She drew on soiled jeans, a sweatshirt and a quilted jacket and headed outdoors like a soldier charging an enemy, marching to the toolshed for rake and hoe, hand shovel, gloves, and wheelbarrow.

Her life had not always felt so lovely. Even now, sometimes it felt bad, like a stomach that was slightly clenched. But years ago it had felt bad all the time, a sour stomach and tight chest that never went away, even though she loved Steven, loved her children, and they were never in want. Still, she felt . . . what? Defeated? Impeded? Stoppered. Like a Chinese girl with bound feet who wanted to run and jump but couldn't, for the pain. She wasn't sure why. Even now, her happiness had some thorns in it—Steven's attitude toward Stevie, for instance. Unresolved, it made her angry with Steven. Over the past years, Steven had changed. He was far less supercilious and arrogant than he had been at first; he made an effort to see her, to listen to her. That was why his response to Stevie made no sense; he had changed enough that he should not be taking it this way: He knew better, for god's sake, he had gay patients. Gay was okay as long as it wasn't his son? It made no sense to her and she had no tolerance for it, yet she had to be forbearing to prevent Steven from humiliating Stevie or Neil, or embarrassing himself. And her.

He just didn't seem to be able to help it. Deep prejudices. Set in what Emily called "the reptile brain," the part that doesn't change, doesn't evolve. Like the brains of the older male chimps who never would wash the sand off the bananas. Old males, stubborn. Was that in the genes?

Bending, Alicia lifted large loose branches off the bed and set them in the wheelbarrow. Each time it filled up, she pushed it into the woods where the mulch pile was hidden. Once she had cleared the branches, she crouched to pull up weeds and deep-rooted sprigs of the linden tree, which sent out new life continuously. She found weeding very satisfying: It was like uprooting evil. In this realm, things were clearly bad or good, which was relaxing. Unlike life. She heaped the "bad" in the wheelbarrow. The afternoon sun grew hotter as it sank, and she went to the toolshed for her old straw hat. She was unaware of the smile on her face, but she felt happy: She loved doing this.

She had never had a garden until they bought this house. A city girl, she had always lived in apartments, and her mother did not spend money on inessentials like houseplants. Not until they moved here and it became possible did she realize she wanted a garden and set about building one. It had been far more costly and laborious than she had anticipated, but now, after twenty years, the garden was beautiful, rich, designed for pleasure. Next to history, it was her greatest joy.

Neither gardens nor history had been in her mind thirty years ago, when she married Steven, or even twenty years ago, when they bought this house.

In a couple of hours, she had finished weeding the bed. She pushed the wheelbarrow to the mulch pile and dumped the final load. She banged her tools together to shake off the dirt and, along with the wheelbarrow, returned them to the toolshed. Glancing at the clean bed, she breathed deeply, as if she were the garden and newly able to breathe. She headed indoors, tossed her soiled gardening clothes in the hamper, and showered.

They were going out this evening, to the Schneiders' for dinner, and she deliberated over what to wear. Enjoying the warm refreshment of the shower, for some reason, her mind kept reverting to the periods in which she had been unhappy—when she was a teenager, then a young married woman, when the children were little—forever, it seemed, before now. Stiff and wary. Not conscious. Did my depression make me a bad mother? A cold wife? Steven didn't seem unhappy. I had no pleasure in my life. I didn't expect it and hadn't arranged my life to include it. Life was duty. Pleasure was an unfamiliar category. My mother knew nothing about pleasure. People of my background did not think about pleasure, they wanted only to survive. We knew about propriety, duty, and endurance. At school, she had had a brief glimmer of the joy of using her mind, but it had disappeared quickly. Her agenda listed marriage as her next duty, and she was a good girl.

She had done well in college, majoring in history. But she thought about herself vaguely, as sequestered girls habitually did, not as a self but as part of a group. Born in 1950, in her teens in the tumultuous sixties, a young woman during the clamor of feminism that filled the seventies, she was insulated from all of it by her close bond with her mother, and the space Neva had created around them. Neva had never since her youth not felt like an accidental survivor, and she encased her child in a shell of affection and xenophobia which contained her tightly. This cocoon held fast despite Alicia's encounters with professors and students at Hunter, and with the bits of the world she glimpsed in newspapers and on television. It was stronger than anything outside it because it was rooted in love, Neva's unending, absolute love for her child.

For Alicia, feminism was something to be renounced in the firmest tones, something that subverted and betrayed the natural order of things, the rules of life. Like girls of earlier eras, she saw her future hovering vaguely in her mind; she knew marriage was inevitable, yet was unable to imagine what it would be like. But she was also unable to imagine any alternative. She knew she would not marry as her mother had (the second time, at least), for security, sensing that her mother would not press her to do so; after all, Neva's first marriage, to Alicia's father, had been for love. The need for security had come later, had been centered, in fact, on Alicia. Neva was pleased that Alicia had a college degree, "in case you need to go to work someday like I did." But when Alicia imagined a career, she saw herself standing in a drab classroom all day, then coming home to an apartment smelling of meat gravy, evoking one of Neva's pot roast dinners, every night. The picture seemed hedged in, narrow, dark.

But marriage had problems too. When she tried to picture it, there were overtones she was glancingly conscious of, a pale sense, never investigated, that husbands expected their wives to obey them and that women had to do so. Some rule. She sensed, but never let the thought seep into the part of her brain that could articulate it, that marriage would trap her in some invisible prison. And that she could not predict it or protect herself from it. It was just a hint, gleaned from, say, Lucille Ball's batting her eyelashes at Desi and apologizing, making up excuses, acting frightened; or from the way even a woman like Katherine Hepburn relaxed at the end of the movie, granting Spencer Tracy some kind of authority over her. It was always implied that Tracy would use his authority only for Hepburn's benefit, but was that the way life really was? Women in television shows all deferred to their husbands. Alicia could not bring herself to think about this. She remembered Mr. Mulrooney yelling at Mrs. Mulrooney through the thin walls separating their apartments; she remembered bruises on Mrs. Mulrooney's face. She brushed these thoughts away.

Arnold Ross often claimed that Neva had him "wrapped around her little finger," but Alicia saw her mother scurrying around to serve and placate him. She did everything the way he wanted her to; they ate what he liked, when he liked. They went only to places he wanted to go to, to movies he chose, to relatives he favored, and only when he wanted to go. When he wanted to stay home, they stayed home to watch the television shows he wanted to see, even if Alicia begged to see Joseph Campbell. He handed Neva a clutch of ten-dollar bills every Friday, as if he was paying her, yet the money was not Neva's, not for Neva—it was for the household, and she had to see to it that he got the kind of dinners and undershirts and beer he wanted from those dollars. Alicia could neither think about these things nor forget them. They shadowed the thought of marriage for her, yet she knew she had to marry.

At a December gathering of the Motyla clan (which was all the family Neva possessed) to celebrate Moishe Motyla's sixty-fifth birthday, Alicia met Steven Gilson, a second cousin of Sean Motyla. Steven was handsome and very, very smart, and he was a doctor!

Neva made a fuss over him, and pressed Alicia to go over and meet him. But Alicia, sought after by boys at school (even Christian boys!), was damned if she'd chase a man, doctor or not. Her attitude convinced Steven to pursue her, impressed by her pride. He was soon smitten. And in time, the combination of his courtship, his looks, his brains, and his profession overwhelmed her scruples. She was awed by him—he was so intelligent that he dared to act supercilious. She was not used to boys smarter than she was. Of course, Steven wasn't a boy, but a man, nine years older than she.

They were married as soon as she was graduated from Hunter, and he urged her not to get a job; his education had taken so long—college, medical school, psychiatric training—that he did not want to waste a minute now that he was finished. He wanted to marry, create a home, and start a family as soon as possible. Alicia was happy to comply: She had no family other than Neva, and both she and Neva felt a sense of emptiness. Now she could create a family for her mother as well as for her husband. What greater satisfaction could there be? Steven's practice was only a little over a year old and did not yet bring in enough to keep him and a wife, but his parents were as eager as he for children and supplemented his income when he married.

They rented a small apartment on West End Avenue and bought basic items of furniture. Alicia became a housewife overnight. She got pregnant almost immediately. Neva was jubilant, as was Steven's family, all of them celebrating their families' accidental, defiant, triumphant survival of the most concerted, comprehensive, unrelenting drive to extinguish a people since the extermination of the Cathars by the Catholic Church. Steven was happy. Alicia thought she was too, but she often had nightmares, dreams of ruin, in which she was alone, trying to find her way through the maze of a bombed city, or a path through a dense, drifting fog. She was often uncomfortable with Steven, but she told herself it was because he was so brilliant, and she unused to deferring to anyone intellectually. Or maybe it was because she was not used to living with a man.

Still, he was kind to her, he seemed to love her, and she felt a pride in her marriage. Two children were born, satisfying the anxious hearts waiting for them, especially the second, a boy. Steven's practice grew, and his parents no longer needed to subsidize them. He joined a prestigious psychiatric institute, where he taught one afternoon a week. They moved to a larger apartment, on Riverside Drive. They were a typical New York Jewish professional couple: They attended concerts and the theater, saw major art shows and movies, ate at restaurants considered "in."

When they had been married for about five years, Steven came home one night disturbed about a patient. He rarely mentioned his patients to her, and never by name, but this evening he was furious, expostulating about a woman named Evelyn who, he said, had attacked him!

"Attacked you? With her fists?" Alicia was incredulous.

"No, no, no. With her tongue, which you women are so skilled in using!" he stormed.

She trembled. Was she a shrew? she wondered. Did she nag him? Was that what he was saying?

"She attacked me verbally, she really bombarded me! It's this damned women's lib stuff. It's infecting everything. She's a new patient—she's only been coming for two months, but I thought we were building a good relationship. Until that day, anyway."

"What day?"

"Oh, I don't know. A couple of weeks ago."

"Why are you telling me about it only now? Why didn't you mention it before?"

"Because today Marisa attacked me too! Saying the same things! She backed Evelyn up!"

Alicia was confused. "Marisa knew what Evelyn said? Had you discussed it with her?" Marisa, Steven's colleague at the institute, was a clinician famed for her articles on psychology.

"No, no!" Steven's irritation spilled over. "She didn't know what Evelyn said, but she said the same things!"

"What did she say?" By now, Alicia was deeply interested.

"Who, Evelyn? She said I was authoritarian. A tyrant! Now, you know how hard I try not to be authoritarian, because of my father, you know how he is and how I feel about him, I always hated his manner. So right off the bat, I know she's inventing an attack. Because I make such an effort not to be . . . But she insisted I was patronizing, said I acted as if I were the authority on every subject. She called me arrogant, supercilious, and said I looked down on women. Then she said she had enough tyrannical males in her life and if I didn't change, she wasn't coming back! Can you imagine? A patient laying down the law to a doctor?"

His handsome face was etched with pain.

"Yes, sort of," she heard herself saying.

"You can!"

"I can imagine how upset that made you," she swiftly amended. She felt like Papageno from "The Magic Flute," with a clothespin on her tongue. She tried to change the subject. "What did you say?"

"I told her she was dismissed as a patient. How dare she try to dictate my behavior! I told her to go find herself some mushy social worker with a psychology license . . ."

Alicia was silent for a moment. "And what did she say?" she asked in a tremulous voice.

"I can't tell you," he said with hauteur.

"Why not?"

"It's obscene."

"Steven!"

"Well, if you insist. She told me to go fuck myself. A real lady, that."

"I see." Why did the thought cross Alicia's mind that this Evelyn sounded as if she didn't need a therapist? "And today?"

"I was at the institute for a meeting." His voice was thin with strain. His description of Evelyn had poured out, but now he began to speak in short jerky phrases. "The committee . . . you know we review new applicants . . . we choose the ones we think will make the best candidates. We were preparing for the fall term. There was one applicant I really objected to . . . I knew the others would probably like her. Well, I thought they might. But she was flaky. She was . . . peculiar . . . but not in an interesting way! But when I raised my objections, Marisa exploded, 'Flaky! She's the most intuitive human being I've ever met! You're saying that because she was involved in

Greenham Common, aren't you? You don't approve of political women!'

"Now, that's not fair! I never said anything like that. And it wasn't why. It was that Greenham was such a . . . a . . . new-agey affair!" Steven raged. "Baby pictures and ribbons!" he added in scorn.

Alicia pictured the hundreds of women, children, and babies camped outside the nuclear weapons storage facility, the women attaching photographs, flowers, ribbons, and ban-the-bomb to signs on the high metal fence. Camped there. For months. Years. A veritable female village. A female protest.

"You know how I loathe new-agey things, they're intellectually bankrupt. So when Marisa said psychology needed to become politically aware—I—well, it's true, I did retreat into superciliousness. I couldn't help it. She must be mad. Psychology has to avoid political involvement. We must be above all that. We have to deal with the psyche, not the polis. And I felt attacked. It's instinctive for me to adopt a supercilious manner when I feel attacked, I've been doing it since the first time kids attacked me in the schoolyard. It's always worked for me, a little Jewish kid in a tough Irish neighborhood in the Bronx . . .

"I . . . I smiled. A supercilious smile, I admit. I said, 'Well, yes, *intuitive* is a more respectful way of saying *flaky*, Marisa, but both indicate weak intellect, I'm afraid. I'd even object if she were a member of Scientists Against Nuclear Weapons, or a serious organization like that . . .' Marisa exploded again. 'Oh, you mean even if it had been a male organization!' she spat. 'Gilson, we have a serious difference of opinion about the degree to which our discipline should be involved in the world, but that is not what I'm objecting to in you. No, you just underlined my objection. And that is that you're arrogant, supercilious, and out of touch'—oh, the way she talks, like a book, she talks in goddamned paragraphs! 'This attitude of yours is offensive and uncalled for—and unfortunately it's shared by other males in this institute—but it's even more reprehensible in you, since you are still young and relatively inexperienced, shallow and lacking in wisdom. You claim for yourself a superiority based merely on your anatomy which, whatever Freud wrote, is not destiny now if it ever was!' Well, that broke the meeting up. Of course she was attacking all the men on the committee as well as our god—Freud! They were all muttering, whispering to each other, calling out, 'Point of order! Point of order!' Goldman called a halt. Said we'd continue next week. Then he said he wanted to speak to me alone."

Goldman, the great Goldman, whom Steven revered! Poor Steven! His stomach must have been twisted with dread, Alicia thought.

"I was nervous waiting for him. It took a while—he had to deal with a lot of after-meeting details. But when he got to me, he put his hand on my arm, he led me to his office, he was pleasant, fatherly. He said I really can't afford to offend Marisa. I'm a junior member, and she has so much cachet. She's published more than anyone else at the institute. She studied with Ernest Jones! Of course she no longer respects him. But Goldman didn't blame me. He blamed feminism. 'The women are all up in arms these days, Steven,' he said. 'And maybe they even have a point, a little point. Marisa, you know, she is a senior person, a person of great repute, her papers on the psychotherapeutic relationship are quoted everywhere . . . And, you know, she is right about some of the men, the older ones, the Europeans, you know how they are, they act as if all the women in the organization are secretaries, or cooks!' He laughed uproariously. 'So she attacks you, huh? Certainly not the worst offender, eh? But an easy target, no? A junior person, only two years with us . . . I am sure you did not mean to insult her. But you are a young man with brilliance, and brilliance is often accompanied by a certain arrogance. Just remember you have to make your career yet; it is not wise to offend . . .'"

Steven might want to apologize to Marisa for any arrogance he might have betrayed and assure her that it was not directed at her, Goldman had said. And in future, Steven might try to tone down his "tendency to superciliousness when questioned" and "deal more honestly with challenge" as Marisa had suggested.

"He didn't say I was arrogant or supercilious, he just quoted her. It was a masterpiece of indirection." Steven smiled. "I felt less reprimanded than corrected, set on the right path."

He had thanked Goldman. "I felt like kissing his hand." Only after he got home did he begin to think about the implications. "I really am arrogant?" he asked Alicia miserably.

This time, she did pity him.

"A little, dear," she said gently, stroking his face.

He frowned. He grimaced. "Supercilious?"

She smiled and nodded.

"Do I patronize you?"

"Always." Until she said it, she had not known it. She had evaded knowing it, as a child evades the monster crouched in the corner of the room as long as the lights are on.

His face scrunched up in pain. "I don't want to be like that! I wanted more than anything not to be like my father! If I'm like him, I must have just slipped into it! How did I slip into it?"

Alicia gazed at him. "You probably imitated your father unconsciously—and maybe you modeled yourself on the older men on the committee. Without thinking. We all imitate other people, even when we try not to. I do things my mother did, I see myself doing them—" she stopped abruptly. "You acted like lots of other men. Men think that behavior is expected of them, or permitted them. Sort of the male mystique."

After that conversation, she saw him trying to change. He would start to say something then check it out with her, one eyebrow raised as if he were asking, Is this okay? He began to hedge his own assertions, unsure of the line between declaring and pronouncing. He asked her to point out when he was being patronizing, and in the kindest way she could find, she did. It had taken some time, a couple of years, but he was much better now. He had slid into the role of authority. And I slid into wifedom. I was only twenty-one; I should have waited, had some fun, worked, taught, traveled. Had sex. Why didn't I do that? He slid into one mode and I slid into its complement, I slid into feeling he was above me, that he had rights over me, that he could tell me what to do or not do, that I needed his permission to do things.

One afternoon, sitting in a fresh pair of jeans and T-shirt in her Steventon kitchen, sipping a lovely hot cup of Lapsang souchong, Alicia's glance fell on a Japanese print hanging on the kitchen wall.

She'd had it for decades, liked it because it was colorful and graceful. She did not think it was valuable. But the circumstances of its framing flashed through her memory.

It happened a year or so into her marriage. Steven's new practice was still sparse, and money was tight. He gave Alicia everything he had left after paying the rent on the apartment and his office, the electric and telephone bills. But what he gave her was barely enough to get the things she was responsible for—food, diaper service, laundry. After Mariette was born, Alicia went out only once a week, when Neva came to the apartment to pick up Alicia and Mariette. They would drop the baby with Neva's old friend Brenda Mulrooney, who was glad to earn an extra two dollars (which Neva could now afford) of an afternoon and who always welcomed Alicia as a lost daughter. Then Neva and Alicia went out to shop and have lunch. It was the high point of the week for both of them: Alicia got away from the baby briefly, and Neva had her first chance in life to play Lady Bountiful, a role that thrilled her.

Alicia and Steven's apartment was still bare and Alicia longed for some art. One day in a bookstore she impulsively bought a Japanese print of a woman—a geisha perhaps, or a lady, she couldn't tell the difference. The print was only ten dollars, but when she took it to be framed, to her horror the framer said it would cost sixty-five dollars to have it done! More than a week's groceries! Because of its size, the man said. Normally, she was prudent and frugal; Steven counted on that and she had never let him down. But she wanted this picture. She decided she would try to save a few dollars a week from her housekeeping money until she could pay for it. She plunged ahead, though she felt a muddy guilt whenever she thought about it.

Her mother was with her when she finally picked it up. Neva admired the print, the frame, her daughter's taste. She went on about it: She had always wanted Japanese prints, she said, but Arnold didn't like that kind of art. She sounded so irritated with Arnold that Alicia could anticipate a scene that she knew she needed to forestall.

"Momma, would you do me a favor? If you talk about the print in front of Steven, would you not say how much the frame cost?"

Her mother's eyes widened for an instant, then her face closed down. She understood, exactly. Had she too lied to Arnold about money? Did every woman have this experience?

Some women have no character at all, the poet wrote. Alicia knew he meant women like her.

•

Steven and Alicia got home from the Schneiders' before midnight, and for once, Steven left the car in the driveway. "I'm catching a quick game early tomorrow morning," he said, a little shamefaced. "Seems silly to put it in the garage."

As they walked to the front door, Alicia stopped and looked up at the sky. Up here, it was a deep black city skies never are, with millions of stars sprinkled across it like diamond dust. Steven stopped, too, and put his arms around her; they stood together, murmuring at the beauty of it. He kissed her, and afterward she let herself lean against him for a moment. Then they went in.

"The Schneiders are really nice, don't you think?" she asked, as they hung up their coats.

"She's nice. He's a bit competitive, it seems to me."

"Really? About what?"

"Everything! Didn't you hear him talking about his tennis game?"

"Yes. You were both talking about tennis."

"I wasn't bragging."

Alicia stood still in the front hall. "Would you like a cup of camomile tea before bed?"

"That would be nice."

He followed her into the kitchen. "You know, he was so . . . such a braggart. Didn't you notice?"

"Steven, the two of you sounded the same to me. You were bragging too."

"I was? And his damned BMW. He kept bragging about his car. A German car, too."

She smiled. "And you bragged about the Volvo."

He was silent for a moment. "Do you really think I'm as bad as he is?"

She turned, setting the warmed teapot on the counter. "I don't know if *bad* is the right word. If that's what I'd call it. You're both very competitive, Steven, you and Stanley Schneider. But a lot of men are."

"What about Charley Gold?"

"No. He's not, that I've ever noticed. But he comes from a different world. Maybe with his relatives he's competitive too. Maybe they argue about high school basketball teams, or farm machines. But I've never seen it."

"What about Tim Halliday?"

"It's hard to say," she shrugged. "No one here is in the same league with him."

"What do you mean?" He sounded angry.

"Steven! He's an artist! He's very rich! He knows so many famous people! He's in a different league from us and Charley, that's all."

"So he doesn't have to be competitive with the mere likes of me, is that what you're saying?"

She sighed. "He doesn't seem to care about golf or tennis scores or cars or the things you care about is what I mean. He's probably competitive with his fellow artists. Artists are notorious for that."

Steven sat down at the kitchen table, where Alicia had laid out cups and saucers, plates, and a platter of toast, with butter and jam. He ate in silence.

"Don't sulk. He might be competitive about New York restaurants, for all I know."

"Aren't women the same way? Don't you compete about—oh, I don't know, your houses, your clothes, your looks?"

"My friends? We don't compete. Lots of women do, sure. It isn't as marked a trait in women, though. Except on television. On TV, they make women talk to each other the way men do and act like men. But real women don't talk like that."

"How come your friends don't compete?"

"We don't want to."

He sat back, staring at her. "Are you saying it's a choice?"

"Of course. We like to make each other feel good, not bad. Competition is an attempt to make yourself feel good at others' expense, but it doesn't really work. You don't feel good, despite all your bragging tonight . . ."

"All my bragging!"

"Steven, I don't care if you brag. It's not a cardinal sin. I'm not criticizing you. You brought this up."

"I don't think I brag."

"Then I guess there's nothing more to be said."

"So why don't you women . . ."

"I told you. We like to make each other feel good. We feel good when our friends feel good. Making a friend feel put down doesn't cheer us up. We want our friends to feel good so we can feel good. We like harmony. Anyway, everybody's different. The things we care about aren't comparable the way BMWs and Volvos are. We care about how happy we are, how fulfilled, how satisfying our lives are . . ."

She finished her tea, set the empty cup down. "Maybe we're less competitive because of our age. We're not young and unsure. Maybe when we were younger we were more competitive. But Jenny's young, and she likes the way we are. We compare things—Maddy's always commenting on how thin we are, or how fat she is . . ."

"Well, she is a big woman . . ."

"Yes, she's a big woman. In every way," Alicia said firmly. "She has the greatest soul of anyone. But we do compete, sort of. I often say I love Jenny's hair and hate this wild wiry hair of mine—and she says she loves my hair." Alicia laughed. "We always like what the other has."

"Your hair isn't always wild: It looks lovely when you comb it back and pin it down."

"But I love my hair wild! Hair is supposed to be dead, but I feel that mine's alive."

"So why do you say you hate it?"

"Because there are days I do. There are days I'd like to have smooth lying-down blond hair like Jenny's. I mean, I'd be a whole different person if I had smooth blond hair like hers, don't you see?"

"No, I don't. Why would you want to be a whole different person? What's wrong with the person you are? You women are always putting yourselves down," Steven concluded. "Gloria Steinem is right: Women have problems with self-esteem—much as I hate feminist jargon."

"A Freudian psychiatrist should be the last person to criticize jargon."

"Ummm. But do you? Have problems with self-esteem?"

"Maybe," she allowed. "But maybe we're just flexible. We let ourselves wonder what it would be like to look like someone else, to have someone else's characteristics."

"That's a perverse form of competition, if you ask me," Steven decided.

"It has exactly the opposite effect from your form."

"What do you mean?"

"You didn't like Stanley Schneider tonight. You probably don't like him, period. And he probably doesn't like you because the two of you compete; you both always try to make each other feel bad about your cars, their mileage, their repairs, your tennis games, whatever. Whereas we make each other feel admired, cherished, attractive. We end up loving each other and feeling good about our lives. You end up disliking each other and feeling bad about your lives. Which one is perverse?"

"I don't feel bad about my life!"

Alicia stood up and began clearing the table. "I'm glad, Steven. Really."

He stood too, to remove dishes from the table to the sink. He examined her face suspiciously, but saw no glimmer of a sarcastic smile. Satisfied, he returned to the argument. "I just don't believe he gets twenty-four miles to a gallon in a two-year-old six-cylinder car!" he said peevishly.

5

Emily swept cracker crumbs from the table into her palm, then tossed them into the sink. Her favorite kind of dinner—no cleanup. And she had enjoyed it: The pear was especially juicy, the cheddar sharp and tasty, the crackers crisp and sprinkled with sesame. A nice burgundy from the last case she'd bought, a good one. A French meal (unless you had to have Roquefort for it to be French). It was even a balanced meal.

She was tired after her long day—a good tired. Being with the women filled her like a meal of nectar and ambrosia. After seeing them, she always felt she'd been to a clinic and had had all her mechanisms readjusted like poor Gittel Steed, brilliant woman with that awful pituitary disease she developed doing anthropology in India. Beautiful before: Rafael Soyer had painted her, tall and exotic, dark hair pulled back. The disease made her extremities grow—arms, legs, nose. And because her pituitary gland didn't work the way it should, a mere cold put her off kilter; she'd have to check into the hospital and have her whole body tuned up. If she'd had friends like mine, she could have skipped the trip, Emily thought, smiling.

And as often happened, a break, an afternoon off, refreshed her, unstoppered her, so what was bottled up inside came pouring out. As if some attar dancing inside her bubbled up when she felt cherished and poured itself out on the page. Most of what she'd done today was good, she thought; except perhaps for the last two phrases (she had known enough to stop then), she would keep it, it would stand. And then, when after a few hours her invention wore down, she practiced. She really should practice every day. Today she put in a good two hours.

A perfect day, a nice supper. Well, one *she* liked; Clea wouldn't have been happy with it. She needed more food than that.

She sat utterly still for a moment, a slant of feeling leveling her, as it always did when she thought about her niece. The word *Clea* was a gap. You'd think I always had her. I feel her goneness.

I remember the first telephone call. July 1980, around four o'clock our time, man from California Vincent Gregorian. Friend of your brother Martin, he said. His executor, he said. Executor! Why?

Plane crash. Martin dead. Martin and his wife Alexa, your brother and his wife, taking off from Tokyo, everyone killed. Terrible thing, tragedy.

My life leaped into my throat. Martin dead. Martin sprang into my eyes as he had sprung into life forty-odd years ago, Blake knew that, babies are shot into existence, like cannonballs from the vagina, glowing pink and fierce, tiny fists clenched tight in terror and rage. Born in the big east bedroom, Momma and Poppa's room then; Mrs. Fenwick, the midwife, carried him out to show us. Still howling but cleaned up and wrapped in a soft blanket whipstitched around the edges by me. When Mrs. Fenwick handed him to me, he stopped crying, and I knew he knew me. I pressed him to me and I thought he looked at me but of course he couldn't see yet. Still, he probably smelled me. That's how I remember Momma now, by her warm musky smell.

Days later, he lay in the tiny crib in the kitchen where it was so hot you could barely breathe. Momma had turned on all six burners and the oven with the door open to make sure he didn't get a chill. Someone tossed something in the step-on garbage can and the lid fell shut with a loud clank, and his entire little body leaped in a spasm; he didn't cry, but his eyes blinked, his mouth opened, his arms flew up, and he turned a little blue with shock, and I caught him up in my arms and told him he was safe and that I would keep him safe forever.

Liar.

Daughter Clea, the man was saying, you're her father's closest living family. Mamie's still alive though, and Alexa had parents, a mother, I think, and a sister, also alive, and maybe a brother, didn't she? They named you guardian in the will, didn't they tell you? They might have, in a letter years ago, when Clea was born. I couldn't remember, it didn't mean anything to me. I named something, I think family important . . . Self-important man, what did he matter in all this? I want to send her to you . . .

Well, of course. We made arrangements: Thursday, Logan, 4:22 p.m.

Emily sank into a chair. Fifty years old and she was about to become a mother. She laughed like Abraham's Sarah.

His tiny rosebud mouth opened and closed involuntarily, like a clam, even when he was not nursing. His tiny fists clenched and unclenched when Momma nursed him, his whole body arced in bliss, it was the most intense experience he'd ever have . . . Momma was tired, she handed him to me, I changed him, bathed him, oiled him, dressed him, set him in his crib, set him on the floor. He lay there, his little arms and legs waving in the air. Later, when he could crawl, he would look backward at me and giggle, wanting me to chase him, thinking himself clever. If I wasn't around, he'd cry. Made Momma crazy. As if she didn't already hate me enough.

Then he was three, running down the hill toward the road where the school bus dropped her off. "Emmy! Emmy!" How he had loved her then! And she him. His hair white as dandelion fluff and his little legs dimpled like a fat bottom. You think that will never change, can never be forgotten, you think love is forever.

"Emmy, Emmy!" he cried, his arms stretched out; he was aching to be grasped, to be picked up and hugged as he reached up and giggled and put his sticky, smudged hands all over her clean schoolgirl's face. "Mama, Emmy home!" he cried, squirming to see if his mother was near him, but of course she was in the house, she had let him out because Emmy was coming. Emmy was his favorite thing in the world. And he was hers. Had that really happened?

•

Emily moved about her bedroom, undressing. She laid her dress over the back of a chair. She didn't hang clothes in her closet until the smell had gone out of them. Her senses were of the utmost importance to her, sound, smell, taste, and touch. Her vision wasn't as good as the other senses. James Joyce divided people into seers and hearers, Shem and Shaun, the pen and the post. He was a hearer, she too. And like Joyce, she loved smells—her father was earth and tobacco, a sexy smell. Duncan was musky like her mother, but mother was perfumed. Even the smells of shit and farts she liked, when they were fresh. It was when smells got old that they got rancid and horrible. All living smells were good, she decided. Bad smells came from decay, old urine, vomit, dead cigars.

What was amazing was how long odors lasted. Considering that they are impalpable, simply air. That time in Boston waiting for an elevator and the doors slid open and a beautifully dressed woman stepped off, the scent of lilac floating behind her like a retinue. All the way up to the twelfth floor, Emily could smell it, although the woman was long gone. The paper the fish was wrapped in, tossed into the trash and left overnight. Ugh.

You could open your closet door and run smack into your own smell, soured. Lilies can perfume a whole house. She hung sachets in her closet and every winter refreshed the lavender in the hope chest left by her great-great-grandfather's first wife. There were still some exquisite old linens left in it—embroidered, edged with lace, appliquéd, wrapped in tissue and sprinkled with lavender flowers. Opening it opening a gate to heaven.

She'd done so for Clea once. Who was unimpressed. Yes, it was a nice smell, but what was all that old stuff for? Who would use it? Why didn't she give it to a museum? Nobody used things like that anymore. Probably true.

Of course smells were gasses, scientists said, measurable substances with names: methane, butane. But some invisible things couldn't be measured, not yet, at least: the waves of feeling that shot between people like wind or arrows, bearing love and hate, interest, dismay, concern, attention, dislike, malignity. The surges of feeling that permeated her community of friends and buoyed them so that when they parted they were still riding the waves, sailing over the seas of their lives like angels.

And days like that one in Nairobi, she and Duncan and Annabel and Roger on the street in that airy city which had been comfortable and easy ten minutes ago and suddenly felt malevolent. A wave of hatred had hit her, and she had stopped dead on the sidewalk. She began to tell the others that they should all go back to the hotel, but it was already too late, that man had Annabel's gold necklace in his eye and was heading for it, threw himself into Annabel like a missile, grabbing at the chain, knocking her down, dragging her along the sidewalk. He got a cheap watch. Would that be enough for his dinner? The streets were suddenly filled with predatory, hungry men on the move. Hungry. Starving. A country that couldn't feed its children.

She pulled a flannel nightgown over her head, remembering Clea that first night in Steventon, in a thin little jersey nightshirt like a T-shirt. It was August, but cold at night, and Emily worried that Clea would freeze. Clea had, and the next night, finicky as she was, she'd taken the flannel nightdress Emily offered her—only temporarily, of course. She had Emily's keen awareness of the material world, but hers was centered on clothes—cut, fabric, color. She was difficult to please.

Emily laid her shoes on the floor beside the closet, letting them air out. She'd put them away in the morning. Twenty pairs of shoes, so extravagant! Oh, I do love shoes. And you need different kinds for teaching, for dress, for working in the garden. When we were children, we had two pairs each. If our feet grew, we had to keep wearing the old shoes even if they hurt. Momma could only afford to buy shoes for the lot of us twice a year, a sensible pair of oxfords at the beginning of school, Mary Janes at Easter. There were so many of us. But even better-off kids had only two pairs. Things were different then. Momma bought herself one pair of shoes every five years; if she had more than one pair, the others were old.

Twenty pairs of shoes. She was as bad as Imelda Marcos. Maybe not. Emily could not remember how many pairs she had. It was unbelievable to her.

She laid her worn underthings in a pile on a hassock to air. Then, sitting at her dressing table, she unpinned her bun; her hair was straight, dark blond mixed with white, pretty; it hung to the middle of her back. Every night as she did this, she remembered watching her grandmother brush her hair fifty strokes. Every night for years. I am part of a line. I haven't continued it—for which they will never forgive me—but I am still part of it. Others did: John had kids before he died, Mamie has five kids. Crighton and I failed to reproduce, (Robert died too young, not his fault). Not a great record, for a family: Five children produce only eight grandchildren. Maddy has nine from her four. Different age. Small families.

She stared at herself in the mirror, suddenly shocked by her hair: She'd once thought herself a rebel, but now she had long hair kept in a bun and brushed it every night. How old-fashioned could you get? Some rebel she'd turned out to be.

Forty-eight, forty-nine, fifty. Emily laid down the brush. When she was a girl, all grown women had long hair. They wound it into a bun, as she did now. Bobbed hair was modern, and only girls in cities had it. After the forties, a few older women had short, permed hair. Girls today had long hair, but they did't brush it. Clea never brushed hers. When Emily was a girl, she had long, thick hair, golden brown and shiny. She wished she had a stripe of white blazing out from dark hair like Maddy Gold. But Emily was a tan person, Maddy had said.

Aging wasn't fun, no matter what the ones insisted who were trying to sell you something: retirement in Florida, moisturizers. People were shown gleeful in ads for paper diapers, buzzers to keep you from feeling alone, despite stiff joints, drab hair and skin dry and old. Or even worse. Look how bent Monica Moody was now, couldn't stand up straight. And Wally Benson could barely walk. Inane people claimed they got better every day. What really happened in aging was that every day you got more and more amenable to dying. Of course, seventy wasn't the end of the world, but it was close enough. Lots of people didn't make it to seventy: Poppa, Martin.

But aging started long before that. Maddy's niece Amy was only thirty-three and the last time Emily had seen her, Amy's glowing, velvety skin was already beginning to dull. Youth could return, though, when someone was happy—the glow could come back.

She wondered how Clea looked these days. Was she old for her age? Poor Clea hadn't had much happiness in her life. The first dish that Emily had served Clea that the child had managed to eat was waffles. With real maple syrup, of course, and homemade country sausage from the Sowinski farm. Clea knew what waffles were, she sometimes went to a Pancake House in L.A. with a girlfriend whose mother was willing to drive them, or who had a chauffeur. Can you imagine having a chauffeur at your disposal at thirteen? My generation didn't have cars at eighteen, much less thirteen. Of course, we weren't rich, no one here was rich then—or now, either, for that matter. Some people are well-to-do, but really rich, no. Maddy makes a lot of money, but she isn't rich. Even the Aldriches, who owned that huge house on Widmer's hill that was turned into an inn after they moved to Marblehead years ago, burned down in the sixties, even their children didn't have their own cars.

But when we were seniors, Johnny Kilman got a car for his eighteenth birthday, a convertible, we were so impressed. The Kilmans didn't stay around here, they moved to New York after he went off to college. Once he got that car, all the girls wanted to go out with him even though he had bad skin. Probably why his parents bought it for him. Mary Williams dated him, I think, or Beth Mayer. I wonder what happened to him. He was a spoiled brat, really, arrogant, snotty. Probably scared. The girls all got married a few years after high school. They moved, Mary, I think to Albany, and Beth to Springfield. I was never in his car, I didn't care about cars, well, I acted as if I didn't. I wanted to be a bohemian, I claimed that material things didn't matter to me. I wonder if they really didn't or if I wouldn't admit that they did. What about now? I say material things don't matter to me and I almost never buy anything, but the truth is, the material world is my first love, and I have everything I want, I have never been in need: I live in what feels like luxury. I'm always warm, never hungry, never without clothing or staff paper or a piano . . . or even a radio. Sitting on the bed, she leaned over and switched on the small Bose on her bedside table. It was tuned to a public radio station that played forties swing late at night.

Jerry Gray

Oh, *String of Pearls*. The music of those days, the dances, high school gym, boys lined up on one side, girls on the other, everybody feeling bottomless dread I bought a big band CD just to remember that doomed nostalgic yearning longing. "Tuxedo Junction," "In the Mood." I still love them. We all, I, wanted wanted wanted . . . but what? I didn't know. And how could I be nostalgic when I was sixteen and hadn't experienced anything? Sick music, really. Why Nietzsche turned against Wagner . . .

Yes, Clea ate two waffles and a whole sausage, she didn't play with her food like the night before, but she still had that look on her face. Sleeping beauty. I thought I'd try serving them with berries and cream some night. Not really a dinner, but so what, if she liked it . . .

Thinking about Clea made Emily's head ache, and she rested it against the headboard of the bed. Old, finished. Concert in two months. Oh, I'll be ready. I always am. But I'm tired. I wonder if she'll come to see me again. Does she ever think of me with love? Will she ever come here again? Will she ever forgive me?

She rose and walked toward the window.

I don't even know what my sin was. Anything, everything.

She pushed the curtain aside and raised the shade, which was drawn halfway down. Raising the shades had for so many years been forbidden in this house that even now she did it with a defiant energy. She peered out but the night was too black to see anything. In daylight, she could see the broad front lawn carved by the drive lined with chestnut trees planted by her great-grandfather. Glorious when they bloomed, in a month and a half, or two. Then that feeling tearing through her, felt like being drawn and quartered, such joy in the beauty, exaltation, a longing to praise a deity who created such beauty, and at the same time, keen sorrow, grief because they wouldn't last, would be gone in ten days and then invisible for a whole year. Like love, can't feel the joy of it without also feeling the sorrow.

Flesh dies. All flesh is grass.

Martin. Poppa.

April in Paris, chestnuts in blossom.

When I was little, this room was Great-Grandma's. Before that, it was hers and Great-Grandpa's, but he passed on, Momma said. Momma never said "died." And one day Great-Grandma too passed on, leaving Emily with a memory of a shrunken, bent body with a black box hanging on it—a hearing aid. Great-Grandma had the tinkling, unfeigned laugh of a small child, chiming delight. And sometimes she told stories about her stepmother, Annie, who took care of seven children with ease, children hanging on her hip, on her legs, in her arms, while she yelled and cooked and cleaned. Great-Grandmother Sarah hated automobiles, those darned newfangled inventions, but had no fear of them and insisted on her right to cross Main Street unhindered, menacing approaching cars with her umbrella. And Emily's Great-Great-Grandmother Gretel from Germany, indefatigable, working as hard as three women and two men, climbing up on the roof to repair leaks with a pail of hot tar and new shingles, whose hope chest, painted in red and green crosses and wreathed roses, passed down through the generations to nestle to this day at the foot of Emily's bed, filled with antique linens. And Great-Great-Uncle Maximilian, who died after falling from an apple tree during harvest season, the doctor arriving too late to help him, his death shocking Great-Aunt Ida, then a child, to her roots. Her first death.

Not her last though. How many children did she lose?

After Great-Grandma died, Grandma and Grandpa moved into this room, filling it through most of Emily's childhood. After Grandpa died, Grandma would let Emily come in and sit with her at night while she brushed her hair and told her about her life, about hard times and hard work, how her momma made butter, how they brought in the hay, how she made her first goose-down quilt, how she and her momma made soap. She told her about the quiet, intense boy her father had been.

Then, when Emily was nearly grown, Momma and Poppa took possession of the room. Momma stayed there after Poppa died in 1960. It was in this room that she threatened Emily after his funeral. Poppa had left the house to his eldest living son, John, not to Momma. This infuriated her, even though he'd included a clause saying she was to be allowed to live in the house as long as she lived. But the worst of all was that John had already died, before Poppa did, but Poppa hadn't changed his will. And John had left the house he knew he was going to inherit to Emily, willing the house they lived in to Cindy, his wife. All this giving and receiving over her head, as if she did not exist, made Emily's mother crazy with rage, even though she knew that John had died suddenly, of a heart attack, and had never expected to die before his mother. She could have accepted his leaving her house to his wife and children; she could have accepted sharing the house with Cindy, two widows together. What she could not stand was having to share it with Emily, her daughter, the one who had defied her, who had gone away to school, gone to Europe, and never married or produced a child. Who had no love for her.

In her rage, she told Emily she would not live in it alone. If Emily planned to inherit and still go on living in Boston, she would move away, live with Mamie in Rochester, New York, leave behind all her friends and relatives and die in loneliness and let the house go to rack and ruin. It was the duty of the unmarried daughter to return home to care for her aging mother and she demanded Emily return to take possession of what was her own. It was more than Amanda could bear that Emily had not only left the farm but also lived in a city, alone. Supporting herself. It broke every rule she knew, and in her own day would have been scandalous. It was scandalous; she could barely hold her head up around her friends.

Emily thought it over. She loved the old house and wanted it to stay in her family. Maybe a nephew or niece would want it when they grew up—it should be available just in case. And her life was at an impasse. Her job in Boston was secure, but she had for some time seen that she would not rise in it. The institute never promoted women. She would never advance beyond teaching the very young and teenaged piano students she was presently assigned. She loved them, but she wanted some older students for master classes. The Boston conservatory was stultifying, dominated by elderly European men who looked down on women. She would enjoy leaving them behind.

And Douglas had gone to New York after she turned down his

marriage proposal. In a fury. I seem to make everybody furious. He had a job at Mannes School of Music, was doing well there, had found a woman who would marry him. But then Phil came along; some years younger than she, but handsome, vivid, full of life, a cellist. But now he too was talking of marriage. Emily heard men's desire for marriage really as a desire for a servant; perhaps she was wrong, but that was how she heard it. A man could work, practice, politick, and socialize best when he felt safe knowing that a woman was at home cleaning the house and his clothes, fetching and carrying, cooking and serving dinner, taking his suits to the dry cleaner. She would wash and iron his shirts and smile and have his children and raise them, and be perfectly happy doing it. All he had to do was bestow an occasional kiss, a hug, even a smile would do. A woman would provide all the comforts Momma did plus something extra, for practically nothing, for room and board and an occasional kind word. Seeing it this way, she was chagrined by talk of marriage; her lovers, who didn't understand her viewpoint, found that upsetting.

Emily compared the sacrifices demanded of her by her mother and by Phil, and decided she had more freedom with her mother. Of course, she didn't have to chose either, to stay in Boston or return to the house, but remaining at the conservatory if Phil (her only friend there now) left or found someone else to marry, seemed too bleak to be endured. After she made up her mind, she flew back to Boston to quit her job and give up her apartment. Phil was terribly hurt. He did not comprehend what she meant when she said she did not want the same life he wanted. Of course she did, he insisted. They would live in New York, they would find a nice apartment, they would concertize. Their friends would be all around them, the music world, opportunities. He'd like children someday, wouldn't she?

She would not.

Emily closed down her Boston life and drove back to the Berkshires, her car piled high with music, records, audiotapes, and books. She moved into her mother's house and made it hers, renovating one wing as a studio. She applied to the Browning School for a teaching job and they were pleased to get her. But she refused to give Amanda what she wanted. She would not act as a dependent unmarried daughter should. When Amanda started to supervise her, Emily stopped her firmly but without anger. She reminded her mother that she had her own income and her own considerable savings, her own car, her own life, and her own rules.

"I'm thirty-six years old and I've lived on my own since I was twenty. I will live here but I will not tolerate your interference."

Amanda gasped, shocked into silence, expecting nothing like this, expecting indeed what had been expected from such daughters in her youth—obedience, meekness, apology, and piety. If, for example, Mrs. Archibald was unavailable on a given Sunday to drive Amanda to church and pick her up, Emily would drive her, but she refused to go into the church herself. Just refused! Said—said, if it could be credited—that she didn't believe that crap and would not give it even lip service! Amanda subsided into the hurt martyrdom in which she lived out her years, and which Emily ignored. Yet her mere presence was enough to deter Emily from bringing home a bedmate. So, together, they created a family hell, or at least purgatory. Emily escaped by going to work at the college or working in her study in the side wing, or seeing friends. It was a relief to both of them when Amanda died. Sometimes she wondered if marriage might have been better.

Gazing across the road at the mountain, which was gray or green or blue, according to the light, she saw the curved hump rising black against the purple night sky. I'd probably be kinder to her now, she thought. Find a kinder way to tell her to back off. Nowadays, I wouldn't try to hurt her. Of course I didn't know I wanted to hurt her then, did I. I was angry at all the years of disapproval she'd heaped on me. I liked hating her. I justified pain—you can always justify things—because I really enjoyed it. I wouldn't now. Maybe the ego subsides, or maybe by now I've been hurt enough myself that I don't care to inflict pain on anyone else or maybe I have more sympathy for her now.

There was a part of me that loved her.

Yes, we had to have all the shades in the house drawn halfway. Grandma had a fit if they were uneven. Come in from marketing, we went in the buggy when I was little, how I loved that, Blackie pulling us, I loved Blackie, sometimes she let me take the reins. We'd come in from town and her angry, sharp little voice would drill into the poor maid: "The shades in the front bedroom are not even with the rest! Go and fix them! We aren't shanty Irish!" A sin, it was. What would the neighbors say?

Clea asked why I didn't leave the shades up. So much lighter.

Emily smiled.

She raised the window a few inches, breathed in the night air, and went back to bed. Sliding her slightly achy body under the blankets, she let herself feel the comfort of the cool sheets, then the warm bed. Every night, sighing with gratitude, she would remind herself that few women her age in the world regularly had a soft bed to lie in, warm blankets, and a full stomach. Grateful for such ease, she closed her eyes as if in prayer, and music entered her head, the same music every night, the children's prayer from Humperdincks's *Hansel and Gretel.*

She slipped into a deep sleep.

6

Tuesday morning, Jenny didn't get out of the house until eleven-thirty. She always picked up the mail and Tim's *New York Times*, which the general store reserved for him. (It sometimes ran out, and Tim could not get through the day without it. He'd drive all day—from one near-by town to another—searching for a copy. Or ask her to do it. If no *Times* was to be found, he was irritable all day.) So it was nearly noon when she met Maddy Gold coming out of the post office carrying a pile of mail.

"I'm late this morning!" Jenny cried. "You too!"

"Yes. Getting lazy in my old age. Even Charley was tired this morning. We both slept in, didn't get up until nine o'clock, then had a leisurely breakfast with the family—Thomas and Sarah and their three kids are here from Los Angeles. So, I asked Parrish and Jean and the kids and Charles to Sunday dinner, and Amy and Don and the kids stopped in to say hello, and Matthew and Carla and their grand-kids stopped by, because Matthew and Thomas were really close in high school. I had all of them for Sunday dinner. Twenty-five people. I was prostrate yesterday," she said, laughing. "There was a time I could have thirty for dinner with one hand tied behind my back, but no more. And I didn't even bake!"

"Oh, Maddy!" Jenny was appalled. "Twenty-five for dinner! I couldn't handle that; I wonder if even Tim could. I've never had more than six. But how nice Thomas and Sarah are here! Are they staying long?"

"They took two weeks off from work. They went to New York, to see the city with the kids; the kids had never been there. They stayed with Lily and Parsons and their kids—it must have been pretty crowded." She laughed. "New York houses aren't meant for overnight guests. They rented a car and drove up here Saturday, and tomorrow they're driving to Boston. They want the kids to see the Freedom Trail and Old Ironsides and Paul Revere's house and the old North Church. They'll be flying home from there."

"So you have a houseful today."

"Only for dinner, and we'll go out tonight. I've learned to be kind to myself, take things a little easier. They all went sightseeing today. They had a carful, so I didn't go. Anyway I've seen everything there is to see up here."

"How nice to run into you. Are you in a hurry?"

"No," Maddy smiled happily. "All I have to do is buy something for my grandniece Amy. She's going to pop any day, and I want to cheer her up. I remember how I felt at nine months, when you're as big as a bear, uncomfortable as a chicken in a downpour. I thought I'd go to Dahlia's in Winchester and see if I can't find her a nice sexy nightgown with a negligee . . ."

Jenny laughed. "That's what got her in this fix in the first place!"

"It's what she needs now, actually," Maddy disagreed. "The negligee, not the nightgown."

Jenny didn't quite get it, but she smiled anyway. "How about having lunch with me at Leah's first?"

Maddy gazed down the row of shops toward Leah's. "Why not? Go get your mail; I'm going to put this stuff in my car, and I'll meet you there."

All Steventon's commercial enterprises sat in a row far back from the main street—a bank, post office, hairdresser, grocery, and general store. At the end of the row stood a Revolutionary-era building of large yellowish stone. Leah Albertson, who had come to Steventon from Connecticut to rent it, fit its large windows with lace curtains, and opened a café, which she named Leah's Ark. She had decorated it with a frieze of animals marching around the walls, just beneath the ceiling, and tucked stuffed animals, which were for sale, on shelves along one wall. She served homemade soups, sandwiches, and desserts.

Jenny and Maddy settled themselves on mismatched old chairs at one of Leah's old tables, set with antique linen tablecloths embroidered in different styles and patterns. It was early and they were alone in the café. They both ordered warm vegetable sandwiches—grilled eggplant, tomato, green pepper, onion, and swiss cheese—and iced tea.

"Lunch at your house was so lovely, Jenny," Maddy said.

"Oh, thanks. It was so good to see you all. You really lift my spirits."

"Our get-togethers seem to do that for all of us. I don't know why, exactly, but I don't question it. We're all so different. I'm so old, and look at you. You're close to Amy's age."

"I'm thirty."

"Well, she's twenty-four, but you're both in your childbearing years . . ."

Jenny colored faintly and looked away.

"Oh, there I go again!" Maddy exclaimed. "Always putting my big foot in something. I didn't mean anything by that, Jenny Halliday! I'm not one of those women who thinks every woman should have baby after baby. Don't pay any attention to me!"

"I didn't think you meant anything," Jenny laughed. "Don't worry. But I have been thinking about it. I mean, if I'm going to have a baby, I should do it pretty soon."

Maddy nodded. "I suppose so. Do you want one?"

"I don't know. Tim doesn't. You know," she added quickly, "he already has a couple of kids. And . . . well, he wouldn't want me talking about it but he's had some trouble with them. You know how things are with kids these days . . . "

"Do I not!"

"Soooo . . ." Jenny let it drop. The waitress arrived with their food, and they started to eat.

Jenny resumed, "Besides, I don't know if I'd be a good mother. I never had a mother. Well, of course I had one, but she died when I was little. I was raised by a German nanny. She was proper, stiff, and humorless and I don't think she was very motherly. Not compared to you all. You women give me more mothering in one afternoon than she did my entire life." She laughed.

"Yes, I guess that's part of what we do for each other. Cherish each other. We need to be cherished . . . by somebody, for heaven's sake!" Maddy smiled.

"Oh, I can picture you with your children," Jenny said warmly. "You must have been a wonderful mother. I wish you'd been my mother . . ."

Maddy smiled, patted her hand. "I'll take you on any terms you'll have me." She took another bite of her sandwich. She wiped her lips, sipped her tea, and spoke, as if she'd been holding her breath all this while: "I wasn't such a good mother, you know."

"I don't believe it."

"I wasn't. I resented my children."

"Why?" Jenny sounded shocked.

"Because I had to work so hard to give them a childhood—and I never had one myself."

Jenny looked puzzled.

"You're so young. You don't know how things used to be. People had large families, and they all turned the oldest girl into a baby minder. Farmwomen were overworked, but even town women worked hard. They worked all the time. They just couldn't take care of the babies too, so they pressed their four- and five-year-old daughters into service. I was the oldest girl in a family of nine. I worked from the time I could walk."

"Oh, Maddy," Jenny lamented.

"Never had a childhood. Never had the freedom to play, run,

and jump, and the only time I could read—my favorite activity—was late at night under the covers with a flashlight."

"That was so unfair!"

"At the time, I just thought it was natural—everyone did it. All except old Emily! She just wouldn't. Until Martin was born, anyway. Of course, she wasn't the oldest, but she drove her mother crazy with her irresponsibility."

"And she didn't have children when she was grown, but you did. Doesn't that seem ironic?"

"No. Makes sense. Old Emily just never bought the package the rest of us bought. Wouldn't be a 'good girl,' then or ever. Did what she wanted to do. I respect that so much. Wish I'd done the same."

"Do you wish you hadn't had children?"

Maddy paused. "Well . . ." She thought. "I can't say that. My children mean so much to me. They all live far away, except Parrish, and I don't see them much, but I love them to pieces."

Jenny listened intently.

"They make me feel complete. They give a reason to my life," Maddy concluded.

"That's what I imagine," Jenny said faintly, staring into space.

"But they were a lot of work," Maddy added. "A real pain in the neck."

Jenny smiled. "So I gather. Tim's really out of patience with his son. They keep trying to get him into rehab—Tim and his ex-wife. Joel—the boy—and his mother Clare went to Hazelton for a while. Not sure how he is now. And his daughter too . . . "

Maddy laid her head in her hand. "Don't tell me."

Jenny looked at her, puzzled.

"When I was a young married woman, back in the fifties, people talked about their children. They'd tell you the kid was getting a tooth or had learned to walk, or was getting straight As in fourth grade. Or was getting married or having a baby, moving house, or getting a new job. But that was it. They never told you Son-in-Law had lost his job or Daughter-in-Law had had a nervous breakdown or Son was on drugs. Mainly because they weren't! Such things were very rare. But now every family has a horror story to tell, kids on drugs, anorexic, dropping out, alcoholics, homosexuals, criminals, getting divorced, whatever. The children don't behave, they fall apart. I have four children, and eight brothers and sisters, all of whom have children, and I can't tell you all the disasters I've lived through in the last twenty years. So which was it for Tim's daughter? Or is there more than one?"

Maddy's half-jocular tone made Jenny smile, but she was uneasy. She knew Tim would be mortified at her betraying his secrets.

"She was anorectic. Polly. She nearly died, she weighed so little. But the worst part—for Tim—was, after he divorced Clare, Polly stopped speaking to him. She wouldn't see him, or stay with him, wouldn't accept his birthday or Christmas gifts. She's nineteen now, he's been divorced for eight years, and she has only just started to take his telephone calls again."

Maddy nodded. Her face was pained. "I'm sorry. I know it's agony for the parents. I know, I am one," she said. "It's just so peculiar, though. How come these things didn't happen in the old days and now they do?"

"I don't know," Jenny said vaguely. "Maybe people repressed things then?"

"People blame the sixties, the sexual revolution, or the war. Everybody has a different explanation."

"Yes." Jenny sounded deflated. "Anyway, the upshot is, he doesn't want to have any more children."

"And you?"

"When I got married, I didn't think I wanted children . . ."

Maddy peered at her. "And now you do?"

Jenny looked away. "This weekend, some friends of mine came up to stay with us. Just Saturday and Sunday. Tim made a great dinner Saturday night and I made brunch Sunday morning. It was fun. Lisa Goethals and I were in art school together, and her husband, Joey Castellano, he's an artist too, but he works for a fashion magazine now, he makes tons of money. She sculpts. Or did. Because now she has a baby and of course can't do sculpture. No room in the house for one thing, no energy left for another. But they brought the baby with them." She looked in Maddy's eyes, and Maddy studied hers, innocent as a child's, pale blue, wide open.

"She was so adorable, their little girl. She's only two months old. I just wanted to keep holding her. Oh, I know, she's a pain in the neck, she cried, she wet, she wouldn't nurse because she wasn't at home and Lisa was getting crazy . . . And Lisa can't work. But still. Those tiny hands, the way she waved them around, the way her fists clenched when Lisa nursed her, the way she kept moving her mouth. I was riveted by her, wondering what's going on in her mind. And then, when she smiles! You feel you've done something wonderful.

"When they left, Tim said, 'Thank god they're gone, one more hour with that brat and I would have had to get blind drunk.' But I . . . I didn't feel that way. And I don't know what to do about it. The crying passes, doesn't it?"

"Ummm, sure," Maddy said.

"So if you had it to do over again, what would you do? Would you have a career?"

Maddy studied her lunch for a while. Then she said softly, "I don't think I could do without them."

"Did Charley help? He seems such a sweetheart."

"Oh, you know how he is: He thinks I'm perfect and perfect people don't need help. Men didn't help in those days. It wasn't expected. And most of them just didn't. And Charley is so sweet, he couldn't get his mind around my misery. He'd listen and put his arms around me and tell me he knew I was just having a bad day and would feel better tomorrow. If he'd let himself understand, it would have made him unhappy, you see—he would have had to do something about it. The worst time for me was when I got pregnant after the other kids were grown, with Benjamin. Here I thought I was through . . . What saved me then was Emily coming back here to live. After twenty years away. She'd been my closest friend, and she still was, and I could talk to her, and she understood. She kept me sane. I was able to return the favor when Clea was here. She's a darling girl, but she gave Emily grief. Still, there's no one Emily loves more. That's the way things are. Ironic to the last comma."

"Comma?"

"Comma. There are no periods. Nothing ends. Things keep on going, generation after generation." Maddy sipped the last of her tea.

"What goes around comes around?"

"Pardon?"

"Nothing. Just an expression. Did Alicia ever need . . . help?"

"Not from me. So far as I know, she hasn't had troubles that serious. Except she seems upset about Steven's relation with Stevie these days. She has . . . my niece-in-law's a psychologist, and she says people have 'issues.' She'd say Alicia has issues with Steven. Except of course, conflicts with another person are always really with yourself . . ."

"Are you saying that my . . . questions . . . about Tim having kids are really my own conflict?"

"I wasn't, but of course, sweetheart, they are. If you were sure you wanted a baby, Tim wouldn't be much of a problem for you."

Jenny laughed. "You are something, Maddy Gold!"

"I suppose that's true," Maddy said wryly.

Jenny laughed again. "I'm an expert at saying nothing. My social training . . . But Maddy, tell me the truth now."

Maddy turned to face her. "Promise."

"If you had your life to live over again, would you have had children?"

"If I could live my life over again . . . you mean in the world the way it is now? Absolutely. If I had to live my life over again in the old world, I'd shoot myself. Once was enough. Once was too much. But in this world, I'd go to college, I wouldn't marry young—of course twenty wasn't considered young in those days—I'd go to law school, get a job in a city, have love affairs, travel in Europe, maybe Asia, it's always fascinated me.

"But I would have married eventually. I've liked my marriage, I like Charley, I like being married, except if I did it again, we'd share the housework, I wouldn't be a servant again, I'd demand cooperation. And I wouldn't have had four children—although if you asked me which of my four I'd do without, I couldn't answer. I wouldn't worry quite so much about cleanliness and disease, things like that. Of course, children did regularly die of rheumatic fever, diphtheria, and polio in those days. Even measles."

She drifted into another place, where she seemed to be talking to herself. "They're the most important people in my life, my children, they're everything to me. I love them profoundly. I know no one else can love them as much as I do. They've filled my life. It hasn't all been sweet, but it's all been rich. Alive.

"They are my most profound experience. My deepest being is in them."

Jenny sat absolutely still. Then her face collapsed into wistfulness. "That's what I thought," she whispered.

Maddy carried the mail and her packages into the house, leafing through the envelopes for orders for Charley. He got excited every time an order arrived, like a child who never tires of ice cream cones. Only one letter was addressed to the Gold Strike, as Charley called his business; she set it on the counter where he'd see it as soon as he came in. The rest she carried to her study: She always paid the bills, had since she was married. Then she sat down at her desk, still in her coat and hat—Maddy always wore a hat in cool weather—and gloves.

She swung around on the chair to face the side yard of the house, the long sweep of lawn, dormant azaleas and rhododendrons lining it, the trees beyond. It made her sad; she disliked the garden when it was dead, brown and spectral, the twisted fingers of the trees reaching for some imagined reward. Summer disguised their longing, filling them with greenery. Or maybe the greenery was what they wanted, the rustle of leaves, the twittering of birds, nests in the branches. Life.

Jenny, imagining me as the ideal mother. What a joke!

If you had it all to do over again, would you do the same things?

Who has it to do over again? And once you know, you know. And once they're born, they exist and you cannot imagine them nonexistent. You are horrified at the thought of their disappearance. Those dear ones, you clutch them. They are your life.

She took her hat off and laid it on the desk, removed her gloves, and stood up to take her coat off. She let it fall on the chair and went over to the chaise against the wall and sat on it, turning sideways to put her feet up. Her mother's old handmade lap rug lay over the back of the chaise, and she pulled it down and covered her legs. She laid her head back against the chair and gazed out at the March grayness. Not even a tiny swelling on those tree limbs, no touch of green yet.

In 1967, Maddy had been forty-three; Thomas was nineteen; Parrish, seventeen; and Lily, her youngest, fourteen, when Maddy had found herself pregnant again. Shock silenced her. She could not believe her situation, kept imagining that her period would arrive a few days late, tomorrow or the next day, although she was regular as the moon and it never came. She burrowed into herself in sullen rage, feeling like a baby in a tantrum, but having to behave like a mother, a wife, a housekeeper. Her body vibrated with resentment. She broke out in a rash, itched miserably, had palpitations. The doctor found nothing wrong, but her heart was a cymbal struck regularly by a gong. Pregnant, pregnant, pregnant.

The news was not just an ordinary shock, but a lightning bolt that cruelly illuminated her past, like huge film lights suddenly switched on over a plain littered with bones. Suddenly she knew that not only did she not want to be pregnant now, she had never wanted to be pregnant, never wanted to raise children. She had never wanted to be a secretary, never wanted to be a housewife. She had not chosen her life, it had been handed to her ready-made, like a prefabricated house, and suddenly, the carefully built structure that was her respectable life collapsed into a heap of rubble, a bombed-out remnant of failure. She had lived in bad faith; she had lived a false life. She capsized into mourning. She took to her bed.

Charley had to draft her mother to come and help out with the children and housework. Maddy, inconsolable, lay on the chaise, gazing out the window as she had when the children were small and played ball or tag on the lawn, their piping voices a constant music in her days. Closing her eyes to hear them better, she would feel the familiar twinge of . . . resentment. She had resented their joy, their carefreeness. She'd envied her children their freedom, their playfulness, their childhood.

It came to her that she begrudged them every joy she worked so hard to supply, and that she was always working against herself, struggling to make life sweeter for them and hating them for it. She had to pry her teeth apart to say yes to them. She wanted, oh how she wanted to say no to everything they asked for, to thwart every desire. They played, they had toys, candy, ice skates, ice cream from Good Humor; when they got a little older, they went to the movies.

Her childhood had contained no such pleasures. It had been Maddy do this, Maddy do that, from the time she could walk. Maddy, watch the baby. Maddy, change Ethan's diaper, or William's or Anne's or Donald's or Eleanor's or Clarence's, well, by then she didn't need to be told to feed the baby, give it bottles, change diapers. Eight children, she the eldest girl. Andrew was a year older than she, but a boy, so he was free, out playing. Munson too, two years younger. They were allowed to be children. That time Munson fell and hit his head and got so mad that when he stood up screaming he held his breath so long he passed out. Momma shrieked, picked up his limp body, then slapped Maddy hard, in the face, leaving a mark that stayed the whole day. It wasn't her fault the baby fell. She'd never forgotten that, never forgiven it, either: She was only four, a baby herself.

And bright as she was in school—always got 100s, always got As, the brightest of the Thaddeuses everyone said—college for a girl was out of the question. Of course, people here didn't send even sons to college in those days. But Andrew and Munson were drafted into the army, and afterward got the GI bill, so they both went to college. That was good, people said, they were bright boys. But everyone knew Maddy was smarter. Yet she had questioned nothing. She had been given so little that she smilingly accepted any spare kindness that fell upon her. Life was hard for everybody. She saw that everywhere. Farming was hard work, harder for women then men. Poor Momma was worked off her feet. She desperately needed Maddy's help; it mattered. She felt good knowing she helped Momma so much.

They made almost everything themselves in those days: Grandma had made all the family's clothes, baked her own bread, even made goose-down comforters. Momma put up vegetables, fruit, whatever they grew—they would have starved winters if she hadn't. Grandma remembered her grandmother and mother churning butter, making soap. She was grateful for having things a little easier than they, but she still worked from early in the morning until late at night, long after the men had stopped and were sitting near the fire with a pipe. And Maddy had done the same. Unlike her mother and grandmother, she didn't make the men's clothes and made the boys' only when they were little. But of course she made her own and Lily's—all women did in those days. Laundry was a big deal then. Hard hard work done on a scrub board with yellow soap. Women had it so much easier these days. Her eyes had wept all by themselves when Lily first showed her a disposable diaper.

In her youth, you took what you could get and bowed to the rest. Things were the way they were, the way they had always been, for men and women. The lives of both were engraved in stone, by law or fate, long before she'd been born. Your role had been written for you by God. No one could escape.

But by the time she was pregnant with Benjamin, she knew better. Revelation fell upon her all at once. She wanted to scream, to shriek, to smack god a good one right in the face. She was forty-four years old, Thomas would be twenty when the baby was born. Twenty years of child-rearing was enough, she'd done her share, no more, not again starting from scratch. By the time the baby was grown, she'd be sixty-odd years old, no life of her own, ever, ever.

She even considered . . . doing something about it. From the first moment she suspected pregnancy, the thought popped into her head. She couldn't help it, it just popped there all by itself. She didn't know who or how, but she knew there were ways. She could ask someone like Sally Torrence, who'd been wild since she was a girl. If Sally hadn't done it herself, she'd surely know someone who had. Someone in Pittsfield, probably. Of course, it was dangerous. Illegal. Women died from it sometimes. But it would be worth it: She'd just as soon die as have another baby.

Because she was considering . . . doing something about it . . . she did not at first tell Charley she was pregnant. But it was hard, not having anyone to talk to about it. She wished she had a friend, a real friend. But a woman with three children, a husband, a mother and father, seven siblings, seven siblings-in-law, and twenty-odd nieces and nephews didn't have time for friends. People had families, not friends. The only friend she'd ever had, Emily Oldfield, had left years ago.

In the end, she gave up the idea of doing anything about it. She couldn't. Suppose Charley found out. He worshiped her; she couldn't bear seeing disappointment in his eyes. Suppose she died from it. He'd never get over her dying that way. She cared too much about Charley to hurt him that way.

All this while, Charley, noticing that she was absent most of the time, answering him in curt phrases, but mainly ignoring him, was wondering if she was in menopause—everyone knew women went crazy in menopause. As a boy, he had heard his mother whisper about Mrs. Gamble, who in menopause drowned her newborn baby, and Mrs. Dowd, who went into a profound depression and had to be hospitalized. Since his childhood, the word *menopause* had struck terror into his heart. He treated Maddy as if she were made of glass. So she had to set him straight.

She gave him the news and resigned herself to never having a life of her own, to following her mother and her mother before her in an infinite line of self-sacrificing, hardworking women whose destinies were indeed their anatomies.

A few months after Maddy became pregnant, Robert Oldfield died of an aneurism. Emily was summoned home. Maddy, visiting the funeral parlor, went up to embrace her old friend. Maddy was showing by then.

"Another on the way?" Emily asked, smiling.

Maddy grimaced. "A surprise for my middle age."

"Oh. Sorry," Emily said.

"Sorry about your father."

"Yes . . . thanks."

"Blackmailing me to stay here."

Maddy's heart lifted. Oh, stay here! Oh, she wished she would! Another visitor approached Emily. There was no time or place to talk that night. She moved away.

They met again at the funeral, and at the gathering that followed it. Again, they could not talk.

But Emily never called her or stopped in, and Maddy, profoundly hurt, assumed she had returned to Boston without getting in touch. Their relationship was really dead and gone. Then a month later, there was Emily coming out of the grocery store.

"Em! You're still here!"

It was Emily's turn to grimace.

"I'm back. I was going to call you this afternoon. After the funeral, things were crazy, with my mother," she said. "We went round and round. *Sturm und Drang*. But I decided in the end to come back to Steventon, so I went back to Boston to quit my job and pack up my apartment."

Maddy's spirits rose enough that she was able to offer her newborn baby some affection. She copied the older children, who adored him, constantly picked him up, held him, kissed him, played with him. She watched them in wonder. This, she concluded, was how normal people were with babies. She was not normal: She had a shriveled heart. Imitating them, she tried to learn how to love. And where had they learned? she wondered. Certainly she had never held and kissed them. From their grandparents, from Charley.

She poured her sorrows out to Emily, who was not shocked. She had never wanted a baby at all, and could easily understand Maddy's not wanting a fourth. And Emily knew how things had been years ago.

"My mother tried to make me tend Mamie and Crighton, but I wouldn't—Robert and John were both older than I, remember. Mamie got stuck with Crighton. But I took Martin, I wanted him, I chose him, I loved him so. I was already thirteen when he was born, I didn't lose my childhood. But otherwise things were the same way in my house—the girls had to do the dishes, make the beds, help with the laundry, with the mending. The boys could go out and play. The boys could stay out at night, we couldn't. I fought back, though; I drove my mother crazy being irresponsible. Her word. I knew I was being stubborn, but I just couldn't do what she wanted."

"I remember."

"You know, when I think about it now, I think my mother didn't really want us—didn't really want children—at all; I'm not sure she wanted to be a mother or even a wife. That's why it makes her so furious that I never married, that I escaped."

"You did! Oh, you did!"

"The way she's acting at the moment, it's hard for me to sympathize with her, but you know, she probably never wanted the life she had. Too late now for her to change it: She's sixty-six, and she's old. Worn out after bearing seven children. I have colleagues at the institute who are older than she and full of life, but they've had different lives. Terrible to have lived the wrong life . . ."

"Oh Emily!" Maddy moaned, "that's how I feel! That's exactly how I feel! As if I've lived the wrong life! Someone else's life! Not the one I was meant to have. Would have chosen if I could choose!"

Emily looked at her friend with profound sympathy. "I'm so sorry, Mad. I suppose you can't change it . . . " Her glance fell onto Maddy's belly. "No."

"Not now," Maddy said grimly. "But someday!"

Maddy gave Benjamin as much love as she could dredge up from what she thought of as her dry little heart—to the furious jealousy of the older kids. She tried to be more generous to the older ones, but mother-child relations, once set, can be impossible to change.

Benjamin became her favorite, her sweetheart, the one who doted on her as she on him. She and Charley took him on vacations with them (explaining to the older children that one was easier to take along than three) and invented little outings for him, picnics, canoeing excursions, movies. She rarely denied him anything. The older children steamed with rage and jealousy—Lily aloud, the boys silently. Benjamin ended up the happiest of her children, the easiest in his skin; yet he was the first to move away from her, to settle clear across the country. And when Thomas married and had children of his own, she saw him pass on the denial she'd practiced. Like tumbleweed, it gathered bulk and speed as it moved onward on its own through another generation. He had resented her denials, but they were engraved on his soul as the virtues she had claimed they were. He still denied himself, adult that he was, and his children as well. She had passed on an unending cycle of misery.

7

While Maddie waited for Benjamin to be born, in 1967, everything exploded.

Charley, a college man himself, wanted his sons to have degrees, and Thomas had started school at UMass in 1966. By the time Benjamin was born, Thomas had stopped washing his hair and let it grow long. He wore only blue jeans, ignoring the nice gabardines she'd bought him for college. He began saying things that upset his father. Maddy didn't pay much attention, she was so busy, she had Charley and three other children, one of them a baby, to tend to; she did all the laundry (including Thomas's) and mending and sewing for herself and Lily and she sent Thomas care packages and put up fruit and vegetables every fall. And the things he said didn't seem so awful to her, but Charley began to get a worried look on his face when he listened to his son.

Things got worse in 1968, when her nephew Ken, Munson's son, the brightest of the young ones, joined Thomas at UMass. The boys were overjoyed at being together at college; Thomas and Ken had loved each other since babyhood. Strange things were happening at other colleges—Charley would read the paper out loud to her in the evening while she mended—uprisings at Columbia, Harvard, Berkeley. Within a month of starting college, Ken too was growing his hair long and smoked pot openly. His mother, Edna, was horribly upset by this. Well, he did look dirty. Both boys started ranting about the "military-industrial complex" (Maddy knew exactly what they meant, she'd often thought the same herself); Ken kept referring to "Amerika," pronouncing it like a foreign word. He called Lyndon Johnson an agent of the devil and said he would not fight in Vietnam. When Munson said a man had a duty to fight for God and country, Ken said he would not fight for a country ruled by the rich for their own profit and well-being without concern for the poor, or worship a god who did not exist. He said his family, the town of Steventon, and their minister were all hypocrites and racists.

He provoked Munson so much that Maddy feared her brother would have a heart attack. Charley was upset by what the boys said, but he was a reasonable man, he thought over their attacks and finally said he could see some justice in Ken's statements. He remembered his World War II and its horrors, and he admitted to Maddy, quietly, in their bedroom one night, that war was such a terrible thing that no country should ever enter one unless it was absolutely necessary—as his war had been, he believed. Hitler had to be stopped. But maybe there was no reason to fight in Southeast Asia. Maybe Charley's being so sane was what kept Thomas from getting as crazy as Ken. But Munson, red in the face, raged around the house, "Never thought I'd raised a coward!" Momma and Poppa were upset too—well, who wouldn't be? They'd never heard such things as that boy was saying and punctuating his sentences with *fuck*, a word that had never been uttered in that family. No one of them, no one in Steventon had ever uttered such a word until Ken Thaddeus did in 1969. In time, Maddy's other brothers, Ken's uncles—Ethan, William, Donald, and Clarence—Charley's brothers too, got up in arms, and her sister Anne too, and Anne's husband, Lincoln. Lincoln said, What would happen to a country whose men just decided they didn't want to fight? The country would collapse, he said. Men had to be soldiers.

In fact, Andrew and Charley were the only ones who had actually fought in a war. Munson was drafted when he was eighteen, in 1944, but he spent the war in Texas, learning to fix jeeps and tanks, training that got him a job with GM in Pittsfield when the war ended. Charley and Andrew had enlisted at nineteen, in 1941. Both, Maddy believed, had seen horrors, not that they said much about them. Charley had bombed Germany from England; when asked about it, he only shook his head. The work had been horribly dangerous, men were lost every night, and he knew that his bombs often hit civilians. At the time, all he could think about was scoring and staying alive, but later he was overwhelmed by the damage he'd done. Andrew was at Guadalcanal, which had been savage and demoralizing. He came back a serious quiet man, like Charley. Andrew was the only one of Maddy's brothers with a profession—he taught math at the high school. And Andrew took Ken's side: He agreed with Charley that war was horrible and shouldn't be waged if it wasn't necessary. What did we have to gain in Vietnam anyway, he wanted to know.

Finally Munson exploded and threw Ken out. He went to live with Andrew and Lilian. Ken knew that Andrew had suffered horribly at Guadalcanal and in a Japanese prison camp afterward, and he kept his mouth shut about Amerika when he was around him and when he was home weekends from college, he'd often stay at Maddy's with Thomas. Charley was such a mild man that Ken had no fear of him, but for the most part, he kept his mouth shut around Charley too. It was Maddy he spoke to, shooting his arrows into the one he thought vulnerable. He'd bring his girlfriend, Willow. She was a women's libber, a brand-new thing to be, a thing all the young women were talking about, and the two of them would talk to Maddy for hours about all the things that were wrong with the country. Maddy listened while she did laundry or ironed or put up peaches or cherries from their trees, or vacuumed or dusted. Often, she agreed with them. Their points were reasonable. But knowing she half agreed with them made them push further. Ken lectured her arrogantly, telling her that women were exploited, enslaved, forced to be a servant class to men, whose property they were, whatever the Constitution said.

Maddy couldn't bear this. It wasn't that he was wrong, but she felt he was saying these things in hate, not love. She wondered why he had so much hate in him, and why he directed it at her. She remembered Munson punishing Ken with a belt, when Ken was a boy, time after time. She'd protested it then—she was Munson's older sister and felt she had the right—and he told her to mind her own business, he was going to raise up obedient kids. He said she spoiled her children by never hitting them or allowing Charley to hit them. Not that Charley ever wanted to, she thought.

Munson having forbidden him the house, Ken's mother, Edna, never saw him anymore, and she missed him, even though his attitude or rather, his beard and long hair, upset her. So one Sunday afternoon, Maddy asked Edna to stop in alone at a time Ken would be there. Maddy had stopped serving huge Sunday dinners after church (they had pretty much stopped going to church, for that matter), and served just a small lunch. Ken, who had noted that no one had gone to church that day, launched into a sermon about hypocrites, who claimed to be religious but never went to church. Edna, who did go to church regularly, defended herself, sending Ken on to a different subject: denying there was a god and a law handed down by god. Such statements reduced Edna to tears. Seeing his mother upset, he began to shout that the ideas that formed women's lives were based on belief in a god who had made men superior to women, and required them to stay that way, which was all part of a plot invented by men to enslave women and subdue nonwhite men. Edna ran from the room with her hands over her ears, weeping her heart out. She'd never heard such things, she'd always been a pliable person. But even Maddy was angry. He lashed these truths at his mother like flicking a whip. Edna never made another effort to see him and Maddy never invited the two of them again. Edna wept to her brother-in-law Andrew about it and Andrew called Ken and castigated him for attacking women, whom Andrew believed to be more vulnerable and fragile than men. He told him he was no longer welcome in his house. Ken hadn't understood that when you destroy your links with women, you burn your bridge back home.

Maddy wanted to weep, wanted to join Edna in the bathroom

and bury her face in a hankie. Not because of what he said, but because of the way he said it. His words stayed in her mind, burned in more every day as she recognized again and again the way her life had happened around her without her choosing it, had made her what she was, had been the wrong life.

Ken said, Nothing was written in stone.

In 1970, Ken was drafted, and in the end, his courage failed him; all his talk about escaping to Canada stuttered into silence. He went into the army, head down. Munson subsided into silent anxiety, Edna into a bewildered dread.

He came back three years later. His beard and long hair were gone, but he was on drugs, and bitter as a peach pit, mean and nasty. He no longer gave tirades; he rarely spoke at all. By then, many of his relatives grudgingly agreed with him about the Vietnam War, if not war in general; they still thought men had to fight, just maybe not in Southeast Asia. But the issue had divided the family, brother from brother, as effectively as the Civil War a century earlier. Half the Thaddeuses no longer spoke to the other half; parents and children had split forever.

This, of course, was not Ken's fault, but it didn't help him. Because half of the family would not speak to him at all, the other half felt guilty about him. Couldn't meet his eyes, not that he looked at anyone. He hung around for a while, but finding no footing, drifted away. After that, he came home only when he was totally broke. He would plead for loans, and for a long time, out of guilt, Munson, Edna, Charley, Andrew, and Maddy extended them. But after a couple of years, Charley, who during all this time had been fetching the drunken Parrish from whatever gutter Parrish had landed in, had been educated by Al-Anon. He called the relatives together and explained the dynamics of addiction, explained that cooperating with the addict encourages the addiction. He told them they all had to stop helping Ken and urge him to get treatment. So they did. But the next time he was broke, Ken sneaked into his parents' house while they were in church and stole the TV, the stereo, the silverware, and Edna's few pieces of jewelry. Munson reported it to the police, naming his son. The police found him easily—he had not bothered to hide—with some of the stolen items still in his possession. Ken went to jail for a while. Edna went berserk and had to be hospitalized.

When he came out of jail, he disappeared. The family hadn't heard from him in over twenty years now. He might well be dead, dependent on heroin as he was. Who knew? He was gone, god knew where, Maddy thought, her heart slowing down as she recalled his brightness, his eager gray eyes smiling up at her. He had had talent. He'd been an adorable toddler, his little legs carrying him up and down the little hill in her side yard, chasing a ball, chirping with laughter. What a handsome young fellow he'd been setting off for college with joy in his intelligent face.

But none of them was the same now, they'd all changed, and he had helped to change them. Now everyone knew that the government lied and lied and was lying still, and that what we did to the people of Vietnam was as bad as anything any oppressor had done anywhere. No longer could Americans bask in the belief that America was indeed the city on a hill, the radiant expression of a new belief in humankind. Ken had enlightened them, but not with goodwill. He had used his opinions and his knowledge to try to crush them; he was as brutal as the men he hated. And that, finally, was what hurt her most about Ken: He became what he hated. His life had been co-opted just like hers. Poor Ken. Poor Munson and Edna. Poor all of us . . .

She lifted her head wearily. The sun was spread across the side lawn, midafternoon it was. Practically the whole day gone and she hadn't accomplished anything. Oh well. She was old now, she didn't have to accomplish something every day. She was still tired from Sunday after all. She told herself she deserved a rest.

It was all years ago, why was she thinking about it now? It was too late to change anything. I've had a good life, she told herself. My marriage is good, my kids and grandkids are healthy, I love my friends. It's just that I'm a little tired. Often these days, she found herself thinking that she would not mind lying down and never having to get up again. The years have been so costly. All the . . . wounds. The children, oh the children. Life was hard.

And I made it harder, she thought, her mouth tightening.

•

Wednesday morning, there were tiny green nodules on the weeping willows along the river. Winter in the Berkshires is long and cold and people hunger for spring. Maddy was so elated by the buds that she decided to leave her office early, stop at the bakery for some Linzer tortes, which she knew Emily could not resist, and stop at her friend's house. Now they were having tea.

"Ummm," Emily said, sipping her fragrant linden tea. "This was a nice idea."

"I knew I'd be taking you away from your work. But it's four-thirty, after all. Time for a rest."

"I don't stop working until dinnertime," Emily said. "Around eight."

"I know that. Are you annoyed I stopped in?"

"No. You know I love to see you. I just couldn't do it every day," Emily said.

"You're as jealous of your time as a man is of a woman."

"You have to be on guard when you work at home. Everyone thinks if a woman is home, she's available." She raised the pot. "More tea?"

Maddy nodded and Emily poured. She had served it in the proper way, even to the silver strainer and the pot of hot water.

"Nobody serves tea like this anymore. You do everything so correctly," Maddy commented.

"I know," Emily lamented. "It's my upbringing."

"We just can't get over it, can we? Even though it's so much trouble and no one cares about it."

"But I've gotten better. You should see how simple my dinners are some nights."

Maddy bit into a Linzer torte. "Ummm," she said. "I had lunch with Jenny yesterday."

"You did! How come?"

Maddy explained. "She's a little confused."

"Yes, I thought she might be, when I met her. So young. So sweet and innocent, New Yorker or not."

"How long have they been up here, four years?"

"Three. They came in 1997."

"That's right. That house was being built in the spring of 1997, and it was finished in the summer. I remember everybody wondering who was going to move in. Some millionaire, they thought."

"Is Tim a millionaire?"

Maddy shrugged. "Probably. Millionaires aren't that unusual nowadays—even I'm a millionaire. So is Clea. Tim's got plenty of money, that's for sure. That house cost a bundle, and there's the pool, the tennis courts, his studio. And the art he has in it looks expensive to me . . . Not that I know anything about art. I guess some artists make money." She finished her tea and moved to what interested her. "The problem is, he doesn't want to have more children, and she thinks she might."

"Oh. Clea's a millionaire? I didn't know that."

Maddy nodded.

"Yes, of course she is, Em. Both her parents had huge insurance policies, and they had money too." She wiped her lips with the linen napkin. "So Jenny's in a quandary, because when they married she agreed not to have children."

"Hard for an artist to have a baby and her art," Emily said shortly.

"You don't sound sympathetic."

"No, I'm not. I had to settle that for myself, and it was hard then. I guess I think of it as the testing ground for women artists. They have to choose, and if they choose a family, they've chosen something else above art and will never accomplish much . . ."

"You mean, women who want families have less talent?"

"No, time. It takes more than talent to be an artist. Much more. You have to have drive, ambition. You have to be relentless."

"Was there any great woman artist with a family? There must be some."

"Well, Clara Schumann. If she's great. George Sand. She's great, but she had servants. But nowadays being an artist and having a family seem to be mutually exclusive."

"Didn't Louise Nevelson have a son? I love her work. What I've seen of it, which is only in photographs. Anyway, don't you think things are different now?"

"The main thing that's different is that housework is not so onerous anymore. Did you ever see that BBC program called *1900 House*? It shows what taking care of a house was like in 1900—not even 1800, or 1700, when most women lived on farms and had three times the work of that 1900 woman . . ."

"Yes! We saw that together. Awful, I remember. Sweeping every day. Coal dust. And everything was so hard to do, like the laundry. But maybe nowadays a woman could do it. Have a family and make great art."

"Maybe," Emily said, but she sounded dubious.

Maddy sighed. The choice had been too cruel for Emily, she thought, and had hardened her too severely for pity. She changed the subject. "I wonder how she'll manage. Jenny. She seems so—fragile to me. There's something childlike about her, don't you think? Sweet and trusting. She'd have a hard time holding her own in a power struggle."

"Yes. Not like Clea."

"Oh, Clea!" Maddy laughed. "She was a tough nut. She beat you hands down. But I wonder if she's that tough dealing with a lover, or a husband."

"That's true. She might not be. She's a darling girl, though.

"I wish she'd come back for your concert. Would you like that?"

"I'd like her coming back for any reason at all. But I don't feel I can ask her."

Maddy gazed at the floor. "You don't?"

"No. I feel she doesn't want to be around me. That she wants complete separation from me. And that I must let her have it if she needs it. I shouldn't press her to come back here. You know?"

"You think if you asked her, she'd come?"

"I think she'd feel an obligation to come, whether she wanted to or not. That's what I don't want to do to her—or myself. To have her appear out of duty. Perfunctorily. I'd hate that."

"Love or nothing at all," Maddy smiled.

"Right."

•

Maddy drove home full of thought. Emily's reminiscing about Clea had brought those years back to her, too. She would dearly like to see the breach between Clea and Emily healed, but wasn't sure whether her intervention would be wise, or how far she should go. What if I called her, she wondered. Would that be intrusive? Well, yes, but was it a forgivable intrusion? She knew where Clea lived, she could surely find her phone number. But then would Clea come as a duty, which would surely upset Emily? Was that worse than her not coming? Would she blame Emily for Maddy's intrusion? Would Emily blame Maddy?

Maddy and Emily had been friends for sixty-odd years and knew almost everything there was to know about each other. Each was central to the other, whatever other ties they had. Maddy knew that Emily was not like other people. Most people were interested mostly in other people and their doings, what they owned and what they owed. And with their own desires and longings, and with things of the world. But Emily's mind was filled with ideas, structures, building blocks she experimented with. Maddy knew Emily's untouchability, saw it and felt it and did not try to change it. She would have said, if challenged, that that was how Emily was: The still core of her was beyond reach, even to her. It sat like a soul on a rock, contemplating the world, a little wistful at times, but mostly contented to be itself, playing with sounds and progressions and rhythms and tones. Only, sometimes, she missed being able to feel Emily, or at least she had, when they were younger.

But by now, Maddy knew the core of Emily, had seen it in her anguish over Clea. The girl had been with Emily for only a few years, but those years constituted the center of Emily's life, the one center she had apart from music. Maddy often thought that Emily's time abroad, her marvelous adventures—at least, so they seemed to Maddy—did not show at all on her quiet friend. No one would guess, looking at her tall, slender body, a little hunched with age, her hair still not gray, but tannish and pulled back into a dowdy bun, that rebellious ideas lurked inside that mind, rebellious feelings as familiar as her own breath. But for all the romance and drama of her early life, Emily's greatest emotion occurred in middle age, after Clea came and after Clea left. Emily had talked about Clea in a way she had never talked about anybody, even her mother. Yet even so, Maddy could only imagine how it was.

Thank heavens she, Maddy, had not had to go through a child's leaving in anger. Parrish had gone off, of course, but not in anger. At least, he didn't act angry. Just irresponsible. None of her children had gone away not speaking and then stayed away, like Iris Hawkins's daughter Lisette, when she was eighteen. It seemed to Maddy that Lisette had simply decided to punish her mother for everything that was wrong with her life. Hadn't Iris raised the child with love? Maddy had thought Iris a better mother than she, by a long shot. She, Maddy, was punitive at heart, no matter how she tried to control it. Yet her kids never rebelled. Who could understand the way children were these days? They spoke to their parents contemptuously, for instance; kids would not have dared do that when Maddy was young. Maddy never dreamed of speaking to her mother that way, nor would her sister or brothers. In Maddy's generation, mothers were blamed for everything—autism, schizophrenia, anorexia, asthma. And girls blamed their mothers for everything from acne to being overweight.

Certainly she had had problems with Parrish: phone calls in the middle of the night, police in one town or another saying he was drunk and lying in his own vomit, come and get him. And poor Charley would get up and get dressed and put on his overcoat and heavy boots and drive the many miles to wherever Parrish was and bring him home. They would set him up with pep talks, help him get a job, and sit back and wait and watch, half sick with dread. He would be okay, unhappy but sober, for a few weeks or months, they never knew how long. But sooner or later he'd disappear, having started in again without their noticing. How often they'd begun to relax, feeling that this time he would make it, and then felt like fools when again he suddenly reeled into the house on a tear again. For five years this went on, until someone told them they were encouraging him, and advised Charley to go to Al-Anon. After that, Charley told Parrish he wasn't going to be rescued next time, he could dry out in the drunk tank and make his way alone. And the next time the police called, Charley stood by his word. It nearly killed him, they were both out of their minds with worry, but they stuck to their guns, the two of them, holding hands and biting their lips, for days afterward.

And Parrish did disappear. He was gone for months. She and Charley had both ended up going to Tom Gamble for help. He'd prescribed Tagamet, a new miracle drug, to calm their stomachs. Cousin Dilly Lang told Maddy that when she, Dilly, was in China, where advertising was nonexistent, she had seen a gigantic billboard in Beijing advertising Tagamet. Seemed the Chinese had ulcers too.

Missing for months, no word of him. She kept seeing his keen eyes, the dark blue of them in his pale face, he, of all her children, looked the most like her. He had been such a sweet little boy, the sweetest of her children, the most loving to her. But she . . . oh, she had failed him, it was all her fault, she knew it.

She blindly turned into her driveway and sat in the car, recovering.

Charley was home. She did not feel, at that moment, that she could face him, and for a moment, she lamented his retirement; life was easier when she did not have to see him all day every day.

She got out of the car and entered the house.

"Maddy?" Charley's voice called from the cellar. "That you?"

"It's me, Charley," she called.

Up the stairs he trudged, his face and hands smudged with old dust. He was grinning. He held out a metal tool she did not recognize. "I finally found that old vise! I been lookin' for it for months, and there it was, on the shelf with the old beach chairs!"

"Oh. Good, dear!"

"I wanted to do a little work on the window-washer handle, see if I could make it easier to use," he explained. "Plane down one end, taper it a bit, you know?"

"Good idea," she said, smiling at his wide-eyed eagerness.

"Any orders in that pile of mail you're carrying?"

"I haven't been through it yet. Want to look?" She offered him the pile.

He hesitated. He liked to get his orders right away, but he did not want to take the mail from her. It seemed . . . bossy, somehow. He turned away. "No. You check it. I'll be down basement, you want me," he explained, returning the way he came. On the stairs, he stopped. "If there's an order in that mail, you'll let me know, won't you?"

"Of course, dear," she called to him. Carrying the mail she'd picked up that morning, she went to her office to open it. Bills, junk mail, tons of it, a letter from Carla. She ripped it open.

> Dear Ma,
>
> It was so nice of you to have all of us for dinner Sunday. It's a real treat for me not to have to cook and you always serve such a delicious meal. It was so good to see Thomas and Sarah and Parrish and Jean and Charles and Amy and Don and all the kids! What a houseful! I hope you and Pa will make the drive over to New York State sometime soon so I can give you a thank-you meal, even though it won't be half as good. Pammie's going to pop any day now! And when she does, I'll be a grandma and you'll be a great-grandma! How about that!
>
> Love,
> Carla

Funny girl. The only one who always said thank you. None of my own children do. She could have picked up the phone, but she always writes. Maybe she doesn't like that kind of contact; maybe she doesn't like talking on the phone, like me. I'd rather get a letter.

She put the note down. Must remember to show it to Charley. No orders for him today. It will offset his disappointment to get a personal letter.

Deciding to rest and read the newspaper, she lay back on her fainting couch and pulled the afghan up to her knees. It occurred to her that Carla, her best niece-in-law, was Catholic. She recalled how horrified Momma would have been by that. Of course, Momma was long dead by the time Matthew had married Carla. But Momma had refused to go to the wedding when Andrew married Joan, who was Catholic too, and a good good woman, as good as Carla. Were they so good because they were Catholic? No, look at Joan Weiss, she was Jewish, and she was just as good. Took soup to people when they were sick, went all the way into Pittsfield to help out at the kitchen of the homeless shelter. It was their nature, these women, they were just saintly by nature. Joan Thaddeus had remembered every family birthday and holiday, and when they'd lived nearby, she'd often sent the children over after school to say hello. Sometimes with some spaghetti sauce or brownies she'd baked, or a layer cake. And she always smiled, always laughed, she was just a happy person. Momma wouldn't go to the wedding, wouldn't let Joan enter her house, relenting only after the grandchildren were born.

Joan was not just a good woman, she was a saint. But Momma didn't know that. She just set her mouth and raised her chin and that was that. Had no doubt whatever of her rightness. Wonder what she thought. She couldn't really have believed that Catholics had horns, could she? What did she think they were, or would do? Hard to imagine. The old folks had such strange ideas. Then of course she was avid to see the babies when they were born, and she ended up loving Joan as much as her own. Her best daughter-in-law. Didn't apologize, though.

Joan was old now but still a saint. Did Catholics feel they had to be saintly, married into these bigoted Yankee families? Were they forced into sainthood? Were Yankees so puritanical, so forbidden to think about their desires, that meanness and hatred became substitutes?

The past unfolded like a frieze, an endless Bayeux Tapestry laid out for her horrified delectation, scene after scene of women leading false lives. Nowhere in those scenes was there a moment when any of them showed, for even an instant, an awareness of their imprisonment. Her mother, Emily's mother, so many aunts, unhappy women all, and mean. Even she, Maddy Thaddeus, had not had more than a tiny intimation of who she was, a wisp of memory of a teacher saying how smart she was, of her brothers and sister deferring to her authority, well, she was older than most of them . . .

No, the insight had come suddenly, in the lightning flash of a phrase on a doctor's lips: You're pregnant, Maddy Gold, congratulations! *NO NO NO NO NO NO. ENOUGH.*

Even now, she remembered the fierce prick of rebellion that had penetrated her, the refusal to accept it, the wild wonder about forbidden things like abortions . . .

She wondered if it would be different for her now. Would she, now that abortion was legal, be able to announce to Charley, to Emily, that she was going to abort a child? Couldn't imagine it.

Only when Emily returned to Steventon and Maddy, and had picked up their friendship, had Maddy been able to talk about how she felt, let it out, all that bitterness, pour it into Emily's ear. It didn't poison Emily. Maddy didn't seem monstrous to her. And her patient calm listening turned Maddy's vileness into something different, not benign exactly, but human. Acceptably human. Within the human range.

Yet she still felt like a monster, resenting her own children. Her innards wanted, wanted hard, to say no to them, to see a shadow of hurt cross their eyes. She had had to fight with herself daily not to do it. How it hurt her to be kind. Deny, deny. No, you can't have an ice cream until you finish your homework, clean your room; you can't go on the school trip unless you save up the money for it, I haven't got a dollar for something like that . . . And Charley on the periphery, trying to get her to ease up a little, sneaking them money on the side, but she'd known, she'd resented him for it, thought he was trying to buy their love, so they'd love him more than her, and they did, it worked . . .

And through it all, she had hated herself for her feelings. What can you do about feelings? You can't make them go away: There they are. They are what they are. The whole business was too much, it was crazy-making, she had cried out and even screamed telling Emily about it. Lucky thing Em lived alone.

Still, even as he undermined her, Charley thought she was right, thought she was the good parent, because she was like his mother, and he like his father, weak. The kids thought she was right, too. Everyone did. Parenting was done Maddy's way in those days. Worse, even. At least she never spanked the children, much less hit them with a strap. And she did lots of giving. She gave them good meals, plentiful, delicious food. She made or bought them nice clothes. She took them to the doctor for shots and checkups (what a blessing when the polio vaccine came in, not to have to worry every summer when they went swimming), took them to the dentist (the damned orthodontist cost a fortune), watched out for them . . . They knew she took care of them. Daddy was on the sidelines. But he was the one they loved.

She had failed as a mother, she announced, weeping, to Emily, she had failed in the worst way.

No, Emily said, you enabled them to survive, and they love you, they know you love them.

Maybe, she said. They're always a little wary of me. But I failed myself, don't you see? I'll never have children again, they're it, and I didn't enjoy them when they were little. That's irrevocable."

Emily sighed. "Ah, Maddy."

Maybe Parrish's alcoholism was rebellion. But thank heavens he recovered. After they stopped taking care of him, after he vanished and lived on the streets wherever . . . he found his way home and to AA. They took him back joyfully, she and Charley, and in time he married again and was a better husband than he'd been to Susan, his first wife. Maddy thought he was a better father now than he'd been to poor Charles, though she wasn't sure. Did his suffering change him? Maybe suffering can enlighten, she thought. It did me. Too bad it came so late.

When Benjamin was in his teens, old enough to stay alone, Maddy again began to imagine having a life of her own. It came to her that she would have liked to be a lawyer, but at fifty-one, she was too old to start such a career. She had not even gone to college, much less law school. She would now face seven years of education, which meant that by the time she became a lawyer, she would be nearly old enough to retire, she told Emily, laughing. But maybe she could sell real estate. She liked houses, and she knew almost everyone in Steventon.

She started working on commission only at Cahill and Cahill; they gave her a list and access to customers. She did not sell a house for two months, but when she sold her first one, in 1976, it was a big one; it went for fifty thousand dollars. That was a lot of money then. Not now, of course. You couldn't find a house for that up here now, she thought. The realty commission was twenty-five hundred dollars, of which she was given half. This impressed her: Twelve hundred dollars for two months' work was very good money in Steventon in 1976, more than most men earned—and Maddy was a woman! Her dry little heart moistened a little: Could it be that she would do well at this?

As Maddy became surer of herself, and better at her work, she grew happier. Whirling through days filled with clients and telephone calls and drives across the county, she had a light heart for the first time in her fifty-six years on earth.

Remembering this part, Maddy forgot her grief and fell asleep with a smile on her face.

8

Emily clutched her coffee cup with both hands, kneeling on the living-room floor, bent over the photograph album. Clea, cross-legged on the floor beside her, leaned against the couch base with a diet soda in one hand, leafing lazily through the pages of the album with the other. She peered warily at her grandparents and great-grandparents, aunts, and uncles, and seemed roused only by photos of her father in his youth and of her parents during a trip east years earlier, pictures that contained her own two-year-old self. There she was, adorable thing with an ecstatic gap-toothed grin, trying to pet a curious goat at the Archibald's farm. Her bottom was fat with diapers under her little red overalls. In another image, her face smeared with mud pie, she grinned in Emily's arms.

"How come I'm here? In Massachusetts? How come you're with me in this picture?" Clea asked.

"Your father was asked to give a lecture at Harvard Medical School, and they decided to take a little vacation at the same time.

They left you with me while they went to New York to see some plays and museums and concerts. And to introduce you to me and vice versa. Of course you don't remember. But I do."

Martin was the only one in the family who listened to music. Besides Poppa. Did he like it because of me? Or did the others dislike it because of me? The gene must be in the family, after all. I couldn't be the only one, could I?

"How old was I?"

"Two. You were here for a week. You were ecstatic, looking at the animals. There were more animals around then, deer and rabbit and cows and ducks, and the Archibalds next door kept goats in those days. You loved them. You were so adorable, all satin skin and brown eyes, you looked like your daddy when he was little, except his eyes were blue. And you hardly cried at all once you got over them leaving—which did take a couple of hours!" she smiled.

In two photos, Clea stood stiff and pouting, dressed in a fancy silk coat and hat, she stood holding hands with her mother; in another, her father held her in his arms.

"I guess the other one was taking the pictures," she said in a forlorn voice.

Emily understood that she wanted a picture of her parents together.

"There is one of them together. Turn the page."

She turned and saw it. She traced her finger over her parents' faces.

"Can I have it?"

Emily hesitated. "You must have one—check your family album."

"I don't. Mom kept meaning to get around to it but she never did. They used to toss photos into a drawer. They're probably in a box in storage with their other stuff. Gregorian said he'd leave everything in storage until I was ready to go through it." She peered up at Emily. "Can I have it?"

Emily was loath to part with the only recent photograph she had of her brother, but she saw the child's face. She then realized that she could duplicate the photo. "Of course. I'll have it copied for you. Take it out."

Clea pulled the photo out of the plastic envelope and stared at it, her forehead wrinkled, studying it as if it contained a hidden message. Then she sighed and turned the album page, once again wearing the glazed expression she had had since Emily first saw her at the airport.

Martin's face in these pictures made Emily's throat constrict. Gone. It was terrible: A person was alive, flesh throbbing, voice pulsing, then in a moment silenced, flesh shredded. A soul gone. Still, every time she looked at Clea, a smile automatically broke across Emily's face. Clea was so like Martin. Pain banged her chest when she thought of her brother dying, yet at the same moment exactly, her heart soared with elation, looking at her niece. Clea, her closest living relative, was, Emily felt sure, lovely, sweet, and smart. She was clearly lovely, perhaps sweet underneath the sullenness, had to be smart, given her parents' genes. But she was difficult. Emily searched her mind for something that might lighten the child's sodden misery, and pounced on her first thought.

"Clea! Shall we go shopping?" That was a treat, wasn't it? Girls loved shopping, she thought, although she hadn't liked it much as a girl, and still didn't. "Your lovely clothes aren't warm enough for this climate. You'll need oodles of things, sweetheart. Nice warm cuzzy pajamas for our cold nights, and a warm robe, maybe fleece, and some cuddly slippers. And warm underwear, you'll be going skiing and skating and sledding!" She hoped. "And school clothes! And warm jackets and coats! We should make a list of what you'll need. School starts in a week and a half."

School.

Clea's face was stony. Leaning against the sofa skirt, she slowly raised her unwilling gaze to her aunt.

"Are there any cool stores around here?

Pale, pale child so tightly wound on the floor, and so thin, so thin . . .

Emily frowned in confusion. "Cool stores?"

"People around here look pretty hicky. I won't wear hicky clothes."

"Hicky?"

"Yeah!" With irritation. "Hick clothes. I only go to cool stores."

Emily's heart stopped. This was going to be a problem, perhaps a major one. Never occurred to me. We won't find clothes in Steventon or Winchester like the ones in Los Angeles. Maybe not even in Boston. People "around here": Whom had she seen "around here" except me and Maddy? We look "hicky"? Don't ask. "I don't know any cool stores, Clea. I kind of doubt there are any."

Clea looked up at her aunt in surprise, entering a datum in her subconscious ledger: Emily is honest. Her mother would have said, "I'm sure we'll find something you like, Clea," in a slightly snarky voice that implied Clea was a spoiled brat. Well, if she was, who made her that way? And who was more spoiled than Alexa herself, who would wear only imported Italian shoes that cost four hundred dollars a pair? Alexa, who . . . was dead.

The child was silent for such a long time that Emily's heart began to beat anxiously. Finally, in a hard, angry voice, the girl said, "I won't wear things that aren't cool."

Sounds like she's going to cry. Were clothes that important to her? Well, I suppose at her age. But right now, they were probably a symbol of everything . . . Nothing here is going to be good enough, Emily thought, nothing is going to console her. Not for a while, anyway. Have to endure it. She's a baby, she'll change. Emily breathed deeply and made her voice light.

"We'll go to the shops and you'll see. Do pajamas and underwear have to be cool? Or just the clothes that show?"

Clea darted a contemptuous glance at this clueless woman. Pajamas and underwear had to be major cool, neat, dope.

Emily read her face. "Well, we'll go to Winchester, and if you don't see anything you like, we'll go to the mall in Pittsfield. Okay? Or if we have to," she continued sturdily, "we'll go to New York! I'll ask Maddy or Alicia to drive us."

Clea saw how hard her aunt was trying, but her heart felt mean. She wanted to hurt Emily; she wanted to make her feel pain, make her cry, and was surprised by a spasm of pity. "Okay," she said quietly.

She turned another page of the photo album. "Is this Daddy?" She pointed to a picture of a tot in a white suit with droopy drawers, leaning against a leggy teenager who knelt beside him with her arm protectively about him. A small horse stood in the background.

"Yes, that's Martin." Emily's voice thickened and Clea glanced up at her. Emily's eyes were wet. "He was just two that day. It was his birthday."

"Is that you with him?"

"Uh-huh. I had taken him for a pony ride over at McCrae's. He loved it."

Clea was surprised at how pretty Emily was in the photograph. She had ivory skin and long, shiny hair, blondish-brown, at least she thought so; the picture was in black and white.

"How come all these pictures are in black and white?"

"That's how film came in the beginning. We didn't have color film until later."

Clea stared at her, amazed. She hadn't known that film had been black and white. "How old were you here?"

"Sixteen."

"Was Daddy spoiled?" Clea demanded.

Emily, nonplussed, gasped a laugh. "Why do you ask that?"

"'Cause my mom always said I was spoiled. Always. And once, after we were arguing and she made me cry, Dad snuck into my room to console me. He told me his mother always said he was spoiled, too."

"Did he?" She considered. "Well, if he said so, it must be true."

"Don't you know?"

"No. I never heard her say that. I was very close to your father when he was little, I really brought him up. My mother was kind of worn out by the time he arrived, she'd already had five children, so I took care of him in the early years. But when I was eighteen, I went to Philadelphia to school. Martin was only four when I left . . . and after that I only came back for holidays . . . then I went to Rome and stayed a long time . . . So I missed seeing him grow up. Still, I don't recall my mother saying he was spoiled. Once he was past babyhood, nothing was good enough for her Martin. She adored him. He was her last, her best, the star of her universe . . . " She stargazed briefly, then came back. "I was the one she called spoiled," she recalled.

"Which kid were you?"

"I was the third."

"The third of six?"

"Uh-huh."

"Did she hate you?"

Emily squirmed. "Sometimes. Probably all parents and children hate each other once in a while, you know? But they love each other too, and you can't forget that. And in those days, you know, all women married and had children. It was expected. Even if some of them would have preferred to do something else. So sometimes they weren't as happy as they might be. I've often thought my mother would have made a great corporation executive. She was so organized, and she organized us—all but me," she recalled, laughing. "She really managed the farm, my father just did the work. She didn't love having children and doing housework, I think, but she did her 'duty,' as she put it. It annoyed her that I was my father's favorite. Families are like that sometimes. My father spent a dollar every week on my piano lessons. She would have liked to have that dollar for other things. A dollar went far in those days! You wouldn't believe!" She laughed. "A pound of ground beef was fifteen cents, a newspaper was a nickel. A new car was eight hundred dollars. A house cost four thousand. You could even get one for less." She leaned back and wiped her eyes with a white linen handkerchief. "When he sent me away to school, she was outraged! I was going to escape!" Emily laughed in a gurgle, as if she were trying to disguise it.

"Escape from what?"

"Her life. A woman's life."

Clea seemed to consider this. "Do all mothers think their daughters are spoiled?"

Emily gazed at her niece. "Some mothers' lives," she said finally, "are so hard . . . they have to give up so much for their children. Most mothers do it willingly. But you can't really blame them if they resent it occasionally, can you? When I think about my mother's life, I weep. So hard, so unremitting, so servile. As I saw it, anyway. Every once in a while a mother . . . especially if her daughter has more than she—which daughters often do—sometimes she'll feel jealous."

"If my mother's life was hard, she made it hard. She did what she liked to do," Clea said grudgingly. "She was always with patients or at the hospital. She was hardly ever home. Well, neither was Dad. They liked to work. I don't understand how a mother could be jealous of her own kid! Why would she have it?"

"They didn't always want to have them," Emily began, then stopped. Not the case here. Clea would not understand. "Not your mother, of course. Unfortunately, one can be jealous of anybody, Clea."

Clea considered this. She remembered feeling jealous of Horhay, Carmela's son. A funny name. But no, it was spelled different: Jorge. She remembered wondering why she was jealous of a Mexican kid who lived in a house like a shack, but she knew, really. It was the way Carmela looked at him. She called Clea "little love," but never looked at her like that. That day they went to Carmela's house, he was lying on a cot under a sheet, a tiny form, just big eyes showing. There was an old woman sitting there with him, but Carmela was so worried, she had to go see him. She stroked his head and gave him water and a pill, and sat beside him, and sang him a song, a Spanish song she often sang to Clea. It was Clea's song, not Horhay's. Jorge's. Clea had turned on her heel and run outdoors, but she was uncomfortable out there with all those strange children staring at her. So she trudged back in, defeated, and sat in the other room where there was nothing to do, no TV or coloring books or games or anything.

"Was my mother jealous of me?"

"I don't know," Emily said. "Your mother had to work very hard to become a doctor. It's especially hard for women, and maybe when she was young she didn't have things as nice as you had."

"But she bought them for me," Clea argued.

Emily really laughed now. "I know! It doesn't make any sense, does it?"

Clea smiled, then looked at her with something like respect in her eyes.

Emily basked in it, whatever it was. "Well, shall we have some lunch?" As she rose, a faint groan emerged from her throat as she straightened her knees to stand up. "What do you like to eat?" Another adventure, she thought, a whole new area to explore! Food!

•

Emily was uncomfortable in bed the night of Clea's arrival. It was still August, but August was often cool in Steventon, as it was that night. She shivered in her thin cotton nightgown and considered searching for the flannels. But she did not move except to pick up the volume of Emily Dickinson that she kept on her bedside table. She did not open it. Her mind was rushing. Funny girl, asking if she's spoiled, what does spoiled mean anyway? What is considered "spoiled" in a place where thirteen-year-olds are driven around by chauffeurs? She had her own phone, too, in her room! Good grief, we had one phone in the house when ten of us lived here and we never quarreled about it. But we didn't use it much. We realized we wanted one during the war, but we had to wait, there was a waiting list for phones, for other things too, refrigerators, cars. Nothing got made during the war, all resources used in the war effort. Rationing. A real strain on poor Momma. Things were different then. We got the phone after the war ended.

Lots of people didn't have phones then and felt no lack. Went centuries, millennia, without such a thing. I remember when Great-Uncle Thomas—was it Thomas?—one of the great-uncles died, Momma wanted to call the relatives to tell them, but they didn't have phones, she had to write instead, she was annoyed. I was seventeen, I felt very grown up, helping her; it was a big job. I didn't like those hostessy tasks she was insistent about. Writing thank-you notes, birthday congratulations to all the relatives. We kept the phone on the little table at the foot of the stairs where it is still. Those days, someone was always speeding down the steps sounding like a brush on a washboard to answer it, and if it was one of the boys running down, half the time he'd fall, accidentally on purpose.

She smiled.

We didn't get an extension until after Mother's heart attack, when she wanted a phone by her bed. It was such an event, she wrote me about it, she who rarely wrote. I was in Rome. She said I could call her and she wouldn't even have to get out of bed. She must have wanted me to call. Did I? Can't remember. I wonder if she was saying that she missed me. I was having a glorious time, too selfish to worry about her. I did call! I spoke to Poppa. I remember him saying it was a mild attack.

It probably hurt her that I didn't come home to see her.

Oh dear.

I was selfish, wasn't I. Still am, I guess.

But I couldn't imagine her missing me. She never showed the least pleasure in my company.

And that's what I still have, one phone up, one down. Why should anyone need more than that? Her own telephone, can you imagine? Surely the kids here don't have their own phones and radios and CD players and television sets; high school kids here don't have cars, do they? or their own entrances to the house like that girlfriend of Clea's? Maybe in Brentwood, California, but I can't believe kids here have those things. I'll ask Maddy. She'd know, with all the children in her family. They might have a radio, maybe a stereo . . . Does she really expect me to get her her own phone when I hardly ever use the one I have? A wasteful expense. I hate waste, goes against all my training. I'd be glad to have an extension put in her room so she can have privacy. But does she really need her own television set? I hardly ever watch the one I have. And we only get three stations here, what is there to watch?

Of course, they were doctors. Probably couldn't have their phone tied up for hours the way teenagers do . . . Maybe that's why.

Finally, she opened the book to a familiar poem:

The Soul selects her own Society—
Then shuts the Door—
To her divine Majority—
Present no more—

Unmoved—she notes the Chariots—pausing
At her low Gate—
Unmoved—an Emperor be kneeling
Upon her Mat—

I've known her—from an ample nation—
Choose One—

Then—close the Valves of her attention—
Like Stone.

She stared at the dark window across from her.

Maybe I should just give her the monthly allowance Gregorian sends and let her do what she wants. But it's—good grief—two thousand dollars a month, how could she spend it? I guess Martin and Alexa left her lots of money. Too much money is not good for the character; neither is too little. Best argument for socialism. Twenty dollars a week, that should be enough for a teenager, shouldn't it? Enough that she'd be able to buy what she wants. Put the rest in a trust account.

Mother would be horrified. She thought *I* was spoiled. Mostly, she hated Poppa's encouraging me. Jealous. Wasn't me she should have been jealous of, was it. Didn't think girls should have careers. Or maybe she pitied me in advance, didn't want my expectations raised when she knew perfectly well that I wouldn't make it, a career in music too hard for a woman. She didn't know much about the world, but she knew that. All females know how hard it is for women in the professions, know it from the time they're teenagers. Very few females in the world of music, even at Curtis. How many women made it? Nadia Boulanger, Wanda Landowska (of course, she was a harpsichordist), Ruth Schlenzinska, she came and went, Rosalyn Tureck. Who else in those days? And she was right, I didn't have it . . .

So sad Mother couldn't have had a career herself. So smart she was, such a terrific manager, probably today she'd go to Harvard, get an MBA and end up managing IBM. Oh, IBM isn't a great company anymore, is it, I'm showing how old-fashioned I am. What is it now, Microsoft. So she might have been jealous on those grounds.

Funny, that never occurred to me before. If it was sympathy, I could forgive her.

It's hard to believe that Alexa was jealous of Clea, though; Alexa had her career, was a highly regarded neurologist. I have never understood what a neurologist is, what they do. Never went to one myself. Nerves. What kind of diseases do you get in your nerves?

Martin a surgeon. Two brilliant parents, wealthy too, by my standards anyway. Obviously, I don't know anything about wealth. When I told Clea she had been rich, she seemed bewildered. No, just middle class, she said, shrugging. Just average. Average! Has she ever been to Arkansas or Mississippi? Well, of course not, neither have you, Emily Oldfield. Doesn't seem to realize that even I am wealthy compared to most of the folks in the world. American children have no idea of how people live in India, in African villages, South America. Comfort is privilege, she doesn't know that. I wonder what she'd make of Bombay. Probably doesn't even know it exists. Maybe someday she'll travel. Learn something about the world.

Oh, she's just a kid, Emily, get off your high horse. Half the people in Winchester have no idea how most of the world lives. Don't want to know. Don't want to have to care. Don't want to feel they should do something about it . . .

Emily slid down in the bed. Pain struck her chest. Heartburn. Oh, Momma. She switched off the lamp.

But sleep would not take her this night. Excited about Clea's arrival, probably. The child herself had immediately fallen into a deep sleep; Emily had checked her earlier. Clea was all tuckered out, poor thing. But Emily was not. Having read that one should not keep trying when sleep is elusive, she sat up, her mind racing still. When Martin was born, Mrs. Foster carried him out of the bedroom, washed off and wrapped in a receiving blanket, to show the other children. She came straight to Emily and laid him in her arms. She knew he was hers.

Then the older boys went off to the war, to ghastly horrors the family read about in the newspapers, events sanitized and glamorized in the movies. Momma and Poppa, Emily and Mamie and Crighton would sit around the radio nights, Poppa following events on a map. Emily would have Martin in her arms or lying on the couch beside her, asleep. Then Robert was killed, Father's namesake, Robert Jr., 1944, Normandy. Carrion, just one more bleeding body in a massacre. Cannon fodder. Feed the weapons. When enough bodies fall, do they form a bridge in the shallows and on the beach for the rest to march on, like soldier ants? Momma lost all heart, she mourned for months, terrified for John, still in the service. Couldn't bear the thought of losing two. She'd already raised five when Martin was born; she was too worn out to take care of him; when he was a little boy, she was bowed down by grief. She never really recovered from it: Robert had always been the light in her eye. Only later did she adopt Martin. Mamie and me, well, we were girls. She didn't like girls much. What had John and Crighton done that she did not prefer them, poor guys? Crighton was a dapper young man, small and graceful. Should have been a dancer, he loved to dance. Not in this family. He married Lily McKee, a Catholic, Mother wouldn't let her into the house. Sort of disinherited him. For years he didn't come home.

Poor John did, though. Guadalcanal, like Maddy's brother Andrew, like him, two years in a Japanese prison camp, at least they had each other, came home skin and bones, like people who'd been in Bergen-Belsen, to a family in pieces. Mother had just found out about Poppa. Took it out on all of us. Of course she was happy he was back alive and not disabled. But Poppa was never home in those days, I was about to go off to Philadelphia, and she was in a state. John never complained, but he got out of here as fast as he could, married Cindy and moved to Ohio. Hardly ever came back to visit. Her brother was killed too, in Italy, bond between them. She became the heir of her family, they took their place in her family line working her father's farm. But Poppa believed in that man stuff, he left the Oldfield house to John, not Momma, passing everything done in the male line, primogeniture, females not really family members. He gave Momma life occupancy. She was outraged when the will was read, forcing her into dependency on her son.

But John was already dead by then, sudden heart attack, Poppa hadn't foreseen that, hadn't thought to change his will. And John had left this house to me, not Momma! I suppose he thought that by the time he died, Momma would be gone. Momma was mortified. No one talked in those days. Especially men. Never explained. Got drunk late at night or had heart attacks but they never said anything. All the years I lived with them, Poppa, my brothers, I had no idea at all what they thought, how they felt. Terrible. What a way to live.

Wonder what their insides felt like. Rage burbling around inside like diarrhea. Hurt, never consoled. Crying hearts could not speak. I'd die. Where would I have been all these years without Maddy, someone I could tell everything to, someone who heard, who saw, who understood. Not that she could make anything better. Or that I expected her to. That was the problem with Douglas. Whenever I told him anything, he felt he was supposed to make it better, and if that wasn't possible, he got annoyed with me for telling him. Duncan didn't do that. Never occurred to him he was supposed to do anything for me: *I* existed for him.

What do men think life is? A test of manliness you win if you never betray a muscle twitch? A thing to get through with the least emotion possible? Of course, our family believed in god, well, I think they did, they went to church once in a while. But how could they? How could John, after what he'd seen and been through, still believe this life was created by a benevolent deity who would reward sufferers in an afterlife? Could he still imagine after Guadalcanal that if he kept everything in, god would paste a gold star on his forehead in heaven? Did Poppa think he was going to hell? I don't think so. He had stopped believing long before. But didn't they want recompense for all their suffering, their hard work, their heartbreak? Didn't they ever want to go on strike against god?

Poor souls, silent suffering, Mother, too, all of them, Thoreau's "lives of quiet desperation." I don't think people live that way anymore. They want more out of life. John and Mamie's kids go for what they want, they get divorced, Ned took cocaine for years, Lia was an alcoholic for a long time, Ellie had a baby by herself. Not great, happy lives maybe, but not silent suffering either. They keep trying to get it right. For all its dislocations, life is better now. I wonder if it ever dawned on Momma or Poppa that life could bring them pleasure. That they had a right to find pleasure, not just survival.

So sad, life wasted like that, seen as something to be endured while doing your duty. Not something to feel and know, to experience and enjoy. A life, a living thing, not a dead duty . . . When after all, it is all you have. Poppa at least reached out for happiness or at least pleasure . . . for a while.

The women were more miserable than the men because the men had the upper hand. But the women had more pleasure in their lives, because they loved their children so much. Most mothers anyway had kids in their hearts and that made them richer. Consoled them for the rest. Men loved their kids, but not in the same way. They didn't devote their lives to them the way the women did. For men, everything was duty and power. Although Poppa cared a lot about me. I could feel it. I wonder why people made things so miserable for themselves. Was it all god? But they invented the god. They wrote the words they said god spoke. They decided what god wanted. Of course, their lives were hard, living was hard on a farm, always the goddamned weather, no days off when you have animals, constant hard work . . .

Progress is a real thing, it sounds so superficial but a washing machine and a drier is not a small advance, it's freedom from slavery. Dishwashers. Funny how I resisted buying one. Clea had to insist, refuse to help me do dishes. She reminded me of myself when I was young, when I simply wouldn't do the chores Momma assigned me . . .

Eventually, Momma came to love Martin. I think she saw how much I loved him and got jealous of the way he loved me. Nasty, but that's what it looked like. Anyway, after I left, she had to take care of him and she came to adore him. I saw it when I came home for holidays. She never imagined that he'd go off and abandon her, probably why she ended up so wretchedly bitter, oh, those miserable last years! He went farther off than John, in Ohio, or Crighton, in Boston, or Mamie, in Florida. Martin went far, the way I did, and like me, he rarely came back. I wonder if he had bad feelings about her the way I did. He brought Alexa here after their honeymoon, en route from Paris to California. He came alone when Poppa died. And he came when Momma died, a little late for her. After Poppa died, I told him Momma was blackmailing me to come back here, saying she'd go live with her sister in Fort Lauderdale if I didn't come back and take care of her, take care of things. It was my house, after all, she whined in that thin, mean voice. He said, Fuck it. He said, You don't need this white elephant on your back. Why would you want to live in a backwater. Stay in Boston, in the middle of things. But it turned out to be just what I needed then. Got me out of a rigid, futureless situation. How could I tell if one of the young ones might want it? I couldn't let it go out of the family. Now it will go to Clea. Who probably won't want it either.

How I loved it here when I was a girl. Things were wilder. I'd sit in the window seat for hours, a score in my lap, looking up every once in a while at cows in the meadow, sheep, goats, rabbits, geese. Life teeming everywhere—wild turkeys in the fall, and deer munching the windfall apples and foxes streaking through the high grass. I still thought I would be a star of some sort, would be discovered. My music appreciated, maybe even loved. By the time Poppa died, I knew I had to have silence and solitude so I could compose. The house was quiet even with Momma here—silent, subdued. It had been crowded with people for so many years, it was strange to find it empty. It's been empty for years now. I would love to see it crammed with life again. Maybe Clea will fill it.

She's in a state of shock, how could she not be? I wish I knew how to help her. Her whole life altered in a couple of weeks, and she only thirteen, not an easy age, junior high freshmen, I see them when I go to the junior high to give music lectures, the boys noisy terrors, wild in the halls, uncontrollable. Girls giggly and nervous. Both crazy with hormones, giggling or yelling at the drop of a hat, on the edge of hysteria. Boys full of crazy machismo, the duel in Tchaikowsky's *Romeo and Juliet* . . .

Shakespeare's Romeo an adolescent punk too, I suppose, how old was Juliet, thirteen, fourteen, Romeo the same or maybe a little older. Had to grow up fast in those days, most of them dead by twenty, all by forty.

I'm glad I don't have to teach kids that age regularly.

Such a shock she's had, losing both parents so suddenly. And they so successful, invulnerable, on top of the world in the morning, dead in the afternoon, a plane rises up from Tokyo like a gorgeous bird and a moment later comes plummeting down, smoke rising from its gorgeous wings, Firebird

Oh god, oh god! I wonder if they were terrified, they must have been, people screaming or does it happen too fast for that, what is it like to be in an explosion, maybe too fast for you to know, I hope so. Glad Mother was gone, never to know, such a shock when I heard, I thought my heart was giving out, what must it have been like for Clea! And now the culture shock of being here. And then coming here to this climate, such a different environment. And to me. She looks in a state of shock, still. Like someone comatose, not yet come to.

When she walked into the terminal with the stewardess, I knew instantly she was Clea, well, they sent photos at Christmas, but when she saw me, her face really fell, oh, she tried to disguise it, but I saw it, and I suppose, who could blame her? Her mother was beautiful, even in her forties, things have changed, Gloria Swanson retired from the movies at forty, considered old then but she was still beautiful too. Women over thirty-five have a richer beauty. Until sixty or so. Some even after. I'm not glamorous, never was. In the photographs, Alexa was very glamorous, terribly thin, with that smooth hair women have in Los Angeles, more finished than women anywhere else, she looked like an actress, not a doctor. Sonia in the English department went to L.A. once, said that the women there all weigh sixteen pounds. But all the women out there can't look like Alexa, can they? Surely some of them must look like me. Of course Martin and Alexa were younger than I, a different generation almost. And I don't dress fashionably, I don't care much about clothes. Every year, I buy one good wool dress or suit. That's it. Our family was never extravagant. Besides, what should I look like? For heaven's sake, I'm fifty years old, am I expected to look like Rita Hayworth?

She's probably never even heard of Rita Hayworth. Thirteen. Ignorant. Don't judge, Emily: You're ignorant too. Do you know the names of today's movie stars or singers? I don't even know the music they listen to, and I should, it's my profession. Meryl Streep, I know her, and Julia somebody with a fat upper lip. I know the men, the men are more famous. De Niro, Newman, Redford. But I'll bet they're not the ones she likes, she probably thinks they're old too. What do I know about raising children? It's going to be rough for a while. Still, I'm so grateful she's here . . .

Martin . . .

A cloud settled on Emily's heart. Feeling uncomfortable, she sat up and sipped from the water glass on the bedside table, then leaned back against the pillow, pain in her face. All the losses. Still, I love my life. It's a wonder, the richness of my life, nobody knows the glory that goes on inside my head. Saves me. Saves me from everything. Like a great chorus, Mozart's Requiem, Verdi's, why am I concentrating on death? Stravinsky's *Les Noces*. That's as violent as battle music, isn't it, he saw marriage as savage female sacrifice but maybe that's the truth of marriage. No: my song is *Der Rosenkavalier*, the great final aria, the Countess's renunciation of her young lover. Yes. That's me.

9

Alicia had walked around the house all week talking to herself. It was just like the old days, she thought grimly, when she needed his approval for something and had to plan her approach, plan every word. Why can't I just say, Steven, I need to talk to you. Or, Steven, we need to talk. Or Steven, I'm really upset. I can say that. I will say that, she decided, standing stock still in the middle of the living room. Steven, I'm upset. She was allowed to be upset, even with him.

This morning she had begun the obsessive litany as soon as she woke up, and continued it through her morning coffee and dressing. What if he just shrugs me off? she thought. What if he doesn't care that I'm upset? What if he uses that superior voice and says, Alicia, I don't care to discuss it.

She got her keys and jacket and went out to the car and drove to the post office for the mail. She stopped at the market for a quart of milk; Steven used milk in his coffee. She'd wait until tomorrow, to get the fish and vegetables; see what he wanted to eat. She drove home.

She glanced around the garden with impatience. Tiny green things were beginning to appear on the trees, reflected by the light, but now there was another cold snap. It frustrated Alicia, who was eager to get to work on her garden. She had nothing to do, which made her feel useless, suspended.

Sitting on her porch with her second cup of coffee, she went through the mail—a pile of junk mail, even though she'd written to the catalog companies and told them she didn't want their ads—such a waste of trees. Years ago we didn't get this stuff, she thought in outrage; the mail used to be just bills and an occasional personal letter. And it was delivered twice a day, morning and night.

She noticed a letter from a company, Marshall Merchant. Wasn't that a publisher? She ripped it open.

> Dear Mrs. Gilson,
>
> I have a house in the Berkshires and have read your history of Steventon. It was extraordinary, I thought, in bringing alive the past of this beautiful area. I have also read your occasional pieces on the history of New England in the New England Heritage. They are also vivid and charming.
>
> I am an editor for Marshall Merchant, and wondered if you would be interested in doing a book for us on some aspect of New England history. If you have such an interest, you can reach me at 212-555-0999.
>
> Sincerely,
> Charlotte West

Alicia dropped the letter into her lap.

Me! Asking me!

She picked it up again, reread it, got up and fetched the portable phone, carried it out to the porch, picked up the letter again, read it and dropped it, picked up the phone . . .

"Emily!" she cried. She told her about the letter. "What should I do? You know I'm not a professional historian. I read history as an undergraduate. I don't have any credentials . . ."

Emily was calm, amused. "They didn't write you because of

your academic credentials. They don't even know them. You might not even have gone to college as far as they know. They wrote you because of what you've done, Alicia. Your book, your articles. And they're good, we all told you how good they are. Not like the usual amateur stuff in that magazine. You write with real feeling, your writing is interesting . . ."

Alicia's eyes filled."I've never had a job in my life."

"Yes you have. You wrote a book. You wrote a book no one wanted—a history of Steventon—and made people want it! That's talent!" Emily laughed.

"Really? Really? How can a woman my age be such a baby, Emily? I'm so frightened."

"You've never been out in the big world. Neither have I. I understand completely. I'd be terrified if someone wrote and asked to hear something of mine . . ."

"You would? You would? Okay, Emily, I'll call her. I will! Thanks, Emily."

"It's nothing, pet. Let me know what happens, okay?"

Alicia dialed the Manhattan number, her hands shaking. The woman answered the phone herself. Alicia explained who she was and said she was interested.

"But," she added quickly, "you have to know I'm not a professional. I mean, I have an undergraduate degree in history, not a PhD."

"Oh, we don't care about that, Ms. Gilson," Charlotte West replied. "I liked what you wrote." She sounded as if she was smiling. Alicia eased a bit.

"What were you thinking about? I mean, what part of New England history were you interested in?"

"Well, that would be up to you. But I particularly liked what you did with the old letters and diaries in your book. You know, finding them in the archives of little local libraries, and describing what women did all day in those days. I found that fascinating."

"Yes," Alicia said. "Me too. They worked so hard. Incredibly hard. Life was hard generally, but for women, it was . . . unbelievable!"

"Yes. I was sort of imagining a book describing the lives women led . . ."

"Oh, I'd love to do that!" Alicia exclaimed.

"Great. Why don't we discuss it over lunch. Do you ever get into the city?"

"I can. Sure."

Charlotte West set up a lunch date, while Alicia's heart beat so hard she wasn't sure she was hearing correctly, and had to ask the woman to repeat herself. She scrawled the date and time on the back of a piece of junk mail.

"My secretary will call you that day and tell you where . . ."

"Oh. I won't be here . . . I'll be at my New York number."

"Give me that one then," the woman suggested, and was gone.

The phone sat silent in Alicia's damp hand.

Could this be happening?

Alicia leaned back in her chaise, pale with shock at what she felt was a world-shaking event, trying to fix the origin of her career—if it could be called that—as a historian. It began during their first trip to the Berkshires, hers and Steven's with the children, who were little then. The look of the place, the feel of it, had hit her with force because it was so beautiful and so green, so hilly and quiet, so unlike the city where she'd spent her life, in the Bronx and Manhattan. It was unlike the Long Island suburbs where her stepfather's sister and some of Steven's relatives lived. It was unlike Washington, D.C., where Steven's college roommate now lived; or Paris, where they went on their honeymoon; or Rome or London or Vienna, where they'd spent some summer vacations. It was like no other place, and it enchanted her with its simplicity and natural beauty, but above all, its age. Not that it was that old. The only old structures in her country were out west—great mysterious Mounds, like the barrows in England, and pueblos. She longed to see them, but she could not imagine Steven agreeing. His interest in the past was limited to the concert halls in Vienna's Musikverein, or Freud's rooms at Berggasse 19 or in London. But she had read about it, and someday—it was in the back of her mind—some distant day, she knew she would get on a plane and fly to New Mexico—maybe with Jenny!—and go to Santa

Fe. They would rent a car and get up at two in the morning and drive to Bandolier and climb the cliff and watch the dawn come up with roses in its arms over the great valley. In that silent throbbing wild, she would stand on top and survey the ground for miles around, assure herself no enemy was approaching, and utter deep in her throat a ululating cry like a bird's to tell those below that all was well. They would go about their business, paint their caves, build their fires, collect water and faggots, clean the ashpits, everything in the community well-ordered and peaceable for serene living. And standing there, she would know what it was like to be a woman there, among those people.

But she was here now, where the old things were mainly houses from the nineteenth century, and a few, like Maddy's and Emily's, from the eighteenth. There was a sign in a field announcing that W. E. B. DuBois had lived there, another on a building on Bridge Street announcing that Elizabeth Blackwell, the first woman doctor in the country, had lived there, and there was a tiny old synagogue tucked away on a back street and always closed. These were the secrets she wanted to unclose now, they carried the air she wanted to breathe.

She came up only seasonally, so it had taken her a few years to get to know the place well. But once the house was furnished and functioning and the children acclimated and at ease, she found that managing the house became routine, and she had the leisure to drive through the countryside, risking unknown roads and directions, letting herself get lost. Imagining herself Edith Wharton, in an open car with Henry James by her side, she would take back roads, dirt roads, and suddenly find herself in deep woods, then, just as suddenly, arriving at a group of houses set in the middle of nowhere. She drove through exquisite old towns that looked as if nothing had changed there in two hundred years. The pastness of the place was what fascinated her: Its containment of a sense of a past that was not forgotten. She envied the place its history.

After five or six years, she knew the area as well as she knew Riverside Drive and the Upper West Side. She took to visiting old houses that were open to the public, noted because they had been the homes of important people or had interesting architecture or typified a gracious, vanished way of life. On weekends, with the children, she and Steven drove to Melville's house in Pittsfield, to the art museums in Williamstown and North Adams, to famous gardens in New York State.

Above all, she was fascinated by people whose ancestors had settled the area, people who still lived here. The first one she met, Homer Carlyle, her handyman, came from a family that had settled in Steventon in the 1700s. From him, she heard about Lil, who was married to Nick Carbone but by birth was a Carlyle and now ran the local grocery store; and Lynn Kellogg, who had married an outsider but still ran her family's horse farm; and Emily Oldfield, whose people had been in the area even longer than the Carlyles.

Everything about these people fascinated Alicia. They might seem ordinary enough to another observer, but not to her. For her, they were haloed with nobility, marked by their heritage. Their backgrounds made them compelling, part of an aristocracy. As she came to know a few of them, she saw that they regarded themselves as special, as an elite whose supremacy was acknowledged by most Steventonians. Emily scoffed at this: It was nonsense, they were just a bunch of overweight hayseeds, proud of their ignorance. But Emily had little to do with anyone, and Alicia privately thought that Emily believed in an aristocracy of one.

The bones of the old families lay in the ancient graveyards. Members of the different families were bound by intermarriage and had lived near each other and gone to school together in Steventon. When they talked about each other, an edge of excitement, glamour, blushed in their voices. Alicia felt this: She saw not saggy overweight or skinny bodies, gray hair, gray skin, dowdiness, or down-home accents, but something magical. She saw that, to each other, they still looked as they did in high school—lovely, desirable, exciting. Their lust for each other rose up as easily as blood to a pinprick; age never veiled their beauty in each others' eyes. Their dealings with each other were sweetened by memories of desire that lingered in present flesh. The past existed so vividly in their imaginations that it annulled the present. To listen to Homer describe Emily Oldfield was almost embarrassing. Emily, though, was not like them. To her they were all old people like herself, remembered vaguely, and, except for Homer, without affection. She had no sentimentality about the past.

When Alicia began to think about writing about the area, she questioned Emily about it. Emily wasn't interested in the past (she spent her life trying to create the future, she said), but she encouraged Alicia. Most of the old families here were obsessed with the past. Most also had family genealogies—Homer did, she knew, and so did Emily. They could help.

Alicia began to spend her days in the old local libraries, examining yellowed documents and fragile newspaper clippings about historical events. In time, she began to feel that she was an expert on this part of the world, part of its present and so part of its past, almost as if she had been born into a family that had settled here in the 1600s. It was that feeling she craved. She wormed her way into archives in tiny country libraries, daybooks held sacred by their custodians, photograph collections in heavy manila folders, folders of handwritten diaries or old letters wrapped in ribbon, thin, casual folders of newspaper clippings. She leaned back in the hard wooden chair in the tiny old Mill Race library, studying its creaky floor and its handsome, polished old wooden bookcases and inhaling the sweet dusty odor of old paper. With her left hand, she combed back her wiry hair; and as she did, she realized she was happy.

In time, Alicia came to believe the move that the she and Steven had made to move to New England was dictated by destiny, a supernatural force that impelled people toward ends mysterious and unknown but intended. She avoided thinking about what kind of force this could be, whether it was inside or outside us, conscious, moral, or all-powerful, but if she'd been pinned down—by Emily, say, who questioned all such formulations—she would have said the force was in ones genes, that it pushed one to the fulfillment of one's capacities, that it hurt like a Chinese infant's bound feet when thwarted, and flowed gratefully like urine after long self-containment when released. Or like an orgasm. That it felt like life. Or death.

And in the Berkshires she had found her destiny. Her education—alas, never used!—now had an outlet. She would create a history, a history of Steventon, not the kind of history she'd seen other places produce, a record of property ownership, descriptions of parcels of land and the names of their owners over time. She wanted to write about the people of the area: How did they come to settle there? What gave them the fortitude to endure snowbound winters? Were their lives austere and grim or filled with natural delights? She wanted to write about the settling and clearing of farms, finding markets for agricultural products—and the emerging future, which no one could foresee but which lately both old and young contemplated gloomily.

She read widely in New England history, concentrating on the western part of Massachusetts. She learned how Steventonians suffered during King Phillip's war, how fervently they supported the Revolution. She read, with some surprise, of the fierce abolitionism of its citizens, and felt its grief over sons lost in the Civil War. She read letters from Emily Oldfield's great-great-uncles, written from the battlefields of that war. She read Edith Wharton's *Summer*, and reread *Ethan Frome*, trying to imagine the wild, rough country and the fierce mountain folk Wharton described. No such seemed to exist any longer: Little here was wild, even in nature. The countryside was tamed and serene, like England's rolling countryside, rather than the fierce and willful landscape of Ireland or Greece. It was not an ideal world: The lovely inn built in 1800 on the village green had been leveled to create a parking lot; the old schoolhouse on Grange Road had been torn down to open up land for a mobile home. She read old letters, and their phrasing stuck in her mind. She sought out old photographs and studied them. She made lists. She interviewed the descendants of the original families, like Emily.

Until the mid-twentieth century, Steventon's main street was a broad, empty, tree-lined avenue; the post office, the bank, and a shop or two sat in neat old clapboard buildings that faced each other across the main boulevard. When cars arrived, Steventonians unused to vehicles approaching without the noisy clopping of horses began to be killed crossing the avenue. So the town moved all its commercial buildings to one side of the street, where they remained still.

For Alicia, these photographs conveyed peace and spaciousness, a world in which little happened, where people had time to think about their lives. They created such a different feeling that she grew intent on imagining the feelings of people in those times. What interested her was not the technological changes—automobiles, airplanes, radios, telephones, elevators—but the different air and its different silence, the sense of serenity and eternality she imagined people felt. Or were they bored? Was the only entertainment singing around the piano of an evening or in the church choir on Sunday morning? Did, perhaps, an occasional wandering theater troupe stop for a night or two in Winchester or Pittsfield? Books were probably the main distraction for most people, but how many read? Church would have been the main social event of the week and, beyond gossip, the weekly newspaper the main source of local knowledge.

Trying to slide into those times, she felt herself expand in the silent space. She wore boots and a long gingham dress as she slowly trudged up Howell's hill in the quiet days of summer under a wide-brimmed straw hat, carrying a basket of peaches. The boots were hand-me-downs and a little too large, and her heels chafed. Or she would climb the same hill, ruddy-faced, white-breathed, in the even quieter days of winter, with snow muffling bird twitter, returning home from "town" hugging a precious pound of coffee. At home, in the dark workshop of a kitchen, she stood, at six in the morning, stirring a great pot of oatmeal to be served with cream from their own cow.

She imagined Greta, Emily's great-great-great-grandmother, rising at four to do the milking. Mostly it was women who did it; did they sit on stools? Greta would pour the milk into a large jug, then set it in a cool place to let the cream rise for butter. Then to the henhouse to cull the eggs—only a dozen today—and carry them in her apron into the house. She had to cook a giant breakfast for the hands and her family, and there were not enough eggs, so she'd make pancakes, sausages, ham, fried potatoes, boiled onions, biscuits, baked beans left over from the night before, ham gravy with raisins. After that, Alicia thought, I'd want to lie down, but Greta would then go to weed the vegetable patch. Vegetables were a lot of work, with all the weeding and watering. Then she'd climb a ladder to mend the roof, that's what she was famous for, work like that. And those huge meals, three a day every day, a roast loin of pork, three fried chickens, a boiled ham, beans, five vegetables, three kinds of potatoes, homemade pickles, biscuits, gravy, pies, cakes, jellies. Ugh. Yet people were thin, look how thin, in the photographs. Perhaps they worked it off, or maybe they didn't always have enough to eat . . .

Once a week I'd do the laundry, an awful job. Maybe I'd do it once a month. Lye soap I made myself, once a year or so. Piling the soiled clothes into a great tin vat, scrubbing them on a washboard, hands worn away over the years, to mere bone and worn-out skin. Housecleaning wouldn't have been onerous, though, at least in the early years. A sweep and a dust. People didn't have much stuff then. There might have been soot stains from the wood stove, did they bother to try to clean them away? On Sunday, I'd dress up in my rusty black silk and a good bonnet for church. Would I wear a silk dress, no matter how old? Or would it just be cotton? Or wool? Sit on a hard pew for four or five or more hours listening to a minister tell you what a sinner you were. Did all of them believe it? Such a hard life: I wonder if they weren't angry most of the time. Probably felt guilty, so sin sold.

But they must have had pleasure in their lives. Just walking around must have been a pleasure, before polluted water and the disappearing ozone and the constant zoom of traffic. Like in Willa Cather's writing, or Elizabeth Gaskell's, seeing the beauty of wildflowers and hills and racing rivers. Maybe the sky here then was like the sky over Africa now, almost transparent, unlike air any place else on earth. Stretching for miles over the Kenyan hills, the Tanzanian mountains, pierced by brilliant yellow birds, tiny green ones . . .

But people were just as mean. All Protestants up here then, and many of them hated Catholics and Jews, didn't even know about Muslims, men thought women were imbeciles . . . well, some still do. Still, life was peaceful, no drugs, no guns. Just imagine that. No drugs or guns! Even when I was young in the Bronx: long lazy days in the sun, quiet streets, the thwack of a bat on a ball, the boys playing in the road having to walk toward the curb when the rare car came through. They walked, they didn't run. Cars drove slowly then. No burning tires screeching. Even I remember that. And whatever farmers thought about women, they had to treat them with some respect, they needed them. Couldn't live without them. The women kept everyone alive. A farm was a business: To succeed, it required two people with foresight, a sense of priorities, and tons of energy and resilience. Some French curé—was it in the eighteenth century?—wrote that without a father, the family suffers, but without a mother, it cannot exist. There was probably love in some families; mothers always love their children . . . Well, usually. All those nasty stepmothers in fairy tales. And lots of absent fathers and ogres. Then as now, family life the first hell . . .

Yet it was women's most enduring satisfaction, love for their children. It fills up all the loving room you have so you never feel need. At least when they're small. So unless a husband was actively oppressive, it wouldn't have mattered what he was like. Because most men don't partake in the parenting. At least nowadays. Could that be true? But most men were actively oppressive. Look at even Elizabeth Cady Stanton's husband, who was better than some. Those women had no one to cherish them. Which is the main thing. In the universe.

•

It was Mrs. Hein (her most favorite teacher ever) who precipitated the event. She had given them an exciting assignment: to question a relative and write a history of their family. "Your mother or father, your grandmother, an aunt or uncle, a cousin—anyone!" Mrs. Hein had explained. "Ask them to tell you about their lives."

Alicia dutifully consulted her mother, her only relative. She did so confidently: Neva revered education and always encouraged Alicia in her schoolwork. Alicia expected an enthusiastic exclamation followed by a long delicious sit-down, with Momma telling her stories.

But Momma was cleaning that day, spring-cleaning, she called it. So Alicia asked her question of her mother's back, as Neva worked in the china closet. She had washed and dried all the Limoges china Arnold Ross had bought her, as she did every spring. She was now replacing it in the cabinet. She handled the dishes reverently, a woman who had waited for luxuries. It seemed to Alicia that her question had stiffened her mother's back, but when she turned slowly to face Alicia, her face was unreadable.

Is she mad at me? Have I done something? . . .

She said, "Just make one up. Or go next door and ask Mrs. Mulrooney for hers. She was born here."

"The teacher said your own family."

"The teacher said." Her mother mocked Alicia's pious tone. "Hah! Can the teacher bring them back?"

Her face was fierce, her mouth an ugly snarl, her eyes like the eyes of a madwoman.

Alicia stared in horror. This woman was not acting like her mother, she didn't know who this woman was. Her mother loved her, tried to help her. "Momma! What am I supposed to do?"

Her mother turned back to the dishes. "I told you. Make it up. You read enough. Or do the Mulrooneys. Theirs is probably bad too but it can't be as bad as ours."

"Why won't you tell me about your momma and poppa?" she nearly wept.

Her mother turned then suddenly and shouted in a loud, thick voice she had never used before, staring into Alicia's face with something like hate: "Because the Nazis killed my momma and poppa, my brother, my whole family! They sent me away, and while I'm gone, behind my back, the whole family, the whole village, one hundred twenty-three people, one hundred twenty-three people—no, one hundred twenty-three and a half, because my cousin Galia was pregnant! They were all killed! And I was here! Without them! You want to write that in your school paper? You want to tell all of them your shame! You want to bring hatred down on the head of your mother!"

Neva turned away to lay another plate atop the others. Alicia could see little tremors in her back; it looked as if her mother were crying deep inside her body.

Alicia stood paralyzed as Neva turned again and bent like a weeping birch over the table, her hands covering her face, tears dripping through her fingers like stalactites in a cave.

Alicia wanted to embrace her mother the way her mother held her when she was upset, but there was something about her today that forbade it. She lay her small hand lightly on her mother's arm.

Neva swung her arm up, throwing Alicia's hand off, stumbled to her bedroom, and threw herself on the bed. Her cries seemed to come from deep in her belly, hoarse and raging. Alicia followed and stood by the bedroom door. Gradually, Neva's sobs came less frequently, and at last she was relatively quiet, although with each new breath, she shuddered a gasp of pain. Finally, silence. Alicia pushed the door open farther. Neva seemed to be asleep.

Alicia made her way slowly back to her own room, dragging her body as if she were maimed.

She didn't remember now what she wrote in her essay.

Alicia knew her mother had come to the United States in 1939, as part of some special child's transport. She knew Neva had lived with the Motylas, relatives transplanted from their village in Poland. But she felt had no curiosity about these facts until the scene at the china closet. She had imbibed enough of the immigrant mentality from her stepfather, Arnold Ross, to know that people came to America to live better, to provide opportunities for their children, to make money. She assumed her mother had come for reasons like these.

But after the revelations of her tenth year, she was consumed with hunger for stories of her mother's life, knowledge of the relatives—a hundred and twenty-three and a half, Neva said?—she had never met or heard of. Yet she did not dare approach Neva again. Neva rose from her bed to make dinner that night, but she walked around like a zombie, barely speaking, even after Mr. Ross came home. He peered at Alicia as if to ask what was wrong, but didn't ask Neva herself, as if he were afraid of her. Yet normally he dominated the household—it was one of the things Alicia disliked about him. It was several days before Neva was herself again. Alicia, fearful of unleashing another fit, moved gingerly around her.

She was grown and married before she dared to raise the subject again. In the years between, she had read everything she could find about the Holocaust, wept over Holocaust accounts until she felt she had no tears left, and seen all the serious Holocaust films. But she had never discussed it with anyone, not Steven and certainly not her mother.

She and Steven were living on Riverside Drive; it was Friday night, which meant nothing to Steven, but was important to Neva, and Alicia had invited her for dinner. Mr. Ross had died, and Neva lived alone. She came happily to help prepare what she called the Sabbath meal—which Steven, an atheist, ignored. He despised the trappings of religion. Neva was cheerful: She was cooking (which she enjoyed) in the Riverside Drive kitchen of her daughter, who had married a doctor, a psychiatrist, and who had two lovely children, a boy and a girl. Neva had never hoped for more for Alicia. She was shaping the matzo balls, while Alicia put finishing touches to the kugel.

"Momma," she began apologetically, "I don't want to upset you, but I need to ask you something."

Neva peered at her over her glasses.

"When you were a girl—1939—you came here from Poland, right?"

Neva nodded. "I came here not able to speak a word of English. They said, 'You're smart,' and put me in school without a word of English. The teachers thought I was an idiot."

Alicia was silent for some time, to show that she had absorbed this new humiliation, done it honor. And when she spoke, she tried to keep her voice expressionless. "Why did your parents send you here? Why didn't they come with you?"

Neva turned toward her a stony gray face. "They were going to come. As soon as Poppa could sell his business, as soon as David finished his school year." She wiped her hands across her face. "Moishe knew, Moishe Motyla, he saw what was coming, but Poppa didn't believe it, he couldn't believe anyone would harm us seriously. He had a good business, people were friendly, we lived in a thriving little town, we had a post office and a train station and a school. We were at home. He thought," she ended bitterly.

"So, 1939? . . ."

"Yes. Moishe wrote, he insisted that Poppa act. There was going to be a war, he said, and Poland would be attacked, and look at what Hitler was doing to the Jews in Germany. I was thirteen, and because I was a girl, it didn't matter about my schooling, so they sent me right away. They decided to wait until the end of the school year to come with David. Moishe wanted Momma to come with me, but she stayed to take care of Poppa and David. I thought then—because I didn't understand and didn't want to go—that Poppa sent me away as punishment for growing breasts. They bothered me, and I saw they bothered him. But soon after I left, the Nazis invaded Poland. I don't know when they arrived at our town. I didn't know anything about it at the time. A young man who escaped after they arrived fled to France and wrote to relatives in the Bronx who knew the Motylas, told them about it. Years later. So I'll never know what I was doing when the Nazis came. I was probably studying mathematics or drying dishes or playing hopscotch. They didn't bother sending anyone to the camps. They marched the whole town to the top of a mountain and ordered them to dig a hole. When a wide trench was dug, the Nazis machine-gunned them; they fell into their graves. Then the Nazis tossed lime over the bodies."

Neva turned her face away, wiping it with the dishtowel. She stared down at the pot of boiling broth.

"When Uncle Moishe told me our family was destroyed, I collapsed. No one understood that then, they didn't know about nervous breakdowns. I kept thinking—What was I doing when they were dying? Playing tag, drinking a Coke, helping Aunt Fanny with the Sabbath meal?

"My grades plummeted. I was a good student once I learned English, but I couldn't read, couldn't think. My teachers told Fanny I wasn't cut out for studying, and anyway as soon as I was sixteen, I could leave school. In 1942, people thought girls stopped learning at adolescence, because of physical development. And my 'physical development' at sixteen made me miserable. I blame my body that I didn't achieve more in life. I was cursed with a zaftig body. I was so happy when you matured and had a slender, small-breasted body. Slight, like your father.

"But no one noticed that there was something terribly wrong with me. Not even I knew. I just knew life had no taste for me anymore. With my low grades, I couldn't go to college, but girls didn't go to college anyway, and I couldn't expect Moishe to pay for it. He didn't send his own daughter to college. Only his sons. They took me out of school—I didn't care. I had studied bookkeeping and I looked for a job and tried to bury my feelings. I was already good at it.

"Too hard for me. I will never get over it." She stopped then and stared hard at Alicia, whose face was wrenched in pity. "Do you understand? Shoah is a true thing. Get that hurt look off your face! Nobody cares that you're hurt! Nobody and no god cares! This really happened and it could happen again. Everything you've read is true—oh, yes, I saw you reading—human beings really did those things to other human beings! You don't think that's the way the world is, do you? You don't want to think it. You want to think it's an ab—what's the word? Aberration. An anomaly. And I didn't want to tell you, I didn't want you to know. You were so young, so innocent. I didn't want it to hurt you so young. I protected you from it so you don't grow up crooked like me, crooked just from knowing it. Like a fish missing a fin: I can't swim straight. My soul is bent.

"But now you know. Now you too have to carry the shame. I tried to protect you! But you had to know. And knowing shames me—and you: to be the victim of such monsters! I wanted you to be free of it but now . . ." She bent her head. "Don't ask me about it again!" she cried angrily.

This information dropped into the stewpot of Alicia's teeming brain and steamed up with mystery, raising questions that could not be asked. This taboo haloed the subject even more with awe and horror. Not for a decade more did people start to speak openly of the Holocaust, speak without shame, expecting sympathy.

When that happened, Alicia was able to more easily. She wished her mother could feel this new openness; if Neva could talk about it, she would be lighter. Sometimes Alicia would hand her an article on the subject. Neva would read it, shaking her head sadly from side to side. She herself would never speak to anyone about such things, she said. It was shameful!

"Why is it shameful, Momma?" Alicia asked gently. "The Jews did nothing shameful."

"To be a victim! A whole people!" Neva roared. "That is not shameful? Are you crazy? Nothing could be more shaming!"

Neva fiercely repudiated victimization, but Alicia believed that victims were predestined—born, not made. Marked like Cain for suffering, with bad karma. They got caught because they showed vulnerability—so it was imperative not to do so. Alicia knew all this because she felt herself a born victim and since girlhood had held herself erect and aloof, careful not to betray her helplessness. She walked tall, tried to appear self-sufficient. And she fooled everyone. Except herself. Still, over the years, she had become a person of dignity, she thought, one who owned herself.

10

Jenny wanted to work on the porch, where she was setting the painting, but it was still too chilly on this last day of March. Even with the electric heaters on, her hands were too icy to draw. So she worked in the studio. She blocked out the forms on the canvas. She needed to do sketches first. She needed models. Just imagining drawing her friends in their company raised her spirits. She knew they would exclaim over her, praise her. She bathed in their praise, a Florida swimming pool of warmth. She'd call Maddy first: The tallest, the heaviest, the oldest, she was the anchor of the picture. Later. Meantime, she drew rough approximations of the four women, in descending order as she thought of it, age the differential.

She worked all day, loving what she was doing, tossing off one sketch after another, getting new ideas with each try. She thought about colors and shadows, scrawled in patches of darkness, left patches of light. She exhausted herself.

A knock on her door. "You ever coming out of there, Jenny my love?"

The door opened and Tim peered in. "Oh, I'm having the most glorious time!" she exclaimed.

"Can I see?" He stepped into the room and she pushed the sketches toward him. He examined them carefully.

"Yes," he said, "there's a terrific feeling in them. But you need models."

"I know," she said, flushed.

He looked at her appraisingly. "You'll be fine, Jen."

"Thanks, Tim. How was your day?"

"Not good. Hit a snag. Snag after snag! Nothing but snags! I have to change my style! Completely! I'm sick of sticks of color, sick of lines. Sick of it!" he cried passionately.

Jenny murmured sympathetically, not worried because Tim regularly had *crises de nerfs*, as he called them.

She pulled his head to hers. "Poor baby."

"Ummm," he snuggled in her neck.

He kissed her, and her blood rose toward his touch. He kept kissing her, and she returned his kisses, and soon he lifted her from her chair and led her to the couch and sat them down on it, still connected at the mouth. He leaned against her, put his hands on her breasts under her sweatshirt.

"Ahhh," Jenny sighed.

He started to make love to her on the couch, which was narrow, and they tumbled onto the floor. They lay on a rag rug to complete the ardent struggle.

They lay spent. After a long while, Tim said, "Wanna eat out?"

"Sure," Jenny said. Thinking, so I'll call Maddy tomorrow.

Later, in the shower, Jenny thought, it's terrible to be married to an artist. Full of her work all the time. At a time she should be—no, was—feeling romantic and loving and melting and should be thinking what a great lover he is or how satisfied she feels, she's thinking, I'll call Maddy tomorrow. Artists only care about their work. They raid the lives of the people they love, everything else is secondary to the work, the work, the work. She stepped back from herself judgmentally.

But Tim is an artist too. He certainly does the same thing. I don't need to feel guilty with him. Was he lying there thinking, tomorrow

I'll try geometric shapes? Circles? Or a black canvas, or . . . whatever? I'll bet he was! She giggled and left the shower smiling.

•

She would be thrilled to sit, Maddy said. Or stand, as the case might be. Jenny had asked her to come at ten Monday morning, and as always, she was prompt. Jenny was ready for her, sketchbook in hand, charcoal and soft pencils nearby. The weather had turned warmer, and she turned on the porch heater, and moved furniture around so that Maddy could stand against the long white wall of the house. Jenny wanted a void, nothingness, behind her figures, not waterfall, garden, or lush nature, just emptiness. The arrangement she intended at this point was the women standing in descending order of age and height—Maddy, Emily, Alicia, and Jenny. Like a police lineup, four suspects. The usual suspects. Or maybe she'd have Maddy stand with her hands on the back of a chair in which Emily would sit, studying a sheet of staff paper. Maybe Alicia would lean against the wall; this arrangement would make her taller than Emily. Jenny would have to experiment. Alicia's hair would halo out, filling the space around her head. Or maybe Jenny would sit like a kid on the floor, sketching. Light would stream from their faces. *The Women*. Take that, Clare Boothe Luce. Or maybe just *Woman*. Take that, de Kooning.

Jenny was excited.

Maddy was game, but unsure of herself. "I've never done this, you know, I hope I can stand still enough. I can't stand for too long at a time, varicose veins, you know, one of the blessings of age." She smiled grimly.

"You'll be fine. Whenever you get tired, just tell me. There's ice water and hot coffee in these thermoses, we can have them whenever we want to take a break. Okay? Oh, I love what you're wearing, that red wool dress, did you choose it purposely?"

Maddy was surprised. "No, I never even thought about it. I guess I thought you might drape me in a sheet or something."

"Maybe I will. Make you a Roman senator."

"It would hide a multitude of faults, heaven knows."

"Not at all. I love your body. It's so . . . there."

"That it is! Always there."

"Do you want music?"

"Oh, I don't care. If you do."

"No, I prefer to concentrate."

"That's fine with me."

Jenny placed Maddy in position, with her hands resting on the back of a wood-framed wicker porch chair. She stepped back, viewed, returned, changed the angle of Maddy's arms, stepped back, viewed, returned, changed the angle of Maddy's chin, did this several more times. She sensed that Maddy was already getting impatient.

"Okay," Jenny said finally and sat down on her stool. She began to sketch swiftly, making simple quick strokes, catching something, then turning the page and starting again. After ten or twelve of these, she picked up a pad of heavier paper and began drawing more slowly, blocking in the figure, then refining it.

After half an hour, Maddy said, "Sorry, but I have to pee. I should have warned you about that."

"It's fine, Mad. Go ahead. Want some coffee?" She went to the table and poured a cup.

"No, but I'd love some water," Maddy said as she disappeared into the house.

"Can I see?" she asked when she returned.

"Would you mind not?" Jenny asked timorously. "I'm not ready for you to see anything."

"Okay," Maddy said cheerfully. She drank her water thirstily. "Have to ensure my next potty break," she explained, laughing.

Indeed, she had to pause for something about every forty-five minutes. Jenny would have preferred a longer stretch, but she let Maddy set the pace. When Maddy tired, her muscles tensed, and Jenny did not want that look. At her break, Maddy would go to the toilet, or just walk up and down the porch, sipping water. Then she'd announce she was ready to start again.

They had worked for almost three hours when Jenny said, "How about a real break?"

"Thank heavens," Maddy sighed. She shook her body as she moved to a chair and sat down. "I don't think I was cut out for this work," she said, gratefully sipping the water Jenny passed her.

"You're doing great," Jenny smiled.

"Really?" She flushed. "Can I see now?"

"Okay." Jenny turned the pad to face her. She was a large block in the corner, a body made up of planes. "Oh, good, no curves!" Maddy cried.

•

Maddy saw that she was a kind of bulwark, a large, strong block standing like a protection for the others, who were merely suggested by scrawled rectangles, and she wondered about this. Was that what Jenny thought her? Maybe because she was the oldest. Because she was anything but a bulwark. She stood where she stood, that was true, but not out of conviction, only out of habit. She was the only one of them who had lived an inauthentic life, so fake that she had not felt like a real person until she was almost fifty. Lived someone else's life, like the babies in fairy tales who were substituted for princes or princesses in a crib: a changeling. Girls were told they were princesses, but it was a lie intended to keep them quiet in their slavery. Talk about redefinitions! Alicia said in Homer, princesses like Nausicaa, even goddesses like Athena, served men, did their laundry, poured their wine. Athena waits on Achilles, Alicia said. All women, told they are princesses, are raised to be servants and become them, and she, Maddy, was one still, although she was disguised as a crackerjack real estate saleswoman.

Of course, she was that too, but she still had to go home and fix dinner and clean up the dishes and mop the kitchen floor. How come being a crackerjack saleswoman didn't exempt her from those things? Men got exempted from those things, ostensibly because they were crackerjack salesmen, or drove trucks, or cleaned sewers. When a woman was in the hospital having a baby, everyone invited her husband for dinner: Poor thing couldn't be expected to cook for himself. And if there were children, her mother took them, he couldn't be expected to take care of them, even though they were his.

She would never get over her resentment of her life. Too much of it had passed while she was still in disguise, a spy in the world, but not knowing what power she spied for . . .

And that had ruined her relationship with her children, which was a real thing, and which should have been good, something shining and hot, like Alicia's relation with Stevie and Mariette. Maddy saw her face when Alicia talked about them, when she was with them; it was suffused with love, like an electric heater sending out warmth . . . And that it was too late to change that, it couldn't be changed, that was why Maddy was inconsolable. Only with Benjamin had things worked out, but he had moved as far away as the others . . .

Maybe she should tell her children, she thought. Just tell them the truth. About who she was, and why she acted as she did, and how she had changed. Would they understand? Could they forgive? Or would her explanation just give them a language for expressing their resentment? And what would she be telling them, after all? I'm terribly sorry I wasn't a more loving mother, but the truth is, I didn't want to have you, didn't want to raise you, resented giving you what I needed myself, so I did it with a dried-up little heart. Although I love you deeply. Now. And always did, even when I was resenting taking care of you. Was that believable?

She wished she could talk to Charley about this, but she knew he wouldn't understand. She could talk to Emily, but Emily didn't know the children the way Charley did, didn't love them the way he did. At least they had him: They felt his affection, and returned it. They all loved him. It was she who'd been left out in the cold, her own doing, yet not, not. She had been slotted into the wrong life . . .

And even when she had pulled herself together, after Benjamin was grown, made herself a career, it was still the wrong career. Maddy knew she had a good brain. Selling real estate was child's play for her. She could have done something better, something more, been a scientist, or a thinker, made a real contribution to humanity. Selling real estate contributed to nothing but her own pocketbook. It was easy, it was gratifying, but it was nothing. Nothing.

Oh well. She could have been born a Jew in Germany in the same year she was born here, or Japanese in Hiroshima a decade later, or in Bhopal decades later. For that matter, she could have drowned in the Great Flood, unchosen by Noah and his nameless wife. She could have been fed and cared for and loved deeply, raised by careful parents, only to die in some war, massacre, or accident. That happened to millions of people. She had no right to her bitterness, nor did it do her any good. It only poisoned what life remained to her. But she could not remove it from her heart.

•

Jenny's voice startled her back to the room. "Good God! It's almost one thirty! We should stop! You must be starved!"

She stretched. "My. I was really gone. In another world."

"You must be hungry. I am. Let me give you some lunch."

"Oh, that's not necessary, Jenny dear." She looked around for her handbag. "I should get home."

"It'll just be a salad. Let me. It will ease my guilt over keeping you so long."

"We figured three hours. It's just a little over that. It's fine. Charley will be wondering . . ."

"Really?" Jenny searched her face. "I'm willing to bet Charley gets up at six and eats lunch at twelve on the dot . . ."

Maddy laughed. "You have his number all right . . ."

"Good! I won't fuss. Promise." They walked into the shiny steel kitchen, and Jenny opened the refrigerator. "How about chicken salad sandwiches? We had chicken last night, and there's lots left over."

"Sounds good to me." Maddy sat down at the kitchen table. It felt good to sit down. "Did you get much done?"

"It was terrific. I'll only need you four or five more times. It was so much fun. I haven't worked from a model since we left New York. Years."

Jenny was dicing chicken. "Want me to chop the celery and onion?" Maddy asked.

"No. You worked hard enough today. I can do this fast."

She did indeed. Maddy wondered where she'd learned to chop that way. It looked professional, if there was such a thing as professional chopping. It was done in a flash.

"Did you hear Alicia's news?"

"Yes! Isn't it great? It must make her so happy. She's been longing for a vocation ever since I've known her."

"A vocation?"

"Yes," Maddy said. "You know. Not just something to do, but something you need to do."

Jenny put her knife down. "Ah."

"We suggested things, years ago. Teaching, working in a shop. She was really happy when she was working on that little book on Steventon . . ."

"Oh, I love that little book!"

"Yes. It's charming. So now . . ."

"She can do it on a larger scale. Emily said—Emily told me about it when I met her at the post office this morning. She said—I didn't quite understand—that it gives Alicia a surrogate past. What did she mean?"

"She has no family," Maddy explained. "The Holocaust." Maddy told her the story of Neva. "The poor woman used to read a Jewish newspaper put out in New York to find notices of Jewish people from Poland who had died, and go to their funerals. All over the city. So she could grieve."

"God!"

"Yes." Maddy shook her head. "She had so much sorrow."

"I feel protected from sorrow. Actually, I feel like a child, like I haven't grown up yet. Maybe because I haven't really felt sorrow. I haven't experienced loss. Well, my mother died, but I was so little I don't even remember it."

"Don't ask for it, my dear. It comes unbidden."

•

On a Sunday morning in April, Alicia told Steven that she wanted to turn the porch into a study for herself. He nodded, said it was a good idea, and went back to his *New York Times*. Having spent some days preparing herself to make this announcement, she sat silent in shock. Could it really be this easy? Would it have been this easy all along if she had just seen her way to it earlier? Just told him, without conceding that he had veto power? He didn't question cost or ask how it would look. Was it that he trusted her or did he not care? She was a little crestfallen, because she had anticipated the entire dialogue. Expecting him to protest the cost, she had planned to drop a small bomb in his lap and tell him she would pay for it herself! Her check for the first payment for the book should cover it, she thought. Maybe she'd scare him a little. Terrify him with the idea that she was now independent.

She called Bob Hawkes Monday morning, and he came to the house that afternoon. She had drawn a plan on graph paper, on a scale of a half inch to the foot, walling up four of the twelve porch windows for bookshelves, adding a fireplace that would abut the living-room fireplace inside. She wanted the floor and roof insulated, electric heat installed, the overhead light fixture removed, outlets added, and a good hardwood floor laid over the existing boards.

He said he could do it and would write an estimate for her.

So easy!

She walked through the rooms of what, she realized, felt for the first time like her house. Before, she had felt herself its caretaker, with rights in it but not control over it. Now she reached out to touch the air.

What enabled Alicia to act in her own behalf was a contract with Marshall Merchant, promising her twenty-five thousand dollars for a manuscript to be delivered in a year and a half, depicting the lives of women in New England in past centuries. The contract promised half the total on signing. The check had not arrived yet, but in Alicia's mind, it was banked and drawing interest, this gigantic sum, more than Neva earned in five years. Alicia had entered it in an account mentally engraved on her back in indelible ink; which so far contained only what she had earned babysitting in high school. It made her back straighter. The new straightness felt like a rest, it relaxed muscles tired of slumping, she felt her back thanking her. Virginia Woolf once wrote that the pounds and pence that concerned Arnold Bennett didn't matter, but later, she had admitted that four hundred pounds a year could save a woman. That wasn't anywhere near twenty-five thousand. (Twenty-five thousand dollars!) But maybe it was. How much had four hundred pounds been worth in the twenties?

She worked most days in county libraries or in her kitchen. She consulted Maddy's nephew Hilly Barrett for advice on buying a computer, and bought one, silently promising to pay Steven back for it when her check arrived. She began entering notes on it, and now had a file on the 1600s, which was very short but of all her files was the one she was proudest of, because she had had to work so hard to find the information in it. She ordered the machine to print. As the pages slid from the printer, she picked them up and read them, tears in her eyes, and began to underline sections she intended to use. Then she called up the file on the 1700s, which was not much longer, and repeated the process. Just like that, she had the beginning of her book. Except for the writing. And the writing was fun. The most fun. Alicia smiled at the waning light of the afternoon, at the plants on her windowsill, at her notes, silently saying, Good day, Good day, how nice to see you. She had embarked.

Writing history is a slow process, but Alicia didn't mind, because she loved it. She sometimes thought that perhaps she was stretching it out, prolonging it, because she enjoyed it so. There was still her life to be attended to—the garden, requiring much hard work, there was Steven, there were her friends, and her usual round of marketing, errands, housework. She had not heard from Stevie. He rarely even called now. He didn't seem to react to the fact that she was his mother, who loved and accepted him; she was Steven's wife, and so was alienated from him just as Steven was. He didn't know about the constant ache in her heart. Sometimes, though, when she was working, she could forget even him, briefly.

Soon after she'd decided to build the room, Alicia had lunch with Jenny and Maddy; Emily couldn't make it that day; one of her students was preparing for a concert and needed last-minute coaching. They were in Winchester, at the Copper Pot, having shrimp salad and tea. Alicia had asked Maddy about the changes that had occurred in Steventon during Maddy's lifetime. Maddy talked for a while, then paused. "It was so quiet then," she recalled. "That was the main difference, I think. It's still quiet compared to New York or Albany, but now you hear cars and trucks passing all the time. They make an impression on me, because there were none years ago. Even after cities were full of cars and noise, it was quiet up here. People still used their horses to draw the haywagons; lots of them still went to town in a surrey, right up till after World War II. The horses were a boon during the war, when gasoline was rationed. The roads were quiet, the town was quiet in a way it never is now, not even at four in the morning.

"Summer days, Main Street was a long sunlit avenue, grand, really, with the trees in full leaf; the town was idyllic. I didn't think that then but I do now. Then, I chafed in its smallness, its lack of opportunity, the boredom of life up here. I was an ambitious kid, but I didn't know what I wanted—just more life, I think. I was young and had no idea what women could do in other places. Up here, you could be a maid or a waitress, that was about it. The law office was the only place that hired a woman as a secretary in those days. That was probably the only secretarial job in Winchester; there were none in Steventon. Banks hired only men. A few women worked in the shops, but they were always daughters in the families that owned the shops."

She paused to sip her tea.

Jenny leaned across the table. "What were you like then, Maddy?"

"Oh, I hate to remember what I was." She patted her lips with her napkin.

"Tell us," Jenny cajoled her.

"Oh," Maddy sounded upset, "I don't like to think about it."

"Why?"

Maddy looked at Jenny and smiled at the wide-eyed, innocent face, so concerned, so sympathetic. She patted Jenny's cheek. "Kids were innocent up here in the mountains. We knew the facts of life, we were farm kids. People think knowledge of sexuality is the loss of innocence. They take the Bible seriously. But of course that has nothing to do with innocence. All farm kids know how animals are made and have seen them being born. There's nothing glamorous about it for them. They're still innocent."

"Until when?" Jenny asked. "When does innocence end?"

"The day you realize that even with good intentions, you will and do hurt others, even willfully hurt others."

"That's original sin?" Jenny asked.

"You were raised Catholic?"

"Sort of."

"I guess you could call it 'original sin.' But isn't there a ritual that's supposed to wash that away?"

"A sacrament. Baptism. Yes."

"Well, it doesn't. You can't wash this away. This is just part of being human."

"So, kids were innocent when you were a girl . . ."

"And I spent my entire childhood taking care of babies. As soon as one child had outgrown diapers, bottles, learning to walk and talk, needing to be calmed down from crying, there was always another one . . . Whatever else it does, taking care of children keeps you innocent. Because children are. Sweet. They may do things that upset you, but never intentionally. They want you to love them—they cry if they think you don't, even for a minute. They don't see themselves, they're not self-conscious. They don't know they have the power to hurt. That's innocence, for me."

"I see." Jenny nodded. "No idea of self."

"Wouldn't you agree, Alicia?"

"Yes. That's why it's nonsense, wicked and useless, to hit children. They don't need it. It doesn't do any good."

"Yes. Yes. And it does do harm. Children tell the truth, as they know it at least, until you teach them fear. Lies come from fear. But I never hurt my siblings, I almost never got angry with them." Saved that for my own children. Quiet anger, the silent slit of a mouth, corners bent down. "I'm trying to explain that I grew older, but inside stayed a child. I didn't see many people outside the family—our family was so huge. The minister, the schoolteacher, the family doctor—they were about the only outsiders we met. And they were all kind, or sort of kind, or maybe not kind but severe, but not violent, not angry. Emily was my only friend, and Emily was much younger than I, a child, and she was like other children. True. Sweet. Showed her feelings. And so that's how I was too. I hadn't seen anything else, really."

Her mouth twisted, she was getting into territory she didn't like. Alicia thought, I know where she's going. I was like that too.

Maddy finished her tea, and looked at her friends' cups. "Do we all want more tea?"

They did, and Alicia hailed the waitress. More tea was fetched.

"So I was a baby. I never learned to fight for myself. Boys maybe did, playing outside, but not girls. I stayed a baby for years and years. Even after I married. Don't know when I grew up. I trusted everyone, I did what people wanted me to do, I wanted approval, I wanted to be loved. So when something hurt me . . . I remember once, we were living with Charley's mother, and she criticized me and he didn't defend me—well, he was so awed by his mother—and I never said a word to him, just went off by myself and cried, and suffered about it for years afterward. Anything Charley did that hurt me, I just cried. I never fought for myself. I never defended myself. I never got mad at anyone. And the result was, I didn't get much respect. Charley doesn't know this, he thinks he respected me then. He respects me now, but he took me pretty much for granted in those days. He was happy, so he thought I was; he did what he wanted and was sure that that was what I wanted too. He didn't realize I was a separate person from him. Because my separateness was inconvenient. If I was a separate person, he'd have to think about me, and men are raised to think only about themselves. It took some years and a lot of hurt—even heartbreak—before I learned to speak up; then it took a fair number of fights before Charley, and some of my relatives, realized I was more than a shadow . . ."

Jenny was appalled. "Hard to believe. You're such a—distinct person! And I always thought Charley adored you!"

Maddy chuckled. "Well, every distinct edge you see, Jenny, cost me pain and sorrow."

"I was like that too," Alicia said sadly. "But I haven't come as far as you, Maddy."

"You're doing pretty well," Maddy said.

"You too!" Jenny exclaimed. "You seem like such strong women! Do we all have to go through this? Do I?"

"It's a toughening process," Alicia mused. "We're raised to be giving, it's expected, and we expect to be made happy by it. And with your children, well, usually, that happens. But you need to get something back."

"But I never realized that . . . moving into yourself—that's what it is, isn't it?—becoming your full self?—means you have to fight and attack, hurt and be hurt. I hate the thought of that," Jenny lamented. "Is it true?"

"Maybe there's another way. I just never found it," Maddy said.

11

It was spring now; the ornamental fruit trees were in their full glory, forsythias and crocuses had soaked up the light, and the daffodils were budding. It was so beautiful that Tim, wanting to share it, had invited two old pals up for the weekend. They were painters he had hung out with in the decades when they were all poor and unknown. He had drunk with Marcus Roth and Ippolyte Imperioli at the White Horse Tavern and eaten with them at the Pink Teacup, back in the days when you could get a good hot meal for practically nothing. He had great affection for them, and asked Jenny to tolerate the heavy smoking, filthy language, and heavy drinking that were sure to characterize the weekend.

Jenny was eager to meet Tim's old friends—she and Tim had been out of New York for some years, so she had never met them. She was excited at the idea of being part of a bohemian atmosphere. The three men were now considered the heart of sixties New York bohemia, and Jenny wanted to experience them, even if it entailed an alcoholic weekend, smoky and filthy-mouthed. As a young girl she had read novels about the bohemian world of artists in Paris in the nineteenth century, and she had always thought that that was the world she wanted to inhabit.

Now all three were stars. Ippolyte was so famous that the Guggenheim was giving him a retrospective in 2002. He was fifteen years older than Tim, so, not young, but still alive—so what an honor! He'd married an Italian countess and had lived with her in Modena for years, but when she died last year he returned to New York. Marcus Roth had been teaching at Yale and living in New Haven for two decades, showing occasionally and receiving critical attention. Then a show he'd had four years ago had been such a huge success, critically and financially, that he retired from teaching, and he too had now moved back to New York. Immediately on their return, both men called Tim.

Tim told Jenny not to worry about food: Ippolyte was a gourmet and Marcus a gourmand, he said; so he'd do the marketing with her, and he'd do the cooking. He bought and bought: two large jars of caviar, hundreds of dollars worth; huge steaks from the prime butcher, piles of sea urchins, scungilli and shrimp. He ordered pickled herring and smoked bluefish online; it arrived in a huge box filled with dry ice. Cheeses of all sorts, including a huge chunk of Roquefort were sent by Dean and DeLuca. He lugged home two cases of wine, one white, one red, and ordered pasta from a shop in Little Italy. Yet the morning of their arrival, when he went out to paint, he was wearing his soiled paint-spotted jeans, and he never changed. Jenny dressed in her New York "artist" uniform: tight black pants and boots and a clinging jersey top, black lipstick and long silver earrings.

The men arrived just before noon, roaring up the long drive in a tiny, dirty foreign car Tim told her was a Ferrari, trunk filled with packages. They slowly unfolded themselves from the car, two old men who looked their age. Ippolyte was huge, and waddled; cadaverous Marcus bent forward as if he were studying the ground for spoor. They reached into their piled-up tied-down trunk even before they said hello and handed Tim, who was standing near them grinning widely, large, thin packages wrapped in brown paper which Jenny recognized as wrapped canvasses. After they laid them in Tim's arms, they both tried to hug him at once. All three nearly fell over, and Jenny laughed as one exclaimed loudly, "Timothy caro, oh caro Timo," while the other kissed Tim on each cheek over and over, saying, "Timola, Timola." They both tried to unwrap the packages immediately. Of course they would, Jenny thought, even before they had been introduced to her. To them, the paintings were all that mattered.

Ippolyte's canvas was large and covered with wild scrawls and sand. Jenny thought it a cross between a de Kooning, a Max Beckmann, and an Anselm Kiefer. It didn't seem original to her, but it was a kind of painting considered "in." He conferred it upon Tim like a priest offering a communion wafer, or Lear handing over his kingdom, and Tim fell over himself praising it, wild with his words, but also, half teasing, insulting it as if he were jealous of it. Which, Jenny thought, he couldn't be—could he? Of course, she realized, the thing was probably worth a hundred thousand dollars. But they weren't thinking about money.

Now Marcus was jealous, and he tried to set his painting into Tim's hands, and Tim put Ippolyte's painting down on the terrace and opened Marcus's, an austere, geometric set of angles and colors, and began exclaiming again with the same exaggeration, the same envy. Hard to like both, Jenny thought, smiling hard. She found them both a little inhuman, but when Tim held the paintings up to her, she cried out with fervor, just as Tim had.

The men smelled rather strongly of alcohol, and she wondered how the trip in the car had been, but they were here, and while the car had a few dents, none of them looked new. When Tim finally introduced Jenny, they threw themselves on her, hugging and kissing and crying out about her beauty, her charm, her glamour, and even her shape—Ippolyte went so far as to stroke her ass. She led them into the house.

The men roared through the house exclaiming alternately about it and Jenny—as if she came with it, was one of its appurtenances. With them, Tim (normally soft-spoken) roared too, and poured wine for them and himself, eyebrow raised at Jenny, who shook her head no. They wandered through the rooms commenting on everything, using sophisticated architectural terms to praise the house, and artist's terms to praise the paintings, speaking of hard edges, planes, color field. Many of the paintings were Tim's (Jenny had hung only two of her own, those that she felt could stand up to Tim's), but many were the two visitors' own earlier work. They looked at them almost impersonally, discussing their former inadequacies and youthful brilliance with what sounded like complete objectivity. They waved cigarettes about as they spoke, dropping ash everywhere, putting the cigarettes out in expensive antique Chinese bowls. They recognized the ethnic source of every piece of African sculpture, and gushed over it, discussing Picasso and Matisse along the way. They were extraordinarily intelligent and learned, which, Jenny thought, you would not guess from their appearance.

She trailed behind them. She could understand why Tim loved them—they were not only very smart, but also warm, effusive, giving. Unlike most men she knew, but like Tim. It made sense that they would be his friends. They acted completely at home from the moment they entered, and when the tour was done, they sat on stools drinking in the kitchen, while Tim fixed seafood with pasta for lunch. Jenny prepared salad, and they ate at the kitchen table, the men praising the lunch hugely and eating hugely too. They drank even more, finishing four bottles of wine by the end of the meal. After which, of course, all three needed a nap.

Jenny sat on her screened porch reading the paper with the heat on while the men slept. It was still chilly out here, but at least the air smelled fresh and clean, while the house was smoky and rank from the cigarettes and cigars they smoked after lunch. Marcus had brought a box of Montecristos for Tim, who exclaimed extravagantly over them, although Jenny had never seen him smoke a cigar. She too had had wine with lunch, which was unusual for her. She'd had only one glass, but now she too began to nod off. Ippolyte was napping on the couch in Tim's studio and Marcus on the one in hers, so there were no free beds, and Jenny went into their bedroom and crawled into bed beside Tim. Even the bedroom room smelled of drink and smoke, although no one had smoked in here. Tim smelled heavily of both. Jenny wondered if she did.

She woke up sooner than the men and went into the kitchen, which hadn't been cleaned up. The whole room smelled; maybe wine had spilled on the floor. She felt a little ill as she wiped up the countertop (Tim was a messy cook). She put away the food that had been left out and slid the soiled dishes into the dishwasher. The room still smelled when she finished, so she found the mop and gave the floor a damp cleaning. It really needed more, she thought, sniffing, when she finished, but that was all it was going to get now.

The noise began again as soon as the men awoke, Ippolyte tottering and scratching, Marcus coughing as if his lungs were about to explode, Tim groaning and passing out aspirins and orange juice. But that was the last nonalcoholic drink to pass their lips. Tim took the Stolichnaya out of the freezer and poured it into tiny cordial glasses, put out the caviar and chopped hard-boiled egg, the herring and bluefish, the cheeses, crackers and toast triangles. The men roared with joy, Tim knew how to live, this was like the old days, and Jenny wondered how, broke as they had been, they had been able to live like this in the old days. Yet she was sure they had. It was the nature of the beast, artist, to live well, whoever footed the bill. She smiled, appreciating this talent, and took some caviar and egg and ice-cold vodka along with them, deciding to join what she could not defeat.

They settled into the living room and talked. The conversation ranged from recent work by younger artists, about which they were surprisingly positive, to their idols of the past, whom they spoke of in awe, simultaneously gleefully exposing their most vicious secrets. They ranted about the disgusting situation in the political world, the nastiness of academia, the beauty of Italy and its great cuisine, and the beauty of Jenny, which was commented on quite regularly. Some of the remarks edged close to seduction, and Jenny glanced at Tim, to check his reaction. But he laughed heartily, looking at her with proprietary pleasure. After some hours had passed in this entertaining fashion, they were quite drunk (Jenny included), and Tim announced that it was near nine and he was going to start dinner. He clambered clumsily to his feet.

"To the kitchen, Jenny dearest," he ordered, and she followed him. They followed her, and Ippolyte grabbed her and pulled her to him and kissed her. His mouth was wet and tasted of Roquefort, which revolted Jenny, who tried to pull away. Tim and Marcus stood stock still howling with laughter. As she slid out of Ippolyte's grasp, Marcus cried, "Hey, how about me?" She smiled at him and evaded him as she approached the refrigerator. She pulled out the salad greens, mushrooms, avocado, and asparagus that Tim had approved for the evening's dish, surrounding herself with food as a shield. She squeezed into a corner of a counter, leaving the main counter space free for Tim, who was buttering steaks and pricking potatoes and drinking vodka and laughing and joking with Ippolyte and Marcus, who surrounded him, falling over him and themselves, telling one more story, one more joke, trying hard to make one more point.

Jenny was drunk enough that she could barely understand the jokes; she had to concentrate to prepare the vegetables the way Tim liked them. She felt wary, on guard. In an alcoholic blur, steaks got broiled, the potatoes baked, everything served in the formal dining room this time, with the good china and the sterling; the men praised it to the skies, and ate and ate and ate and drank four more bottles of wine. Then they all went back to the living room to continue the blast. What enormous capacities they had, she thought, knowing she was falling-down drunk despite having had only a fraction of what they had drunk. Her head ached, and she wanted to go to bed, but she was leery of losing control. They were now gossiping about everyone in the art world, telling vicious stories about even each other: Everything sent them rolling over with laughter. Finally, Jenny stumbled to her feet and headed for the bedroom.

"Leaving us, sweet?" Tim called.

"No, no, come back, you must stay, oh bella donna, mia cara, stay and be beautiful for us!"

"Yes, stay, you gorgeous creature," Marcus bubbled.

"I'm just going to pee," she apologized, and ran. She went into the bedroom and used the toilet there, then closed the bedroom door. She wanted to lock it, but that seemed . . . paranoid, somehow. Unfriendly. Besides, Tim would eventually want to come in. She got undressed nervously, kept looking at the door. She put on flannel pajamas and buttoned them up to her neck. She slid into the rumpled bed, but had trouble falling asleep—she kept imagining she was hearing the knob turn on the door. At last she slept. She was having a nightmare when she was wakened by Ippolyte clambering into the bed beside her.

•

"Finish that last blueberry waffle," Emily ordered.

"I can't. Maybe half."

"Okay, we'll split it."

"Great." Jenny grinned, cutting the waffle in half. "I feel terrible just barging in on you like this on a Sunday morning."

"Nonsense. I love having company for breakfast. It was a fun surprise."

Jenny, who did not know whether to believe this or ascribe it to graceful flattery, regarded Emily steadily. "Really?"

"Really."

"I was just desperate. I didn't know what else to do."

"It sounds hopeless. So what did you do then?"

"Well, I tried to push Ippolyte off the bed, but he's huge, he weighs a ton, I couldn't move him an inch. And I didn't want to hurt him. I mean, I like the guys, they're fun; I just can't stand the way they treat me. If that makes any sense . . ." she drifted off, looking to Emily for response.

Emily nodded.

"I had an experience of that kind of male energy," Emily recalled. "My friend Dinah Russoff fell in love with a rabbi, a Canadian, head of some kind of sect or cult, I'm not sure what. She was moving up there to live with him, although he was already living with two other women, but she said she didn't care. So his group came down to Boston to help her, to pack her things up in a rented van. And she had a party for them, inviting all her Boston friends. They stayed in her apartment, they all had their wives—or whatever—with them, I don't know where they all slept, but there they were. They were all pretty young and good-looking, and there was music and wine, and after a while, Dinah asked them to dance.

"'You gotta see this,' she told us, 'they're great!' So they put on a record of some kind of Jewish music, I don't know what to call it, klezmer, maybe, and the guys stood in a circle in her living room and danced. And their eyes were so bright, and they were so happy and so alive and pink in the face, they were gorgeous, they made you want to be with them, well, they made me want to, and I kept watching them, so vivid, so full of energy, singing and kicking and bouncing and smiling, and I thought maybe I'd go with her to Toronto, join the commune or whatever it was, just to be in the same world with those men. And then I looked at the rest of us. We were all sitting around in a circle, watching. We were all women except for one or two Boston male friends of Dinah's. The Canadian women were all sitting cross-legged in the front row, watching the men, smiling, singing, clapping, and they all wore old-fashioned skirts down to their ankles like from the 1800s, and head scarves covering their hair, and no makeup, and they all looked meek and mild, and suddenly I realized that that was what they had to be to have men like that, and my heart stopped for a moment and I thought the cost was too high. I don't know why it is, but for men, freedom and joy and high spirits seem to depend on women being completely subdued. It occurred to me that Dinah wouldn't last up there—and she didn't. She was back in six months complaining that the rabbi kept her awake by banging one of the other women in the next room every night—and she couldn't concentrate on her spiritual development."

Jenny laughed.

"The men are great," she concluded. "What isn't is the way they see women, the way they treat women. It is the same with Ippolyte and Marcus.

"So I leaped out of bed dragging the duvet with me. Damned if I was going to leave it for him—anyway, he was too drunk and had too much insulation to notice, or to freeze. He was saying, 'Jenny, darling, stay,' but his head fell on the pillow and he fell asleep while he was talking." Jenny laughed. "I went into the living room. Tim was dead to the world, sitting on the floor leaning back against the couch with his mouth open, snoring. Very loudly. All that smoking. Marcus was lying down across the room, all curled up like a fetus, with his thumb in his mouth. Or anyway, near it.

"I thought I'd sleep in my studio, where Marcus had been, but it stank of dead cigar, the worst smell I know. There were a couple of extinguished cigar butts in a ceramic dish, an ornament I keep on a table. I tried Tim's studio too, but it was even worse, because somebody had thrown up in there. I didn't look for the vomit, but I sure could smell it. So I went out to the porch, which was really cold in the middle of the night, but the air was fresh, and I wrapped the duvet around me and threw myself on the couch and tried to sleep. I couldn't lock the door, it locks only from the other side. But I figured they might not look out there.

"I woke up about ten. The house was quiet. No one was in the living room. I tiptoed around in my slippers. Ippolyte was in Tim's and my bed, Marcus was on the couch in my studio, and Tim was gone. I assume he was in his studio. Ippolyte and Marcus were sound asleep, snoring. I couldn't face it—the stinky house, the cleaning up, the vomit—and I couldn't face them. I was so disgusted . . .

"But I had nowhere to go. I'm hung over myself, not up to driving all the way to Connecticut to my father's, who would probably have a stroke from the shock of seeing me anyway. Or back to the city, where I still have some friends. I could have gone to a motel, I suppose, but I thought of you, Em. I hoped I wouldn't be intruding on you, that you wouldn't mind. So, here I am . . ."

"I'm glad you came here. I'd hate to think of you driving around aimlessly, without a place to go."

"Oh, what a mess!" Jenny lamented, laying her head in her hand.

"Oh, it's not so bad," Emily said consolingly. "They meant no harm. They don't know they misbehaved: They're unevolved."

"Yes," Jenny said thoughtfully. "That's how they feel—like dinosaurs. From the dark ages. But don't you think there's a kind of willfulness in being unenlightened after all these years of feminism?"

"Of course. But men like that—I've known them—pay no attention to feminism. They are totally self-involved, each one thinks he's the center of the earth, and they dislike being distracted from themselves. A world-famous author, a man some men consider a great humanist, told me he disliked feminism because it was inconvenient for him. Can you imagine? He values women so little that he is annoyed if they don't make things easy for him. Men like that really believe women were created for them. And men like that are convinced that they love women, and that women love them. They don't realize they treat us like appurtenances."

"Are they typical? Is this what bohemian life is like? Do you know? Are there bohemians in music? Did you know people like that in Rome?"

"Yes, of course. In Rome, at Curtis . . . lots of them. But musicians can't drink like that. They have to perform, they have to be technically perfect, they can't afford to drink. They wreck their talent if they do. But I observed scenes like that."

"Really!" Jenny had anticipated it, yet the answer shocked her. "I wonder what you were like as a girl," she mused. "I wish I'd known you then. Or when you were my age. I bet we would've been friends. Tell me about Curtis. Tell me about then."

Emily gazed at her for a few moments. "Curtis was glorious for me, a glorious place. I love music schools! I love walking down a hall and hearing people practicing, each one in a different instrument, in a different room. You hear pianos, violins, French horns, flutes, sopranos practicing scales . . . A total chaos of sound, yet it never turns into conflict. Chaotic coexistence. Like outer space. Or an anthill. I think of it as anarchy, and anarchy is my ideal.

"I was a naïve kid. We all were, really. In the forties, you know, America was a very different place. Very . . . provincial. Compared to today's kids, we were utterly innocent. And ignorant: We knew nothing. No one had the kind of skinny figure youngsters strive for today, or fancy haircuts, or glitzy clothes. We were all just ordinary people, pretty enough because we were young, but our bodies had lumps and bumps and we had unkempt hair. And most of us had been—well, kind of unpopular in high school, because we were musicians, solitaries, committed. I was sort of popular, but only because my family had a kind of cachet. But my only close friend was Maddy, who was six years older than I. Which is a lot at that time of life . . .

"At Curtis, my family didn't matter, but I was still well liked. So that really mattered to me. The kids there cared about the same things I did. They were all crazy about music, obsessed with it, centered on it, like me. So we were friends. I even had boyfriends, something I hadn't been interested in before . . . And one in particular, Duncan Cade, another pianist, he's somewhat famous now . . ."

"Yes. I've heard of him. He specializes in French music, doesn't he?"

"Yes. Ravel, Debussy, Poulenc, Faure, Martin . . . Actually, I was the one who introduced him to French music. Anyway, Duncan came from Illinois and had felt out of things there. We were all happy to be together, happy to feel like, instead of unlike, each other. We had to work hard to stay at Curtis; we were all practicing for some competition or other. I wanted to enter them as a composer, but my teachers insisted I enter piano competitions as well. They insisted I could win. But that put Duncan and me in competition with each other, we all were of course, but it was hard when you had to compete against your lover . . ." Emily said, unembarrassed.

Jenny nodded, wide-eyed. Emily had a lover?

"For me it was terrible to compete against him. Some days I thought I played better than he, and that made me feel queasy with remorse; and other days he sounded better, and I would hate him. So I began to question things . . . what life was about, goals, what mattered and what didn't. You know, how adolescents do; I was not quite eighteen when I got to Curtis, but very very young, undeveloped physically—I had no breasts to speak of until then. I was not at all mature. And I had accepted my parents' beliefs for the most part: I thought our country was the best country in the world, the most moral; I believed we were on God's side in World War II and that the Axis powers were evil; I believed there was equality between men and women, whites and blacks . . . and tolerance for all religions. I didn't question much.

"Nobody did. We were a country of innocents. We believed that our government was honest with us, that our rulers were acting for our good, that the United States shone among nations for its high moral virtue and godliness. I stopped believing in any god even before I left home, after I read Nietzsche and Schopenhauer and Tom Paine, whose books were just lying in the bookcase at home, though I don't think anyone in the family had ever read them. I don't know where they came from. But I read them and I started to question. Only religion at first.

"You're so young, Jenny, you were only five when the Vietnam War ended, you can't know how different things were in this country before it. That war ended American innocence. After it, no one, not even rigid right-wing people, really believed that government was devoted to the welfare of the people, or was honest and righteous. In fact it's the radical right nowadays that claims the government is spying on us in black helicopters or something . . . I'm getting off the point.

"I knew, partly because I lived abroad, but also because I read a lot, that Europeans did not feel the same way about their governments. They were too used to being preyed upon and robbed by nobles and their armies . . . They knew that the real war was between the rich and the poor, and that the rich got rich by robbing the poor, by living on them like parasites. Americans were like children compared to Europeans. And I one of the most naïve.

"Anyway, competition was the first value I questioned. You know, competition is equated with the American way, is considered an absolute good. My high school emphasized it. Probably because the kids—we were mainly farm kids—weren't great competitors. We liked to get along. But they wanted us to compete with each other, to vie for higher grades, and especially wanted the football team to strive to defeat other teams . . .

"But at Curtis I saw that everyone loses in competitions: The loser feels bad because he lost, he's a loser; the winner feels bad because he's alone, lonely, and everybody envies him. He tries to find satisfaction in that but it's a recipe for misery. I wanted to withdraw from the La Salle Prize and the Prix de Rome, but Duncan wouldn't let me. He said that if I quit, he would too. But I knew he wanted to win some prize, any prize, with every fiber in his body. So I didn't quit. Not formally. I just didn't try as hard as I could."

Emily stopped suddenly. "I don't know why I'm telling you all this. I'm leading up to the bohemians, but I'm certainly taking the long way round. How about more coffee?"

Jenny stood up. "I'll make it. We finished the first pot. Please go on. This is fascinating. All this stuff about you I never knew."

Emily shrugged. "It isn't important. At least, not to anyone but me."

"It's interesting," Jenny insisted, washing out the pot. "Go on," she urged.

"In the end, Duncan won the La Salle and a lesser French prize and I didn't win any. My teachers knew what I'd done. One of them, Madame Glasnova, took me aside and reproached me bitterly. She told me that if you sacrifice your talent for a man, you will spend your life sacrificing. She told me I had made a terrible mistake. But Duncan didn't even notice. Strange . . .

"But I won the Prix de Rome for composition! The one I really wanted. I had to compete for that, too, but it didn't feel like competition. You don't compose in competition. You know? When you're writing music, you're not thinking about how other people write music, or comparing what you do with what they do. At least, I don't. I can only focus on my own work. And I did. And I won.

"If I'd been male, that would have been the beginning of big things for me, but as it was . . . Still, in a way, I didn't care. I like my quiet life. I like burrowing in here, safe, away from the blasting world. But bohemia . . . yes, there were a few bohemians at Curtis and, later, in Rome. I was very excited when I first went to their parties, at being part of the wild crowd. Even then, one earring, blue hair, drugs . . . But most of us just drank. I couldn't drink. One drink and I started yawning. So I kept it to a minimum. Duncan could hold it, but when he got drunk, he would wander off to be with the guys. He would simply ignore me. The parties were for the men. The women were stage dressing—there as the men's adornments, their jewels, to be shown off and ignored. I remember feeling terribly abandoned. Guys gave me attention, but the leering kind that made you feel appropriated, dirty. They would skewer you with a look and ask you to get into bed. It was taken for granted that they were irresistible. Or could command you. Young women were prey in that world. Isn't that what you said you felt like? Prey. Yes. Men use us for one thing or another. They don't see us as people with interests and abilities apart from our bodies. They didn't know how to talk to us. They see women instrumentally. I think they see each other instrumentally. They relate to people in terms of 'what use can I make of this person?' And the only use they can think of for women is sex. Or typing their papers, or serving them in some other way. Sex and servitude. As I recall." She smiled ruefully. "I like to think things are different now. The world has changed so."

"Maybe they are. These guys are old. Ippolyte is over seventy and Marcus is close to it."

"So they're part of a passing generation."

"It would be nice to think so," Jenny grimaced. "Did you ever kiss someone who'd been eating Roquefort? Ugh!"

Emily laughed. "I can imagine." She paused. "So what are you going to do?"

"I guess I have to go back home. I don't know what to say. I don't know how to act. I feel like such a fool, but this morning, I just didn't feel I could stay there for one more minute. It isn't that I don't like them. They're smart and funny. But I don't like the way they relate to me. And Tim is different when they are around."

"You know," Emily mused, "I'll bet they've barely noticed you were gone. Why don't you pick up three copies of the *Times*, and pretend you've been at the newspaper shop?"

"Tim knows it closes at noon. But then, he'll be hung over, he'll be out of it. They'll all be out of it. Good idea, Emily! I'll do it!" she cried. "Right after this cup of coffee," she added, smiling, as she poured the newly brewed coffee into their cups, savoring the aroma as if it were new to her.

•

Jenny drove home through a glorious June day and walked into the house bowed under the weight of three copies of the Sunday *New York Times*, to find the men, baggy-eyed and with sallow skin, stumbling around the dirty kitchen. They greeted her painfully: Tim said he'd wondered where she was, but he should have known she would be a perfect wife and get the *Times* before they were all gone. He'd made coffee and squeezed orange juice, but anything more was beyond him. She took over like a loving mother, told the men to sit down in the dining room, and put out the bagels and cream cheese and lox she'd also picked up, and a coffeecake she'd bought on Friday. They leaned into her care gratefully, heads throbbing, unsure about what had occurred the night before. They were a little uneasy.

Jenny did not want to clean up after this trio of bad boys, but it had to be done if she was to resume her life in this house. So she started to clean the kitchen. But when the men finished breakfast, Tim came into the kitchen to make Bloody Marys for them.

"There's no horseradish!" he complained angrily, turning from the refrigerator.

"I guess it slipped your mind when you were buying the wine and brandy and caviar," she said.

He glanced at her a little suspiciously.

She looked back and stopped wiping down the counter. "And before you start drinking again, Tim, please get rid of the vomit and the dead cigars. The smell permeates the house."

"What vomit?" he asked in irritation.

"In your studio. Can't you smell it from here?"

He went out to the studio, then marched back, yelling as he went. "Ugh, god, Ippolyte, is that your excreta? Get your guinea ass in here, man, you are going to clean it up, not I, you wop bastard, and Marcus, get your kike ass in here and get rid of these dead butts before my wife throws up all over the three of us, you lousy drunks, you slobs, you verminous waste from the shallows of a viscous slough of despond . . ."

Ippolyte and Marcus followed him, running, then cried out in disgust when the studio door was opened, Ippolyte holding his hands up to his fat cheeks, Marcus drooping and moaning as if he was dying. "How can I, I'm so sick!" he cried. "I'm going to throw up!" he shrieked.

Ippolyte tried to press Jenny into the task, telling her he did not know how, did not know where, even as she pushed a bucket into his hands, with a roll of paper towels and a plastic bottle of detergent. "Ew, god, the smell of that is worse than the vomit," he cried, backing away from it.

She went out to the porch. She had left the duvet there, and she wrapped it around her now, thinking she needed a room of her own. She needed a place of refuge in her own house.

It was a long time before she sensed the men trailing back into the living room, sounding subdued. She did not feel like speaking to them, and stayed where she was. She heard Tim calling her, and at last he opened the door and peered out.

"Oh, there you are, luv," he said genially. "We're going out, down to Rolly's to have some Bloody Marys. Want to come?"

She looked at him for a moment. "No," she said quietly.

Ippolyte pushed the door open behind Tim. "Jenny! Jenny darling! You sweet poor girl! We are so sorry! We are such slobs!" he cried.

Marcus came stumbling out behind him.

"Forgive us, dear Jenny." He fell into Jenny's arms. "Such a sweetheart you are! Forgive us stupid old men who get drunk in your house, can you forgive us?"

She murmured, "Of course," and they embraced her, they begged her to accompany them for a wee hair of the dog, and when she said no, they insisted.

"I have to clean up," she explained.

"No, no, we have done it," they both protested. "It is all done, the house is immaculate!"

She stood firm, walking to the door with them, watching the three of them pile into the dented rusty Ferrari and drive off to drink someplace where they would not have to clean up after themselves. She went back into the house. Three half-made Bloody Marys stood on the counter. She tossed them out, then set to work with sponge and mop and her strongest cleanser, cleaning the kitchen, dining, and living rooms and the two studios and the bedroom. The whole fucking house, she thought. And the whole time, she muttered, "What do they do in their own houses?" knowing that somehow, some way, however or wherever they lived, they had some woman to clean up after them.

12

Emily cleaned up the few dishes Jenny had missed.

"Bad enough I come barging in on you on a quiet Sunday morning, without leaving you with a stack of dirty dishes," she'd said, insisting on washing up.

She was a sweet girl. Emily was glad she'd stopped in. There were times when she felt lonely. This morning might have been one of them, who knows? She didn't let herself know things like that. But now she wasn't lonely: She'd had enough company to satisfy her for the whole day.

She didn't like to admit to loneliness. She had made her bed, as her father often said, and now she had to lie in it. He was adamant that people had to do that. That attitude had ruined his own life, she thought. Then brushed that thought away.

Talking to Jenny about "bohemian" parties had reminded Emily of some of Duncan's less charming qualities, things she preferred to forget. Like the way he simply assumed that she would pick up his shirts from the laundry and keep the tiny refrigerator in their Rome apartment (of course, her parents did not know she was living with Duncan in Rome) stocked with milk and beer. Mostly these days she thought of him as he had appeared years ago in his promotional photographs, young, smiling, open-faced, elegant in his morning coat. They were almost all famous now, the boys she'd gone to school with. There had been few girls, and only one had achieved any distinction—Ariel Godenborg, a Danish flautist. They didn't say flautist anymore, did they? It *was* an ugly word. Flutist. But the boys performed regularly at the great concert halls of the world—the Leipzig Gewandhaus, the Amsterdam Concertgebouw, Prince Albert Hall, Carnegie Hall . . .

They were men now, as old as she or older, wrinkled, jowled, thick, thin, elegant, whatever, they had shelves of records and CDs, they were famous, treated like great men, with deference, reverence. Hard to imagine now their flirting in those years, clustering around her demanding her attention. That's what boys did in her day: They were like performing monkeys leaping around a girl, wanting a smile, a laugh, not expecting much more. They didn't know how to talk to girls; they didn't seem to know that girls had minds capable of thought. They saw girls as audience. She had enjoyed them within limits: It got boring playing Mom in Look Mom, No Hands. And they probably never learned. Their marriages—she had followed them over the years—had not been successful. Duncan was now married to a twenty-odd-year-old woman.

Young people were different now, she thought. She saw them on campus, two youngsters lovely in their youth, head to head, in intense conversation. Boys and girls were best friends, they told each other everything, they argued, they were people together. As often as not, it was the girl who was holding forth, speaking passionately while the boy listened. That couldn't have happened when she was young. She viewed them with a wistful envy, wishing things could have been like that for her. And sometimes they stayed best friends even after they ceased being lovers, like Roz Capek, her brilliant cello student, and that love of a violist, Paul McConaghy. The two of them had gone on, some years ago, to marry other people, but remained best friends to this day. She'd had an e-mail from Roz just last month. Playing in Cleveland, aiming for Vienna. Fat chance!

Yes, and boys talked about their feelings these days, and so they understood when girls did. And girls played sports, and so understood all that fervor—which Emily did not. Both were full human beings, she felt, which her generation had not been. Not been allowed to be. Not been able to be. Whatever.

It wasn't true that nothing changes. Sometimes there were splendid profound changes. But love was still opaque.

The kitchen straightened, she went to her study and prepared to work on an andante section that had been humming in her head. It was about love, but was not right. When she thought about it, most great "love" music wasn't about love at all, it was about renunciation. The *Liebestod* bemoaned the end of love:

so did the great trio ending *Der Rosenkavalier*.

Most of the popular love songs of Emily's day were in fact about the yearning for love, about *longing*. But what about love itself, satisfied and blooming? Did it have no music? Was it complete unto itself, a smug little isolationist world that held only the two lovers and needed nothing else? No! the Tchaikowsky *Romeo and Juliet*,the duet of themes, *that* was about love. Two not-identical voices, in perfect harmony. Like D. H. Lawrence's two eagles fucking in midair. That was what was needed. The andante should be a duet!

Emily set to work.

•

In early May, Maddy sold the old Hewitt place. It was still called that by the old-timers even though there hadn't been any Hewitts living there since 1943. The Kaminskys, who had owned it for fifteen years, had restored it to its original elegance—restoring moldings, replacing fixtures, furnaces, the roof, adding bathrooms and spiffing up the old ones, and landscaping it nicely. They got it perfect, and then got divorced. In compensation, Maddy had gotten a million dollars for them. This was absurd, of course. A million dollars for an old farmhouse and the twenty acres of land remaining to it! Maddy remembered when Nana Hewitt sold it, putting it for the first time out of the family. She was old and poor and was going to live with her granddaughter, but she wanted a little money of her own. There was no Social Security for people like Nana, who had worked like an ox, but never got paid. The house was terribly run down and she was happy to get six thousand dollars for it at the time. It had been sold several times since, the price soaring each time. Where would it end? Maddy asked Charley, How could people afford such prices? Just the mortgage payments would break most people.

It was her first million-dollar sale, although prices had been creeping up for years, and several houses in the area had gone for more than half a million. Maddy had long been prosperous, but in the past decade, she'd grown really rich. She would get sixty thousand dollars from this sale. She'd give twenty thousand to Lacey Glidden, who had helped show the place, and be left with forty thousand. A nice few days' work.

Money meant little to Maddy. She didn't need it. She'd wanted the listing and worked for the sale because it would have mortified her if any other Steventon broker had had the listing or sold the house. It was a matter of pride.

"What is the world coming to, Charley?" she asked again.

"Rack and ruin, looks like," he said.

Maddy worried her lower lip.

"What are you going to do with all that money?" Charley asked.

"I'm going to set up trust funds for the grandchildren. So they can all go to college. The way things are going, it will cost a hundred thousand dollars to go to college for four years by the time they're grown up."

"Yeah," he nodded. "That's a good idea." He didn't care about money either. They had plenty for their own limited wants. Neither of them had expensive tastes. They didn't like to travel—Charley didn't even want to go to Florida in the winter, as many of their retired friends did. He liked being home, comfortable, safe. At the moment, he was reading his paper. He liked sitting quietly in his easy chair on a Sunday afternoon, reading the Sunday paper—the local one, not that encyclopedia of a *New York Times*. He wished he could smoke in the house: He would like a pipe right now. He had been considering moving his body out to the garage when Maddy came in with news of the sale.

"You don't seem especially happy," he opined.

"No. I don't, do I?"

"Why is that, Maddy?" He searched her face.

"I don't know. It's just that . . . things seem to have gone too far. Don't you think?"

"They went too far for me twenty-five years ago," Charley said dryly. "The world and me parted ways back then. I only go back for short visits. Don't like it much. I like you, though. And I like the kids, even if sometimes I suspect they're part of *it* . . ."

His humor was always like this, dry and simple; he rarely cracked a smile.

"Twenty-five years ago," she mused. "The end of the war?"

"Yup. Artificial date. Might as well say the beginning of the war, whenever that was. When did it begin, do you remember? That war sort of crept up on us. It was years in the coming. Maybe I should use Kent State. That was in 1970, thirty years ago May. But I can't remember when kids started wearing beards and smoking pot. Was it 1968 or thereabouts?"

"You really think Vietnam was that significant?"

"I don't know what was *significant*. I only know the world changed in ways I don't like, and it seems to me it started then."

"*What* don't you like? You seem pretty happy to me. You seem to get along all right."

"I don't like kids in beards. Or long hair . . ."

"But practically nobody has those anymore . . ."

"Sure they do. It's everywhere now. Look at Jerry Long, Mark Szypanski, Henry Gold, my cousin . . ."

"Ummm." She hadn't realized. She was used to it, probably. Whereas once, beards and long hair stood out, were shocking.

"I don't like people putting down this country."

"And do they?"

"They did. Some still do. They say *Amerika*," he complained.

She frowned at him.

"Well, all right," he conceded. "I haven't heard anything like that in a while. I'm thinking of the past. I never got over it, though. But people are cynical now, from the politicians on down, in a way they didn't use to be. Nobody even bothers to pretend to uphold the old virtues anymore except when they're running for office. Politicians use the words, but not one of them is actually honest, faithful, including in marriage. I don't even know if they're decent. Everybody basically agrees that money is the only thing that matters . . ."

"And sex."

"And sex. It's downright embarrassing, Maddy, what they put on TV and in the movies these days . . ."

She nodded, half agreeing with him. "But it isn't cynicism, is it? If the politicians really are immoral, greedy, promiscuous, unfaithful, it isn't cynical to say they are, is it? Look at the corporations: Once we thought of them as the backbone of the country. Remember when they used to say what's good for General Motors was good for the country? Of course, it wasn't true then, and certainly isn't now, but now they wouldn't even dare to say it, it's so ridiculous. Now we know corporations have no more loyalty to this country than any other company. They'd sell us out in a New York minute to make more money. IBM and ITT and Ford were helping the Germans all through World War II. It isn't cynicism. It's . . ."

"It's worse than cynicism! It's downright immorality!"

"Greed," she mumbled. "But that isn't how people are, the people we know. Our kids, our friends, our brothers and sisters—they don't care only about sex and money."

"Sure they do. I don't know how much. It would be easier to tell if any of them had more than just enough to get by," he smiled. "About sex, I don't know. Look at all the divorces. Even in our family—our nieces and nephews. How many? Six?"

"Yes. But is divorce really so bad? I mean, remember how Parrish treated Susan? Going off on drunken sprees all the time, disappearing, turning up in some gutter, the police calling from everywhere, Boston, Albany, Pittsfield. Remember? And we would have to go get him and drag him home. And Susan sitting in that house with a baby to feed and no money. She had to get a job and leave Charles with her mother or with me. Remember? Would you have wanted her to stay with him?"

He set his jaw. "Well, now, Maddy, I never said this at the time. I agree with you that Parrish treated her really bad, that Susan was justified in what she did. But the truth is, part of me would have really loved her for hanging in there with him, seeing him through, loving him enough to be there for him through all of it, like we were. I would have been her slave to the death, I would have worshipped the ground she walked on . . ."

"Now, Charley, don't exaggerate. And if that's true, how come you didn't go over there more when it was going on? Go over and ask her if she needed something from the store, or something in the house repaired, or some money. What about that?"

"I did!" Indignantly.

"Yes. A few times in all those years."

"Mmm."

"Anyway, he's our son. That's different."

"Why? Only because people act like it's different. Once upon a time they wouldn't have thought it was different. Once upon a time, marriage ties were as binding as blood ties. No one got divorced."

"Yes," Maddy mused. "And plenty of people lived real miserable lives, as I recall. Remember high school, reading Thoreau? Most folk 'live lives of quiet desperation'?"

"Umm. You think they're happier now?"

"Yes, to tell you the truth. And what about when Parrish came back and sobered up and got Nancy pregnant? Should Susan have stood by him then?"

"I'm not sayin he's right in any way," he said stubbornly. "He was wrong completely. And I'm not . . . judging Susan. I just wish things were different. The way they used to be."

"But they were that way because laws made them that way, not because people were better or had different desires."

He nodded slowly. "You're right," he said wearily. "I guess people were always the way they are now. Sad that we need laws to make us act like our better selves."

Maddy sighed and dropped her hands in her lap. She gazed out the window. Charley returned to his paper. Then he put it down.

"I treat Parrish all right, don't I?"

"You treat him fine."

"And Susan? I'm okay to her, amn't I? She didn't stand by him, but she's stood by us."

"Yes. You're nice to Susan."

"Well, then . . ."

"You're not so nice to Nancy."

"Ummm," he grumbled.

"She can feel you don't like her. She doesn't know why."

"I can't stand that voice of hers, yap yap yap, like a little dog, you know how little dogs bark in those shrill voices all the time . . . But I treat her decently just the same. Don't tell me I don't. I make an effort. I don't have to make an effort with Susan, she's a good girl. She used to bring Charles round to see us when he was little, she never cut us out of his life the way Alceste did my brother Bill and his wife. Bill and Candy haven't seen their grandkids in ten years. It's a crime!" He was working up some passion now. "Things like that didn't happen in my father's day. No woman would have dared!—" He stopped suddenly.

"Because in those days, she would have needed Bill and Candy to help her support the kids," Maddy said calmly. "She would have had to take whatever they handed out. Bill and Candy were awful to her when she and Billy were splitting. They blamed her. They didn't know Billy had another woman over in New York State. Remember how they acted? What did they expect? You can't take sides in these things. Nowadays a woman like Alceste can support her kids herself and doesn't have to kowtow to hostile relatives."

"She should! They're the grandparents!"

She did not answer, and his words hung in the room. The memory of his brother's behavior also hung there, shaming him. "Oh, I suppose you're right," he admitted shamefaced. "Maddy, you know I never opposed women working. Except when their kids needed them. Did I ever try to stop you ?"

"No. Not once the kids were grown," she said, staring off into the distance.

"Well, then . . ."

"You're a good man, Charley. You know I think that. Just a little old-fashioned. You think women should take care of the children."

"Well, I do!" He was a little red-faced. "Don't they nurse them out of their bodies? Doesn't that show that nature intended them to take care of the children?"

"It certainly shows that nature intended women to *feed* them when they're babies. Beyond that . . ." she drifted into silence.

He was silent too, waiting.

"I don't want to fight with you, Charley. We had our fights years ago."

"We did, didn't we? But they weren't too bad, were they? Was I a monster, Maddy?"

"No, my dear. You were part of your time."

"And you're happy now, aren't you?"

She gazed at him in amazement. "I'm as happy as I can be, dear."

Content with that, he returned to his newspaper. She sat shaking her head: We've been married for fifty-four years, and he still doesn't know me. It's astonishing. Of course she understood: He doesn't want to know about a problem he can't correct. He loves it when I need him to fix a light switch. He hates that he can't fix my life.

•

Was it Vietnam? thought Maddy. The angry boys, growing their hair long and refusing to shave. Funny how upset people got about that. I took Benjamin to the barber one afternoon, I'd been busy and his hair was a little longer than usual, and Carl—our barber for how many years?—the neighborhood barber, we'd known him for thirty years, he *snarled* at me and Benjamin, bared his teeth, muttering about long-haired hippies. Went out of business within the year, people won't go back to someone who frightens them. Long hair unhinged him. Drove him mad. I never understood what it meant; it was only hair. Edna got upset about it, so did Charley. Still does. Is it because he's so fastidious? A quiet Sunday, we're home alone, and he shaves and puts on a white shirt. No tie, and his cuffs are rolled up, but still . . . thank heaven I don't have to iron them anymore. Has it been a burden to him to stay neat? Is that what this is about? Makes no sense.

Not trusting the government, not believing it. Yes. That did change, then, he's right about that. We were innocents before. Emily says Europeans never trust their governments. All that history, tyrannical kings, centuries of oppression, taxation, military corvée. And look what governments do. The French government didn't test blood even after it knew about AIDS. And later lied about it. All governments lie. We found out during the Vietnam War, didn't we. Wasn't bad enough that we went into those little villages and burned those tragic souls alive, then lied about it afterward. I say *we*, but who is we? Is *we* our government? Supposedly means us, all of us, but who actually did these things, who's responsible? Certain men in government, that's who. They took the boys we gave birth to and nursed and held, we kissed their satin skin and put our fingers in their tiny hands and played peek-a-boo with them and taught them to walk and talk and be good people, they took them and retaught them, taught them to be killers, torturers breaking peoples' bodies with electric shock, half drowning them, throwing acid on them, firing napalm at them, dropping bombs on them. Killed innocent peasants for no reason whatever. Vietnam, but also Chile, Panama, Guatemala, Iran. Made our children into killers and just left them that way afterward, did nothing to heal them, just left them, killers without a cause. And the ones who could bear it did and the rest fell apart like our poor Kenny, became drug addicts and shock victims. Kenny felt too much. Men aren't supposed to feel; that's what did him in. I wonder where he is. If he is still alive.

Charley wants upright behavior in his leaders, and upright support in us, but he doesn't think about what the government did to

Kenny, he thinks Kenny was disloyal, a traitor. He hates Clinton, oh how he hates Clinton, because of that girl, Monica, he can't get over that. I bet it's really because I'd never do that for him. Hate it. Disgusts me. And Clinton did it in the Oval Office. Hah.

There was a smile on Maddy's face. Charley looked up just then, saw the smile, smiled back, and returned to his paper looking utterly content.

Marriage, she thought, noticing, amused. He thinks he knows me. Of course I think I know him too. But I do. Right now, his stomach is settling down again, his weather storms up indoors when outdoors is gusty. Tries not to show it. He's sweet, my Charley, even if we don't always agree. He's seventy-nine years old, what can you expect? He hasn't kept up the way I have, he doesn't read the New York papers, he doesn't have my friends, they keep me aware. Younger blood. Our generation will have to pass away before things can really change.

All the changes aren't bad. Much more tolerance. Of course people are still bigoted, but it's not as rampant, it's not respectable anymore. Keep your racism to yourself. Jews didn't live here years ago, wouldn't have been happy, would have been excluded. At least we've always accepted blacks up here, probably because we have so few. Charley hates divorce, but as far as I'm concerned, it's a blessing. How many women, Mother's friends, were stuck in horrible marriages, couldn't get out, miserable for life, poor Gertrude Hanwacker, Emily's first piano teacher, married to that unpleasant old man, old even then, so rich and tight, wouldn't give her money for gas for her car. Wanted to keep her home. At least she *had* a car, lots of women were locked in the house. She paid for it herself, giving piano lessons. She had to have a car to get to her students, so she could earn money of her own to do what she wanted. Left her son a nice nest egg after the father cut him off. Wretch. Left his money to the church, you'd think he'd been a good man, he probably thought he was, laid down the law at home and in the office, always right . . .

Nobody's always right. That's part of what it was about, the revolution. Deconstruction, isn't that what Alicia called it? I don't know anything about it except it teaches that nobody's absolute, no one's infallible. Wonder if the pope has heard of it. Every movement forward also contains a movement backward. Everything contains its opposite, I've always thought that. A *is* non-A, no matter what the logicians say. So maybe what Emily says is true, everybody's a bad parent and a good one at the same time, if you're one you're the other, can't avoid it. She tries to comfort me. That's where it hit men, because so many of them insisted they were always right. Can't get away with it anymore. Even if their wives allow it, their kids don't.

Yes, I can see that some men might not be happy with the changes. But they were great for us, for women. Freed us. To the degree we're free. Not free yet. Sister Teresa who taught with Emily at Browning, tiny little woman, used to stand in Emily's living room with her head high, as if she was holding a flag, and declaim, "Women will not be free until no woman in the world has to fear a man's fist, until all women can walk the streets of the world without fear." Well, that will never happen. Not in my lifetime anyway. I've lived in Steventon all my life and there's practically no crime here, but I wouldn't walk out at night alone here, much less in New York City. She was a fierce one, Teresa, in our lives so vividly for a time, then gone, out to change the world. Emily called her the "fierce nun." Taught history until Browning got rid of her. Too fierce for them. Wonder where she is now.

But it wasn't Vietnam that changed things for women, was it? It just started around the same time. Everything happening at the same time. Feminism was separate from everything else, run by women, fought by women, cheered by women, nobody else cared. But thank heavens! Thank heavens it happened in my lifetime. My poor mother, my grandmother didn't have it, but they needed it. I bless the day it was born.

Most things that changed are better now. So why am I so uncomfortable in the new world? The kids seem superficial, don't they? So materialistic. The culture is stupid. At least it seems so to me. The kids at the market can't add or subtract. I ask for a quarter of a pound of fish because Charley doesn't like fish and I do, and they didn't know what that would be on the scale. The music as well, the words to their music are vile. How could good changes have such bad results?

The other day at Jenny's, Alicia was telling us about her friend Fern, at Harvard in 1968. She said the students took over some buildings in protest and talked about burning down Widener Library. When Fern told Alicia about it, Alicia was horrified, couldn't believe anyone would want to burn down a library.

And Fern said, "I can see their point of view. We're so burdened by the past, it's so full of horror and ugliness. We call it *morality*, but *read* the literature of the past, *read* the Bible, *read* Homer, they teach male dominance, hatred, cruelty, and murder!"

But Alicia was appalled that her friend seemed tolerant of burning down libraries. She had stayed upset for years, but she saw Fern in New York a few months ago. Teaching at the University of Pennsylvania and now she's the one who's appalled! She says the kids are hideously ignorant, they know absolutely nothing, that it is as if the past simply had been eradicated. They can't add, they can't spell, they don't know how to use a period or a comma, they don't even really know how to read. "They didn't *have* to burn down the library," she told Alicia. "They just stopped reading the books!"

Fern says she hates the new world. The music is loud and foul-mouthed, the clothes look like underwear. The kids' hair hangs in their faces, messy and unwashed. The noise. The drive for money and sex. A million dollars for a house like mine. When I think how our parents struggled, thrifty and careful, and we, too, in our early years. No one here felt rich, no one thought we were living in expensive houses. Now our children can't afford to live in the houses they grew up in.

A person can live too long.

•

Tim was very careful around Jenny for the next few days, but he said nothing. She was distant to him, rarely speaking. She spent her time in her studio, although she could still detect a tinge of stink. She kept the windows wide open, despite a chilly spring. She wasn't angry, exactly. She didn't know what she was, only that she felt as distant from Tim as if he were a stranger. Indeed, she felt he *was* a stranger, because a funny thing had happened over the weekend, a new thought had popped into her head: What if I left him?

It struck like lightning across her mind, leaving a long burn scar.

It was uncalled for, unwished for. She had never before had even an inkling of such a thought. She had for so long adored glamorous, famous, handsome, charming (and rich, she recalled ruefully, wondering if that had influenced her) Tim Halliday, who taught a class in oils one day a week at the Studio School, that when he began laying siege to her, she had felt like a bowling pin hit at high speed. Her spirits had spiraled to the moon, she literally walked on air and heard the music of the spheres. He was Prince Charming, and that he had selected her, was courting her intensely, stubbornly, was obvious to everyone. Everyone envied her, girls and boys alike; they all wished something like that would happen to them. And when she and Tim married, she floated like a princess entering a kingdom as its mistress, entering a new, strange land in which it was a given that she would eat peaches and cream and drink champagne forever and ever amen. For Tim Halliday presided as king, monarch of the art world. *Everyone* invited him to their parties; everyone came to his. His name, and now hers, too, regularly appeared in society columns.

Jenny, in her early twenties, slim and blond and lovely, was a desirable consort for such a king, and she was photographed for social notes in newspapers and magazines. Caught in a whirl of parties and endowed with fame, wealth, and glamour, which were no less celebrated for being vicarious, she had for some years drifted through the days calling what she reaped a reward. She thought (hadn't her culture been telling her this all her life?) that wealth, fame, and glamour were ample recompense for the new invasions into her life; she thought they were exactly what she wanted. She thought she had what she wanted; she thought she wanted what she had. Until one morning when she woke up with a slight hangover (although they normally drank lightly, her intake seemed to be increasing) and a stomach twisted in dread at yet another scheduled luncheon, at which she would help to plan a charity ball (she had been invited on the committee because Tim would be a guest of honor at the event), followed by yet another cocktail party at the splendid apartment of another city notable, and tickets for the latest ballet sensation. But that day she felt she would give anything, anything, anything to do nothing but sit home and paint. Or read. She hadn't read a book in a year. Claiming illness, she got out of the luncheon, the cocktail party, the ballet. Tim was fine with it. He was a bit tired himself, he said. He painted all day, as he always did, and they both went to bed early that night. They made love for the first time in weeks.

The next day, Jenny got dressed and walked the ten blocks to his studio in Chelsea. She took the freight elevator up to his floor and sidled in. He was working, sweating, staring at the canvas as if he hated it.

"Jenny, luv!"

She walked up to him and put her arms around him. "Tim, how would you feel if you were never, never, never again asked to be a guest of honor at a charity banquet?"

"Never?" he roared. "I'd be delirious!"

"Really?" She drew back from him. "Really?"

"Why, sweet one, have you begun to get bored?"

"Oh, Tim. I can't stand it. There's nothing in it. What everyone's wearing and where they got their clothes and where to eat and the latest sensation, there's nothing in it for me, gossip about people I don't care about . . . Can't we stop?"

"Jenny, dearest, it all just happened. I didn't plan it. It wasn't so bad before, but when I married *you*, well, they adored you—quite rightly, of course—and they saw us as this fairy-tale couple. You know they always have to have one, a couple who makes their delusions seem true. They picked us up and made us the center of something. I thought you loved it! You certainly did well at it! Better than I do. Maybe it's flattering, but it's hard to work in such a circus. And you know if I'm about anything, I'm about my work."

"Okay. I'm happy you feel that way. I do too. I'm going to the Cape, to my father's summer house for a week or two. I don't know how else to get away from all of it. If I'm gone, it will all go on without me, and they'll get used to that, and we'll be out. Is that okay with you?"

"Good idea, yes. But do you have to leave *me*? Can't you just *pretend* to be out of town? Not answer the phone?"

"No. I'm not good at lying. Don't really know how. Or not answer the phone. And people might drop in."

"All right, luv. I'll come up and see you over the weekend, how's that?"

"Terrific." She buried her head in his chest. "Tim," she muttered into his sweatshirt, "I love you."

"Ummm. Me too, babe."

•

It was while walking with her along an empty road in Welfleet that weekend that Tim had come up with the idea of leaving New York, and building his dream house. He'd done sketches for it years ago, when he could not afford to build it. Now he realized that he could, he'd been selling like hotcakes, every major modern museum wanted his work, every major collector. "I might as well do it while I'm hot," he explained.

A cold chill stopped her. "Oh, Tim, do you think you're hot because we're so popular? Because we're social? That one has to do with the other?"

"Maybe," he answered breezily, "maybe. It's a strange world, luv." Then he announced smugly, "But at this moment I'm so hot that leaving town can only make me more desirable."

"I hope you're right." Jenny was seized by guilt and fear. "Suppose you're not?"

"I am," he said, grinning from ear to ear.

Tim had gone to camp in the Berkshires as a boy and remembered loving the area. After searching, they found land in Steventon. Tim hired an architect he admired, Paul Oku, with whom he designed the house and built it. Then Jenny and Tim moved there, giving up his Chelsea loft—although he did take a small one in Tribeca, on North Moore. His willingness to end their celebrity life, to—as she felt it—accede to her demand, endeared him to her even more. Her love for him felt bottomless. She was bound to him for life. It had never occurred to her to leave him. So where did the idea come from in a bolt?

What kind of person was she even to think for an instant of leaving Tim? Dread and horror filled her: What kind of person was she to betray the man she loved, who had after all done nothing terrible, merely been drunk and inconsiderate with his friends for a weekend? She needed to talk to someone about herself, about her wretched character. But she shrank from revealing it. Revealing it, she felt, would be a betrayal; she shrank from criticizing Tim in even the mildest way. She was shaken, her sense of herself was wavery as an ancient mirror, her face a blur in a flickering landscape.

She did nothing, and when Tim, tired of the strain between them, put his arm around her shoulders as she was preparing a salad for dinner one evening, she did not shrug it off.

"Listen, love, I, *we*, were horribly inconsiderate last weekend. I never realized before how we acted together. But seeing your face as we went through our antics . . . You know, if there were women around when we had our drunken get-togethers, they were . . . well, girls we didn't respect very much. We didn't worry about their feelings. I never realized before what a mess we made. Sorry you had to clean it up." His face was etched in apology.

She glanced sideways at him briefly, then walked away from his arm. "It wasn't just the mess, the stink, and the fact that it was left to me to clean up," she said, not having recognized until that second that what she was about to say was true, "it was the way you treated me."

"Jenny, love! How! Was I gross?"

She turned and gazed at him. "Do you not mind that your friends put their greasy hands all over me? Kissed me with their Roquefort mouths? I felt like a whore you were pimping."

"Jenny! That's disgusting! How can you say a thing like that!"

"That's how you acted. And so did they. As if I were a whore you'd hired for the weekend, for communal use."

At this, her emotion rose to her throat like bile and she left the room, went to her studio, and locked the door. She sagged onto the chaise, her heart beating loudly, frightening her. These words had come out of her mouth without her even having thought them. They were lying there in her mind, in ambush, waiting to surprise her. She wouldn't have uttered them if she had known they were coming. Oh, what would she do now, now that they were out? How could she face him, how could she live with him again? It was unforgivable.

Tim did not knock on the door, did not call her name. The house was silent. Jenny fell asleep on her chaise, hungry.

13

Emily was resting after a long day of teaching, sitting in her study, a cup of tea in her hands, and gazing out at the periwinkle sky of a May evening. Now she was home, too tired to work, but the work consumed her thoughts. She was working on a difficult section, intended to express anguish but not despair. She was finding it hard to moderate the emotion. She'd used diminished sevenths and some dissonant triads plus major sevenths, stretched into augmented chords like violin strings about to break. Anguish was different from despair, she thought; anguish can contain an iota of hope, and that hope was what made it so painful. What she wanted was the kind of feeling Thelonious Monk could get, when he aimed over and over for the one note that would bring a sense of harmony and repose, and over and over hitting the wrong note, hitting it hard, with desperate strain, then finally, out of the murk, striking the right key, letting it soar for a moment, brief respite from agony, and sing, at rest. She kept thinking of the great chord Wagner came up with as the first note of act 3 of *Tristan and Isolde*

but there was no hope left in that chord. It expressed how she felt when Clea left. How long had she had her? Just a few years, really, 1980 to 1982. Then back and forth a few more years, at boarding school and college, home for vacations. Then gone as if she'd never been. Only a little longer than she'd had Martin. Seemed fated.

•

Two weeks after her arrival, Clea was calmer and easier to talk to. But Emily, still unsure, consulted her expert on children, Maddy: "Your kids didn't demand things like that, did they, Maddy? I mean, I could understand that she might want a radio in her room, but a television and a stereo system and a telephone? When there is a perfectly good television set and telephone downstairs that are hardly ever used? I can sort of understand the stereo system—mine is in my study, and I really don't encourage her going in there—although I've never forbidden it . . ."

"No, my kids had radios, but that's all. When we were growing up, not one of us had her own radio—there was only the one in the living room. The whole family sat around listening to it on Sunday nights. Oh, I think Lily wanted her own stereo when she was in high school. The boys couldn't have cared less. But that was a generation ago, Emily. The grandchildren are another story. It's a different world now. They don't have just radios and TVs and stereo systems and their own phones, they have VCRs and cell phones and expect their own cars by the time they're sixteen. That's the way it is now. Not just the children of well-to-do people either—Debby Dew was telling me her daughter's stereo system just cost her a hundred dollars to repair, and she has to waitress two nights to earn a hundred dollars!"

"God," Emily mused. "That reminds me of when I lived in Boston in the sixties. I sometimes ate lunch at the counter in the Brigham's in Harvard Square. And one day, I had a waitress—she seemed ancient to me, withered, tired, missing teeth, dyed black hair to hide the gray—but she was probably only in her fifties. She was chatting with another waitress, and told her, with great pride, that her son, on his spring break, was driving down to Florida with his friends. Here she was, slaving away behind a lunch counter to give her oaf of a son money to throw beer on girls in a Fort Lauderdale T-shirt contest . . . and she didn't mind. She was happy to do it! I was outraged for her. Besides, I thought she was giving him bad values."

"Poor soul," Maddy said, but she laughed. "But she wanted him to have those bad values. She wanted him spoiled. It was the hallmark of her success. No?"

"Absolutely."

So Clea got everything she wanted, and after that spent hours at night lying on her bed, talking to her California girlfriends on the telephone. The telephone bill was paid from her allowance, which was a good thing, as the amount shocked Emily speechless. After that, raising Clea became a group problem, shared with Maddy and Alicia during long conversations in 1980 and 1981.

"All this money . . . all this . . . *stuff* . . . it's so different from when I was young. No one had anything much. Houses were rather bare. Most houses. Does all this have some greater meaning that I'm not seeing?" Emily asked Alicia.

"I don't know. It's a little terrifying, isn't it? I know what you mean. We had nothing when I was young, either."

"I had three blouses and two skirts. I had two dresses, a winter dress and a summer dress. I had the brown oxford school shoes my mother bought me every fall, and the Mary Janes she bought me every Easter. My mother had five dresses in her closet, and all of them were old . . ."

"Yes. Same with me, even though I'm younger—probably because my parents were immigrants. I had a few more things than you, but the same two pairs of shoes. But I had a pair of slacks. Bet you didn't have those." Alicia laughed.

"Good heavens, no!" Emily laughed too. "When I came home in pants for my father's funeral in 1967, my mother was appalled. She couldn't believe I would go out of doors in pants. She never in her life had worn pants. She had a closetful of rayon print dresses, some thirty years old, but not a single pair of jeans or pants . . . and no low-heeled shoes. She wore high heels to clean the house! The only liberty she allowed herself at home was not wearing a girdle. She'd run around mopping and dusting and scrubbing in high heels with her stockings on but rolled down and tied in a knot above the ankle. She looked ridiculous."

"My mother told me if I was going to wear pants outdoors, I should be sure to wear a girdle."

"Mine too! I guess they felt the female body was shameful."

Maddy frowned. "They sure did. I remember."

Emily mused, "Now young women go out in what looks like underwear."

"Things have changed so much just in our lifetimes. In seventy years the world has changed completely. You know, I have this friend, Kay Winter, who teaches Women in Literature at a Catholic college in Westchester. In one class last year, she was discussing Kate Chopin's *The Awakening* and Edith Wharton's *Summer*, and the girls had trouble understanding what the heroines' problems were. Why should one of these heroines drown herself for sex and the other marry a fat old man she didn't love? They couldn't understand it.

"Kay said she asked them, 'Don't you worry after you've had unprotected sex?' And they looked at each other and shrugged. They seemed bewildered. 'You mean AIDS?' one of them piped up. They had no conception of what she was talking about! 'What about pregnancy?' She asked. And Kay swore they looked at her as if she was crazy. Fear of pregnancy had never entered their minds!

"Catholic girls," Alicia emphasized. "The same girls, ten or fifteen years earlier, Kay says, could hardly mention contraception or abortion, the subjects were so taboo. Twenty years ago, they wouldn't admit to having had sex, it was so shameful. Not a hundred years ago, twenty! I was in my late twenties and now I'm headed toward fifty. Things have changed that fast."

"Would they have abortions, do you think?"

"They'd rather not, but they know they can. I gather they use birth control, also taboo for Catholics. Far cry from our youth, huh Emily? Think about it, Emily! Sex without worry. Remember how we worried every damn month if we were even a day late? Even after I was married, I worried. I didn't want a big family.

"Kay says it has major implications for literature," Alicia mused. "If they don't know how important virginity before marriage used to be, how will they ever comprehend eighteenth- and nineteenth-century British novels? Because what's at the center of half the plots is the female hymen! In one fell swoop, the classic canon made obsolete!"

"The way Homer was for us," Emily said. "It was hard, wasn't it, to care anything about the Achaeans or the Trojans, or who killed whom?"

"Yes. The only familiar thing was Achilles sulking in his tent because Agamemnon took the woman he wanted," Maddy laughed.

"For how many centuries have girls been constrained, scared out of their minds by the fear of losing their virginity? And in one generation, blotto!"

"It's no wonder so many people freak out . . ."

"Like who? What do you mean?"

"Oh, you know, the rigid religious people—born-again Christians and fanatic Muslims and Jews and Hindus. People who think the new world is corrupt and sinful, who think sex is sinful, who find the independence of women anathema . . ."

"Mmm. Yeah. More than half the world, when you come to think of it."

"Do you think things will ever change back?"

Emily looked at her with a raised eyebrow. "Are you kidding?"

They both laughed. "Well, most of the changes are for the better," Alicia sighed.

"People can breathe better now," Emily agreed, "but along the way, there's been some terrible wrenching. And for some people, it still goes on. Think about born-again Christians storing up weapons ready to defend themselves against our own government, fanatic Muslims willing to kill to set up theocratic states, men who think nothing of oppressing women as if they were bugs, think about their rage. All because of the innocuous fact that women can now control their pregnancies even if they're raped, even when they're forced. They have a tiny bit of freedom they've never had in history."

The women were silent contemplating that, contemplating their own anxious pasts. Just a little dread floated in the air.

•

Clea was full of rage too, Emily recalled, remembering how the girl had lashed out at her in public. The first time that day in Gilley's, where Emily had taken her to buy underwear, she had exploded. Why? Suddenly, she was standing there screaming at Emily that she would not wear hick clothes, was Emily so clueless that she could not see the difference between what Clea wore and these rags? Raised in the decorum of a past age, Emily was mortified; the saleswomen stood stock still, staring, shocked at the girl's behavior, peering at Emily to see how she was taking it. Emily knew she must have turned white, red, then white again.

She tried for dignity, turning to Clea and saying, in a calm voice, "If you don't like these clothes, we'll go elsewhere. There's no need to shout."

And saw, as Clea blushed and glanced away, that the girl had tears in her eyes, that the eruption had burst out of her like pus, from her sickness of heart.

So Emily immediately forgave her, and led her out of the store and home again, heartsick herself. She called Alicia, who in those days came up to Steventon only weekends and summers. She lived in New York, had a daughter, and might know what to do.

Alicia invited Emily and Clea to New York, embraced Clea like a daughter, made her kids double up in Stevie's bunk beds, and gave her guests Mariette's room. She took them to stores she liked—Saks, Bendel's, Bergdorf's, Charivari. Clea adored Mariette, who was only nine, she loved New York—a far cry from Steventon. She loved the clothes, too: "Cool things, like, really rad!" Alicia took them to see *Annie* on Broadway, which Clea loved, as Alicia had known she would. And Clea had come back calmer, perhaps because she now knew that Emily would try to please her, or at least was open to her desires.

Clea started school a week later, instantly becoming one of the most popular girls in her class, her Hollywood-tinged background giving her a neon halo in the eyes of her classmates. She made good grades, too. Well, Emily thought, she should: Both her parents had been very bright, it was in her genes. She even accepted Emily's gift of a mountain bike, terrified as she was of it—children in Brentwood, California, weren't allowed to ride bikes; they were considered too dangerous. Clea had looked at Emily questioningly when Emily first suggested a bike.

"Well, don't, if you don't want to," Emily had said. "But you know, once I start work in September, I won't be here to drive you to your friends' houses or pick you up. You'll have to get around on your own, and you know what that's like here. You'll have to walk."

A bus ran between Pittsfield and New York twice a day; another circled Winchester every hour or so, but it went nowhere near Steventon. There were buses to take old folks to the senior center in Winchester, and one for the youngsters at the camp for the developmentally disabled. There was a school bus mornings and afternoons. Otherwise, the only means of transportation was the automobile, the bicycle, or feet.

Clea thought about it and accepted the bike, and she was soon zipping around Steventon with joy, developing hard muscles in her calves from the hills, strengthening her lungs. Emily realized then that it wasn't just in Brentwood that bikes were unusual; few teenagers in Steventon rode them: They had cars or hitched rides with older siblings. Clea felt free, independent, and proud of herself.

She hung with a crowd, the style then in the eighties, boys and girls together, *hanging out*, as they called it. They would troop to the movies or help in ecology drives on weekends—cleaning the riverbank of debris, or cleaning the river itself from rowboats. They went canoeing in groups. But mostly they just lolled at someone's house, listening to music and talking, girls and boys together. Emily was pleased that they frequently gathered at her house, which they did partly because Clea had an extraordinary allowance and could afford cases of soft drinks and snacks. Emily could see those drinks and snacks on the children, most of whom were very big bodied for their age. But Clea stayed slender.

Emily recognized the names of many of Clea's friends—Arkwright, Kellogg, Carlyle—and deduced that she was in the "in crowd." If Clea had any notion of this, she never referred to it.

The Kellogg girl, Nancy, introduced Clea to her aunt, Lynn Kellogg, who had married Harley Winship, and with him ran a horse farm and riding school. They raised thoroughbreds and offered lessons, and Harley, who had once been a champion steeplechaser, was known for training jumpers and their riders. Clea had done some riding at a camp in California and loved it, and was soon taking lessons from Lynn. She spent several afternoons a week at the stable, learning everything she could about horses.

Within months, Emily had come to believe that she was blessed with the ideal adolescent: Auntie's happy kid. She was smart, beautiful, healthy, and given to healthy pursuits. She was popular. What more could anyone ask? Emily glowed: She had family, sweet young glowing company, someone who reminded her of her darling brother Martin, but bore no shadow of cruel Amanda, hurtful Mamie, dull John, uninterested Robert, vapid Crighton. Emily felt she had become a mother the easy way—no childbirth, no baby spit-up or diapers, just a beautiful child deposited on her doorstep at a time in her life when she could appreciate her.

Two years later, when Clea was fifteen, her friends started to break into couples, going out on dates. The telephone rang constantly: Clea was in demand. But dating seemed to hold less attraction for her than riding. She spent most afternoons and weekends at the Kellogg farm, and had progressed after two years to entering competitions. She won several ribbons, coming in second at her last show, in upstate New York. Once in a while, she would go out with a group of friends on a Friday night, to a bar. She did not drink, but that's where they went, she explained. There was nowhere else to go. Emily remembered. When Emily asked why she didn't go out with her friends more often, Clea said ruefully that they weren't much fun anymore, they'd broken into couples and were "all moony" all the time. She didn't care for any of the boys: They were all silly or pimpled or fat, she said. And she didn't enjoy drinking and somebody always got drunk. It was boring.

One December evening, Clea wasn't home by five thirty. She often stayed at the tack room after riding, grooming the horses, chatting with Lynn and Harley, cleaning the stable. But they had an unwritten agreement that Clea would get home before dark. If she had to stay late or dawdled too long, Lynn or Harley would drive her home, or she'd call Emily to drive over and pick her up, putting her bike in the trunk of the car. Emily was terrified of Clea's riding on the dangerously curved mountain roads with only a bike light.

Emily hadn't cooked that night; she'd bought a spit-roasted chicken and different kinds of salad from Lil at the local grocery. Clea had long ago urged her to stop cooking. Emily had never enjoyed it, and she wasn't especially good at it, although for years she had dutifully done what her mother had, cooking dinner every night. Her mother hadn't been an especially good cook either, not like Maddy. Aunt and niece both enjoyed fast food, but Emily disapproved of it. Suddenly Emily realized it was possible to buy prepared foods that were not full of fat and sugar. "Boughten food," as she called it, was not much better than her own cooking, but it was easier. It was a huge relief after all these years to stop cooking. She had almost erased the memory of Sunday mornings, her mother standing in the kitchen steam, a fragrant roast in the oven. She would peel vegetables, strain applesauce, mash potatoes, have pie crusts cooling on the windowsill, while the children went to church with Grandma, and the huge meal was waiting when they returned, often with the minister in tow. Momma, pink-faced, would smile at the minister but speak sharply to the children. She would be as steamed as the kitchen. She hated cooking Sunday dinner all day long, and everybody knew it.

No, it wasn't that the dinner Emily had labored over was getting cold. But she was worried. Clea knew how Emily felt about her staying out past dark. There were no streetlights in Steventon and riding a bike up and down the hills and around curves full of blind spots was even dangerous after the leaves had fallen, despite her bike light. Clea had been taking driving lessons, and Emily decided that night to get her a car as soon as Clea was sixteen. She would be less worried if Clea was in a car. A car was armor. Thinking of her precious girl, her fragile arms and legs, delicate skin and vulnerable bones, being scratched, bruised, broken, tightened her stomach. She began to sweat, thinking about speeding pickups full of redneck boys lumbering down country roads . . .

She put down her pencil. She couldn't work. She rose and went to her study window, searching for a tiny bike light in the unbroken darkness. She set the dining-room table. She poured herself a glass of water. It was ten of six. Where could the child be?

She walked to the center hall and picked up the telephone. She knew the number by heart now, Clea had gone to the stable so often for so long. Lynn answered.

After an exchange of greetings, Emily asked anxiously: "Is Clea still there, by any chance?"

"No," said Lynn in some surprise. "She left over an hour ago—at least I thought she did. She was out to the stable with Harley, somethin' wrong with the mare, but she was leavin' right after, she said. Harley's not back either, come to think of it. Maybe the mare is sick. Wait a minute." She put the phone down, and Emily heard a door open and close. Then Lynn picked up the phone. "Emily? Maybe I should take a walk over to the stable myself. Can't think where they've got to. I'll call you back."

Now Emily's stomach sank deeper into the pit of dread. She sat on a step, slumped over, waiting. It seemed hours, but her watch insisted that only fifteen minutes had passed, when the phone rang.

"Lynn?"

"They're not out there, Emily. But her bike's gone, so she should be home soon. And the car is gone too; Harley probly drove her home because it was dark. Put her bike in the car. I know he don't like her riding home on that bike in the dark. Or maybe he went to see Walter—the vet—the mare don't look so good. Stuff drippin' from her eyes."

Emily heard the rattle of bike wheels, the slap of a chain. She breathed a prayer to an unnamed deity, announced that Clea was home and tried to hang up. But Lynn held her:

"Listen, ask her where Harley went, will ya? If she knows. Call me back if you find out, okay? "

"Sure. Bye Lynn."

Emily ran to the kitchen. The door was opening and Clea was in the doorway. Emily's heart rushed in relief and her arms lifted to embrace the girl.

"WHERE HAVE YOU BEEN, CLEA OLDFIELD?" she exploded.

Clea raised an eyebrow at her aunt. "Sorry?"

"It's dark! Look how dark it is! It's been dark for hours and hours! I've been so worried!"

"You know my name is Rossi-Oldfield, Emily," the girl corrected her crossly. "Don't claim more of me than you deserve." She put her books down on the kitchen table. "I'm sorry I'm late, but it hasn't been dark for hours and hours. I don't know why you have to exaggerate. The Kelloggs' mare is sick and Harley and I got to talking about it, and time just flew. Then it was dark, and he said he'd drive me home and then he couldn't get the car started. So it took a while . . . What's for dinner?" she asked more cheerfully.

"And where is Harley now?" her aunt demanded.

Clea shrugged. "Home, I guess. He just dropped me off."

"Okay." Emily sighed. Her anger had evaporated. "It's just that I was anxious. Wash your hands, dolly, dinner's on the table."

"Okay, Aunt Em," the girl said agreeably. "I just have to run upstairs for a minute."

Emily had put the platters of food on the table before she remembered to call Lynn Kellogg.

Lynn answered at the first ring.

"Clea just got home, Lynn. She said Harley dropped her off like you thought."

"Yes, he's home now. Don't we get all discombobulated over nothing, though? All this uproar over a bike having a flat. Harley tried to fix it, but it got dark and he drove her home. It's just the winter. I hate the winter. I hate the dark."

"Yes," Emily murmured.

Emily waited until dinner was over, and they were clearing away the dessert plates. Then, casually, she asked, "Did your bike have a flat?"

"No. Why?"

"I spoke to Lynn a little while ago. She was worried about you, and asked me to call if you got home safely. She said Harley told her you had a flat and by the time he fixed it, it was dark."

Clea looked uncomfortable, stopped, mused. "Oh, that was the other day. Monday or Tuesday. She misunderstood. He fixed it the other day."

"You didn't mention it," Emily said. "That you'd had a flat."

"I forgot," Clea said shortly.

Clea spoke into a long silence. "He drove me home tonight because it was dark," she said, too loudly.

Emily put the dishes down on the sink. "Clea, it got dark a little after four. You got home at six-thirty. What were you doing all that time?"

Clea slammed her milk glass onto the kitchen table. "What is this, an interrogation? Are you checking up on me? Or are you just venting? I understand you were worried. But I was working in the barn and, like, talking to Harley, and it got late, okay? We were, like, worried about Ruby. She doesn't look right. Give me a break!" she cried, storming out of the room.

Emily's heart stopped. Holding on to the table, she let herself down into a chair. Clea had not raised her voice to her aunt since that day at Gilley's two years ago, a lifetime ago. Why was she so angry at being questioned?

Clea's unexpected behavior cast a tinge of suspicion on the

events of the past year, as Emily rewound them in her mind, refocusing. She recalled Clea's huge excitement at becoming friendly with Nancy Kellogg and discovering that Nancy's aunt had a horse farm and taught jumping. She recalled how swiftly she became infatuated with the Winships, or Kelloggs, as they were known, especially Lynn. She was full of Lynn, Lynn, Lynn, as the older woman introduced her to jumping, taught her about grooming, offered her milk and cookies, and gave her apples and sugar for the horses. But over the year, that changed. As Clea's skills improved, Harley took over her training, and now she spoke only of him; Harley says I can be really good, Harley thinks I can do show jumping, Harley thinks I can compete, Harley thinks, Harley says . . .

No. Impossible.

Not impossible that she had a crush on him, no. But that he would act on it—married to Lynn Kellogg these many years, and Clea only a child of fifteen: impossible.

But why else did she have such disdain for boys her own age? Emily had thought that strange. Clea was not so mature herself that she would find boys her own age too young. Yet she argued that they were immature and silly; she would go out with them only in a group.

And here I was so grateful that she didn't go to bars with the other kids—though sometimes she did, if Nancy, Cookie, or Ginger, whoever had a car, picked her up and drove her home. Clea said she went just to be with her girlfriends, and drank only Coke. The only other place for them to hang out around here was the 7-Eleven over in New York State, and that was a rough place at night. Even in Emily's youth, there had been a crowd of boys, and a girl or two, who hung out in roadhouses and got drunk and had automobile accidents. In her sophomore year in high school, Owen Heaney had been killed after such an evening. He was sixteen, like Emily. A thousand years ago.

It was understandable that Clea did not enjoy going to bars, even with her friends. Emily hadn't liked it at her age. It all made sense.

She walked to the front hall and called upstairs. "Clea, do you want to watch TV down here tonight?" Sometimes, when there was a program both of them liked, they watched together. Tonight there was *Hill Street Blues*.

The girl's enthusiastic response told her that the whole thing was already forgotten.

14

Alicia spiraled through the next few days, sailing on the high of her phone call with Marshall Merchant's editor, avoiding the troughs of her reluctance to confront Steven. Planning to stay overnight in the city on Wednesday, she asked Steven to get concert tickets for them for that night—the Juilliard Quartet, one of his favorite groups, was performing, and she had not been to a concert since last summer. Meantime, he would be up this weekend, and she determined they would have a serious talk on Friday night. Friday nights he was tired, but Saturdays he played tennis, and Sunday he left—no time seemed right for a disturbing conversation.

Yet the mere thought of it depressed her. Dejected, she slumped in her chair, questioning if she had really changed after all. Fifteen or so years ago when she had examined her character, she had found it wanting. She thought she had since become more honest, braver. But now she wondered if she wasn't as weak and passive as ever.

She had looked into herself when she was furnishing the Steventon house. A great deal of money was involved—they had to buy new furniture, rugs, household equipment. She discussed every major expense with Steven; anything he vetoed was out. She resented this even though she was the one who gave him the veto power. She had to remind herself that if she did not like something, it was also out, so they were equal. Weren't they? But she couldn't equate the two, because Steven never saw the things she didn't like. So he only vetoed things she did like. And when he vetoed something, she never argued, never pleaded the case for or insisted on that darling overpriced slipper chair. She just let it go.

Somehow, equality between them never computed. She remembered understating the prices of a few pieces she liked, fearing he would consider them too dear. And the cost of things she knew he'd like, the leather office chair in his study for example, she overstated. Sometimes she went so far as to have the salesperson write up a fake bill. And all the while she was doing this, she hated herself. She didn't understand how she had become this kind of person. She remembered harboring the highest of ideals for herself as a girl, certain she would always be honest, true to herself, true to others. How had she become a coward? For that's what she was, she knew it, she felt like one.

She recalled reading about a woman whom Muhammad was initiating into Islam. (What was her name? Hind, Alicia thought.) He gave her the rules: "You shall have but one God."

"We grant you that," she replied.

"You shall not steal."

"Abu Sufyan is a stingy man. I only stole provisions from him."

"That is not theft," Muhammad said.

That was not theft. That was marriage to a stingy man. She realized the books she had spent her life reading never demanded courage from women. It was accepted that women would be cowardly, it was even preferred. For if women were not cowardly, how could men save them? And men had to save them. But in those books, men always acceded instantly to the heroine's every desire because they were gentlemen. Whereas in life, men rarely wanted what women wanted. So was the whole thing just lies? The entire moral life of the species as depicted in literature, was it merely invention? Were women cowards, or did men just portray them that way?

What was required of women was to be good servants: That was the crux. What made a woman good was not honesty or courage, but the ability to dissimulate, to enable men to feel strong and in charge on every occasion, act out orgasm, dependency, humility. Wasn't that what Neva did? Neva was a perfect role model. Alicia didn't remember her real father, who had died young from his suffering as a slave for Daimler-Benz during the war. He had had only a few years of freedom before cancer struck him down. Neva, grief-stricken when he died, was a practical woman, and immediately found a job for five dollars a week, leaving Alicia with Mrs. Mulrooney during the day. She got the job through a cousin of Moishe who was a salesman for Arnold Ross. Mr. Ross owned a large prosperous shop in Brooklyn that sold and rented medical equipment. Neva started out as a bookkeeper—she had learned the skill in the excellent New York City high school she attended until she was sixteen—but within a year, she was managing Mr. Ross's shop. A year after that, he asked her out for dinner.

Alicia was five years old the day Momma came home from work a half hour early, all excited. She got all dolled up in a dress Alicia didn't remember, Neva not having worn it since Mordechai's funeral—black and draped across the breast. Alicia thought it very beautiful. Mr. Ross was taking Momma out to dinner, Neva explained; she seemed to be having trouble catching her breath. Alicia eyed her. At six on the dot, there was a knock at the door. Neva took Alicia's hand and led her to the door and introduced her to a large, gruff man. He looked down and said, "Hello, little girl," in a deep, rough voice. Alicia turned her head away, refusing to look at him. Neva took Alicia's hand and led her to Mrs. Mulrooney's apartment.

Mrs. Mulrooney swept the door open instantly, as if she had been waiting for Neva's knock. She craned her neck to see past Neva to the man standing behind her, crying loudly, "Neva, how beau-tee-ful you look!" as if *beautiful* were three words. She laid her hand on Alicia's shoulder and drew her gently in, saying "Come in, sweetheart, come in, dearie," and to Neva, "Have a swell time!"

The man came again the next week and the week after that. Alicia half liked and half didn't like being at the Mulrooney's for dinner. Days, she went there after kindergarten, had lunch and her nap and played with the littlest Mulrooneys, Tommy, Eileen, and Christopher. They played with the games Momma bought her, fitting letters together, writing on her chalkboard. When Eileen or Tommy was cranky, Alicia colored in her coloring book. But sometimes Tommy threw the game pieces around, or Eileen wanted to color with her but strayed outside the lines, ruining the picture. In the afternoon they had milk and cookies. Then Momma came home, and Alicia happily returned to her own quiet, orderly home. At night at the Mulrooney's, Mr. Mulrooney and all seven children were home, and it was so noisy Alicia could barely hear her favorite TV programs. Still, she liked Billy Mulrooney, who was nine; he was cute and he sneaked glances at her and giggled. And Mrs. Mulrooney served exotic foods that Neva never had—canned spaghetti or ravioli, franks and beans, or Spam with canned potatoes and canned string beans, all of which Alicia loved. And when Alicia ate over, Mrs. Mulrooney bought them ice cream pops for dessert, sending Billy down to the corner stationery store after dinner to get one for each child, eight all together. That cost a lot of money, Alicia knew. Neva never had money to spare for a pop. And Alicia understood that the treat was especially for her. That made her like Mrs. Mulrooney. She understood what Neva meant when she said Mrs. Mulrooney had a good heart.

Then one day, Neva told Alicia that she and Mr. Ross were going to get married, that he would become her papa, Momma's husband. And Alicia said he would never be her papa, and she would never call him that. Neva, agitated, said, "Darling it's for you, you're so smart, you have to go to college, I want you to have pretty clothes, things I never had, I can never earn enough for those things, please be good, it's all for you, Lischen."

"No," Alicia said, and ran into the bedroom. (The bedroom was hers; Momma slept on the living-room couch.) She lay on the bed and sobbed, or tried to. She could not dredge up sobs loud enough to make Neva come in. It was bad enough that Neva went out without her, leaving her with somebody else, but now she wanted to move a stranger into their lives. Alicia would not have it. She wanted her mother all to herself. She was not going to let this change occur.

But it did. Somehow, no matter how she sulked or cried—methods of control she had occasionally used before and that had always worked—Neva ignored her feelings. Neva bought herself a new blue dress with a hat, and a new dress, coat, hat, and Mary Janes for Alicia, and one day the man came and they all went out to a big building in a busy part of the city, a big building with long corridors and lots of doors, and Mrs. Mulrooney came (but not her children) and she was wearing a hat with big flowers on it and there were some people Alicia didn't know, and a man said something to her mother and Mr. Ross put a ring on Neva's finger (and he kissed her!), and they went out to a restaurant. Alicia refused to eat, but Momma hardly seemed to notice.

And then, Momma went away. She left Alicia with Mrs. Mulrooney for a whole week, during which Alicia could not eat even the Spam or canned macaroni and cheese she loved. She lay curled on the couch in Mrs. Mulrooney's ragged apartment. Her heart was broken.

Momma came back, but Alicia never got over her betrayal, the momentous fact that Momma had abandoned her for a big gruff man she hated. That betrayal became the central fact of her life. The most bitter part of it was that Alicia knew that Neva didn't love Mr. Ross. Her betrayal was for money! Even if she called it security, it was money. Worst of all, it was money for Alicia. Even when Alicia was too young to have words to say this, she thought this. She had no scale on which to measure her mother's sin—or sacrifice.

Still, who would not call Neva a good woman? She was a paragon. She waited on Mr. Ross like an obedient servant, she gave him two sons—what more could a man ask? She was faithful and loyal, and a good cook to boot. She was careful with his money, asking only that her daughter be educated. She gave him his money's worth. So did it mean anything that she did not love him, that she had never loved him, that she could never do more than lie meekly in his bed?

Was Alicia like her mother? She loved Steven, didn't she? She thought she did. At first, she had been awed by him—he was so smart, so knowing! And good-looking too, and a doctor! What more could a girl ask? How could she know that all that intellect masked fear and an unquenchable drive to be the solution to all problems. He wanted to be the answer to all need for her, his mother, his patients, and his children. He wanted to be the cork that filled the hole in the dam, the wall that stood between them and chaos. She loved him for the wish, even as she deplored it as deluded and foolish. Because of it, she forgave his occasional arrogance, the steady sense he emitted of being separate from other people, above them—even his family. Alicia wasn't Neva, nor was her marriage like Neva's. But like Neva, she lied. Neva lied every time she got in bed with Arnold Ross. Like a prostitute, Alicia thought, bitterly. She lied by not telling Arnold about his sons' misbehavior, but that was the right thing to do. The boys were sweet, and Arnold was inclined to punish. Nor did she tell him about Alicia's increasingly sassy mouth (although he heard it for himself) or how much Alicia's new skirt had cost. She saved up for it from her housekeeping money, and lied, lied, lied. She lied to keep Arnold tractable.

Alicia lied to keep Steven tractable.

Is that theft?

How had Neva, such a good woman, become a symbol of something contemptible for her daughter? If she were alive, Alicia's image of her would crush her, would break her heart. It would make Neva cry to learn that her daughter wanted above all to avoid being like her. Alicia urgently wanted to stop lying, concealing. She believed that lying was a sign she feared Steven, felt unequal to him, acknowledged a power differential between them. But in fact he had no power over her except what she gave him. She didn't have to give him power, she reminded herself, trying to shut up the voice that repeated that he supported her, he paid her way. She realized that despite her efforts, she had not fully conquered her frailty. Today she geared her up courage. She would confront Steven, on Friday night, whether he liked it or not.

•

"Bad traffic tonight?" Alicia asked as Steven removed his coat.

"Not too bad. It's lighter if I leave late. On Fridays, you have to leave the city before noon or wait till after dinner. From about one in the afternoon until seven or eight at night, it's wall-to-wall cars. I saw my last patient at six, left at seven twenty, had dinner on the road. So it wasn't too bad."

It was eleven-thirty when he arrived. He drove faster than Alicia. It always took her three and a half hours. "So you had dinner. Where did you eat?"

"That Italian place in Lavinia. Il Giardino. It's not too bad."

"What did you have? Do you want anything now?"

"No. Just some water, please." He threw himself on a chair in the living room. She fetched the water, putting in a handful of ice cubes, knowing he liked it that way but wondering why he couldn't fetch his own water. Irritated, she did not sit in the living room with him, but went back to sorting papers at the kitchen table. For ten minutes or so, he turned pages in his newspaper. Then he came to her.

"How was your week?" he asked, sitting down opposite her at the kitchen table.

"Well, it was wonderful! I told you about the letter!"

"Yes, that was nice. It'll give you something to do."

She looked up. "Something to do?"

He was startled. "I beg your pardon?"

"Writing a book is not just something to do, Steven, like make-work, like knitting or needlepointing or crocheting or any of the things women who are bored out of their skulls with the stupid business of housekeeping do to pass the time," she said, her voice tilting higher and higher. "It's something I need to do, like it's my destiny!"

"Destiny? Don't you think that's a bit of an exaggeration?" he asked mildly.

She hesitated. "Oh. I suppose. But I mean . . ." She looked back down at her files. Her eyes filled and, wiping her arm across them, she turned away from him.

He was looking at her. He reached across the table and laid his hand on hers, lightly. "I didn't mean to make light of your . . . work."

"Yes, you did," she said in a thick voice.

He removed his hand. He pondered. "Did I?"

"Yes!" she cried. "You always do. You don't understand!"

"What don't I understand?"

"My need . . . to do something. To be something. To have something matter. No. To matter myself."

It was on his lips to say, "Do you think you don't matter?" but he heard how it sounded and he stopped. "You matter to me," he said.

"That's not enough," she said, swinging her head from side to side.

He blinked, and she saw the arrow hit. "Would it be enough for you to matter to me? If you did nothing else?" she asked, eager to heal the wound.

"No, I guess not," he said after a long pause.

She blew her nose and cleared her throat. "This wasn't what I wanted to talk about. This wasn't the discussion we were supposed to be having. And it started so well!" she lamented.

"It started well?"

"You came to me. You don't often come to me."

"Oh, Alicia." He laid his head in his hands. "Don't I?"

"No. But at least you listen to me these days. You didn't use to."

"I know," he said grimly. "You've told me."

"So did other people. You listened to them, Evelyn and Marisa."

"They don't love me."

Is that what he thought? Was it true? Was it because she loved him that she couldn't get angry with him?

"They changed you, though."

"I changed me. Evelyn and Marisa pointed things out. They were brutal. Evelyn felt I acted superior; Marisa had to work with me, and I guess she found me oppressive. But she was good for me. You know all that. You're kinder than they are. And I thank you for being kind, darling," he said.

"Oh, Steven," she wailed. "I don't want to be kind tonight. I want to fight. Well, I don't want to have a fight, but I want to say something that will change you. Will make you change. The way Marisa did." She used her name as if she knew her, although she had never met the legendary creature who worked alongside Steven at the institute. The one who complained until he listened. Who changed him. She really ought to meet her sometime, to thank her.

He stiffened. "Ah," he said. He withdrew his hands.

"Yes, that's better," she agreed. "It's about Stevie," she said quickly.

"Yes," he said, too softly for her to hear more than a mumble of agreement.

"Steven, Stevie is your son!" she began.

"Will you please not labor the obvious, Alicia? And his name is Steven, not Stevie. He's not ten years old anymore."

She ignored him. "He looks like you, his voice is your voice; when he telephones, I think it's you. He has your keen mind. He loves you."

Steven stared straight ahead.

"You are a psychiatrist, I don't need to tell you that a person's sexuality is not under their control . . ."

"Nonsense. One's inclinations may not be, but one's behavior is."

"Oh, Steven. Do you expect him to stay celibate?"

"It would be preferable."

She sighed.

"I have nothing to say on this issue," he said coldly, standing up. "I despise his choice in life and his lifestyle. I am thinking about writing him out of my will. I don't want to discuss this further." He went out of the kitchen and into the hall that led to the bedroom. She heard him shut the bedroom door.

Well, that was effective, Alicia.

She sat on, toying with her pencil. She stared into space. What could she do if he would not even discuss it? She had tried to tell him how strongly she felt about it, how she couldn't abide his treatment of the son she loved so intensely. Should she threaten to leave? Would she leave him over this? Did it mean that much to her?

She wasn't sure. She didn't know how she felt. Either she couldn't feel her feelings or several feelings were at war inside her. A thin high wail was going on inside her head, like a wire twanging in the wind. Part of her wanted to leave and run to Stevie, embrace him, stay with him forever. But that wasn't what Stevie wanted. He loved Neil. Was her love for Stevie abnormal? Was it incestuous? Was that why she was so upset?

The thought stopped her heart.

Stop thinking about this.

She sipped her tea. It was cold. She closed up the file in front of her, and slipped it onto the shelf behind the table. The kitchen table was her desk, the bookshelves near it, her storage area. Her new office would soon be ready. Then, she'd feel like a real professional. Someday.

•

So strange, Emily thought, raising her head from the staff paper, that the composers who wrote the most seductive music, the music of eros, lush and rhythmic and sexy as hell, were men who never had sex—Tchaikowsky, Brahms, Ravel. Or rarely. Maybe they went to prostitutes. Did they have male prostitutes in Tschaikowsky's day? Probably always. I don't know about Ravel, but I'd guess . . . Well, they surely had sex with themselves, maybe that's all it takes. Maybe erotic music is the music of masturbation. Because in masturbation you can maintain your fantasies in full living color—why the high is so high. Whereas when another person is involved, your fantasies have to recede a little. So this section, she thought, regarding the notes she had just written, maybe it will sound like theirs, because that's the kind of sex I'm used to. Or maybe it will be adulterated because I've had the other kind. Not that it was so great. Different for men. They always make sure they get their climaxes.

But Wagner puts the lie to my theory, doesn't he. Those gorgeous Wesendonck songs. Did he ever screw Mathilde? Still, he screwed other women. He knew what sex was like. Stravinsky's climaxes always seem to come with a female being gored to death. *Rite*, *Noces*. Do you suppose he was a sexual sadist? Or just a realist. He probably saw that sex was death for the female because it means pregnancy and the end of her individuality, her freedom. It's funny though, how sex is always seen through the female, even when a male is having it. Puccini. He *was* his women. He swooned in them. Madame Bovary, *c'est moi*. It's always women who have sex in art, who experience the great "surrender." How men see it. Strange. Can't a man swoon?—*le petit mort*?

She was sitting in her great armchair in her study, with her writing board across her knees, and she put the paper aside and rubbed her hand over her eyes. Remembering Artur Schneidel staring at her across the room, back at Curtis. Handsome darkness, his reputation a red flag in the school, no girl could consider herself unwarned. But he never tried anything with her. He treated her as if she were special. Talked to her differently, with respect. As if only she understood, appreciated music as he did. She had noticed it then, wondered about it, felt honored. She adored him, would have given him everything she had, but he never put out a hand. The way he sat looking at her when he played Stravinsky's *Lyke-Wake* for them, first time any of them had heard it. Watching her. She wasn't aware of his gaze until "Western Wind" began, startling her to her root, making her look up wildly, juddering. And saw him across the room, smiling, nodding his head as if his expectations had been fulfilled. He'd expected it to shock her; he was pleased it did. Her shock confirmed his sense of her specialness. Well, he was right: It shocked her so much she went back to her room and wrote her own version.

•

Emily was slicing cheese and laying it on top of the two slices of bread lying in the cast iron pan. The bread and bacon and cheese would be her dinner, with a salad of chicory, red onion, and mandarin oranges. It was a meal she liked.

She was slicing the cheese when she stopped dead, remembering the other morning after she'd given Toby a two-hour prep for his concert and was walking along the campus to the parking lot. The trees had the haze of May on them, as if the air was pale green. A green thought in a green shade. Here and there a splendid blotch of pink or purple flamed up from a flowering plum or cherry tree. She heard her name called, and turned to let John Hammer catch up with her, the dean, a man her own age whose hair and beard were pure white, whose belly had the rotund curve of a well-fed, bibulous man. (Why was it that bellies like that looked okay on a man but horrible on a woman?) She liked him, he was one of the few at Browning who knew something about her, who respected her work and kept track of her. He came to all her concerts, he knew she composed, he liked her work.

"Emily! Haven't seen you in ages. What are you doing on campus on a Saturday?"

"Preparing Toby Bisceglie for a concert. He's playing at the Westboro Town Hall on Sunday."

"He any good?"

"Very."

"Concert material? The circuit?"

She shrugged. "It's hard to know. He should go to New York to study. Just playing well isn't enough. Success in that world has to do with where you train, how you look, how audiences perceive you . . ."

"And who you know and how much money there is behind you . . ." he nodded.

"That matters in everything, doesn't it?"

"Does it not? So what are you writing these days, Emily?" he asked.

"A trio," she said. "I'm calling it the *Eros* Trio," she added, smiling. She often said things like this, expecting no reaction from people;

most didn't really listen to her and she didn't care if they did. Simply hearing the word *Eros* meant nothing to them, although they knew the word if they saw it written.

But John picked it up. "Aha!" he exploded in glee. "Yes!" He looked at her lasciviously. "Oh, you are still juicy, Emily Oldfield," he grinned, tapping her affectionately on the shoulder as he separated from her, heading for his own car. "You always were," he called back.

She smiled, wondering. Am I juicy? Most people don't see me that way. Dried up old spinster, Clea said. Didn't mean to hurt me. Or maybe she did. I shouldn't be hurt by a cliché like that. But that she could perceive me that way, even for a minute . . .

How did you want her to see you, Emily?

With love.

And did you see her that way?

No. Slut.

She stopped dead, turned the heat off the sandwiches, and sat down, clutching a hanky to her mouth.

15

By the end of May, Jenny had finished most of the sketches she needed of Maddy and Alicia. She hadn't done Emily, who had been too busy to sit; once the semester ended and Emily had given her concert, she promised to give Jenny all the time she needed.

These days, Jenny had to make an effort to concentrate on anything, even painting, and she worked slowly, but doggedly. Ever since her cruel accusation, Tim had essentially not spoken to her. They had occupied the same house and eaten together, but their exchanges were minimal. After two weeks of silence, Jenny felt as if her skin were covered with bloody welts. She couldn't stand it. She no longer cared who was wrong, or if anyone was wrong. She wanted this to end.

"Tim," she said gently, one late April evening after dinner, "can't we talk about what's between us?"

"I'm afraid to talk to you," he said coldly. "I might be accused of something else vile."

"I gather you found my accusation unbearable."

"What do you think?"

"But why? Unless it touched the truth."

"Why? Why?" he shouted, rising, carrying his plate into the kitchen. "Stupid bloody woman! Why do you think?"

She blanched, sitting still at the table. She heard him wash and rinse his plate, then return it to the cabinet. He did not even put his dishes in the dishwasher anymore. Now he was washing the pots he'd used to cook his rather elaborate dinner, drying them on paper towels and putting them away. She'd opened a can of fruit salad for herself—she was never hungry these days. She got up and stood in the kitchen door. "I can't go on like this. I can't stand it. I would like to end it."

He did not even face her, but stood at the sink scrubbing a frying pan. "I don't enjoy it, if that's what you mean. As to ending it, I don't know how."

"By talking about it."

"I don't want to talk to you," he spat. "And I'm not going to. I'm going to New York tomorrow morning, early."

She stood there, waiting, but he said nothing more. When he had cleaned up, he left the kitchen. He had been sleeping in his studio for the past weeks, and he went out there now, vigorously silent.

Jenny's head fell and tears ran down her cheeks, but she made no sound. Some chance words: She didn't even know where they had come from. At the time they felt true. But she had not even thought them before she said them. Had she been unfair? She had been hurt by the way he acted. Hurt and something else, frightened, maybe, but maybe things like that were common in marriage, maybe she should have let it go. Unthinkable things suddenly seemed to be happening, as if she'd taken one step too far along an overgrown pathway and fallen into an abyss she had not known was there. She cast her mind back to the drunken weekend, tried to remember how it felt, how Tim acted, so that the word *pimp* could drift across her mind, the word *whore*. It dizzied her, and the memory felt like something she'd dreamed, not something that had happened. It was all a mirage, and Tim's crazy anger seemed to be over nothing, a tempest in a teapot, a tantrum over a lost penny. Whatever had happened was certainly not worth destroying their whole—their everything—for. Was it? But the reality of it seemed a rift between them that could never be healed.

They had been happy. Hadn't they? So why was he willing to toss it all out? Had she hurt him that much? But how? What did what she said mean to him? She had thrown a metaphor at him, had not meant anything serious, it was inconceivable that it could be serious. Yet he took it seriously. She wanted to run out to his studio, to bang on the door until he opened it, to throw herself at him, to weep, to beg his forgiveness, to cling to him the way they once clung together . . .

But she couldn't. She had been hurt, too. She had a right to her anger. That was the problem, wasn't it? He could not bear her being angry. Of course, she had never been angry with him before.

She went back to the dining room and fetched her dish and silverware and carried them to the dishwasher. She rinsed out the fruit can and carried it to the metal recycle bin. She turned out the kitchen lights, locked the front door, and went into their bedroom. Her mind was clicking away. I hurt him, but he hurt me, he must know that, how could it not hurt me, I told him how it felt, I have a right to my anger too, as he does, but if it is going to end, we have to talk. She talked herself back into a state of dignity, all the while fighting off the fact that she had just realized: She had never been angry with him before. This was the first time she had been angry with him, and this was his reaction. Was she not allowed to get angry with him? Had she sensed this? Was that why, in all their seven years of marriage, she had never done so? Was it that—rather than the lack of a reason for anger—that had restrained her? Were some things off limits for him? Was that why he would never discuss Clare, his former wife, the mother of his children? Or the wife before that, whom he never mentioned, whose name Jenny didn't even know? Was he ready to end this marriage too, now that she had crossed the line?

She lay back on the bed, staring at the ceiling, thinking. She came to no conclusion. She did not know enough. She didn't know her own husband, after seven years.

She sensed his absence the next morning when she got up. After she had drunk her coffee, she tiptoed out to his studio. The door was locked, but she had a key, and she opened the door, peered in. Empty. She walked to the garage and peeked through the window. He had taken the little Mercedes. She was glad he'd left her the stuffy old Volvo, which she preferred. He was gone.

Would he come back?

Jenny pulled her back up as straight as she could. She went indoors and dressed quickly and called Alicia. "Would it be okay if I came over for a little while? I need to talk to you."

"Of course," Alicia said, hearing the panic in Jenny's voice.

"Oh, Alicia!" Jenny burst out when she entered. "I don't know how I drove here, I don't know how I'm walking. I feel like I'm held together with Scotch tape and bobby pins. I'm trembling inside and out, I'm a wreck."

Alicia drew her in, embraced her, sat her down, poured coffee.

It took quite a while to tell the whole thing, it had turned into such a complicated story. Why was that? No one had intended that; it just happened. Or was it predetermined to happen because of the pattern of their genes or their characters? "Maybe it was always going to happen, maybe it was inevitable, but I'm afraid I did something irrevocable. I'm afraid Tim will never forgive me," Jenny concluded, sniffling.

Alicia patted Jenny's hand softly; she struggled to think clearly. "It was an awful thing to say," she began, bringing fresh tears to Jenny's eyes, "but so was his behavior that night. He acted as if you were just a woman who happened to be present when the guys got together. As if he bore no responsibility for you."

"But does he? Am I not responsible for myself? I mean, we think of ourselves as enlightened, as having a feminist marriage. He doesn't expect me to serve him, clean up after him, do his laundry, that sort of thing. He doesn't see himself as my owner, my controller."

"But he does support you. Completely. No?"

"Yes," Jenny admitted, mortified. "But he's fifty-five. I'm thirty-one, I was twenty-five when we got married. I couldn't earn much money at that age—unless I was a lawyer or in the market or something, I guess. But not as an artist. And he knows that, knew that: He struggled for twenty-odd years. He didn't start to make money until he was forty-five or thereabouts. His first marriage broke up over money. Or the lack of it. That's what he said. He said she was spoiled, unwilling to be poor. He knew, when we got married, that I would be dependent on him . . . You think that matters?"

"Of course it matters. It's part of the power pattern."

"Power pattern?"

"The arrangement of powers between you. You have some, he has some. A really equal relationship requires equal powers on both sides. He has the money; you balance that with your youth and beauty and dependency. He feels so much desire for you, and so much pleasure in your dependency, that he's happy to support you. You make him feel strong, needed."

"He used to," Jenny said, her nose thick with phlegm, tears pouring down her face. "But I hate your lining it up that way, like items in a list, as if we were opposing armies, or companies in a takeover, or something like that."

"But it is like that, Jenny," Alicia said. "Sorry. It's not that I'm transforming something passionate and emotional into something measurable that can be laid out on a graph. That's the way things are. I know what a shock it is the first time you discover that what you thought was all about love is really all about power. You know, in the years when girls are first learning about love, boys are learning that only power matters in the male world, and that men are supposed to control women—through power. They have an edge on us in this way of thinking. It's all new to us when we stumble into it—if we stumble into it. God knows there are plenty of battered women around who still think it's all about love. What he's doing now is making a move in a power struggle. He's using his power to bring you to your knees. He wants to be sure you'll never again accuse him of pimping for you. Or to make sure you never get angry with him again. He's punishing you, even though he was the one in the wrong, to make sure you learn your position."

"But I did hurt him."

"Yes. But he also hurt you. Which he is refusing to deal with. He's acting as if your attack on him was more serious than the way he treated you. As if he had the right to treat you that way. As if what he did was negligible. And it wasn't. In fact, it was far more serious than what you said. He treated you as if you didn't matter: Maybe part of him feels that way. You're not treating him as if he doesn't matter, you're taking him seriously. You're saying, I care about you, and look how you behaved."

Jenny stared at Alicia. "When you put it that way . . ."

Alicia sipped her coffee. She smiled at Jenny. Jenny smiled back, her smile changing her damp face into a child's, sweet and trusting.

"So I was right to hold on to myself. Not to throw myself at his feet. That's what I really wanted to do. I couldn't stand his being angry at me." Tears threatened, and Alicia took Jenny's hand and, holding her chin high, announced, "Damn straight!"

Jenny's back straightened.

"You must hold on to yourself. He'll be back. I can't believe he's ready to abandon you for this—if he is, then I don't know what held you two together."

Jenny nodded.

"I have to be strong," she said, like a fourth grader repeating the teacher's lesson.

"You have to feel right. You have to believe you have rights."

Jenny took a deep breath. "Oh, Alicia," she said, "I feel so much better! I can't believe it! I was feeling like a whiny kid whose mother had gone off and left her alone . . ."

"Or father."

"Yes. Of course," she nodded. "I understand. My father never was around. You're wonderful."

"Really," Alicia drawled sarcastically. "I can tell you exactly what's going on, I knew the minute you explained it that he was making a power struggle out of this, but can I deal with things like this myself?" She hit her forehead with her palm.

"Steven?"

"He won't talk to me about Stevie. That's the same thing, isn't it? But it's had me cowed for two years! Jenny, you helped me while I was helping you!"

"Isn't life wonderful?" Jenny said, with enthusiasm.

Alicia could not quite subscribe to that sentiment, but she did believe, profoundly, in the circular nature of loving giving. She had been awed at discovering the circularity of political protest. Her history professor at Hunter had given an entire lecture to point out that women were drawn to the abolition movement because they sensed that their condition was also slavery, though disguised. They became abolitionists in great numbers in America in the early nineteenth century, and tried to speak publicly against slavery, but were hooted off platforms, had objects hurled at them, were called filthy names. Men refused to let them speak, not accepting women's right to speak from a platform. It wasn't done. So female abolitionists were driven first of all to defend their right to speak. In the process, they became feminists, fighting for their own rights, women's rights.

Alicia had been a little disappointed to learn that women entered the fight for rights through a side door. It seemed women always put other people before themselves. She knew that the second wave of feminists had begun by fighting for men's right not to fight in an absurd and pointless war; these women only moved on to fight for themselves because the men they supported treated them as subsidiary. They *had* to start fighting for themselves. She mentioned this to the professor, who smiled and said, "Yes, but these things always go round and round. That's my point. Women in England, inspired by the nineteenth-century American women fighting for the vote (which they thought would end their oppression), developed a more forceful campaign that involved violence against property. They used violence against things, not people, and silent protest.

"Their campaign inspired Mahatma Gandhi, who went to England to study it. When he returned home, he started a campaign of his own, calling it *satyagraha*. He renounced violence against people. Hundreds of Indian women supported it over a long period, and eventually Gandhi was victorious: He overthrew British rule, despite England's hugely superior weaponry, despite its army and its organization and its money. Later on, Martin Luther King Jr. was so impressed by Gandhi that he went to India to speak to him, returning to the United States to start a nonviolent movement for the rights of African Americans. And he won too—in time, and at the cost of his life. A host of laws were passed by Congress decreeing that African Americans were not to be denied rights, and that denial of rights on ground of color was to be punished. A southern senator added sex to the bill, comically, assuming this would assure the bill's defeat. But it didn't, and women's rights, too, were secured.

"And," Alicia's professor continued, "once women provoked the second wave of feminism, they, as well as blacks, used these laws to overthrow old customs that excluded them from jobs, schools, clubs, the military, and access to credit. So old fights for rights fed new fights for rights in a circle that continues today, as women in places like Africa and India now fight for their rights, using techniques developed by oppressed people over the centuries, asserting they too are human beings with human rights. The weapons of the powerless were handed from one powerless group to the next, in a circle that came back to hearten the ones who started it." Alicia's heart expanded at this. She sat there, adoring her teacher, adoring even more the lesson, believing just a little that there was justice in the world.

•

Now, with Jenny gone, Alicia sat energized in her kitchen, remembering this. I had forgotten, she whispered to herself. Remembering gave her courage. Here it was, mid-May; she had let more than a month go by and said nothing to Steven. She had even let him make love to her, although not with much ardor on her part. He was depriving her of her son, and she was letting him do it. It had to stop.

The next night, he arrived after nine, a little tired but cheerful, as he usually was on arriving in Steventon. She offered him food. She offered him a scotch. They did not drink much except in company, and his eyebrows lifted. "That's a nice idea. Yeah. I'd like a little scotch." He fixed drinks for them (in his accounting system, that was a male job), scotch on ice for him, with soda for her. They sat in the comfortable "keeping" room of their old house. The balmy weather of the past couple of days had ended; it was damp and chilly that night, and Alicia had built a fire. This made the evening special, as fires always do. Steven was content; a quiet smile hovered on his face. "How was your week? Is your tooth better or still bothering you?"

"I went to the dentist yesterday. It's not a cavity, just a sensitive tooth. He gave me some special toothpaste. It's okay—I was just worried it might be a cavity. Thanks for asking."

He shrugged. "Of course."

"And your patient? Is she okay?"

He shook his head. "She's still alive. I called her this morning. But I'm worried, Lish. She attempted suicide before, before she came to me. And she's very depressed."

"Any special reason?"

"Life!" he exclaimed. "Do we need special reasons for depression? Isn't life enough? Horrible parents, terrible husband, rotten kids, disaster upon disaster. She's seen it all."

"Everyone's life isn't that frightful."

"Life is hard. Painful. Agonizing."

"Yes."

"Hers was harder than most."

"So you don't blame her."

He shrugged again. "What's to blame? I understand why she's sad. But she has some bright spots in her life—her talent, a couple of good friends. Enough."

"Would that be enough for you?"

"I don't know. I feel it should be enough to live for. But I'm not she—as you are no doubt pointing out."

"Are her kids really rotten?"

"Well, one of them's an addict. He's hopeless. The other's not too bad, but scarred by the home life. The violence of the father. The mother's passivity. She can't forgive her own mother. Blames her for her hard life."

Alicia sighed. "Poor thing."

"Yes."

"Steven."

"Yes, dear?"

"You have to talk to me."

"I am talking to you."

"About Stevie."

He uncrossed his legs as if he were about to stand.

"No, don't! Don't get up and leave! Don't run out on me! You have to do this!"

He leaned back in the chair, but clutched his drink as if preparing to get up.

"Your attitude deprives me of my son, who is not rotten, not an addict, not blameful, nothing bad. He's a sweet, good boy who loves males, not females. He can't help that."

"How do you know what he can help or not help? You're an expert on perversion now?"

"He was always gay. He was gay when he was a little boy. I saw it, even if you didn't. He was born that way."

Steven was silent.

"Steven." Peremptory.

"Steven." Pleading.

She went to him. She sat near him on the corner of the couch cushion. She slid her arm around his back. She took his drink out of his hand and placed it on the side table. She caressed his face with her hand.

He took her hand and kissed it. Tears stood in his eyes. "I just can't stand it," he gasped, wiping his eyes.

"Why? What does it mean to you?"

"You know I'm not religious. That I think religion's a load of crap, the most divisive force in the world. And as women's libbers love to point out, the very bulwark of patriarchy. But I was raised in a religious home. My father—well, he might have been unscrupulous in business, but he was so grateful our family was spared, not that we didn't lose family, but no one that close . . . he, his parents, his siblings were here, my mother's family too, all of them were here for decades before Hitler came to power. He felt guilty that he hadn't shared the suffering, and grateful that he hadn't, and proud that some of us were left, that we could rebuild a Jewish community in this country . . . He had four sons. You know that. I was the youngest. We all did well. He was enormously proud of that. That's how he was. You hardly knew him. My mother was like that too. Very pious. She was so old when you met her . . . she was old when I was born, almost fifty.

"It was everything to them to have sons, who were needed to carry on the tradition. You needed girls because Jewishness is passed on through the girls, but only men were true Jews, only men could be rabbis, could make up a minion, only men could touch the Torah, kiss it, carry it . . . My father was so proud he had sons. He almost burst every Passover, with all of us around the dinner table. It felt so . . . sacred . . . even now, remembering it . . . him asking the questions, all the boys answering . . ."

Steven let go of Alicia's hand, and she moved away, back to her chair. He picked up his drink and sipped. "That we don't participate in those rituals is my decision, I know. I've always appreciated your understanding of my dislike of religion. Your mother, I know, was hurt by it. But in spite of that, even though I don't accept religion, I have just a tinge of feeling, a . . . twinge. And when Stevie was born, I didn't think, I felt: I have a son to carry on. I didn't feel that about Mariette. Not at all."

"And you do have a son. Who carries on. Not the tradition, you didn't raise him to be religious. But your name."

He turned white. He glared at her. "But he won't pass it on, will he?" he said in a furious whisper. "Will he?"

She sat stunned. For a time, she couldn't speak. Then she whispered, too, as if what they were discussing was unspeakable. "But you don't care about that! You've often said so! It's all nonsense, you said, passing on a name. And your name isn't even your father's name, they changed it, and your father's name was changed when they left Russia . . ."

Steven closed his eyes. "I know."

She stood up and went into the kitchen, then poured fresh drinks and brought them into the sitting room. She pried his empty glass out of his hand and put the fresh drink in it. He didn't seem to notice.

"Sip your drink," she ordered.

He wet his lips.

"It's all totally irrational," she began.

He nodded.

"You—considering your profession—must feel like a fool."

He nodded again.

"You can't undo this knot?"

He cleared his throat. He sipped his drink. "I haven't been able to."

"Have you talked to anyone? Another shrink, I mean."

He shook his head no.

"Can you?"

He glanced at her almost in surprise. "I suppose. I hadn't thought about it."

"You didn't want it to go away?"

"It's painful. I'd prefer not to deal with it. If you hadn't said . . . if it weren't hurting you, I probably wouldn't deal with it."

"But it is hurting me. And it's hurting Stevie. Horribly."

He covered his eyes. "I want to stay angry. I want to hate him."

"I know that feeling," she said.

He raised his head. "You do?" He sounded astonished.

"Yes."

"That seems inconceivable to me."

"I hated my mother. For marrying my stepfather. I hated him for marrying her, but I was more angry with her. My hating her hurt my mother and I wanted to hurt her. I suppose I wanted to punish her for marrying him. And she said she did it for me! To secure my future. I hated that most of all. I couldn't bear to hate her most of the time; I hated him until he died. That wasn't fair: He wasn't a sweet man, but he didn't deserve hatred. He was good to me in his own way. Paid for things. Didn't complain. For Momma's sake, I suppose. He didn't want to give her grief. And after he died, I still held him against her."

"How we . . ." he dropped his hand in despair.

"What?"

"Punish the ones we love."

She nodded.

"I want a grandson!" he announced suddenly.

She gazed at him. "Chances are Mariette will give you one."

He stared at her, then covered his eyes again.

Oh God, she thought. Don't tell me. It isn't her child he wants, it's Stevie's. Hers isn't good enough. All that ancient shit is still swirling around in his reptile brain. Don't tell me about it, Steven. I don't want to know.

He raised his head, wiped his eyes. "Of course you're right." He looked drained. He hated what was in there as much as she did.

"Try to forgive yourself," she sighed.

"Ah, Alicia."

"It's in me too. All that old stuff. In the reptile brain. All the prejudices, the superstitions. Hard to get rid of all of it. Maybe we never will. But our kids don't have it."

He tried to smile, failed. He looked at her. "Are you sure?"

She stared at him numbly.

"Will we ever be rid of it?"

He reached out for her, and she for him, and they embraced each other like children, clutching at each other in a desperate time. They sat there for a long time.

"I love you, Steven."

"I love you, Alicia. Ask Stevie to come up some weekend so I can try to explain . . . make amends . . . ask forgiveness . . . something. As soon as he can. Alone, please. Just this once. After that . . ."

Tears spurted out of Alicia's eyes. "I will," she said.

16

The day after Clea came home late, Emily called Maddy and asked to meet her for lunch. Maddy kept fanning herself with her menu; she was still having hot flashes, although they should have passed by now. But maybe because she'd had a baby so late, she was going into menopause only now, 1982, when she was already fifty-seven years old.

Emily closed her menu. The waitress arrived with her pad.

"Chicken salad sandwich, please, Mary," Maddy said. "And hot tea with lemon."

"The same for me please, Mary," said Emily. This occurred regularly—their ordering the same thing unintentionally.

They passed their menus to the waitress. Maddy folded her hands on the table before her. She sighed.

Emily looked up expectantly.

"Benjamin's talking about dropping out of school," Maddy said.

"What?"

Maddy nodded. "Charley is so upset he keeps belching; I just know he's getting an ulcer. And I can't talk to him."

"Charley? Or Benjamin?"

"Benjamin. He just turns his face away from me. I don't get it. You know, they're your darling babies, they adore you, they cry when you leave the room, they're inconsolable when you go out, and then suddenly they can't stand you, they turn their faces away from you." Her voice thickened, her eyes gleamed wet.

"What does he want to do?"

Maddy grimaced. "Join a rock band, what else? You know, he's been playing the guitar, we bought him a pretty good one last Christmas, but he isn't that good, Emily, believe me. Who ever gave him the idea he was good enough to play in a band, I don't know!"

Maddy dug in her handbag and found a handkerchief, and used that to fan herself. Her face and neck were a deep pink.

"What did you say?"

"Nothing. I was gobsmacked."

"And Charley?"

"He looked up startled, then got the saddest expression you ever saw on his face. Then he said—so pathetically it would make a stone weep—'Oh. And you were doing so well in school, I thought you'd be the first in the family to go to Harvard.' That stopped Benjamin dead: His jaw dropped. So did the subject. So I don't know."

Emily laughed. "Maybe that did the trick."

"You think? We'll see, I guess."

"If he's not a terrific player, it won't last long anyway. Music is a killer world. You have to be awfully good as well as awfully determined."

Maddy gazed at her friend. "Of course. You're right. I probably shouldn't worry."

The waitress arrived with their tea and sandwiches.

"Thank you, Mary." They both smiled at her.

They ate.

"So what's up with you?"

Emily sipped her tea, set the cup down in the saucer, wiped her lips with her napkin.

"Maddy," she began tentatively, "do you think it's possible that Clea . . . Clea and Harley . . . could be . . ."

"Involved?" cried Maddy. "Absolutely not! How could they? She's only a kid, she's fifteen! 'Jailbait,' didn't they use to call them that? And Harley's almost fifty, isn't he? Well, he's in his forties, anyway. And look at him—such a wimp. Clea has too much taste to get involved with a simpleton like him."

Emily hung on Maddy's words as if they were iron hooks. "Really?"

Maddy's gaze pierced Emily's heart. She put her hand over her friend's. "Really. It's not possible. Put it out of your mind."

"Oh," Emily said, squeezing her forehead into a washboard, "I hope you're right."

•

She buried the late arrival in her memory. Sometimes, it's best just to leave things alone, she concluded. Winter passed, spring burgeoned with its usual heart-stopping beauty, and Clea had her sixteenth birthday and finished her sophomore year of high school.

Emily wanted to give her a party, a "sweet sixteen" with boys and music and dancing, but Clea vetoed that. She shocked Emily by saying that if they had boys, they'd have to have beer. She imagined that Emily wouldn't like boys getting sloshed at her house; Emily said she wouldn't serve alcohol to minors. Clea had never told her that people got drunk at the parties she went to, and Emily wanted to question her further, but Clea preempted the attempt. She announced gaily that she'd like a pajama party with girlfriends. So Emily had the pleasure of a party for her niece after all. She had also quietly arranged to buy Clea a car, a little Pinto, which was what Clea wanted. And the party went well and she loved her new car, and life seemed fine in June of 1983.

By early summer, Emily was sure she had taken the right course. Whatever had caused Clea's lie, it was insignificant. It had passed, and now aunt and niece were on an even keel. They lived happily together. Clea did not want to go to camp, travel over the summer, or even take a trip back to California to see her old friends. She wanted to work at the Kellogg farm, taking care of the horses and jumping. Emily, awed at her commitment, agreed.

Emily herself planned to devote the summer to a project she had never mentioned to anyone—but then, she rarely discussed her work with anyone—she wanted to write a symphony. She had written concerti and chamber pieces and parts of an opera, but had never tackled anything as large as a symphony. Writing such a thing was harder because aside from her solo piano pieces and some trios, she was unable to hear her work performed. It was her own fault, she knew. She could approach people and pressure (or persuade) them to perform her work. She had a few old friends who were now famous, and she knew two faculty members who knew Seiji Ozawa. But she had never done it. She explained this to herself by claiming it was the result of what she privately called her "craziness," feelings she never spoke of and rarely even contemplated.

At the beginning, when she was working toward winning competitions, she had presented herself as a pianist more than as a composer, for the excellent reason that she had composed very little. But even after she won the Prix de Rome as a composer, she still downplayed composing in writing to her parents and friends, because in 1952, no one she knew believed women could write music—after all, some were grudging even in granting that women could play it. Emily's family had no conception of what composers *did*, really. It was bad enough—strange, an oddity—that she played the piano. She had been implicitly seasoned to reticence about her profession.

In the face of the roaring egos and narcissism of male performers in Rome and Boston, she remained reticent. Her fellow musicians regarded her as a superlative performer who lacked the charisma of a star, and she silently accepted their definition, keeping her own counsel. And life went on, and she never spoke. Sometimes she thought about "going public," but after so many years, everything in her shrank from public display. Her anxieties had grown like a mussel community expanding on a single rock; she silently dreaded discovering that her work was not really first rate. And she preferred invisibility, obscurity, to the ignominy of being second rate.

But this summer, she decided to challenge her feelings: She would write something long and complex, something she would yearn to hear. Maybe that would force the issue.

And she was happier that summer than usual, working well, steadily, feeling confident of the beauty and strength of what she was doing, and watching Clea grow cockier and stronger every day, Clea happy too, always humming to herself, inseparable from the Kelloggs (as Emily thought of them) and their horses.

•

As the school year ended, Emily was dividing her time between her students, who were preparing for their final concert of the semester, and practicing for her own part in it. Her students were playing études by Chopin, Scriabin, and Oldfield, and after the break, three of them would play the *Eros* Trio, which she had just finished, for violin, flute, and cello. They were excited and enthusiastic about it; they thought she was cutting edge. Privately she smiled at their eagerness, but of course it pleased her deeply. She would play Beethoven's Sonata, op. 27 no. 1, which she knew would be popular.

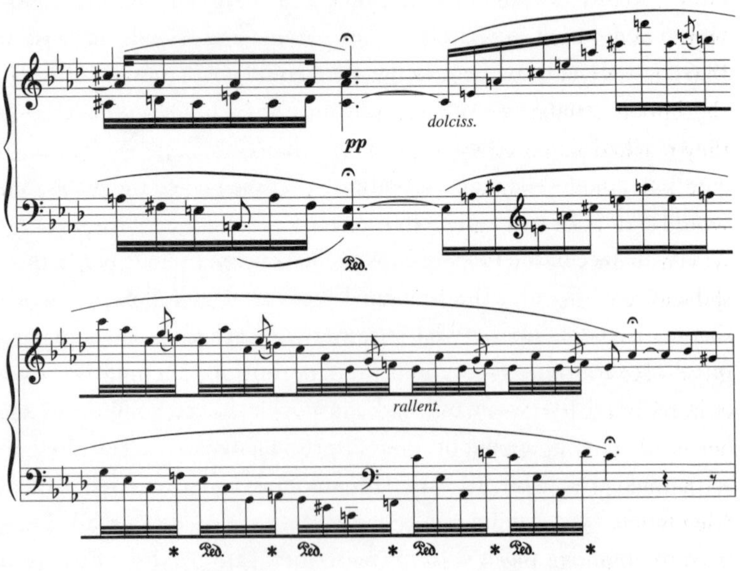

In the second half, she would play some waltzes of her own, and finish the evening with Ravel's *Alborada del gracioso*.

She did not want to end the concert with her own work, as if it were a high point.

As she walked from the studio to her car on a May afternoon after rehearsal, she was smiling, remembering the interaction of the guys in the trio—they always called each other "the guys." They were young: Leonard and Michael were in their early twenties, and Marian was twenty-one. They had argued amiably about the rhythms and dynamics of certain passages, turning to her only when they reached an impasse. She had enjoyed their arguments; they were cute kids, their arguments made sense, and who knew?, maybe she would like their reading better than her own. So she listened and waved them away when they turned to her. But now, recalling it, she was remembering also her own arguments back in the days when she was twenty and twenty-one and doing ensemble work with "the guys." How different it was now. The men didn't bully Marian, didn't ally against her, didn't look at each other superciliously over her head, as boys did in her day. One of them was as likely to ally with Marian against the other boy as not; but this bunch were friends, and the ground would immediately shift again. Few men tried to dominate Emily now, mainly, she thought, because she usually played alone, but if she played with strangers, it could still occur with men her own age. For a moment, she had to stop, her heart hurt so: If only I'd been born later! But then she shrugged, and walked on to her car.

That was how Maddy felt, she knew. If only Maddy had been born after everyone understood that children were to be loved, that they were not little lumps of sin one had to discipline into shape—for that was how people had treated children when Maddy and Emily were young. She remembered adults standing and shaking their pointed fingers in the face of a child—What are you up to young man, young lady!—always sure of the worst. Emily always told Maddy to let it go, forget it, she had made her life a rich, full thing, she had done well in the end, let the past go. But she knew it was probably impossible.

It was hard to think about the past, about one professor after another laughing in her face when she said she wanted to study composition. But when Ralph Kirkpatrick had come to give a master class, he treated her with respect, had taken her seriously, even though she had rebelled and played a Gershwin prelude instead of Bach or Beethoven. And later, Schneidel looked her in the eye, gave a hard, short nod, and she was in, studying with the most exalted composer in the place! Forget the others. The humiliation. A girl with those men was like a used Kotex hanging in a public place for them to see, smell, turn away from in disgust. That's how they felt; that's what they communicated to her. You had to chew your inner lip and keep yourself from crying and go on and on, try to keep your back from slumping. You used to have such good posture, Emily, what's wrong with you? her mother had said when she came home the first time. Not with any sympathy, of course. It was Emily's own fault.

Forget it. You have made a fine life for yourself.

Sure. I've never even tried to have my music played in public. Couldn't bear even the thought of them laughing. Turning away. That bored, indifferent look. A *woman*! Composing? Who does she think she is?

Angelo La Mariana, her first piano teacher, told her she had promise. He recorded her playing the *Spinning Song*, she played it so easily, she thought it was a baby piece until he brought her a record of Alfred Cortot playing it. He gave her *Etude* magazine for Christmas, and every month she read it all the way through, barely understanding much of it but accepting all of it as divine scripture, not ever having heard the music of most of the composers whose names etched themselves in her memory, Mendelssohn, Schubert, Scriabin, Rachmaninoff. Until one day she raised her head in shock, realizing that every one of them was a man, that women could not be composers, or at least, they weren't. Not ever. Was there even one woman? she asked Angelo. He hesitated. No answer. One day she found a piece in one of those books Poppa was always buying for her, *One Hundred Great Hits of the Past*, something like that, he didn't know they weren't serious, there was a piece by someone called Cecile Chaminade. Was that a woman? Could it have been? It was a pretty piece but trivial oh oh oh . . .

Her head started to ache as she reached her car. She stood there for a moment to clear it, gazing around at the campus in full May flower, shocking bursts of pink and purple and yellow everywhere, tree buds that light tender green still, starting to open, and under the trees the students, the young, lovely, like spring, walking hand in hand, talking animatedly, full of fervor, full of the energy and illusions of youth. The illusion that things would be different for them. I thought that too when I was young.

But maybe things would be for these kids.

Then she discovered Clara Schumann and Fanny Mendelssohn and finally heard some of their music, but she found it small. Woman's music. That is to say, unimportant. Unoriginal. Uninspiring. And when her only friend, Natasha argued, saying, You've only heard a couple of pieces, only what they let you hear, you have to do research, look it up for yourself! What about Mrs. H. H. Beach? Did Mrs. H. H. Beach have a first name? Not that Emily could find. Now, of course, everyone knew of Amy Beach. Now she was getting popular. Hah! A hundred years later! It felt like a hundred years later when her colleague Gena Raps found Marie Ferranc and Elisabeth de la Guerre and the Boulanger sisters and a host of others and began to think it was all a giant conspiracy, that it wasn't that women couldn't compose, it was that men refused to take them seriously. Could this be true? All through history? That sounded paranoid. Couldn't be. It was crazy.

Years of agonizing, writing her music secretly, showing it to no one, afraid, and even that fear was shameful, it denied her dignity, it made her a tremulous child. It had all become habit—keeping to herself, working alone, telling no one. Only Maddy knew, and even to her, Emily did not make it sound important. Yet it was her very breath.

In another world, maybe she would even have risked connecting herself to someone, love, marriage, maybe even motherhood . . . Oh, maybe not. Because even if men were different, she wasn't. She was the old person, the woman her mother had raised her to be, expected her to be . . . A servant of men. Couldn't get rid of it. Leap up and cook the dinner. Leap up and fetch the milk.

Maddy said she'd lived the wrong life. But I haven't lived *all* of my life. Is that different? Can a woman live a whole life? Is that allowed? Can a woman do work she thinks is important and still have children, a loving family? Even now?

She opened the door of her car and sat down on the driver's seat with her legs outside; it was hot in the car. She sat there with the door open, the window rolled down, AC turned on high. She breathed deeply. Let it go. Don't poison your life with anger. Forget it. It's over.

The hell it is.

She laughed grimly, pulled her legs inside the car, closed the door, and turned the AC down a bit. She sat letting the breeze cool her face. Go ahead, use the damned AC. The hell with the environment. I'll be dead before it will. And who cares, anyway. Who cares about anything. Not me.

•

Emily was tired, a good tired, the kind of tiredness that came from putting in three solid hours of practice, and finally getting those trills in the first Chopin "Ballade" to roll from her fingers like waterfalls. She had had them down years ago, but had lost them in the years she did not play them. Now she felt completely satisfied. Tiredness was less satisfying if it didn't involve success, and it didn't always. The piano remained a challenge for her, even after all these years. Probably wouldn't be fun if it hadn't. She wondered if for people with astonishing technical abilities, like Horowitz or Richter, the challenge disappeared. Did they get bored then? I don't have to worry, she thought; my technique is not *that* great. Good, but not great. I wonder if I could have made it concertizing, if I hadn't blown that contest. It wasn't a life I especially wanted: How could I have composed if every night I was in a different city, living on airplanes, constantly practicing and meeting new people and going to parties, if I never had silence and solitude? Pondering this, she could not help envisioning the pleasures of such a life—the parties, the praise, the fame, the recordings, the wealth—and sadness shadowed her face.

She brushed it away. It was a little after four; she had time for a nap before Maddy came at six. They were going to dinner and a movie. Some picture Maddy wanted to see. Maddy followed these things. These days there were few movies older women could enjoy: Most films seemed to be violent outer-space conflicts or farcical comedies about stupid adolescents in love or lust—whatever they called it these days. We old women are a group no one wants, Emily thought: We don't spend money, we don't buy junk, and no one cares about us. We're reduced to watching the same films over and over again. What had there been lately? *Mrs. Dalloway*, *Antonia's Line*, *Tea with Mussolini*. We like movies in which people converse, feel emotions and subtly express them. Movies that reflect life as we know it. I wonder what kind of life youngsters know? I can't imagine what they think life is. A race for nooky and green? How can I find out? You can't ask them, can you.

I wonder how Clea is. Is she like that? I can't believe she is. Well, look at what she does. No one who works for a women's health clinic is greedy or on the make. No, she's a girl with principles. After all.

She sat, feeling bruised, for a few minutes, then pushed away the feeling. Nap. Nap, nap, nap. She got up and went to the fainting couch in her studio. She never napped in bed. That was something one didn't do in her mother's house, in her mother's generation. Don't know why. Naps were taken on sofas, fainting couches, hammocks, lawns. Never on beds. Mother always napped around four in the afternoon on the living-room couch, waking in a stertorous jerk about an hour later. Everyone had to tiptoe around her, but she would have been scandalized by anyone napping in a bed. Emily lay down on the couch and threw a lap rug over her legs. She was asleep almost immediately.

The doorbell woke her, and she leaped up, looked at her watch, god, I slept a long time, it's quarter of six. She went to the door and let Maddy in.

"You been sleeping?"

Emily nodded. "Since four o'clock," she answered, still groggy.

"You look it. Go wash your face, Emily Jane. You won't be able to sleep tonight."

"Ummm," she mumbled, heading for the downstairs toilet.

Maddy sat down in the living room and studied it. Nothing ever changes in this house, she thought. It looked today much as it had in the time of Emily's great-grandmother. The lamps were changed, of course, when electricity came in. And a radio was introduced in the thirties; telephone was added after the war, 1948 or 1949, and one was still kept in the same place in the hall. Phone lines had come late to the mountains. In the late fifties, TV arrived, replacing the radio, which was exiled to the kitchen, a stranger there—a walnut cabinet beside a sink and stove. And the living room suffered from the loss; the radio had burled walnut doors with carved moldings, stood on delicate carved legs, and was small and unobtrusive, whereas the television was large and bulky, its doors dark mahogany veneer, the rabbit ears on top. Ugly.

By Emily's time, the elegant old radio with its tubes had been exiled to the basement or the barn, replaced by a portable on a kitchen countertop. Fifteen years ago, Emily had invested in an expensive FM-AM radio with a record player and tape deck for her study. It was worth it, she said: There was fine music on the radio now in this area. And some years ago, she bought a CD player. Funny, all the changes were concerned with . . . what do they call it? Media? Communications? Information? Now, of course, the Internet.

Clea's arrival had forced Emily to move some furniture around, add some lamps, and make the room more comfortable. Clea had been appalled by the room, by the whole house. She was used to up-to-date California houses that emphasized comfort. Comfort had never been the primary purpose of New England houses: Front rooms, or parlors, as people used to call them, were made to impress, with chairs draped with antimacassars, tables covered with precious (at least to their owners) objets d'art, the harmonium, the family Bible, and a good carpet. They were meant to advertise the owner's respectability, propriety. The main guest in sitting rooms was the minister, after all. Or visitors after a death.

Clea's influence had been good, Maddy thought; it was a comfortable room now, one you'd enjoy sitting in to read the evening paper. Even so, it had remained the same for twenty years; even the dust fell in habitual patterns.

Emily returned, looking fresher. "Would you like a drink, Mad?"

"Okay. A little scotch, maybe."

Emily fetched the drinks and sat down across from Maddy.

"I was just thinking how nothing changes in your house."

"I know. I hardly ever use this room. Only when I watch TV, which isn't very often. Usually I don't even come in here."

"Do things change in the rooms you use?"

"Actually, no. Not much. I get a new CD every once in a while. A new book. Otherwise . . . things are the way I like them. No point in changing them."

"No. That's the thing, isn't it. When you get to our age, you are who you want to be, and your life is what you want it to be, and your house is the way you want it to be."

"Which makes it the best time in your life!" Emily laughed.

"I guess. But your house turns into a museum."

"That's okay. So is Paris a museum. And Toledo and Assisi. It's still the best time in your life *if* you can ignore the aches and pains, the difficulty climbing stairs, the fact that you don't drive as well as you used to, and that it takes you seven whole minutes to bend down, pick something up, and get up again!"

They both laughed.

"Suppose you were our age and you weren't the person you had wanted to become?"

Emily shivered. "Ohhh." Then piped up, "Like who?"

Maddy shrugged. "Oh, I don't know. Ethel Elberry, say."

"I think Ethel is exactly who she wants to be. She's always right. She always wanted to be always right, and now she is."

"You're wicked, Emily Jane."

"You're the only person who calls me that. The only person who ever called me that, except my mother. I hate it!"

"I know, that's why I do it. You impress me so much, I have to take you down a peg when I talk to you."

Emily snorted.

"I called Clea," Maddy announced suddenly.

Emily sat perfectly still. "You did?"

"Yes. I told her you miss her. She said you never call her. I told her you thought she would rather not hear from you. She didn't say anything to that. I said you were giving a concert later this month. I said it would be nice if she came."

Only Emily's eyes moved as Maddy spoke, following each gesture of her friend's hands. She hung on Maddy.

"And? . . ."

"She said she might. I said Alicia was having a little party for you afterward and would like her to be there. She said she'd think about it."

Emily sat in silence. Finally, she roused herself. "How was she? How was everything?"

"Fine, she said."

More silence.

"Do you think she'll come?"

"Yes. I do. I'm telling you because I want you to know what I did. I hope you don't think I'm a terrible buttinsky. You know I feel responsible for you in some absurd way. You're still the little girl I used to walk home from school. I know it's irrational. Forgive me."

"I understand, Maddy. It's all right. It's fine. I appreciate the effort."

Maddy sighed, relieved. "It would be nice if she came."

Emily's voice was wistful. "Oh, I'd love to see her."

"Well, maybe you will." Maddy was all business again. "Shall we go? Do you want to eat at the Hutch? The movie starts at 8:20."

"Let's."

•

Maddy was right, Emily couldn't sleep that night. She lay in bed conjuring Clea, imagining how she looked now, how she *was* now. A different person. Had to be. Emily's fists were clenched. When she became aware of this, she tried to relax them, but they soon clenched again. She sat up. She would have liked a cigarette. Even after thirty years of not smoking, she hadn't lost the urge. She got up, put on her slippers, and went downstairs and poured a little scotch in a glass, added ice. She sat in the cold living room, by the window. She had not done this since she was a teenager. No. She did it again when Clea was a teenager. In 1982 and 1983 . . .

•

Emily had shoved to the back of her mind Clea's lateness that night, and the lie she had told. Yet in a part of Emily's brain, in the file cabinet where the unconsciously selected things that would never be forgotten were filed, the event still rested, quiescent. A lie, to Emily, was significant. A lie had caused her to break up with Duncan: He showed up late for a concert one evening and apologized, saying he'd called her several times, but she must have been out at the market or something, because he got no answer. She did not tell him she'd been in all afternoon, working on a piece for flute and cello. She looked at him and wondered why he lied. Was he afraid of her? A lie, to Emily, meant fear. It meant a concealment of something that felt wrong. She never discussed this with him, but the next week, she moved out of their apartment, found rooms on her own. He was bewildered; he never understood her departure. He acted horribly hurt. She later found out that the afternoon he lied about calling her, he had met with a director of programming for the Concertgebouw, who was planning a concert series for the hall, and wanted Duncan to participate. No reason to hide that from her, unless he felt she would be jealous. Since she would not, since she had in fact sacrificed her pianistic career to his long ago, she had to deduce that he felt threatened by her still, was jealous of her and projecting it onto her. In other words, he had bad feelings about her. She could not live with him under those circumstances, and she decided she had been right to leave.

For Emily, Clea's lie held a great significance—Clea had never lied to her before, that she knew of—but she did not probe further. Clea was a child; she let it go. And life went on as ever. Clea was showing fairly regularly now, and Harley had supplanted Lynn as the central person in her life. She was obsessed with riding, it was the entire world to her. She wanted her own horse; she would board it at the farm. Emily had agreed, and Clea and Harley had been spending Saturdays traveling to local horse shows, looking for the right horse. Clea was neglecting her schoolwork, which upset Emily, but she managed to earn As without any work, so it was hard to criticize her. She was almost never home; she seemed to live at the Kelloggs'. She often ate with them, and on some Saturday nights, when she and Harley got back late, she would sleep in their guest bedroom. Their own daughters were long grown and gone, but Lynn told Emily on the phone that having Clea around was like having another daughter. The Kelloggs loved Clea, and she them.

Emily missed Clea when she was gone, but she was obsessed, too, with her symphony. She was having trouble with the final movement. She could not get it to sound as wrenched and awkward as she wanted, without *being* wrenched and awkward. She wanted the feeling of struggle she heard in Thelonious Monk's music: He often completed a phrase with a hard, smashed note that sounded wrong, repeated the phrase with another hard, smashed, wrong note, and went through this three or more times until finally, like the sun finally rising, he'd pause and hit the *right* note—the one that brought harmony, rest, what people now called closure. Hard-won peace was restored like the sun finally rising after many false starts, but purchased at a terrible price in strain. Every hour she was not teaching Emily had spent in her study, experimenting with sounds of struggle. She was in her study that Saturday in May when the doorbell rang.

Lynn Kellogg stood on the step. Emily had rarely seen Lynn since her wedding, although she occasionally ran into her at the post office or the grocery store. Emily saw in shock that she was old! But of course she was. So was Emily. Lynn must be in her midforties.

Overcoming her surprise, Emily invited Lynn in. She looked like a bag lady, Emily thought. Something was wrong with her. Was she ill? Her hair was ragged, her eyes were sunk in dark pockets, her cheeks sank in as if she were toothless. She did not smile.

She sat on the edge of a hard-backed chair in the living room. "I'm sorry, Emily," she began.

Emily frowned. "For what?"

"Barging in on you this way. Interrupting your day. Ruining your life," she added, bursting into tears.

Emily's heart stopped. Was something wrong with Clea?

Lynn blew her nose, wiped her eyes, stopped crying. "Well, I suppose it's only my life that's ruined."

In that instant, a world of knowledge passed through Emily's brain. By the time she could breathe again, she knew what Lynn had come to say.

"I know enough about you to know that what I have to tell you isn't going to make you happy. You've lived here all these many years, and not a single breath of scandal has ever crossed your name. Everyone knows you are a good upstanding Christian woman."

Emily's face reflected distress at this description, but Lynn did not notice.

"Your niece is having an affair with my husband!" she cried, exploding in tears again.

No. No. It could not be.

"No," Emily murmured.

Lynn was crying. Emily's body reverberated.

It was true. She knew it. How did she know it? And if she'd known it, why did she do nothing about it? *Did* she know it?

Occam's razor. Simplest explanation. It explained everything. Things she had not even thought to question.

"Yes!" Lynn shouted.

"Are you sure?" Emily asked stupidly.

"Of course I'm sure! Would I be here otherwise?"

Emily buried her face in her hands. Lynn barely noticed. She was crying, fishing in her bag for tissues, blowing her nose, crying again.

"Oh, that's terrible," Emily moaned.

"You aren't going to deny it?" Lynn cried. "You aren't going to ask me how I know? Did you know about it? Has she told you about it? Have you two been laughing at me behind my back?" In a spasm of rage, she shrieked, she pulled at her hair, she wept like a waterfall.

It occurred to Emily that in television dramas, people hugged people who were crying like this, but such a gesture went against her entire upbringing, and she could not make herself do it. She sat watching Lynn, an expression of pity on her face. As the woman calmed, Emily began to speak.

"No, of course not, Lynn. I had no idea. But when you said it—I just knew you were telling the truth. I hardly ever see Clea anymore, she's always at your place. I suddenly realized how possible it was that . . . But of course I did not know. I would not have permitted it. This is terrible, awful! She's only a child, Harley is a married man, it's statutory rape, you must know that! It's horrible!"

"Oh, so you're making out it's all *his* fault!"

"I think my niece is behaving immorally, Lynn, but Harley's behavior is shocking. My god, he's almost fifty years old, isn't he?"

"He's forty-five," she said sourly. "Two years younger than me, you don't need to remind me. But what did you expect, the way she tried to seduce him. Those eyes she made at him, the way she'd look at him so adoringly, what did you expect?" Lynn's tears were gone; in their place was a cold rage. "Little bitch!"

"Lynn, please don't talk about Clea that way. I understand your distress. I'm distressed too. But Harley is certainly the more responsible party: He *is* the adult! Clea is only sixteen, she'll be seventeen this month."

"She's a little snake! After all the time I gave her, all the attention I lavished on her, after all I did for her, she turns on me like this! I treated her as if she was my own daughter, she had a home with us, poor little orphan, I thought, stuck in a house with a dried-up old spinster, I fed her, I gave her a bed, I taught her to ride! I'll never forgive her, never forget this, ungrateful little bitch—"

"Lynn, stop! Or I'll have to ask you to leave!"

Lynn looked at her with narrowed eyes, an enemy ready to attack. "Don't you want to know how I found out about little Miss Butter-Won't-Melt-in-Her-Mouth?"

"Yes, but I want you to stop calling Clea names."

"They're off together. I suppose you know that. They went up to Saratoga early this morning."

"I know. I know they've been looking for a horse. I thought you usually went with them—"

"Hah! They don't want my company! They're probably in El Cheapo Motel by now!"

At the thought, Emily shuddered. Was Clea being subjected to such a demeaning experience? Could it be against her will? She was only a baby, missing her father. She adored Harley, who had taken advantage of her to soil her innocence . . . Terrible.

"They went off before I was even up this morning," Lynn continued, lighting a cigarette without asking permission. Emily did not have the heart to stop her. "Later in the day, I thought I'd give the tack room a good cleaning, vacuum it and stuff. That doesn't get done very often. And I found this!"

She pulled from her purse a pair of tiny underpants. She dangled them in front of Emily. They were pale lilac, with lace, and Emily knew they were Clea's. Clea loved fancy underwear. She had . . . for the last year, Emily realized. She grimaced.

"There's only one person around the farm these'd fit," said the substantially bodied Lynn. "Nancy is built like me, and the rest of the workers are boys. And there's only one way these pants got into my tack room!"

"We-ell," Emily said, her forehead crinkling, "that's not really proof, is it? Maybe she got dirty working there and took a shower. You have a shower stall there, don't you?"

"And *forgot* to put her underpants back on? Hah!" Lynn puffed furiously. Smoke rose, filling the room.

"There was a long dark hair on the pillow on the couch in the tack room. I go in there all the time, it had to be from yesterday, I had a dentist appointment yesterday and didn't work with the horses at all. So it was recent. But Harley's blond, well, blondish gray—and I'm gray, as you can see, and Nancy has brown hair and the guys have short hair. The only person around with long dark hair is Clea!" she concluded triumphantly.

Emily sat looking at her hands in her lap.

"I am so sorry, Lynn," she said miserably.

"What are you going to do about it, Emily Oldfield!"

Emily looked up. "I don't know. What are *you* going to do?"

"I'm going to throw that girl off my farm and throw her saddle after her. I'll not have her in my house again, or in my stables, or on my land! Let her rot in hell!"

"I see," Emily mumbled. "And Harley? What are you going to do about him? Are you going to turn him in to the police?"

Lynn paled. "He's my husband!" Her face wrinkled anxiously. "You wouldn't prosecute him!"

Emily felt like being cruel. "I don't know. When I know more about the situation, I'll decide. If I find he took advantage of an innocent child to amuse himself—"

"Well, I just want to tell you, if you do, I'll blacken your niece's name as far as Pittsfield, Emily Oldfield! I'll make sure she can't hold her head up anywhere in these mountains, Oldfield or not! Rossi-Oldfield!" she simpered. "Fancy-nancy! You know how big and spread out my family is, we're everywhere in this county, and I'll make sure she can never live here again!"

"You'll be blackening Harley's name even more," Emily said coldly, standing up. "I think you should leave now."

Lynn stood up also; despite her threats, she was a little intimidated by Emily Oldfield. "Are you?"

"What?"

"Going to prosecute?"

"I told you, I have to know more before I decide. I will let you know if I decide to do so. Now, please." She gestured toward the door. "Go. Take your cigarette with you. Don't leave the butt here."

Lynn shook ashes onto the rug and stomped to the door. She slammed it behind her, and stomped down the steps to the driveway, where her car sat. She drove off in a shriek of burning rubber.

Emily calmly opened the door and all the windows. She walked around with a large towel, waving it about. Her heart was beating calmly; her face was impassive; had she spoken, her voice would have been level. But her entire body was shaking.

17

Maddy dressed carefully in a long black dress with narrow gold trim at the neckline and cuff, a gold pendant, gold earrings, a diamond ring and one with an opal, both set in yellow gold. She dressed like this only once or twice a year, for great occasions, and she was nervous, wanting to get everything right. Charley came into the bedroom as she was finishing up, and threw his arms out: "Maddy, you're gorgeous!"

She harrumphed, but two tiny spots of pink appeared high on her cheeks. Charley was wearing a dinner jacket. Most people in Steventon did not dress so formally for a concert, but Maddy insisted that whenever they attended one of Emily's concerts, they dress up.

"We have to set the tone," Maddy explained. "People up here wear overalls to everything. They'd wear 'em to a wedding if they were let. We have to honor Em. Show 'em what's proper."

At first Charley had demurred—he was younger then, and stubborn. He gave in because Maddy was more stubborn than he, but he'd felt a fool dressing up, Mrs. Gold's pet ape. But when Maddy sailed into the theater in her finery looking like a proud old ocean liner that has perhaps been superseded by more technically efficient ships, but cannot be matched in class or luxury, she awed him, and made him happy to be beside her. Now he dressed up willingly.

The others—Alicia and Steven, Jenny and Tim—always followed Maddy in this, as long as they'd been going to the concerts, and the six of them had set the tone. These days many of the audience dressed similarly, which made the concerts a great occasion for the college.

"Don't forget the flowers!" Maddy called out to Charley as they left the house, and he darted back in, coming out with a wrapped bouquet. "We shouldn't bring up Parrish," she said, as they got in the car. "We don't want to upset Emily tonight."

Charley gave her a look. As if he were likely to bring up their personal problems with her friends. He barely talked to his own friends—except about this, of course; he might mention Parrish. But he knew Maddy was admonishing him to remind herself to repress her own emotions.

"I won't, don't worry, Mad. Have you heard from Jean?"

"Just what I told you this morning. They're sending him for a CT-scan. Trying to pinpoint where the tumor originated. They think it's the lung. All those years of smoking . . ." Her voice caught. "Oh, Charley," her voice broke, "He's only fifty!"

"He stopped smoking twenty-two years ago," Charley protested. "Doesn't that count?"

"I guess not." She pulled a hanky out of her evening bag and dabbed her cheeks. "Nothing off for good behavior in nature. And if it's the lung, it's already metastasized. Lung cancer is almost always fatal anyway. If it's metastasized . . ." Her voice caught again; she said loudly, "I'm not going to talk about it anymore! I don't want to think about it!"

Charley patted her hand, lying on the car seat beside her, and she grabbed at his, held it tightly. "Oh, Charley."

"Sweetheart, try to think positively," he urged.

"I know, I know," she muttered miserably. "I don't want to spoil

Emily's night." She raised her head high and pressed her lips together. "Talk to me. Tell me something cheerful."

He pondered. "I sold four hundred dollars' worth of stuff last month, Mad. Pretty damn good for that little ad I run, don't you think?"

"Amazing, Charley."

"Thinking maybe I'll branch out."

"Into what?"

"Joe Ball was telling me he knows where there's tons of snow equipment, going for a song. Shovels, ice scrapers, stuff like that."

"Umm. Good idea."

"Well, I'll look into it, anyway."

"Do that, dear."

"My brother Warren and Karen are going to Machu Picchu next month. Sounds pretty interesting. They go to the Galápagos Islands first. Where Darwin studied animal life. Might like to do that someday."

"Would you? Why don't we go with them?"

He turned swiftly. "Now?"

"Oh, no," she said hastily. "We can't go now. Not until . . . we know something more. Can't leave now."

"But we could go on our own sometime."

"If you want to, dear. They go to the islands on a boat, don't they? I wonder if you get seasick. Do you have to live on the boat? I wonder if it rocks a lot."

As Maddy pondered these questions, Charley saw the chances of their going on this journey recede. He smiled wryly. This always happened. Maddy was afraid of the unfamiliar. She had been terrified of everything when she was young; her father was such a terror. And her mother such a disapproving, judgmental woman. It was a wonder she was so sweet-natured. She'd gotten over most of her terrors over the years, but not of traveling. That one time they went to London and Paris, when he was made partner, it was a disaster. Tell the truth, he wasn't so crazy himself about being in a place where he didn't know the language. Even in England, well, he could read the signs, but as far as he was concerned, whatever the people spoke, it wasn't English—

he couldn't understand them. And that driving on the wrong side of the street! Not for him. He'd really rather watch a travel video of the Galápagos. Almost as good as going there. Neither of them was a very good traveler. They preferred the comforts of home.

Charley parked the Olds in the field near the campus theater, then helped Maddy out. "Oh, what a gentleman," she exclaimed, and a surge of contentment welled in his chest. He held her against him for a moment before they joined the crowd walking toward the hall.

•

Steven's smile of appreciation greeted Alicia as she entered the kitchen. "You look terrific, kid," he said, and when she replied that he looked pretty terrific himself, he preened a little. He had stayed thin and agile—from tennis—through the years, and wore his dinner jacket well. She had found an old emerald green chiffon at the back of her closet, bought for some New York function years ago, and not worn since. It flowed from her hips like water, making her every movement a sexy dance. She waltzed up to him and straightened his tie, then remained leaning against him for just a moment. She moved when they heard Stevie's footsteps in the hall. Both greeted their son with brilliant smiles. The family had had a long confrontation the night before and all day today and were feeling like a sore gum. They were exhausted, but relieved to be in harmony as a family for the first time in several years. Alicia and Steven were also full of a sense of virtue for having done the right thing and bringing it off—which one couldn't always count on.

Stevie was relieved to be back in his father's favor, and he loved his mother for her joy in that. Mostly, though, he felt a silent triumph at his father's admission of irrationality. Stevie, of course, had known since babyhood that his father was often irrational, but never expected him to confess to it. Besides, he had had four years of exile to mull over the situation and decide whether to forgive. He was pleased but distant—but then, he had always felt distant from his father. His father was a distant man; Stevie wondered how, being so aloof and superior, his father could help his patients. Yet Stevie had noticed a slight thaw in his father's treatment of Alicia, which gratified him for her sake. He had often wondered how his mother could love a man so supercilious. Maybe he was different in bed, Stevie thought, unable to twist his imagination around such a picture.

In any case, Stevie was, this evening, amenable to his mother's wish to attend a concert, have a pleasant evening, and show off her handsome son and their renewed family unity. Stevie had often heard Emily play and always enjoyed it, so he was not rebellious about it. But he missed Neil and wished he could have brought him. It was necessary to go through this alone, he knew; Neil would have been in the way of the shame-filled confessing, the raging and arguing and weeping that had filled the day and a half since Stevie had arrived; he would have been miserable.

Alicia picked up a cashmere shawl in green and gold paisley that blended with her dress, and a bunch of flowers that were standing in a bowl of water. She wrapped them in foil, then pink paper. She glanced at the kitchen clock. "Quarter past. I told Jenny we'd pick her up at 7:20. So let's go. Why don't you drive, Stevie?"

Steven's body jerked but he said nothing. Stevie knew his mother did not like his father's driving; she said he was unresponsive to other drivers and inconsiderate, but Steven always insisted on driving, even after he'd had a drink or two. The boy did not like being caught between them this way.

"Er . . . if you want, Dad," he said, diplomatically.

"Sure. It'll make your mother happy," he said, with only a little sarcasm.

"It will," she asserted unconditionally. Then she insisted that Steven sit in front with his son, taking the backseat herself. Stevie wondered what would have happened if Neil had been there; would his father have been relegated to the backseat? Stevie reminded himself that he was leaving tomorrow, and in his own car, while his father would go back in his Saab. Thank god, he thought. Even at best, this house was full of traps for him. He wondered idly if Mariette felt the same way.

"I wonder if Tim's back," Alicia said vaguely from exile.

Steven turned toward her. "Back from where?"

"Oh," Alicia paused, "he's been away for a while. In New York. On business. I'm not sure he's back."

"Is that why we're picking up Jenny?"

"Yes, dear," Alicia smiled.

Her smile had a self-satisfied edge. When she had offered Jenny a ride, she had been unsure what the emotional climate of her family would be that night, and a little worried about it. But things were fine . . .

She directed her son to Jenny's house. Stevie didn't really know Jenny, a relative newcomer: He had not been in Steventon for years. He'd met her once, he thought. "Pretty, blond, short?"

"Yes. Young."

"The difference in age isn't a problem for you guys?"

"Well, Tim's not so young," Steven answered, not realizing that Stevie's "guys" was a reference to his mother's friends. "He's my age or thereabouts. The women all like Jenny, don't they, Lish?"

"We love her. In a way, I suppose she's like a daughter to us, but she's had experiences we haven't. She's lived in New York, well, we did too, but she was in society, you know. And she's traveled more than we have, than I have, or Maddy. She's known a lot of famous people. She's bright. Just—she hasn't lived much, yet. So she's more cheerful, lighter hearted than we are. Which is nice for us."

Stevie hooted. "Mom, are you saying life is depressing?"

Her voice was low, resonant. "Well, it does tend to make you sad. It hurts. Don't you find that?"

There was utter silence in the car.

"All lives?" Stevie finally asked.

"Oh, forget I said it, Stevie," Alicia said with asperity. "Just forget it. It was stupid."

Steven turned to look at her, but said nothing.

"A cloud passed over the moon," she explained.

He turned back.

They reached Jenny's house. "This is where she lives?" Stevie asked in amazement. He whistled. "Some house."

"Yes. Tim designed it himself," Steven said with a little pride.

Alicia got out of the car and walked up to the door. She stood there for a moment until it opened. A figure stood outlined against the light, Alicia walked in, and the figure threw her arms about her.

The door closed. A minute later, both women emerged, Jenny pulling on a light shawl, a bunch of flowers drooping in her hand.

"Steven, hi. How nice of you to pick me up," she chirped as she got into the car. "I've never gotten used to driving these dark roads at night. I always forget to turn on my brights! I drive like an old woman, an inch at a time, always expecting the road to end," she laughed.

"How are you, Jenny? Good to see you. You remember my son, Stevie? Steven, I should say. He's a little big for a diminutive. How tall are you now, Stevie?"

"Six two," he said in a low voice. "Hi, Jenny." He reached out his hand to Jenny. "Most people call me Steve."

"Really? I hadn't realized," Steven said.

"Me neither," said Alicia. "I'll try to remember. Steve. I like it."

She would like it if it were Mohandrasagama, Steve thought, smiling.

"I wonder if Emily's real nervous," Jenny said nervously.

"She says she doesn't get too nervous before concerts."

"I don't believe it. When I was a girl, my father made me take piano lessons, and every time I had to perform in the school auditorium, my hands would get ice cold. I could hardly move them."

"They have warming gloves for that," Steven put in.

"I wish I'd known." Jenny laughed.

"So Tim's in New York?"

"Yes. Seeing his dealer."

"Where does he stay when he's in the city? Which hotel?" Steven wanted to know.

"We still have a little apartment there. Just two rooms, a pied-a-terre, you know. A kitchen he calls a cooking closet. He doesn't cook there. Although sometimes I think he'd cook if all he had was an open fire and a tin can."

"Tim's a gourmet cook," Steven told his son.

"Really? Neil is too. My partner," Steve explained to Jenny. "He doesn't have time to cook very often, he doesn't get home until late—he's a lawyer. Well, we both are. But when he does, it's a treat."

"Yes, I've found it's very nice to have a cook for a partner." Jenny laughed.

"Sure is. Where do we park, Mom? Are we close to where we're going?"

"No, not here. Drive on to the next field . . . yes, just here—turn right."

They got out and walked toward the theater, the two men together, the two women trailing them, talking in low voices.

"Not a word," Jenny was saying. "I can't get over it. What does he expect me to feel, or think?"

Alicia shook her head. "Awful."

"Is he leaving me? Is that what's happening? I refuse to call him. But I'm going to have to, soon. I'm running out of money."

Alicia laughed. "They always get you there," she said.

Jenny mused, "The hell he will," she said stubbornly. "I can use my own money. What I got for my picture. Why not? That's what it's for. I don't mean the bills on the house, they'd wipe out my little windfall in a week. But at least I can afford to buy myself food."

"Good for you!" The strong enthusiasm in Alicia's voice surprised Jenny.

They reached the theater and found Maddy and Charley, who had arrived earlier and had saved seats. Welcomes and kisses were shared all around.

"How beautiful you both look!" Maddy said to Jenny and Alicia. Jenny was also wearing black, a thin black sheath that, like a sundress, bared her shoulders. She had a beautiful shape, and it showed in this outfit. "You could be a model, Jenny," Maddy said. "And Stevie . . ."

"He's Steve, now, Mad," Alicia said.

"Of course." Maddy beamed at him. "How nice you look. How nice that you came."

"My pleasure," Steve said, kissing and hugging Maddy. "And a pleasure to see you."

They sat down again. "Have you seen Clea?" Maddy whispered to Alicia. "I've been looking, but haven't spotted her."

Alicia began to search the room, but the lights dimmed and a young woman entered and sat at the piano. The music began.

•

Alicia, nervous and anxious about her party, left the moment after the flowers had been delivered and Emily and her students had taken their final bow. Maddy and Jenny went with Alicia in her car, leaving the men to wait for Emily so they could accompany her in Charley's car.

Alicia had prepared all the food: She had hired Sean Schwartz to serve and clean up, so she had to get home to let him in, and to supervise putting out the food. There was so much work involved in giving a party. Of course, she told the women, she enjoyed it, since she didn't do it often. Sean was already at the house, waiting.

"Hello, honey," Alicia said, "have you been here long?"

"Just got here." The young man smiled. They kissed hello.

"How's your mother?"

"Sends her love. She'll be here after the concert."

Alicia unlocked the door. "Come in. You know Ms. Halliday, don't you? And Ms. Gold?"

"Sure thing. Hi, Jenny! How've you been? How do you do, Ms. Gold?"

He and Jenny high-fived each other; Maddy smiled hello and gave him an curious glance. "I hear you've got a new job."

"Yeah. Sous-chef at Gleason House. But only on weekends."

"Still . . ."

"Sure, it's something."

Alicia led the young man into the dining room and explained what he was to do. The other women, in the kitchen, opened the refrigerator and pulled out everything that looked like party food. They were buzzing excitedly.

"Did you see her? Are you sure?"

"Lish, you want butter on the table?"

"Well, it looked like her. But it's been so long—I can't be sure. She said she'd come, didn't she?"

"Yes, thanks, I'll give you a plate for it."

"How about this pasta salad? Should it go in this bowl?"

"But who was that she was with?" Jenny asked, sounding awed. "So elegant!"

"No, use this one. Thanks, Maddy."

"That black woman? I don't know."

"This roast beef looks delicious. And the platter is beautiful! Is it an antique? Where did you find it?"

"She was stunning!" Jenny declared.

"Thanks. I like it too. I bought it at that little antique store near the copper place. A hundred years ago, though. They don't have such nice things there anymore."

"Roast beef too? There are meatballs . . ."

"And a platter of chicken, and a salmon mousse. And a platter of grilled vegetables."

"You could feed an army!"

"She certainly was," Alicia agreed. "And if that was Clea, she was pretty stunning herself. A far cry from the way she looked last time I saw her."

"She was pregnant then, wasn't she?"

"Jenny, could you put this bread in that basket?"

"Sure."

"No. The baby had just been born. But she was, you know, sad, and alone, and on the outs with the world . . . Not in the best shape."

"Did you grill these veggies yourself?"

"Yes, it's not hard. Just brush on a little olive oil and put them under the broiler."

"Yes, after you've spent three hours cutting them up!" Maddy said sourly.

"That's true," Alicia laughed.

Sean's handsome face appeared among them. "I've laid out all the plates and napkins and flatware, Ms. Gilson. What would you like me to do now?"

"Oh! A lot of appetizers need to be put out in the living room. On the cocktail table, okay? Or any other available table." She reached deep into the refrigerator and pulled out containers of olives, baba ghanoush, cheeses wrapped in plastic. "There are crackers on the counter over there. And, oh, Sean! There's a whole salmon on a big oval platter in the refrigerator in the garage. Will you get it and put it in the center of the table? And there are drinks in there too, wine and beer and seltzer . . ."

"Sure thing, Ms. Gilson," said the young man, and went.

"But if it was Clea, don't you think she would have come up and said hello? At intermission?"

"Maybe she felt funny . . ."

"Why would she?"

"When did you see her last?"

"Let's see . . . she went away to college in '83 or '84 . . ."

"Shall we put the desserts on the sideboard? The table is full."

"Great."

"It was 1983. The year Benjamin won his letter."

"And she had finished her sophomore year . . ."

"So, 1985."

"And that summer she met Kevin . . ."

"Cookies too? Three cakes and cookies too?"

"Oh, don't forget the cheesecake."

"My god, how many people are you expecting?

"And got pregnant."

"So she had the baby in 1986."

"About forty. Maybe more. I invited the music department, all the students and some of the administration, and all our friends. I wanted them to honor Emily as she deserves."

"So. Fourteen years ago."

"Fourteen years! You haven't seen her in fourteen years!" Jenny was flabbergasted. "Has Emily?"

"They should be here soon, no?"

Maddy shook her head. "It was a pretty bad break."

"I guess so! What caused it?"

"Well, you know, there's always a long line of people waiting to congratulate the musicians. And there were a lot of musicians. Wasn't Emily's trio wonderful?"

All activity stopped. Unconsciously, the women had formed a circle.

"It was great!" Jenny said.

"I loved it!" Maddy agreed.

"I was amazed! So beautiful and so strong and so new! At least, it seemed new to me."

"She's a wonder."

"She's a genius," Maddy assured them.

"I think you're right," said Alicia.

The circle broke up.

"She loved the flowers," Jenny said, "didn't she?"

"Oh, she did. And there were so many!"

"Yes, that was great!"

"The pregnancy. It was the pregnancy that caused it. That time. There'd been trouble off and on . . ."

They returned to fetching and placing and rearranging. "Is Emily that . . . puritanical?" Jenny asked hesitantly.

They all stopped again, looking at her.

"Oh! I see what you mean," Alicia said, nodding her head. "No! It wasn't that she got pregnant. It was that she insisted on having it. Emily wanted her to have an abortion. She wanted her to finish college and have a career. Clea was so bright! But she insisted on quitting school and keeping the baby. Emily couldn't bear it. She couldn't understand how Clea could throw away her life. That's how she saw it."

"Especially when it turned out Clea didn't want the man, just the baby," Maddy added.

They all laughed. "How times have changed!" Maddy said, almost to herself, shaking her head.

"Emily threw her out?" Jenny asked incredulously.

"Oh, of course not. She finally accepted what Clea wanted. She planned to take care of Clea and the baby, to keep them there at her house . . ."

"But Clea had means. You know, an inheritance. She was rich in her own right. Rich kids can do what they want, you know? And she was angry with Emily. Angry at her opposition, and at other things that had happened earlier . . ."

"What?"

Maddy shrugged. "Oh, just stuff that happens, you know. When a kid grows up. She felt Emily had bad feelings about her."

"And did she?"

Maddy stood stock still. "Maybe. Maybe a little."

"So she left."

"With the baby. Broke Emily's heart. Because, of course, once the baby was born . . .well, you know how it is with babies. One sight of them and you're lost—in love—forever."

"And she never came back!"

Maddy shook her head. "Guess she was really angry. Or maybe it was more than that. I don't know. I'm not privy to Clea's feelings. But whenever Emily called her, she was cold and brusque, didn't seem to want to talk. Eventually, Em stopped calling."

"How terrible!" Jenny's pale face seemed to be facing a world full of people who went off without a word. "How cruel."

"Well, she was just a kid, you know. Unsure of herself. And maybe it was harder being a mother alone than she'd thought it would be. And maybe she didn't want to admit Emily was right."

"So how old is the baby now? Was it a boy or a girl?"

"A girl. Fourteen, no?"

"Well, she must have been there, then. Did you see her?"

Alicia and Maddy both dropped everything and gathered around Jenny.

"No!"

"She was there?"

"There was a teenage girl with them. She looked older than fourteen but . . . she had long straight dark hair. She was very beautiful. You didn't notice her?"

"I didn't see them at all," Alicia confessed with irritation. "I'm so blind."

"I wasn't sure. It could have been Clea that I saw. But the last time I saw Clea she was twenty. There was this . . . mature woman . . ." Maddy faltered.

"Well, Emily's shown me pictures of Clea. I thought this woman looked like her."

"You have that artist's eye. You can see resemblances . . ."

"Maybe . . ."

The front doorbell rang; people began to arrive. Alicia ran to greet her guests; Maddy and Jenny trailed behind her to offer second greetings, deserting the kitchen, which was empty when the door from the garage to the kitchen opened and Emily walked in, Charley and Steven behind her. Jenny, in the foyer behind the other women, heard them, turned and saw them, and called Alicia. Immediately the women rushed to Emily, hugged and kissed her, crowing, congratulating, praising, blessing. Emily's smile was brilliant. The men, standing around, looked a little uneasy. Steven took Alicia by the arm and whispered.

"Clea was in the car behind us. She followed us over. Did you know she was coming?"

"We hoped. We weren't sure."

The garage door opened again and three women slowly entered. The women in the kitchen stood gazing at them in silence. First was a woman in her thirties, with short dark hair and beautiful skin, dressed in dark pants and a short jacket over a gray turtlenecked sweater. Behind her was a girl who looked seventeen or eighteen, slender and dark, with long straight hair, in jeans. And finally, an exquisite dark-skinned woman with a long neck, her hair in a short Afro, wearing a brilliant dashiki. Emily smiled at them with tears in her eyes. She took the arm of the thirty-year-old and led her forward.

"Clea, you remember Maddy and Alicia. My friends."

"Her friends too," Alicia said, stepping forward to embrace her. Clea clung to her for a long time, her face buried in Alicia's hair.

Maddy stepped up. "Hiya, sweetheart," she said and grabbed the woman. Clea grinned. "Hiya, Maddy, you are just the same!"

"And this is our newest friend, Jenny."

Jenny stepped forward. "I've heard so much about you!"

Clea rolled her eyes. "Oh, God forbid!"

The women laughed at the old-fashioned expression, but Jenny cried, "Oh, it was all wonderful!" and stepped forward to embrace her. Clea returned the embrace, saying, "Hey, you're around my age. What are you doing with these old fogies?"

Everyone laughed.

"I love these old fogies!" Jenny cried. "They're my best friends."

"I'm just jealous," Clea said. "I know what kind of friends they can be."

"And of course you remember Mr. Gold and Dr. Gilson, and Steve Gilson . . ."

"We said hello at the concert. While we were waiting for Emily. She had a zillion people lined up to congratulate her. As she should! I recognized them. They haven't changed much," Clea said, "except Steve."

"Yeah. I remember you too. Especially that time we went skiing."

Clea laughed wholeheartedly. "Did you go down! We were really lucky you didn't break something! But you looked so funny! I'll never forget it! And then we all followed you! One big heap of us!"

Clea recovered herself.

"Oh! Everybody! I want you to meet my daughter, Martine."

The pink-faced young woman smiled shyly at them, revealing braces. "Hi, everybody. Mom's told me all about you."

The women were on her in an instant, shrieking with wonder, "You're so tall, so grown up for fourteen"—embracing, complimenting—"so lovely, such gorgeous skin, just like your mother's, such beautiful hair." Steven walked toward the counter, rolling his eyes.

"And this," Clea said, making it sound as if she'd saved the best for last, "is my partner, Hallie."

Again the chorus of women went into action, embracing Hallie, telling her how lovely she was, how statuesque, how gorgeous her apparel, and soon the lips of the somewhat distant woman were trembling on the brink of a smile, then smiling, then she was beaming; then she was embracing them back. Very gradually the group dispersed and was swallowed up by the party, which went on for hours and ended—after most people had left, around one in the morning—with the women dancing, then standing in a circle clapping and howling with laughter while Maddy did the flamenco by herself, spinning dramatically in the center of the room.

18

For several weeks afterward, the women spoke of little else but the concert, the party, Clea and Martine and Hallie. The relationships that had emerged or changed were to them major events, as momentous as the end of a war and the conditions of the peace treaty. They filled their airwaves, telephonic and personal, with delightful, not terrifying, matter. Wasn't it wonderful, they asked each other repeatedly, that Steven had accepted Steve's sexuality and reconciled with him? That Clea had forgiven Emily, at least enough to attend her concert and stay at her house overnight? Was it not miraculous that these people were again in communication with each other instead of in exile? And was that Hallie not extraordinary? Gorgeous and brilliant, a physician! So impressive. And wasn't it wonderful that she and Clea worked together in the women's clinic, that they had founded it together! Two gorgeous women who were so good, saints even. They made the women proud. And for six years they had lived together, together raised Martine, who was a darling girl, wasn't she? Adorable and sweet and shy. Those cute braces on her teeth, how darling! What a surprise that Clea would turn out to love women: Did men's behavior turn her against them, do you think? Or was her inclination always there but concealed?

Jenny, having learned the full story at last, suggested that maybe Clea had turned to women because every time she got involved with a man, she got in trouble. They laughed, but wondered if there was anything to it. Could Emily have a bias against men? No, they concluded—she had loved her father. Their understanding of homosexuality was based entirely on observation of relatives, neighbors, and friends over the years, which is to say it was not scientific. But Alicia said there was no scientific knowledge of homosexuality, just prejudice disguised as fact, and they believed her. She claimed that sexual preference was inborn, and immutable, basing that on her observation of her son. But Jenny, remembering certain woman friends, thought it varied. You could be one thing, then another, or even both at once. Some people could, anyway. They all nodded, having known similar cases. In the end, they agreed that they knew nothing, and that it didn't matter. People were what they said they were, for the time being, anyway. Anyway, Clea and Hallie seemed beautifully attuned to each other, and Martine seemed to love both of them. The women approved. With whole hearts.

Life remained imperfect, of course: Steven had accepted Steve, but now he had to accept Neil, and the men had to learn to speak to each other. Emily and Clea still had much to discuss. Doors had been opened but people still had to find a way to sit together in the same space. Only one door seemed closed—that between Jenny and Tim; and that worried all of them. But they didn't harp on it. They called Jenny regularly, as always, without mentioning Tim. They knew she would tell them if anything new happened. The other dark spots in their Eden—Emily's obscurity as a composer, Jenny's uncertainty about parenthood, and above all, Parrish's lung cancer—were not subject to their control. That was engraved on all their psyches.

•

Emily and Clea had not had time, the night of the concert, to do much more than embrace each other with trembling lips, tears spilling down Emily's cheeks when she met Martine and realized she'd missed Martine's entire childhood. But when Clea and Hallie drove Emily back to the Oldfield house that night after the party, and she asked if they wouldn't stay with her overnight, they quickly agreed, laughing.

"I don't know what we would have done if you hadn't asked," Clea said.

"It's past two, and our budget doesn't run to motels," Hallie said, smiling. "Not that I think there are any hereabouts."

"Besides, I want to see your house," Martine offered. "Mommy says it's fabulous."

"She does?" Emily's head twisted swiftly. "She didn't think that when she first saw it."

"No. Mommy was a spoiled California brat when she first saw it, and didn't know how to appreciate beauty, only the Hollywood version of it," Clea remarked.

"The truth is, Martine, Mommy was in a state of shock when she first saw it. She was a little girl, younger than you, who had just had a terrible, terrible shock. She had lost both her parents in one instant, was suddenly transported to a strange new world, and was holding herself together with great courage," Emily corrected her.

The three guests stood behind the car during this exchange, in a circle around Emily as if she were offering the true gospel to a crowd of believers. They fished their overnight cases out of the trunk, and headed for the house. Out of habit, Clea had parked in back, and they went in through the kitchen door.

After Clea and Emily showed the house to Martine and Hallie, they settled down in the kitchen. Hallie stretched out on the daybed, Clea in the rocker, Emily in the old cushioned armchair her father always sat in. Martine sat on a kitchen chair until Emily nodded at her, patted the wide cushion of the armchair and summoned her with her head. Martine leaped up, went to sit beside Emily, and soon leaned her head against her great-aunt's chest. Drinking icy seltzer, they talked.

Emily was deeply impressed by Hallie. In Emily's family, as in so many others, becoming a physician was considered the height of success. And she knew, she told Hallie, what kinds of obstacles are put in the way of women who aspire to professions men long ago took over as their own.

"Yes," Hallie agreed vaguely.

"And isn't it true," Emily urged, "that women were the healers in the very beginning, for millennia, until men decided to exclude them? Men began to require licenses for certain kinds of work. They built schools, requiring education for the licenses, but refused to admit women to the schools. When this did not suffice, they ran witch hunts and burned them."

Hallie agreed, but without passion, seemingly uninterested. Yes, she said, once upon a time, men had tried to keep women out of everything. And yes, med school and interning had been a bitch, because of the way men treat women, but also because of the whole tone, the rigid hierarchy of medical schools and hospitals, the long hours, the difficulty of the work. But she was finished with all that and preferred to forget it. "I have to say, my best teachers were men, and men have helped me all along the way. And now I work with women, our clinic is almost entirely staffed by women, most of our patients are women. And when I do have to deal with men, they treat me with respect. Things have changed, Emily. They have to be nice if they want me to refer patients to them. Anyway, they're a new generation of male."

"Our biggest enemies are the insurance companies, and there, we deal with women as often as men," Clea said. "Petty officials with veto power. How we hate them."

"Especially because we are trying mainly to help poor women," Hallie put in, "for their sake and the sake of their children. They need decent care, timely. Among poor women, serious illnesses like kidney trouble, breast cancer, uterine cancer, ovarian cancer, are often diagnosed too late to be cured. They walk around for years with diabetes, sickle-cell anemia, and heart problems, feeling lousy but not getting help. It makes us crazy. Poor women don't get prenatal care—vitamins, calcium, tests for various diseases—and poor children are often underweight, with severe disabilities, and sometimes even worse, addicted to heroin or crack, with AIDS."

"Oh," Emily said faintly. "That's so hard."

"I feel like a missionary, you know?" Hallie said. "Like someone standing on a street corner holding up a big sign urging them to accept not Jesus, but health! All I need is a Salvation Army band and a Bible!" she laughed. "I beg them, please come in and let me help you! Their kids would be healthier—especially the women with AIDS, there are drugs now to help their fetuses—but try to get them to come in! Women with tuberculosis, well, you know what's been happening with TB, it's developed strains impervious to our medicines. Clea's been brilliant about this, she's had these catchy ads put together and pasted them up in places where our kind of women will see them—street corners, buses, bus stops, any standing object near social services buildings . . ."

Clea laughed. "It took some imagination, believe me. But Raneesha, my assistant, is a terrific help there. She knows exactly where those women go! And," glancing at Martine, "Martine helps me put them up. On a Saturday afternoon we go around town and sneak them on walls and posts and ask storekeepers to take them . . ."

Martine giggled, covering her mouth.

"People aren't too eager to have posters on their walls," Clea grinned. "But I'm an old hand at breaking rules."

"You're the original rule breaker," Emily laughed.

"But on the buses you have to get permission. They like to sell their space, not give it away. If I put them on the bus doors, they're torn down the same day. But the bus-authority people have some social conscience. They let us put ads in a few buses. Some organizations help us."

"Our clinic's grown hugely in the past ten years," Hallie offered. "We started out seeing twenty to forty patients a week; now we see four hundred."

"We're aiming for a thousand. We figure we have the space to grow that much. Our offices are in a cheap part of town; we don't have much but we do have space."

"For a long time, that was all we had." Hallie laughed.

"Yeah. Our equipment sucked."

"They didn't even have an EKG machine," Martine put in, for a moment forgetting herself. "Some clinic!"

Emily caught a flash of silver: braces. The child was self-conscious. She leaned over and kissed the girl on the cheek.

"Hell, we didn't even have antiseptic. We had to beg, borrow, and steal."

"Mommy bought stuff herself. Out of her own money."

"Well, I had the money. And I figured Mom and Dad would have approved."

"They certainly would," Emily said, impressed. "You're wonderful, you girls. You women," she corrected herself.

Hallie stood up. "Well this woman is about to collapse. I got up at five this morning, and I need toothpicks to keep my eyes open. Do you mind if I cop out?" she asked Clea.

"Of course not, sweetheart," Clea said, reaching toward her. They kissed lightly, then Hallie bent and kissed Emily's cheek. "I'm so happy, I can't tell you, to meet you after all this time. And your concert was amazing. I'll see you in the morning." She patted Martine's cheek. "You look as tired as I feel, honey. Why don't you come up with me?"

Martine kissed Emily good night, clinging to her a little, then kissed her mother, said "Night, Mom," and went up holding Hallie's hand.

•

Silence fell in the kitchen. Emily's mind drifted to the silences between her parents in the days before her father was caught out, the night upon night of silent rage.

"I can't tell you how happy I am to see you," she said.

Clea got up, went to Emily, and embraced her. "I'm sorry it's been so long."

Emily looked at her with an expression of longing on her face. Why, she wanted to ask. But stayed silent.

Clea returned her look, mute. She crouched on the floor in front of Emily, lightly holding Emily's hands. They remained in this position, speechless, for some time.

Finally, Clea's voice, gravelly and breaking, like a hard-bowed cello, sounded in Emily's ear. "One day. Some day. We'll talk about it. Be able to talk about it.

Emily nodded in acquiescence. She felt unable to demand more. They embraced and went upstairs to bed.

•

The next afternoon, after a late breakfast of waffles and sausages (how could Emily forget a child's favorite meal?) Clea and Hallie packed the car and prepared to leave. Emily didn't want to let Clea go, she held her hands and embraced her as Hallie put their bags in the car; Martine was still at the Archibalds' visiting with the goats. "I wish you could stay longer."

"Yeah. But the clinic—you know."

"It's too bad you live so far from here."

"Would you like me to come up for a weekend?"

Emily's face opened and shone. "Could you? I'd love it!"

"Sure. Hallie will enjoy a weekend alone. And Martine's no problem. She has so many friends, she's out all the time anyway. I'll work it out and call you. I'll come up on a Friday night and leave Sunday afternoon. Okay?"

"Oh, Clea!" Emily hugged her. "That would make me so happy! I'll cook dinner, so we can just stay home and talk. If you don't mind," she added, laughing. "You remember my cooking."

"You made a good lamb stew. And that dish you called boiled chicken was good. You should just change the name; it sounds awful. You cooked better than my mother. Whenever our maids were sick, we had pasta. It was the only thing my mother knew how to cook. She did that well, though—al dente, not mush. And a light sauce. Lightly applied. My father couldn't cook at all. I don't know what was wrong with him. He says his mother wouldn't let him in the kitchen. Hallie's son is a great cook. When he's visiting, we eat like royalty. There's Martine. We have to go. See ya," she said, kissing Emily one last time.

Emily stood on the porch waving at the departing car and was still standing there after it had turned onto the road and disappeared.

•

For weeks afterward, the women praised Alicia for the wonderful food, the variety, the bounty of it, the hard work (which they fully appreciated) and planning, the beauty of the many spread tables. And the smoothness and efficiency of it all. Alicia was gratified. She understood that her friends would have thanked her if the food had been mediocre, scanty, or had been served haphazardly. But their praise of her was extravagant, generous, felt: She could feel that they meant it, and knew it was deserved.

She understood the function of praise among them. They had been lovely at thirty, yet never called beautiful; now, in their fifties, or seventies, they called each other beautiful. And saw beauty in each other. They sought and seized on special qualities in every man or woman they met, they lingered over, caressed, people they sensed needed something. Everyone was singled out and made much of, for reasons they shared without speaking: Everyone deserved it, everyone needed it, and the women were full of love and wanted to embrace others. Praise made their social world an enchanted place, where people who had reached an age at which dancing was difficult could dance in their spirits. They made each other feel accepted, at home, wanted. Facts were important, but less so than feelings. Each person who walked in the door had something special: a new tie, a beautiful shirt, a new hairdo, glowing eyes or skin; it was important to embroider upon it. A stranger, especially one who was cold hearted or cold-eyed, might suspect hypocrisy, but hypocrisy had nothing to do with this world where language was used to create a bond, a sense of community, a loving embrace in the face of what was never mentioned but which they all knew as a huge black sky, a cosmos of encompassing cruelty and indifference, the shining malevolence of the stars, the cold malevolence of an indifferent ocean. None of them had escaped being slapped down by that malevolence: wounded, cut, maimed, drowned, frozen. But they had survived the slapping down, and they knew that what mattered was not what was lost but what was left, and what they could make of it.

•

One of the people who had attended Emily's concert, who came up and stood on line to shake her hand afterward, was Andrei Sikorsky, who for years had conducted the Accademia orchestra in Kiev. Since the fall of the USSR, he had guest-conducted European orchestras and was now visiting the United States. He was trying to build an

American reputation. He introduced himself to Emily, praising her. He loved the *Eros* Trio, he said. It was original, delicate, moving, passionate, strong. And her other work? Was it like that? He would like to hear or see more. What could she offer him? She had recorded nothing for orchestra, she told him, although she was working on a symphony. She had tapes of college concerts, herself playing her own works on the piano, and of her students, performing a cello sonata, a flute sonata, and a work for flute, oboe, clarinet, and guitar. She had the score of an opera; two movements of a symphony. She could have them copied and sent to him. He asked that she do so, and gave her his New York address.

This small overture left her with a fluttering heart and trembling hands—at least for a few days. Then she forgot about it. One good thing about age, she thought, was the way things faded. She did not remain stuck on the horn of a quarter moon, dangling in space. She took a nap and it vanished from memory. Jenny and Alicia, however, did not forget about it. They called regularly, asking for news, and only stopped when, after some months, she still had heard nothing from Andrei. They stopped, not because they had lost interest or hope, but because they feared upsetting Emily.

•

Jenny had her own problems. On a gorgeous morning in June, the garden bursting with color and life, Tim called.

"Jenny, luv, it's me."

She was speechless.

"Jenny?"

"Tim? It's you? Where are you?"

"New York. Our place. Listen. Do you want me to come home?"

"I think the question is, Do you want to come home? I didn't ask you to leave."

"I think we should talk."

"I see. After two months, you think we should talk."

"If you don't want me to come, just say so. You don't have to be sarcastic."

"Sarcasm seems to me the only response to someone who ran away from conflict two months ago and hasn't made a peep since.

Pretty cowardly, it seems to me. Pretty adolescent for a grown man."

"All right, Jenny! Never mind! I'm sorry I called!" The phone crashed in her ear.

She wept, castigating herself.

But he did come home the next day, driving up to the house around noon. From her studio she heard a car door slam and recognized it as the sound of the Mercedes, a sound that, in the past, had raised her spirits. Today, she felt only dread. She had been trying to find the right composition for the painting she was working on, but in an irritated, impatient frame of mind, hated everything she had done. At the sound of the car, she raised her charcoal from the paper, but remained where she was, sitting cross-legged on the floor. The door to her studio soon opened, and Tim stood there. She knew that would be the important moment, and blanked out her mind so she would be sure to feel her body. She turned and saw him . . . and felt a frisson of pleasure, a wavelet of desire. Only a little; but it was pleasure, not indifference or anger. Sometimes you don't know what you feel until you feel it. She had feared she would feel nothing, or would feel rage or at worst, indifference. She stared at a face she knew she loved.

"Hello, Tim."

"Hello, luv," he said, sheepishly. He took a step into the room. "I have been a chimpanzee's asshole," he confessed.

She stood up, wiping her charcoal-blackened hands on a towel. "Don't insult animals. Especially chimps." She took a deep breath. "You want some tea?"

"Love some."

As she passed in front of him to walk through the doorway, he touched her arm, but she evaded his touch and kept walking. She loved him, yes, she wanted to embrace him, to weep on his chest, but she would not let herself. You cannot hold yourself cheap, she reminded herself. Something has to be settled between us—exactly what, though, she didn't know.

She prepared tea in the kitchen and put it on a tray with some little cakes. "Will you carry this out to the porch?"

Her territory. Her porch.

She sat on the chaise, he in the rocker; they sipped tea and took tiny bites out of the cakes. They gazed out at the life that surrounded them, the greens of the trees, the movement of birds, the brilliance of the flowers. They were silent.

Tim finished his cake and wiped his fingers on his napkin. He set his teacup down on the table. He cleared his throat. "I don't think I know how to explain it."

"I wish you'd try."

He gave a small sigh of exasperation. "I can't read you. Are you at all glad to see me?"

"Did you expect me to fall to my knees with gratitude that you've deigned to return? You've been gone almost two months. What do you think I've felt during that time? You left without a word, without an argument, without any reason. Without a word for two months."

"You're exaggerating. It wasn't two months."

She gave him a look.

"It's been six and a half weeks."

"Oh, a gross exaggeration! Sorry."

He shook his head, dismissing it.

"It isn't up to me to say anything," Jenny said, "It's up to you: to explain why you left and why you came back. Both are utterly mysterious to me."

"Jenny, luv, you know why I went."

"I do not. I know I said something that hurt you, or angered you, or whatever it did. But I also know you acted in a way that upset me. You refused to deal with either; you just left."

He sighed. "You're right. I couldn't deal with it. Any of it. It was so awful, what you said. Yet . . . I recognized some kind of rightness in it. Which was what I couldn't stand. I remembered how we were years ago, the bully boys—if any women were present. I vaguely remembered that we treated them—well, like unnecessary appurtenances." He looked at her imploringly. "We never meant any harm. We were just being bad boys, you know. We acted the way we thought bad boys acted. The way we thought women expected us to act. We were *artists* together . . ."

"Adolescents. I understand."

"The women accepted it, usually. Sometimes a girl would leave . . . or pass out."

"They expected no better."

"Probably," he admitted, lowering his eyes. "I'm ashamed of myself, if that makes you feel any better."

"It does."

"You think I should be ashamed of myself."

"For the way you have regularly treated women, yes. For the way you treated me, I expect more than shame."

"Yes." He put his hand on his forehead. "I didn't realize, you see."

She just looked at him.

"I didn't know we were doing that. Treating you badly. We were drunk, Jenny!"

"And that means . . ."

"We were just being silly . . . I had no idea you felt . . . I didn't really know they were making moves on you. I didn't know it at all. I would've smashed them! Really!"

"You saw it. You saw Ippolyte . . ."

"Maybe I was looking, but I didn't see. And do you think they'd consciously make a move on you, on my wife, if they weren't drunk out of their minds?"

"Probably not. But they were, and they did."

He laid his head in his hands. "Oh, god. What can I say?"

"Not much. You've taught me that I can't count on you to be there for me when you're drunk. I have to watch out for myself. I have to be willing to insult your friends. And if I drink—even in my own house—I have to remember I might as well be in some bar in Providence, surrounded by predators waiting to leap on me. I was thinking, that night, that I had no place to go. No room of my own with a lock on the door. There was my studio, but one of them was using it . . ."

He lifted his head. "Oh, god . . ."

"Even our bed wasn't safe. I was sleeping in it when Ippolyte came and joined me. And he was too heavy for me to push him out. I had to come out here to the porch. It was freezing cold . . ."

"Oh, Jenny. Jesus, I'm sorry."

"That was bad. But it wasn't the worst. The worst is that you got angry with me for telling you. Angry enough to punish me by leaving."

"That's not what I was doing! I was just so upset!"

"And I wasn't?"

"Oh," he murmured, rocking, his head in his hand, his eyes downcast.

"So what's your excuse for leaving?"

"I couldn't deal with it. I couldn't deal with your anger, and I couldn't deal with my own. I was angry as hell at your—well, you essentially said I was pimping for you . . ."

"I didn't essentially say that. I said that."

"Well, yes. It infuriated me."

"So you punished me."

He was silent for a long time.

"You can't admit that?"

He raised his head and looked at her. "I guess you must be right. I didn't think of it that way. But maybe that's what I was doing."

"I'm not allowed to get angry with you?"

"It's not that . . ."

"What is it then?"

"Listen, Jenny. What can I do? I want to make amends. What can I do?"

"Am I not allowed to get angry with you?" she persisted.

He slammed his hand down on the wooden arm of the rocker. "No! All right! If you insist on fighting, we'll fight! No! I don't like you to get angry with me! Is there something strange about that?"

"What I want to know is, if I should get angry with you again, are you going to take off for foreign places?"

"I don't know! How do I know what I'll do on some hypothetical occasion about some hypothetical problem?"

"I want you to recognize there are two problems here. One is the way you feel about women in general . . ."

He groaned. "Jesus, are you going to turn this into some feminist discussion of principle?"

" . . . and me in particular. The second is the way you act when we're in conflict."

"You seem to have thought this out all nice and neatly. I suppose you had help from your women friends? Is one of them a shrink or something? Seems unlikely," he muttered. "Such a bunch of old hags."

Jenny's heart stopped. She could not speak.

He looked at her and paused.

"Sorry, Jen. But they are, you know. Well, Alicia's not bad. But the other two . . ."

"Alicia's younger than you are, Tim," she said softly.

He looked away.

"I thought you liked my friends."

"They're all right. For a bunch of old hags."

Jenny stood up.

"Where are you going?"

"Inside."

"You're ending this discussion?"

"I don't feel I have anything more to say."

"Because I insulted your friends? Christ, I didn't mean anything. They are old. You have to admit they're no glamour girls."

"To me they're beautiful." Her cheeks were wet.

"Oh, Jesus," he muttered, shaking his head.

"And your friends are Adonises?" she asked sharply.

"My friends! . . . You don't judge men that way! . . . They're great artists, Jenny, famous, world famous!"

"And my friends are great human beings."

He sighed deeply. "I'm sorry," he said in exasperation.

Jenny sat down again.

He came over and crouched in front of her. He took her hands in his.

"Jenny, I apologize. I'm crude, a boor, I've been insensitive. I won't do it again. I swear."

She raised her eyes to him, but her face drooped. "We just don't think alike at all."

"I shouldn't drink. I don't handle it well. Clare . . . she always got angry when I drank. That's why I asked if you could accept the drinking, I knew we'd get drunk and act up, it's always been that way. I didn't want you to get mad the way Clare always did. It happened more often years ago. We saw each other more when they lived in New York, before they went off to exile . . ."

Jenny looked at him but said nothing.

"I won't ask them here again. When I want to see them, I'll go into the city. I'll stay with one of them. I won't expose you to such shit again . . ."

"And you won't play power games again?" she asked sadly.

He dropped her hands. "*That's NOT WHAT I WAS doing!*"

She looked at him.

"I wasn't playing a power game!"

She said nothing.

"I can't fight," he said falteringly. "I just can't. Not with you. Right now, I'm not fighting with you. I can't. I couldn't defend myself, so I had to go away."

Jenny looked at him unbelievingly.

"What would have happened if we'd had a serious talk?"

"I couldn't. I can't speak when I'm upset."

"Angry, you mean."

He shut down. His lips pressed together. After a time, he said, "When I was younger, when I was married to Clare, I used to smash things. I smashed furniture, bottles, I wrecked every vase in the house. She used to say it was a good thing I didn't paint still lifes." He grinned appealingly.

She wondered if he thought he was cute. She wanted to ask him, but didn't dare. What would happen if she did? He was looking at her like some naughty boy caught in mid-act, his face turned sideways, his eyebrows raised in appeal, his mouth a near smile.

Please, Tim, don't, she thought.

He reached his hand out to her. She did not take it.

Don't destroy all my respect for you.

He sulked. He pulled himself up, sat back in the chair. "Well, you want me to stay or not? I can go back. I was staying at Ippolyte's. He has a loft now, in Chelsea."

"That's why you look so puffy."

"Puffy? Do I?"

"Sure. Look at yourself in the mirror. You must've gained ten pounds."

He leaped up and ran to the bathroom, was gone some time. He returned, crestfallen. "I'll have to go on a diet."

"You just have to stop drinking for a while."

He grimaced, then cheered up. "What's for dinner?"

She shrugged. "I haven't been cooking. There's nothing in the house but fruit and cheese."

"Shall we go to the market?"

So. She stirred. "You're staying?"

"Is it okay?"

"Yes," she said.

"Jenny, I love you!"

"But what does that mean to you? That's what I don't know."

"It means I love you. That doesn't seem so hard to understand."

She sat, staring at the floor.

"Does it?"

She raised her eyes. "This is the first time we've had a real fight. In seven years. Because this was the first time I did something that deeply offended you. And I did what I did because you did something that deeply offended me. But I was here. I told you what it was. I stayed here. I waited for you to speak. You took off. Just like you used to run away from home all the time when you were a kid. To press your will. You don't want to fight, you want to win. You want to overwhelm me, force me to my knees, make me beg you to return . . ."

"Well, if I wanted that, I certainly didn't get it," he said sarcastically. "You never called anyone! You didn't even try to find out where I was."

"How do you know that?"

"I know." He nodded.

She kept her face straight, but inwardly, smiled. "When I saw you standing there, my heart was glad," she said tentatively. "I was so glad you were you, that you were back, that you were here . . . But now . . ."

"What!" he barked.

"I don't know." She made a gesture of futility. "I don't know how I feel. I don't know anything."

"Jenny." He moved closer to her.

She looked at him without expression. He gathered her in his arms. Where he touched her, her skin tingled. Her head collapsed onto his shoulder. "Jenny, love," he said, kissing her hair.

She began to cry then, slowly but more and more intensely, sobbing out the weeks of silence and the dread she still felt. Nor did the dread completely vanish after he began to stroke her, or even after she began to stroke him, or even after they embraced hard and fell into a kiss that went on and on and on, and began to let their bodies touch too, and even after that . . . She shivered at the passing thought that the dread might never go away again.

19

Several weeks passed before Clea called, but Emily, trusting that she would, worked on her symphony with a new excitement. She might get to hear it played yet! When Clea called in late June, Emily's spirits jumped with anticipation. She freshened up Clea's old room, stripped the sheets, which had been used only once, and put on clean ones, hung clean towels in all the bathrooms, shopped for lamb and vegetables, even though it was not a season for stew. It occurred to her that the chintz curtains that had been hanging there for the past eighteen years or so were a little . . . sad, and she drove to Lenox to Country Curtains and bought lace ones, matching those in the rest of the house. She tossed the chintz bedspread she had thought so cute before Clea arrived and bought an antique linen spread with lace insets. She tossed the cute rug with little animals woven into it, and transferred an antique kilim from another bedroom to Clea's. She went to Grovers' Farm and bought a huge bouquet of just-cut peonies and irises, set them in a wide pitcher on a table in Clea's room. Then she rested.

Clea drove up the first Friday in July, arriving around seven. She looked very different from the girl who had left fourteen years before. Her body had thickened, her face had aged. Before, she had been cute; now she was beautiful. She had a quiet dignity she had not possessed earlier. Of course, she had a few wrinkles and an edge of plumpness too, but to Emily's fond eye, these made her even more beautiful.

Emily, too, was older, of course, but not more beautiful. She was a little bent, more lined and grayer. Her body looked more fragile. Looking at Emily made Clea's heart stop for a moment.

They embraced and Clea accepted a gin and tonic; Emily poured herself a scotch. They sat in the kitchen, facing each other across the table.

"Oh, Clea," Emily said tremulously, her eyes liquefying.

"Don't cry now, Em," Clea said. "I won't be able to stand it if you cry."

Emily wiped tears from her cheeks. "I'll try. I can't promise."

Clea reached across the table and took her hands. "It was my fault. I had this idea . . . I felt you were somehow or other against me . . . I wanted to call you so many times. I thought of you. But I wouldn't have been able to bear it if I heard that distant tone in your voice, that edge of disapproval. I was a stupid kid, full of rebellion. I took everything out on you. But nothing was your fault."

"Yes it was. It was my fault. I couldn't understand why you would want to have a baby instead of finishing school. It seemed so perverse, which made me think you were doing it just to hurt me, to defy me and my life and all of what I stood for. I couldn't understand it any other way. I thought it was about me, when it was about you. I couldn't understand how after all that fighting and struggling, all the work of all the women over all the years, all the effort women put into getting the vote, getting accepted by schools, forcing companies to give us jobs, making ourselves legitimate, changing our possibilities, you would choose a life exactly like my mother's, like Maddy's mother's, like Maddy's when Maddy regrets it every day of her life—like all women in those days, when I knew (and I thought you had to know) how unhappy they'd been. Women who never got to go to college or develop their minds, consigned to a life of servitude to children and husband . . . How they resented their children, even though they'd sacrificed for them and loved them! That was what I was feeling; but you didn't, couldn't, understand that. It meant something so different for you. I felt you were denying the fact that I'd had to sacrifice, the fact that I might have liked to have had a man and a child in my life and had given that up . . .

"My problem was that I couldn't see that it wasn't the same thing for you, that changing times had changed even that fundamental state. That having a baby wasn't the end of your life the way it was of women earlier, would have been for me. My mother always said that having my oldest brother—her first child—ended her life. She meant it ended her life as an individual, a person with volition, with possibilities. After she gave birth, she was a mother, a wife, not a person."

"I should have seen that," Clea responded. "I should have understood. You tried to explain. But I was hard against you. I had this conviction that you would oppose anything I wanted. Because of things that had happened earlier . . ."

"Yes. I understand. And you were right."

Clea paused, her eyebrows raised a little. She started again. "It took me a long time—probably until Martine was starting her teens and getting—stubborn, willful, whatever—when she began to oppose me about things—to see how hard you'd tried to give me whatever I wanted. When Martine made impossible demands, I saw how patient you'd been. I began to see you more clearly then."

"She's so adorable."

Clea flushed with pleasure. "She is, isn't she? She's my darling girl. I love her so much . . ."

"And you're glad you had her."

Clea nodded. "But of course you had no way of knowing that things would be different for me. Why should they be? After all, look how people acted when Lynn slandered me . . . they acted exactly as they would have a hundred years earlier."

"Yes, I know. I'll never forget it. I'm sure you won't either. Oh, I knew things had changed, of course. That women could go to professional schools and get decent jobs and earn enough to support themselves . . . but I didn't think motherhood itself had changed, that the very notion of it was different, that it would be possible for a woman to have a child and a life of her own as well . . . In that, I thought things were the way they'd always been. And I really panicked when you wouldn't marry the boy. Whatever happened to him, anyway? In my day, not marrying the father of your baby would have relegated you to—well, to prostitution, really, or its equivalent: marriage to anyone who would support you, whether you cared for him or not. You would not have been accepted by any respectable family. You wouldn't have been allowed inside their door. No decent community would have had you, not even as a servant. You would have been an outcast. I don't know how you would have lived."

"Well, but now there are lots of communities," Clea said, "Women's and lesbian communities. With women's rules, not men's. The idea that women should be virgins when they marry and remain chaste in marriage comes from men, not women. It's based on the belief that women are property, goods, new or used—men's way of seeing them—and that women should offer themselves to buyers as new and unused. For centuries, women tried to abide by men's rules because they had to or starve. But now we can follow our own rules and still find work. And we love all our children, accept them all, the way they do in matrilineal societies. Hallie has a son, I told you that, didn't I? Evan's in his early twenties, in graduate school. He's gorgeous and very smart. Martine is crazy about him. They get along. He never had a father either—I mean one he knew."

Clea sipped her gin. "Josh. I don't know what happened to Josh. When I told him I was pregnant, he was furious. He wasn't ready for fatherhood, he said. He wanted me to have an abortion. I have nothing against abortion, but . . . you know, my folks had just been killed, just a few years before. I think it'd been in my mind to have a baby as soon as I could because . . . it was my way of replacing my parents. Sort of replacing them. I needed kin. So I couldn't abort her. I wanted this baby more than I can tell you now."

"You told me then. I just couldn't hear it."

"He said he'd pay for an abortion, but nothing else. I told him to get lost, and he did." Clea laughed.

"You never saw him again?"

"No. And he could have found me. I was at school in Northampton when I got pregnant. When I left school, I came here and stayed with you. He could have found me. He'd come here with me that Thanksgiving, one Christmas, remember? But he never came, and after I left here, he never called you, did he?"

"No. Not that I knew where you were at first. You left in such anger." Emily got teary again. She wiped her eyes and blew her nose. "Where did you go?" she asked in a thick, nasal voice. "How did you manage? I was sick with worry."

"I went to New York. To the city. You know, Em, I had money—Mom and Dad's money. I wasn't some desperate kid. I found a tiny apartment in Greenwich Village, and I took courses at NYU and met people my age and did things in the city. I took Martine with me whenever I could, and I found a woman who'd keep her when I couldn't. You can do anything if you have money. I finished NYU and went on to get a degree in medical administration. But you knew that. I'd called you by then."

"Yes. Thank heavens. Oh, thank heavens you called me, darling," Emily said, grabbing Clea's hand. "I'd had nightmares about you every night until you called."

"Yes. I'd begun to regret being so . . . precipitated. Regret my—what's the cliché these days?—rush to judgment."

"I can understand it. And I'm sorry that I deserved your judgment."

"No. I was unfair to you."

They sat in silence for a while.

Then Emily asked, "Hungry?"

"Yeah, actually. What's for dinner?"

"Your favorite," Emily said, rising.

"Fast food?" Clea joked.

"Do you still eat it?"

"Very rarely. Only when Martine drags me." She laughed. "With a medical background, I know how bad it is for you."

Emily got the stew out of the refrigerator and spooned it into a pot, which she covered and put on a low flame. Clea rose and set the dining-room table. Emily set a loaf of French bread in a basket. Clea put out butter. Emily sliced tomatoes and basil, put them on a plate, and lightly poured olive oil over them.

"What kind of job could you get with your degree?" Emily asked, putting salt and pepper on the table.

"I could work in any hospital. In management. I have medical training as well as business training. Sometimes I think about getting an MD and becoming ambitious, you know, to work in a prestigious hospital, a big hospital, to make a couple of hundred K a year. But other times I remind myself how much I love my life, and just settle down. We started the clinic with nothing and we've built it into something really wonderful. Because of us, a whole neighborhood around Bridgeport has healthier babies and children and women. We serve only women and children, but the men are better off too, because we advise the women about diet, exercise, healthy living, and they worry about their men and they buy the food, they prepare it. Thing is, in social service, you tend to burn out. In this country, everything you try to do for poor people is a struggle. That wears you out.

"Right now, Hallie's the ambitious one. There's a part of her that would like to earn real money and make a name for herself and, most important, really use her brain, in ways she can't now. She's awfully brilliant. Our salaries are laughable. She's dedicated, but she has nothing and she hates taking money from me. I support us on my trust fund. I'm always afraid that one day she's going to leave and go into regular practice . . ."

"How courageous you both are," Emily said softly.

"Not me. I've got a cushion. But she is."

"What will happen if she leaves?"

"I don't know. I'm not sure our relationship could survive that . . ."

"You don't love her that much?"

"I love her to bits. But you know, Em, love is part of a context. It can't stand alone. You of all people should know that. You didn't reject men because you didn't love them, you rejected the context they came in. Remember that old song, 'If I were a carpenter, would you still love me?' That always got me, that song, the way it implies that a woman should love a man no matter what he does or how they live, that she should accept his life as her life and be satisfied by it. I couldn't do that. If Hallie worked at some huge hospital, made a couple of hundred thou a year—as she could, and as part of her would like to—she'd be a different woman, she'd have a different life. It's a life that, right now, I wouldn't want to share. It's a different life from mine. Mine is tied to the clinic, to the neighborhood."

They were standing in the kitchen, as they had hundreds of times before, Clea leaning on the stove, Emily standing at it, stirring the stew with a wooden spoon.

"You know," Clea went on, "I remember in college anthropology studying simple societies in which people marry for economic reasons. You know, the women weave and the men make boats—or men weave and women make boats, or whatever—and everybody needs cloth and boats. The partners have the same context, the same culture; they need each other economically, and marriage makes sense. Marriage is for economic survival: Sexual fidelity is not always required. In some societies, it's not even expected. Well, we don't have that kind of context. We don't need each other's skills; often we're rivals, really. Yet we expect our marriages to be as stable as those in simple societies. And we make no allowance for love affairs, as most simple societies do, well, anyway, the matrilineal ones. I think we expect too much of marriage."

"You always were a rebel," Emily said admiringly, shaking her head. "You thought for yourself. I remember you defending adultery . . ." She laughed.

"Much to your horror," Clea said, surprised that her aunt had raised the subject. "But *adultery* is a word I don't use. A concept I don't accept."

"I know." Emily sipped her drink, set her glass down hard. "But I don't think I understood. Back then."

"Well, to me the word has an archaic context, a view of life in which some people, namely men, own other people, namely women. You know, in ancient law, adultery was a crime that only women could commit. The only way a man could commit it was to have sex with a woman who was married to another man, appropriate another man's property. I don't feel like that, and I don't think other people should. I don't think anyone belongs to anyone else."

"Yes. I guess. I have such a different context. And the truth is, when we were going through . . . the Harley business, I'd forgotten what it meant to me."

"Forgotten?"

"You know, things get defined for you when you're a child, and they continue to have that meaning even if it's an eccentric personal meaning, long after they should. You forget how they took on that connotation . . . That was the problem between us. That was why you felt . . . that I was against you. I was."

Clea cast her mind back. "So it was the Harley business that set us at odds?"

"Yes. I didn't realize it at the time. I didn't realize it until a few weeks ago. I'd forgotten the past. I'd wanted to forget, and I did. The thing that colored everything was that my father had an affair when I was a young teenager, twelve and thirteen. It was a terrible event in my childhood, but I buried it. Still, it infected my feelings about you and Harley . . ."

The stew was hot, the Caprese salad and the bread and butter were on the table. "We can eat," Emily offered. She had opened a bottle of red wine and wiggled it at Clea. "Want some?"

"Yes. I don't have to drive home. Mmm, that stew smells delicious."

As they moved toward the dining room, Clea put her arm around Emily's waist, and they walked together. Emily laid her head on Clea's shoulder—the girl was that much taller than she now.

"You've gotten taller and I've shrunk," she noted.

"You have, it's true! Someone told me people did that, and I didn't believe them. But you have. It's nice. Makes me feel you're manageable somehow, even though I know you're not."

They both laughed, sat down at the table.

"Whatever happened to Harley, do you know?" Clea asked.

"Well, some years later, he got involved with another girl. You were long gone, of course. I heard about it from Homer Carlyle. The girl was a Carlyle, so this time, Lynn couldn't get away with maligning her—the Carlyle family is even more widespread than the Kelloggs, and they can be just as mean. And of course, this was the second time, since Lynn had seen to it that everyone had heard about you. Even with you, most people blamed Harley—you were so young. Everyone but the kids . . . the teenagers. You know how kids are—supermoral, judgmental, mean. They were cruel in my day and they were cruel in yours. They hadn't yet discovered their own frailties.

"This girl was even younger than you, twelve or thirteen, and her family had Harley charged with statutory rape. They had some sort of evidence. Well, she was pregnant, and I guess by then they had DNA testing. He pleaded guilty. He didn't go to jail, but he had to do some sort of community service, and he was shamed in the eyes of the whole community. He had to pay a fine. I don't know if he felt ashamed, but Lynn certainly did.

"The girl had an abortion and her parents sent her away to a private school in Connecticut. Lynn held on to Harley, though. He's still with her. He looks like . . . he looks debauched. I think he drinks. Lynn kept him but she wrote him out of her will, Homer said. The farm goes directly to her girls when she dies. She looks awful too. I can't imagine what it must be like, the two of them sitting down to dinner every night, facing each other, alone together. I can't imagine what they feel. You know, I had a friend, Mary, who was unhappily married back in the days when you couldn't get a divorce if your husband didn't want one. And her husband didn't. She said the worst part was that living with someone she hated made her hate herself. And that was horrible to live with. You'd think that's how Lynn would feel." Emily shuddered.

"Maybe she doesn't hate him."

Emily looked at Clea. "How could she not? She's my mother's kind of woman. What matters most to her is her image in the community." Emily chewed for a while. "Do you really think it's acceptable, Harley's behavior?"

"I think Harley has rights over his own body. I don't think Lynn owns it. I don't know what to say about the fact that he stays with her even though she feels she owns his body. Or the fact that she wants him even though he challenges her on that. Or that he stays with her when his body at least clearly wants someone else. It sounds mostly miserable.

"I mean, if he really believes he owns his own body, he should leave her. Act on his beliefs. But anyway, now I think that most of the things he said then he said because he wanted to screw me. He said he believed he owned his own body because it suited his desires at the moment. I don't think he really believes anything. He doesn't think, he has impulses, that's all. I'll never forget how for months he was saying he'd love me forever, how he said it on Monday, and on Tuesday after Lynn found out, he ducked and hid when he saw me. In those days I believed that a person could promise to love forever, and I was busy loving him forever." She laughed. "He broke my heart."

"Did he? He certainly broke Lynn's."

"I guess. You promise to love forever when you marry, don't you? But I don't believe Lynn loves Harley so much as she feels she owns him. That's the only excuse I can come up with for his behavior."

"You and Hallie didn't make any such promise?"

"No, we didn't. I love her, and it feels as if I always will, but I have come to see how long forever can be . . ." Clea laughed again. "And how contingent love is. Except mother love. I think that stands."

"Yes. Aunt love too."

"Same thing," Clea smiled, squeezing Emily's hand, which lay on the table.

"And sometimes, father love."

"Yes. My father loved me the same way my mother did."

"Mine loved me more than my mother."

"It's unusual, though, isn't it?"

"It seems to be getting more common. The younger generation of men, the men raised by feminists, love their children like mothers."

Clea's eyes filled. "That's nice, if it's true."

Emily paused. "Are you . . . are you considering . . . changing your lifestyle?"

Clea laughed. "No. No! But I look at Evan, whose father is just . . . *negligent* is the word, I guess. Or selfish. He just doesn't think about Evan. He's divorced from Hallie, so he doesn't think he owes his son anything. The son belongs to the mother, in his cosmology. I see how it hurts Evan. I want to hit Dirk, slap him in the face, kick him in the shins, something. I want to hug Evan. But I don't do anything."

"Ah. Dessert?" Emily asked, standing up and removing some plates.

"What is it?" Clea rose and took the rest of the dishes into the kitchen.

"Hot-fudge sundaes."

"You're kidding."

"No. With real whipped cream."

"Yay!" Clea cried. "My most favorite favorite!"

"I suspected that," Emily smiled, scooping ice cream into bowls.

"How can you make hot fudge at home?"

Emily smiled. "Nowadays, it comes in a microwavable plastic container. You were the one who made me buy the microwave, remember?" she said, inserting a plastic container of fudge sauce into the machine. "Now I'm telling you about the latest innovations!"

A few seconds later, she removed the container and squeezed clumps of hot fudge onto the ice cream. She pulled a bowl of whipped cream from the fridge. "Voilà!"

"Oh, Em! A miracle!"

Clea carried the bowls into the dining room.

"Tea or coffee?" asked Emily.

"No. Just ice water," Clea answered, picking up her glass and bringing it into the kitchen. "What a meal! You outdid yourself!"

"Well, keep it in memory. The next one will probably come from the grocery store."

"I like those too. I'm not fussy."

"What?"

"I am? Am I?"

"Well, you sure used to be."

Clea stood, a little smile playing on her face. "Well. That's good. I'm glad I'm not an accepting slob."

They sat down and devoured their desserts.

Clea leaned back, sighing deeply. "I don't usually eat this much."

"Me either. Usually I have a pear and some cheese and crackers. Or potato pancakes—they sell them frozen, did you know that?—and applesauce. I love that."

Clea was silent for a while. Then she asked, "Your father was unfaithful to your mother?""

"Yes." Emily's body tensed, although her face didn't change. "Just before the war. The real war, World War II."

"Why was that 'the real war'? Aren't all wars real?"

"For the poor soldiers fighting them, I guess. But not for the country. We weren't assured of winning World War II. I mean we could have lost and losing would have been devastating, for Europe especially, but for us too. If we had lost, the world would have changed. That wasn't true of later wars. They didn't matter to us as a nation. They mattered to the other countries, but not us. We even did lose the Vietnamese War, and it didn't matter. We didn't risk much of anything in Korea, in Panama, in the gulf, in Grenada . . ."

"I see."

"We started building weapons even before we entered the war in 1941. People knew it was coming. Munitions factories were gearing up in the late thirties. It wasn't a surprise, December 7 notwithstanding. It appears now that FDR set that up to reconcile the isolationists. At least, that's what some people think . . . I'm wandering. You can see I'm not eager to talk about this . . ." She cleared her throat. She drank some water. "My father was working with a friend of his to build a gyroscope. It's a gizmo used to hold cameras steady in airplanes, and maybe bomb sights as well . . .They were brand new then, a recent invention. He was working on it and stayed out late every night. At first, my mother was fine with it; she'd keep his dinner warm in the oven. She thought that if the war department bought his device, we would get a lot of money. Actually they did, and we did. It put our family firmly into the middle class, I mean economically. We'd always been middle class in New England terms, farm terms. But we'd never had any money, only land. After that, we were comfortable, we had a bank account . . ."

Clea watched her, concentrating.

Emily glanced at her, grimaced. "Yes. Okay . . . At some point, my mother began to act moody. I grew aware of this gradually. I came to realize—I don't remember when or how—that she was sitting in the kitchen in the dark every night, waiting for my father. So I began to wait up, too, hiding behind my bedroom door, leaving it slightly ajar. One night, when he came in, she began to yell. I slipped downstairs and hid in the front room to listen. She kept at him until he admitted he was seeing a woman. When I heard that, I ran upstairs, I hid my head under my pillow, I cried, I was outraged. Humiliated. But I wasn't angry with my father, my beloved father, the only one in the family except Martin who loved me, who paid for my piano lessons. No. I blamed the woman. I blamed her, not for taking my father away from my mother, but for taking him away from me. I couldn't forgive her."

Clea said nothing for a while. "But in time he came back to you, didn't he?"

"Not really. My mother gave him an ultimatum: that woman or her—us—this house and his life here. So he ended the affair, he gave in to her. But he never forgave her, or us; he was distant for the rest of his life. He still didn't come home at night, he just worked on the gyroscope. Maybe he wasn't blaming us, maybe he just didn't care about life anymore. The only time he came to life after that was when I was about to be graduated from high school and he announced he wanted me to go to Curtis. I often wondered if my mother regretted her pyrrhic victory."

"And what do you think?"

Emily shrugged. "No, I don't think she did. I don't think she cared how he felt or even how she felt. I don't think she ever thought about love. She only cared about respectability and duty, about presenting the proper exterior to the world. She was never going to have any satisfaction in life; that had been denied her at birth; she knew she'd never have the chance to live her own life. Her duty was to fit into society properly: All of life was appearances. To be respectable and hold your head up in a repectable community was all that mattered."

"Weird sense of life."

"Yes. But very common once, you know? And people do, don't

they? Have odd senses of life. Do you remember Maddy's uncle Philip? He was brought up like all our parents, his father had a heavy hand with a belt, on the boys at least. And times were hard, life was hard. For everyone. Just having enough to eat was something to be grateful for, and people didn't, sometimes.

"Philip married Marie Considine back in the twenties. Well, they had to get married. That was the first scandal. He adored Marie, but she didn't adore him, and she had been so demoralized by being pregnant and not married that she had had a kind of nervous breakdown. She never forgave Philip. He got a job in the gravel pit, some helper's job that paid ten dollars a week or so, and they lived with her folks, but the Considines looked down on him as a failure and a debaucher. He just bowed his head and accepted it. He thought he deserved it.

"When the baby was born, they moved to a little apartment in Winchester, over a store. By now Philip was working at the mill and was earning a little bit more. Marie was still teary and resentful but she took care of the house and the baby and Philip, with a sour face, my mother said. They had a couple more kids, and Philip worked two jobs to pay the bills, eventually making a decent living. They weren't rich, but they were able to buy a little house in Hood Falls. I remember him from those days. He scared us kids. He'd look at us with such angry eyes, and when he spoke to us, he'd bark. His kids were scared of him, too. He didn't hit them—Marie wouldn't have it—but he seemed to hate them. They were never close to their father.

"The time came when life was a little easier for them, but Philip always worried about money. Frugal Marie would have liked a little luxury in her life, but she never really got it and she never complained. Grandchildren were born, and then grew up. Marie died in her eighties, she had had a long life, she got to hold two grandbabies in her arms. Philip went on living.

"He was terrible with babies. I always thought he was afraid of them—their spontaneity, their wildness. He barked at babies, made them cry, even his own grandchildren. But he did it rarely enough that the grandchildren didn't grow up afraid of him, and when they had babies of their own, they laid siege to him. They brought him their babies; they laid them in his arms. They said, 'Grandpa, this is your great-granddaughter, or great-grandson, and you have to love her.' 'Oh?' he would ask. 'What's that?' The grandkids are the new generation, they love their babies to pieces, they don't see them as sinful creatures who have to be broken or ungrateful parasites or drains on a pitiful income. Babies are helpless, innocent, need love. And the way they acted affected Philip who was old and alone and whom they included in every family get-together.

"And he came to understand that babies existed to be loved! It was an idea he'd never before entertained. He'd never even imagined such a thing. He tried it. He smiled at the babies and they gurgled back. When they started to walk, he played with them, and they giggled and ran and played peek-a-boo with him. And he loved it!

"And one day, talking to Maddy, he said his great-grandkids were *fun*. Maddy said it was a word he'd never used before, she'd never heard it from his lips. It was a new concept to him, fun. That life could be fun was not part of his parents' culture, not part of his, either. Life was real, life was earnest, but life was not fun. And pretty soon, he was saying other things were fun: He loved to play bocce with some other old guys in the summer, and now, instead of moaning about how badly he'd played (as he'd always done), he began to crow about how much fun it was. And he started to enjoy the family arguments, which always exist, you know, the gossip. He'd listen, and confess to Maddy that it was fun, listening, wondering how it would all come out. In his nineties, he totally changed his personality! He'd joined the modern world!"

Clea laughed, both at the story and at Emily's astonished recital of it.

"But those were concepts my parents couldn't have imagined—that children were to be loved, that life could be fun. God! For them, everything was serious. They always worried so about survival. Life was grim. The best you could do was your duty. And I was raised that way too."

"But you're not like that."

"You don't think so?"

"Look what you did! You did exactly what you wanted to do. No matter what they thought!"

Emily mused. "Yes . . ." she said doubtfully. "But that isn't what I'm getting at. It's that our concept of what life is has changed. Life has always been hard. People in older times had a harder time than we did. Life still is terribly hard for most people on the globe. In India, Africa, South America, Asia. In most places, survival is a daily struggle. And the rules society developed, the way it conceived of things, were based on the sense that life was hard and survival not guaranteed. Both personal survival and survival of the group, the clan, the community, the race, whatever. People could imagine entire communities being destroyed. Like in the story of the Flood.

"But the industrial revolution, I guess, changed that in some places in the world. In most of Europe, and here, for most communities, survival isn't really an issue. Personal survival is: You worry about your kids, about accidents. But not about polio, which when I was young was a terrible threat, or measles, or starvation. Starvation, never. We don't even have any concept of what starvation is. Even though there are people starving in our country. But they're around the corner, you don't see them. How can we know what starvation is? Look at our supermarkets, with their heaps of food, rainbow colors heaped to the ceiling! So we feel no terror for our group, we know it will survive. And that changes the rules. The values. And our generations—mine, and yours too—because huge changes take a long time to percolate through—are dealing with that. With the consequences of a different sense of what life is, of survival. It's hard to imagine how life seemed to my mother, to earlier generations. Because it's a different vision from ours. And mine is different from yours. Which is astounding. In the past, from parent to child, life didn't change much; neither did vision. Parent and child saw things, felt them, pretty much the same. And now they don't. At least, I think so. That's what I think," Emily finished lamely.

"Sounds like you've been doing a lot of thinking."

"I had lots of time after you left."

"Oh, Em . . ." Clea reached out for her aunt.

"No no," Emily said, raising her hand. "I'm not reproaching you.

I'm just telling you what happened. Thinking about why you left, how you felt about things, thinking about how I felt, how my mother felt, it came to me that we might as well have come from foreign countries. We had such different backgrounds, the times had changed that much. Just in our lifetimes. One of the main differences was economic: Things were harder for my parents than for me, but then easier for my parents than for theirs, and things were incomparably easier for you . . . economically."

"But that was because of Mommy and Daddy," Clea offered. "If they hadn't died . . ."

"Do you think that whatever you did, they wouldn't have helped you?"

"No. You're right."

"It's as if there is a world mind, and from my mother's generation to yours, it has changed more several times. As if people from my grandmother's generation would not be able to comprehend, say, Martine."

"That's probably true," Clea murmured. "I can hardly believe the way people felt in your mother's day—when you tell me about it. It's really foreign to me."

"And that was one of the problems between us . . ."

"Sure."

"I'm not discounting my irrationality about . . . infidelity."

"You weren't irrational. You just accepted the standards of your period."

"I *was* irrational. Because I blamed you, not Harley. No—I blamed Harley, but I blamed you more. I blamed him for seducing a child, but I blamed you as if you were a woman, full grown and aware of her seductive powers. That was what was irrational."

"What it felt like to me . . . was as if you just couldn't get over what I'd done. I had this feeling that if you lived to be a hundred, you'd still be harboring this simmering anger against me . . ."

"Yes. That is how I was. I'm so sorry, sweetheart. It's gone now."

"I can tell." Clea smiled in delight. "And I'm sure glad!"

"And do you feel the same way now? What about if Hallie had an affair? Would you feel it was okay?"

"Okay? Yes. I mean, that isn't really relevant. I'd be angry, or hurt, or whatever. But I would certainly feel she had the right to one, if she chose. As do I. We own ourselves. That's all I ever meant. I might even be able to tolerate it. It's not sexual fidelity that matters to me, it's a question of primary loyalty. I'd always want that from someone I was involved with. When I said you owned yourself, I meant that I was not answerable to Lynn. I didn't feel responsible for guarding Lynn's marriage, or Harley's virtue. I was responsible for myself, that's all. Harley did as he chose, so did I. I had no obligation to her. I didn't own his body."

"I guess . . ."

"You seem doubtful still."

"I don't know. I guess I think friendship is a factor."

"I guess it could be. But I didn't feel I was hurting Lynn. If I had intended to take him away from her, I might have. But I didn't intend that."

"She'd been very good to you."

Clea looked suspiciously at her aunt. "Are you still on about this?"

Emily looked startled. "Actually, no. I don't care about it anymore. I'm just thinking about your position, in principle. Don't you think it's complex?"

"Maybe. It didn't seem so to me then. I never wished Lynn any harm. And it made Harley so happy to be with me that he was nicer to her than usual. I didn't feel I was harming her. But she obviously felt that his screwing around took something away from her. As if there was only so much to go around." Clea barked a laugh. "A funny way to see sex."

Emily nodded. "Especially since . . . well, Belinda Cox told me later—after the affair with the Carlyle girl—that Lynn didn't particularly like sex."

"Likely. Whatever happened to the Carlyle girl?"

"Her family was opposed to abortion, but they let her have one. She was only thirteen. She went away to school, but I don't think she went to college. I think she left school to get married when she was still in her teens. I'm not sure."

Clea was staring into the distance.

"What are you thinking, darling?"

Clea blinked. "About you telling me—remember when I said how I loved Harley, and I would forever, you said I'd get over it? You said a person survived a broken heart. I thought that was the most horrible thing I'd ever heard. I thought you were cold as ice." She laughed without mirth.

"Amazing, how fragile love is," Emily mused.

"Yes. Was it for you? Did you forget the men you loved?"

"Yes. Except one I loved but never slept with. Him I still love. Funny, isn't it?"

"Do you think love endures only when it's not sexual?"

"I don't know. I only know my own experience. There were plenty of men I liked but didn't sleep with. I don't remember them. I loved the few I slept with, but the only one I remember with love is the one I didn't sleep with. But it seems that even the most enduring love—between parent and child—can maybe fade."

"Who do you mean?"

"Well, your father. I adored him and I really raised him from the time he was born until I went away. And he adored me when he was a baby. But I don't think he remembered that when he was grown."

"Yes, he did," Clea said. "Whenever he mentioned your name, his voice got this foggy quality. 'My big sister Em,' he'd say, in this yearning tone. It pissed my mother off, I'll tell you!" Clea laughed.

"Really!" Emily glowed. "He really did?"

"It predisposed me to like you when I came. Except I fought off the feeling, just out of sheer perversity!"

They laughed.

"Tell me about Martine."

"Oh, she's adorable, I love her to pieces, she's a pain in the neck, she drives me crazy . . ."

"Oh, tell me, tell me," Emily giggled in delight.

And Clea did.

20

For days after her son's weekend visit, Alicia walked with a bounce, as if she were wearing air-soled shoes; she felt taller than before, lighter, straighter, smarter, abler. A miracle had happened, something that could not have been expected in the normal course of events—and she had made it happen. Steven had accepted Stevie—Steve; she had to remember to call him that—even though he was queer, gay, whatever it was. Steven had embraced his son, talked to him! Because of her, Alicia. She felt giddy in the head, while the rest of her felt grounded, solid, firmly set on earth. She was not a woman with no character at all. She had brought together two of the three people she most loved on earth; she had painted a rainbow over their lives, healing the family. And they, her husband and her son both, saw her differently now, too, she could see it. They saw a little space around her: She took up some room. They might be grateful to her, but that wasn't important, that wasn't what she wanted, and that would fade. What would last was that they had a sense of her as a person who could make something happen. She was not just a loving, indulgent mother, a loving tolerant wife, as they had seen her before. She was a person with a force field and desires of her own, not a mere function of their lives.

In this sense, she was newborn.

This new Alicia was quieter than the old one, abler, much more able. She spent July making final preparations for her new room, which was almost finished. She sat at the kitchen table transferring notes from file cards onto the computer with efficient speed, cross-referencing her files. She was so competent that at times she was a pain in the neck to herself. She concealed her efficiency a bit, so as not to be a pain in the neck to others. If she wasn't telling one lie, she was telling another, she thought wryly, amused.

Steven was happier though now. She could see this. She occasionally caught him looking at her with affection; but also, he smiled more often and more easily, he was less burdened. She found him humming the theme from the first movement of Mozart's Thirty-Ninth Symphony Sunday as he helped her in the garden. And that was new!—his helping her in the garden. She was weeding the herb bed. The locust tree that grew near it had sent out shoots that had rooted in the bed, and they were too entrenched for her to pull out by herself, so she asked Steven for help. He was able to dig them out for her, and was surprised, exclaimed at their length and strength and stubbornness. Although he had started out a bit suspicious at her saying she did not have the strength to pull out the roots, he found them almost impossible to remove himself. And so he believed she really needed his help. And when he was at last able to extract one, he felt a spurt of satisfaction with himself. He had been humming. It was a beautiful day, puffs of cloud scudding across a pale blue sky. A tiny one-person plane hovered overhead. It must be fun to be up there, Alicia thought, to look down on all the greenness here and feel the target of envious earthly eyes. She was happy, even though she hated the way she thanked Steven, why did she have to put so much fervor into her thanks? Why was she so humble? But he had never worked outdoors before, and it was so nice, so cozy, working beside him, having someone there to say something to: "That's a bitch of a root, isn't it?" or "Will you look at how many weeds sprang up here in just a month?" And his humming. It made her so happy, how could she help sounding like a refugee taken in from the cold and fed?

Satisfaction spread through her like warm urine in a diaper—but it stayed warm. She had discovered a new cache of material, a box of letters from an old Eastchester family that had long resided on a shelf in the basement of the library in a tiny hamlet called Greenage. There were letters from the paterfamilias to his wife, from her to him, from her to her daughter, a few to her son, from the children to their parents. The letters covered a thirty-year period at the very beginning of the nineteenth century, but what made them so interesting was that the wife was an intelligent woman, smart about everything—the weather, the crops, the children, her husband's business. Alicia felt she'd made a discovery like the English Paston letters, only smaller; and thank heaven, this family did not beat their daughter to force her to submit to their marriage plans for her. It was great that the Paston girl had had spirit and had resisted, but how much more wonderful it was that this daughter picked out her own husband, and won her parents' approval.

Stevie—Steve—called, saying what a fine time he'd had, how good it was, how grateful he was to his mother for her efforts with his father, how grateful he was to his father for coming around. Yes, he said, he would come up with Neil, sometime next month. Promise, yes. Love you, he said.

That was the next hurdle. She would have to work on Steven beforehand, find a way to teach him what was rude and what could pass as his normal aloof behavior. He didn't seem to know the difference. Strange. If he didn't know that, how could he judge what was neurotic and what just eccentric? Did he simply assume that all his patients' behavior was neurotic?

Emily had told her about an uncle of Maddy's who didn't know that children were supposed to be loved, who didn't know that people were permitted to have pleasure in life, who had always worn a face of disapproving sternness. Would Steven have judged him to be merely neurotic when he was really just ignorant? He had been raised with a particular worldview and retained it. That he had been able to change it when the world changed, at ninety-plus years of age made him eminently sane, it seemed to Alicia.

Poor men. They were socialized so poorly. They must be horribly confused. After all, look at their fathers! Men who concealed their emotions, withdrew from their families, men who exploded, shouted, got drunk, hit people, beat children! Funny, Shakespeare, who could create a Hotspur, a Hal, an Antony, a Falstaff, a Coriolanus, a Julius Caesar, and an Octavius Caesar, never created one of the kind of men who seemed to populate the earth nowadays. Nor did Homer, or Virgil, or any of those guys. People got their models from the movies nowadays, and from television, where men were mostly violent and silent.

She put down the shovel and wiped her face with a hand. Warm today. Beautiful. The sun beat on her back, warming her cockles, whatever cockles were. What were they? All the way to her bone marrow didn't sound nearly as good.

It occurred to her that the new Alicia was just as consumed with thoughts about how to deal with Steven as the old one. Was this an improvement? Was she a controller? Was that what this was all about? Why did she worry so much about Steven? What would happen if she stopped? If she just let him be, and was herself? He'd offend Neil, who wouldn't return, which would make it hard for Steve to visit, as well. Well, maybe she was controlling but only in the interests of a happy, harmonious home. Why was that so hard to achieve?

She stopped working and stood back to gaze at what she had done. She had sharpened the edges of all the shrub beds. She decided to stop for the day. A shower would feel wonderful now. And a cup of tea and a ginger cookie. Wonderful!

She carried her tools to the toolshed, went indoors, examined her gardening clothes, and pulled them off right there in the hallway, then stuffed them into the washing machine. In panties and bra, she headed for her bathroom, walking through her orderly light-filled rooms, loving the order, the peace, the light, like a convent, she thought, walking through the cloisters as the bells called her to worship, serene in her devotion to her deity—whatever it was. She had one, she was sure of that. Harmony, maybe? Love? Life as a set of connections holding everyone in their embrace, connections that had to be adjusted, balanced, tightened, loosened, reaffirmed, but that provided all the meaning anyone needed, and all anyone had.

•

Jenny was finding herself newly incompetent. She was continually dropping things, tripping, making mistakes, leaving the marketing list on the kitchen counter and forgetting half the groceries, hitting her finger with the hammer, smearing paint all over her arm or face. Tim was back, but nothing was settled—and she had let this happen. He had gone away when he wanted to, returned when he wanted to, stopped speaking to her when he wanted to, resumed when he wanted to, and she was passive, simply letting it all happen, without holding him to account. Well, she had tried. But he was too wily for her. Or too . . . something. She didn't know how to press him to think about his behavior. He wasn't particularly introspective, hadn't ever been, artist or not.

But she was profoundly grateful he was back. That's what galled her the most—her own pitiful need for him, her eager embrace of the prodigal. It was affecting her work, she felt. Everything she painted looked awful to her, stiff or lifeless or awkward. For this reason, she stopped painting the women and embarked on a series of still lifes, small paintings of fruit or vegetables or flowers, of a doorway in afternoon light, a bicycle leaning against a pale wall.

These paintings had some charm, but she felt she was making them with the top of her head. She stopped, midafternoon one day in late July, put all her brushes to soak in turps, turned her canvases to the wall. She began to take walks in the woods around the house. One day, she got in the car and drove to the Kellogg farm and rented a horse for an hour. As she was riding along the bridle path, trying to take pleasure in the sun slanting through the trees, the wildflowers poking up along the border of the path, she remembered the story she had heard about the Kellogg man, whatever his name was, and poor Clea years ago. She had seen no middle-aged man or woman; a boy had brought her the horse. But the memory brought Clea to mind, and their meeting at Alicia's party.

They had hit it off splendidly, she and Hallie and Clea, as if they had been old friends who had met again. The young women were closer to her in age than her Steventon friends, more serious than her old New York friends; intelligent, fun, good company. Before they parted, they had urged her to come down to Connecticut to visit them, see the clinic, spend some time. It came to her that this was something she really felt like doing, the first thing she'd felt like doing since the trouble with Tim began.

That evening, as Tim lay in bed watching *Nightline*, Jenny puttered around the kitchen (as Tim would put it), then took the opportunity to call Clea from there. They had a long chat. Clea and Hallie would be delighted to see her; Martine had fallen in love with Jenny too. They had a big old house with plenty of room. Jenny should come and bring a sketchbook and charcoal, perhaps the impulse to make art would return. She might like to sketch some of their patients: They had remarkable faces, these women, they had suffered more than most people Clea or Jenny would know. Some were spectrally thin, others obese. Extremes. Jenny began to get excited. She had never spent much time on portraits—she had done an occasional sketch in art classes with live models, but had never felt drawn to it. She wanted to try again. They chose a few possible dates and Jenny said she'd get back to Clea soon.

But when she went into the bedroom, she said nothing to Tim. She was so excited that her face reflected happiness, eagerness. Sensing this, she said nothing, not wanting Tim to know her feelings were for something other than him. But he saw her heightened mood and took it personally; it cheered him. He knew she had been low since his return. He had not addressed it, though. He felt that ignoring feelings was the best response to them. He wanted things to go back to the way they'd been before his friends had visited, and couldn't really understand why this didn't just happen. He wanted to go back in time and cancel the visit, undo it, the way you canceled a train ticket. Jenny insisted that you couldn't cancel a ticket after you'd taken the journey. Which made sense, of course. But that was still what he wanted.

So this night, he welcomed her with open arms, assuming that her cheer meant her anger had finally dissipated and they could start anew. Maybe their "Lost weekend," as Tim called their time apart, after an old movie, was really lost.

Jenny knew exactly what he was doing, and she let him do it. They made love, but for the first time since she'd been with him, she failed to reach orgasm. She faked it so Tim wouldn't know, but filed this fact away for future thought. Several days later she brought up her plan to visit Clea, Hallie, and Martine. She mentioned it at the dinner table. Tim, a bite of steak tartare halfway to his lips, put it down again.

"You're leaving me?"

"Not leaving you. Going for a visit."

"For how long?"

"I'm not sure. I want to see their clinic, see what they do."

"Why? You planning to become a nurse?"

"No!" She laughed. "I'm just interested. What's wrong with you?"

"I don't want you to go."

"Ummm," she mused. "It's just that I'm not working well. I feel . . . drained. I thought a change might help."

"Are you getting even with me?" he asked suspiciously. "Is that what this is about?"

"Getting even? . . ." She was puzzled, then realized what he was suggesting. "No, of course not. I just need a break."

"I wish you wouldn't go."

"I need to," she insisted.

"Will you forget me?" he whined.

"Of course not, silly," she said, patting his arm. "I'll miss you."

"You will?"

"Did you miss me while you were away?"

"Horribly. And you never even called! Never tried to find me!"

Jenny laughed. "Served you right."

He smiled wryly. "I guess."

"So, what did Preston say about the weeping birch?" Jenny asked. Tim gave her the horticulturalist's diagnosis of their sick tree. He did not object to her changing the subject; he would have done the same. He was pleased that she seemed to have decided to do things his way. They never talked about her trip again; one Friday morning in mid-June, dressed and carrying a small suitcase, she popped her head into his studio and said good-bye. He kissed her a little coolly, but did not try to stop her.

That was all right.

It was a long drive to Bridgeport, along a meandering two-lane road. Jenny drove in a state of bliss, cooled by the wind from the open moonroof, basking in the sun-warmed air blessing her head. She was shocked at how elated she felt, how free! Was she feeling free of Tim? Did he feel oppressive to her? When had that started? It wasn't long ago that he had seemed to fulfill her every desire. Maybe it wasn't freedom from Tim she was feeling, just the joy of breaking with routine. You set up your life the way you want it, and first thing you know, it's become a rut, stifling, smothering. Maybe she just loved being in the car alone, sailing alone on an unknown adventure.

She arrived in Bridgeport in the early afternoon. Clea had said she would come home from the clinic early to meet her at the house. Clea's directions were perfect, and Jenny came upon a big old-fashioned Victorian house, with a gallery all around the lower level, a round tower on one corner, and a sprawling lawn with huge old trees shading it. The house was a little shabby, it needed paint, the shutters needed scraping and painting, the lawn was unkempt. It looked like a real home.

She left the Volvo in the dirt driveway behind Clea's Honda and carried her bag up the front steps. Clea threw the door open the moment Jenny's foot touched the first step, ran out and embraced her, then bent and grabbed her bag. Jenny felt again a surge of trusting affection.

"How was the trip? It's long, isn't it?"

"Not bad. I was in such a state of bliss! I haven't gone off on my own in a car in . . . maybe I never did! I've either forgotten what a joy it is or I never knew! No wonder Americans love their cars!"

"Me too. I love starting out early in the morning alone in the car. It feels like the epitome of freedom. The wandering cowboy hitting the road. Hitting Route 66, where anything can happen. The American myth," Clea laughed.

Inside, the house looked exactly as Jenny had imagined—comfortable, easy, pleasant. Barely decorated, just lived in. Clea pointed in a circle: "Well, this is it. Living room, dining room, kitchen, library down here—and a half bath. There are five bedrooms upstairs. Most of them are small, and two are really tiny, but I hope you won't mind. We don't want you to hide out in your room, anyway. Want to put your bag down and freshen up? I'll carry it for you. No, it's fine, it's not heavy at all. It's a gorgeous day, isn't it? I'm so glad you came! I'd like Emily to come down, but she's such a nerve-wracking driver that I'd worry the whole time."

"I could bring her down sometime."

"Would you? Brilliant! We'd love it!"

"You spent time in England?" Jenny asked, commenting obliquely on the "brilliant."

Clea got it. "Yeah, actually. Don't know why. We like it and often take our vacations there. The Lake District, Devon and Cornwall, the Cotswolds. Hallie loves the east coast, but then she's weird: It's so flat and bleak, with the smell of the sea everywhere . . . Actually, I like it too. Have you been there?"

"Yes. You mean around Aldeburgh? The land of George Crabbe and Benjamin Britten? Yes, I went there once. Drove over with a friend who adored Crabbe. She said it's a tragedy he's forgotten, but the truth is he's forgotten even there. But that area is so real compared to the Cotswolds. My father used to take me to England on vacations, London, Oxford, Cambridge, Stratford. And Tim likes it. Sometimes we fly over around Christmas, just to go to the theater."

"The people seem more . . . civilized . . . than us."

"They do, don't they? They're probably not, though. Football hooligans, India, South Africa. They have some blots in their account book too."

"Yeah. But they're polite. Like American southerners. Politeness can make up for an awful lot of sins. Especially when you can't see the sins. So, this is your room."

The room was airy and immaculate, with a polished wood floor, a rag rug by the bed, and two curtainless windows. There was a bed, a chair, a dresser with a mirror, and a round table, covered with a fringed cloth, a lamp, and heaped with books. There were framed sketches on the walls that looked to be by a child.

"Who's the artist?"

"Martine. I love her stuff. I know it's just kid art, but I like it better than anything I see in museums. But then I'm an ignoramus about art, Jenny. Don't be upset."

"No," Jenny said, examining the pictures. "I can see why you like them. They're lovely, really charming. I love them too."

Clea's color rose a little, and she turned away.

"Our worst feature is the bathroom. There's only one up here. At least it's big . . . but it's old and tatty. We keep intending to modernize, at least put in two sinks and a stall shower, but we never have the money. And we all love that huge old bathtub with the claw feet. It's just down the hall," She led the way. "Here."

She threw open a door, and went into a large bathroom with a huge old tub on legs, a wide sink, a toilet, and a dresser on which was placed a pitcher and bowl, some hand towels, dried flowers. "Here are your towels, I put them on the dresser. They're a different color from the others, so you won't get mixed up. I'll wait for you downstairs. What would you like to drink?"

"Oh, anything cold."

"Iced tea?"

"Perfect!"

"Okay. See you in ten." Clea ran down the stairs. She was quick in her motions, in everything she did. Probably why she was so thin. She moved like a person doing things she enjoys. Jenny used the bathroom, pausing to gaze out the wide window into a large yard with an old barn, some broad old maples and oaks, and a bed of tiger lilies that had sprung up haphazardly near the barn. The whole place made her feel serene; she wondered at this, coming from the work of art she lived in, with its perfect lawn and sculptured gardens. She felt easy, at home, which she rarely felt in her own house.

Lately she'd been thinking that she hadn't chosen her life, she'd chosen a man, and was living the life he created. So maybe sometimes it felt like a prison. And her mind snapped to Dr. Edwards, her professor in freshman English, talking to the students about *The Scarlet*

Letter. She had asked the class why at the end Hester chooses to return to a town that ostracizes her. The students made guesses, but when they thought about it, they were puzzled. Dr. Edwards said that our lives, whether we admit it or not, always end up being a prison. Hester chose one in which she could be of use. That had shocked Jenny; it was one of those ideas that penetrated her spine, or so it felt, as she wondered swiftly, thumbing through her brain as if it were a book with pages, to find somewhere some other choice, a life that keeps on being chosen, doesn't become imprisonment. Thin with experience at eighteen, she had assured herself that art, a life dedicated to art, would retain the incense of daily sacrifice to a beloved god, would remain free . . .

•

The weekend was mainly talk, talk of the excited sort that happens when smart people who love ideas encounter each other. Like people beginning a love affair, they were high on their own emotions, and wine, and their brains, which had them jabbering nonstop all day Saturday and Sunday, no matter what else they were doing. Martine, who had at first rolled her eyes at her mother, ended up becoming as involved as they were, as they questioned socialism, and why the Soviet version failed (Clea reminded them how both Rosa Luxemburg and Emma Goldman advised Lenin that socialism could not be imposed from above but had to grow from the roots, from the people themselves; and how he dismissed them). They argued about how an economically fair system had to be constituted as if it were to succeed, and they described in horror the future of capitalism if socialist ideas completely vanished. After many hours of laughter, passion, weeping, and shouting, they agreed with fervor that capitalism could only become fascism, that was its future, and that was what was happening now, in their day: They were watching fascism grow.

They did not stop talking when they drove to the clinic and gave Jenny a tour, drove to the grocery store and bought food for dinner, took a long walk in the woods in a park near their house, cooked a dinner of pasta with clams, green salad with parmesan cheese, and raspberry torte, and ate it with relish. They talked and talked more, pounding chair arms until three in the morning. Sunday, they drove to the Sound, and walked through a park there, had lunch at a little seafood shack, while debating Freudianism. Like socialism, it was obsolete yet alive and persistent, and the three women had read innumerable works on the subject by feminists and nonfeminists. Like most women, they were passionate in their dislike of the misogynist doctrine, but Hallie defended certain aspects of it: "Hovering attention," she said. "Who else ever suggested a man pay that much attention to his patients?" She laughed. "And the idea of an unconscious . . ."

"That's as old as myth!" Clea objected. "Lots of people have suggested an unconscious . . ."

All were united in condemning penis envy, clamoring that the truth was uterus envy. All condemned Freud's stupidity and ignorance—and he a doctor!—of the clitoris, and agreed that it (which did not depend on a penis to arouse it), not the vagina, was the seat of female pleasure. The clitoris, to which Hallie almost sang a hymn of praise as the only organ in mammals dedicated to nothing but sexual pleasure, was, she said, an organ protected and safe inside its sheathe, unlike the penis, and more dependable than drugs in delivering ecstasy. Her celebration, accompanied by loud laughter and braying, came close to embarrassing Martine, who nevertheless would not leave their company, even when urged.

They interrupted each other, yet heard each other out, arguing as if they had a serious stake in the issue, as if on their rightness or wrongness hinged the very future of the world. By Sunday night, they were exhausted, but exhilarated, and didn't want to stop.

"I could keep this up forever," Clea said.

"Me too. I never get to talk this way, with anyone! I've been longing for this kind of talk all my life."

"Well, stay on. Come to the clinic with us tomorrow, we'll put you to work. There's always something to be done," said Hallie. "Stay a while."

Jenny thought. "I will."

The talk continued through the week, if with less intensity, interrupted as it was by endless tasks. Hallie saw patients until eight at night most days, except for her mornings, spent at the hospital.

Clea managed the clinic, overseeing its systems, employees, supplies, and anything else that had a place in the bright airy building at the end of a strip mall. Clea supervised Jenny, who replenished supplies from the storeroom, made appointments when the receptionist went to lunch or took a break, calmed agitated patients or their children, holding babies when Clea thought it best the mother not be present—mostly when a baby had to have a shot. Mothers, she explained, tended to cry when their babies cried, upsetting the babies even more.

Holding the babies felt strange. They fit into her arms as if her arms had been especially constructed just for this, and she felt utterly experienced at it, even though she had never done it before. She was careful to support the necks of the newborns and not to touch the top of their skulls. She studied their faces with awe, seeing character, personality, and a fierce life force in each new infant she encountered. She bottle-fed a couple, whose tiny hands clenched and unclenched with ferocious nervousness as they nursed, and she thought about the nervous, starved way squirrels nibbled on nuts. That's basically what we are, she kept thinking, starving animals.

She loved being at the clinic—"loved" didn't cover it; it was totally engrossing, she forgot herself entirely for the hours she was there, and she loved the patients, even the difficult ones. When there was nothing she was skilled enough to help with, she sat in the foyer, sketching the patients who'd allow it, sketching the employees, catching quick impressions of Hallie in her white coat, Clea in her jeans. She sketched babies, who carried her over into another realm of experience. The answer to all need, Maddy had said. Yes, she could see that.

On their way home (they took separate cars because Hallie had to go to the hospital and Clea had to do errands) one of them would stop at a food shop that specialized in takeout food, and pick up dinner. At home, tired and quietly eating, they caught up with Martine's news, always giving her food for her soul—praise, a pat of affection, ten minutes of completely attentive interest. They desultorily discussed the patients, and their headaches, tiredness, sore feet, their serious and troubling diseases. And once refreshed with food and a glass of wine, they leaned back and continued their talks, this week on the volatile subjects of politics—the presidential campaign had heated up—television, and movies. They were disgusted with both candidates; Bush, whom they called Dubya, who lied about his conservatism, and Gore, who in terror of sounding too liberal sounded like a Bush twin. They were aghast at Bush's stupidity, wondered how such a man dared to run for president, and were even more aghast at people who supported him. Round and round they went, agreeing with each other, outraged at almost everything. They talked about violence on television, sex on television; Jenny told them what Maddy and Emily had told her about censorship of sexual matters in "their day." Now, it's progressive ideas that are censored, Clea said. From the news, from programming, even from newspapers and magazines, she said. Anything left wing, anything feminist, anything that might really affect the system, was silenced. Censorship of political matters outside the mainstream was worse than sex had been in olden times, she said. But whether mentioned or not, sex existed, you couldn't forget it, even censored, whereas most people in the country had probably never heard a progressive idea in their lives.

The week flew by. Jenny was reluctant to stay longer, however much she was enjoying her visit, because she didn't want to—as she said—rub Tim's nose in it. Yet (she had to admit to herself) she had in some way intended to get even: She had not called him at all that week and she did not call to tell him she was returning. But as she set out Friday morning, after the others had gone to work and school, she saw that it was not natural for her to go a week without calling him. It was not natural to the person she had become in her marriage; although it was perfectly natural to the girl Jenny had once been. So what am I doing? Getting revenge, or regressing?

She left early in the day and again turned her face to the open road, wondering if she would feel the same elation she had felt coming. She didn't. It was only the setting out, she surmised, the embarkation on the aventure, not the return. But she felt extremely content. Happy, tired, used up, satiated with the many different pleasures of the week, she was ready to return to a less demanding life. Yet something had changed in her: Passages within her body were wired to the babies she'd held, and she now understood that she had to have a child. How Tim would react to this was unknown, but Maddy was right. It no longer mattered how he felt. She had to have a child. With him or against his will.

21

In early July, Maddy and Charley, not conscious of the sweltering New York humidity, were sitting with Jean in a waiting room at Sloan-Kettering. Parrish was being processed for admission. Maddy had insisted her son come to a New York specialist, one of three Steven Gilson had found for them. Parrish had seen all of them and chosen one to care for him: This oncologist was associated with Sloan-Kettering. Maddy felt that their doctors in the Berkshires were fine for most things, but when the problem was as serious as cancer, you should go to the people who knew most about it. Although treatment in New York City would enormously complicate their lives, Parrish and Jean simply obeyed her—as they had passively obeyed her ever since Parrish had fallen ill. They were like two children wandering in the forest, and Maddy their guide. Not that she knew more than they; she was just more used to gathering herself together and coping. She took care of everything. She had said whatever it cost, she would pay for it; she would rent them an apartment or pay for a hotel, whatever it took. After all, she repeated frequently, what was money for?

As soon as Lily heard that her brother was ill and being treated in New York, she offered to put up the family up in her Manhattan apartment. Alicia had already taken care of that. She explained that their Riverside Drive apartment sat mostly empty. Steven rose early every morning, left at seven-thirty, and didn't return until nine or ten, or even later, some nights. He went to Steventon every weekend. So if they wanted to stay in town while Parrish was receiving treatment, they could use the two empty bedrooms: Jean could have one, and Maddy and Charley the other. There were televisions in all the bedrooms, and each had its own bath, so they would be comfortable.

Maddy apologized to Lily, explaining that they could have Alicia's apartment essentially to themselves, without bothering anyone. Lily was graceful about it, had the family to dinner, and offered space to any other family members who wanted to visit. Maddy was grateful for Alicia's invitation and offered to make dinner for Steven on the nights he came home wanting to eat. But Steven refused, graciously. He said Maddy would be too exhausted after a day spent sitting in a hospital, to market in unfamiliar territory and cook in an unfamiliar kitchen. Besides, he was used to eating at the Harvard Club with some friends or at a local bistro where he was known. Still, he liked the Golds and enjoyed Charley's company at night when he got home. The old man was smarter than he seemed, and easy in himself, so easy to be around.

They planned to stay in New York for the one week each month while Parrish was hospitalized for chemotherapy. When he was released, they would take him home to the Berkshires to rest up for the next onslaught. But things did not work out that way. Nine-year-old Madeleine, back in Steventon with Jean's sister Arlene, got sick, something strange with her stomach. Parrish and Jean's older kids then started having difficulties in school—one had been truant, the other began talking back and acting out. The children had never been without their parents, and they were reacting. Maddy insisted that Charley drive Jean back to Massachusetts and stay to help her out—three kids are a handful for a single parent, she said, especially one already worried sick about her husband. Charley could do errands for Jean, babysit, and perform whatever chores Parrish would normally do. Charley was happy to do it. He was uncomfortable in New York, it was too big and noisy and impersonal for him. He was homesick. He went back with Jean, whose face settled into a permanent frown of anxiety, and became her mainstay. The two formed a bond during this time, one that would never be broken.

Maddy stayed in New York. She would not leave Parrish's side. She sat in his room, in a corner, reading one or another giant Trollope novel. She did not speak to him much, but she was alert to his every need. She used the nurse's kitchen to make him tea, or bought him soft drinks from the machine in the hall. When he could not eat the hospital food (and he often could not), she would walk up to First Avenue and stop at one of the tens of restaurants near the hospital, to find something that might appeal to him. After she left him for the evening, she shopped on upper Broadway, and spent the night making a nourishing soup for him. She made him a lamb and barley broth, a rich chicken broth with rice. He was able to eat these, and she believed he gained strength from them. She answered his phone when he was resting. She sat by him when he slept, smiled at him, stroked his hand. She played cards with him when he felt well.

Lily came several times the first week, Parsons came once, and Parrish and Jean's children brought video games on their computers to play with Parrish. They were the ones he enjoyed the most. Maddy oversaw everything like a fairy godmother with a bleeding heart, weeping because she had no magic wand.

In Steventon, Alicia invited Charley for dinner one night after his return. He was a wreck, as tired and old as she had ever seen him.

"How's Parrish?" she asked.

"Oh, Lisha, I don't know. I'm just a useless old man. Maddy knows. Don't ask me."

When Parrish came out of the hospital after his first week of chemo, he was so sick that Maddy was afraid to take him home, and they remained at Alicia's for a couple of days. He could not swallow, and the hospital readmitted him through Urgent Care, their emergency room. He had thrush, and he needed hospitalization for another week. After it was better, Maddy drove them up to the mountains. Parrish was silent during the trip. They would have to turn around and come back in just ten days.

After a couple of months of this, Maddy told Emily that all life felt suspended. She felt as if she were in prison, or at war, someplace where she was alive but not living her life. "You know you have a life, you know you are still, somehow, in it, but . . . You know how the sky looks when a storm hovers over the mountain, not yet arrived, but coming? That's how it feels: like a storm suspended for a time."

The women gathered around Maddy and Parrish once he was home. They took Parrish and Jean trays of lasagna, stuffed cabbage, boeuf a la mode, desserts, soups, anything to tempt the pale, thin patient to eat and to save his anxious wife from cooking. But Parrish had mouth sores and couldn't eat most of the time. Maddy and Jean made him cold soups, milkshakes, aloe on ice. Maddy in turn was given help. Her friends had her for lunch, had her and Charley for dinner, tried to divert them. An endless stream of gifts poured into the two households—books on cancer, meditation tapes, amulets, Mozart CDs, flowers, video games. Jean read all the books; Parrish wouldn't touch them, he wouldn't listen to a tape or use them to meditate. But he did play video games.

"He thinks he's going to die," Maddy said tearfully to Emily one night in September when they were dining alone at Emily's. "I can see it in him."

"Is he going to die?" Emily asked. "Is it a fact? Or a supposition?"

"Who knows?" Maddy replied. "But it doesn't look good. He had a CT scan; the first two months of chemo didn't shrink the tumor at all. It's spread even farther. It's in his lymph nodes."

"I'm so sorry, Maddy," Emily said.

"Thanks," Maddy said, a sob in her throat. "The poor baby's had such a hard life. It's all my fault."

"Oh, Maddy!"

"No, it is! If I hadn't been so punitive, he'd never have started drinking the way he did, and all that smoking. His health would be better now . . ."

"Maddy, I'm getting really angry with you. You don't know

what it was that started Parrish drinking. You don't even know that his drinking helped to give him lung cancer. Most likely, his smoking did that. Are you responsible for his smoking too?"

Maddy began to weep.

"Maddy!" Emily yelled. "What you are doing is putting yourself at the center of your children's lives! Making their problems seem to be about you, instead of them! By assuming so much guilt, you're giving yourself ten times more power than you ever had!" Emily gazed at her severely.

Maddy stared at her white-faced.

Emily, studying Maddy's face, melted. She put her arms around her friend. "I didn't mean to hurt you."

Maddy removed Emily's arms. "But you're right, aren't you? I've been so blind. I'm doing the same thing my mother did—she acted martyred, as if everything we were or weren't came from her, drained her spirit, cost her her life."

"Of course, in a way that's true."

"Some mother fish eat their young; midge daughters eat their mothers. Is that what you mean? But what am I doing when I insist that everything they do is my fault? Am I eating them?"

"Oh, I don't know! Drop the metaphor. You're taking responsibility for their lives, for everything they do. You're denying them any power at all."

Maddy plopped down on a sofa. "You're right," she said grimly, staring into space.

"You don't have to get mad at me for being right. It happens rarely enough," Emily muttered.

Maddy smiled at her, and Emily smiled back, ruefully. Maddy reached out her hands to Emily, who grabbed them and held on.

"Sit," Maddy ordered, and Emily joined her on the sofa, their hands still clasped.

"What a jerk," Maddy said.

"You or me?"

"Me."

Emily considered. "What do you say we order in? Chinese, pizza, or chicken?"

"You pick. You pick and you call. I'll make drinks. We'll toast the future!"

"How about," Emily suggested, "we just toast the present. Now. Today."

Maddy gazed at her. "Never thought of that."

•

Of course, Jenny would not be able to proceed "with Tim or against his will" after all. Driving home, she had thought about not telling him of her decision to have a child. It would make sense not to tell him. He was entirely capable of becoming . . . well, incapable, if he really didn't want a child. Not even in pique, just unconscious stubbornness. Sometimes it happened anyway, when he'd had a bit too much to drink or was a little angry with her. He never, of course, said he was angry, but there was a strong degree of coincidence between her rare refusals to do something his way and his later inability to make love to her. It didn't matter how petty the issue was. It infuriated him, for instance, that she habitually cut lettuce instead of tearing it. He didn't say so, or act angry; he always made a joke of it, but it was a joke with an edge. What did you call this—probability, was that it? For instance, he liked his underwear folded in a complicated way she was too impatient to undertake, so when she was the one to empty the drier, she simply laid his stuff unfolded on the bed. And on laundry night, he always claimed tiredness or a headache. At least, she thought so. She hadn't kept track on paper, which was the only way she could be sure.

Still, she could not in good conscience get pregnant behind his back, as it were. He would have to help raise a child; he had to approve the having of it. If he didn't . . . Jenny would have to think further about her marriage.

The wheel shuddered under her hands as this thought had passed through her mind as she returned home from Bridgeport. She felt she had undergone a sea change, to be able to think such a thought. When had this happened? How?

Still, as she pulled into her driveway, she was happy to see her beautiful house and even happier to see Tim. He must have heard her car, because he was standing in front of the house when she drove up, waiting for her, and he pounced on her as she left the car. Her body thrust itself into his arms; they embraced wildly, as if months had passed since they'd seen each other, and he half carried her to the bedroom. To say something then would have crushed his desire, and besides, it was not even in her mind at that moment. The break had been good; it had done its work. She felt refreshed and new, full of energy, and when he led her into the bedroom, she felt as she had in the old days, chosen by a god. How could she not lean into the beautiful mindless ecstasy of passion, one of the great experiences of life? Something that cannot be coerced, willed, manufactured, begged for, wilfully produced or reproduced: something that happens rarely enough in any life.

But lying there with him afterward, both of them damp and sleepy with pleasure, the thought popped back soon enough, bringing a guilty dread with it. She had stopped taking her pills the day she decided, four days into her stay with Clea and Hallie. It was possible that she was into her fertile period. Since she had been on the pill for years, she hadn't paid attention to her cycles. They hadn't mattered.

She had to tell him soon. What would she do if he did become impotent? On the other hand, she couldn't force a baby down his throat. It wouldn't be fair. She lay, replete, breathing deeply, his right hand fastened on her left thigh, her left hand clasping his right arm, the two of them a static image of love fulfilled, a perfect couple, while Tim slept.

•

Two months had passed since Emily had sent Andrei Sikorsky the tapes of her recorded work when he called in July, voluble with apology—he'd been traveling—Berlin, Vienna, Pittsburgh, Cleveland. He'd listened to her tapes; he loved her work and wanted to give her a premiere. How was her symphony coming?

Emily had to sit down. Her voice surprised her by remaining calm and steady, unlike her pulse. The symphony was essentially finished, she said, as calmly as if people asked her about it every day. A little polishing here and there, she thought. But she had no tape of it . . .

He would read the score, he said, if she could fax him a copy. It was fine with him that no one had heard it, he wanted to be the first, he had just been appointed music director in Cleveland, he was so happy, it was so great to be in the city of Szell and Leinsdorf and Boulez, such an honor, he wanted to do something major, he wanted to celebrate an American in this most American city . . .

Emily closed her eyes. She was silent as he ran on.

"I can send you the score in a couple of weeks," she said finally.

"Wonderful! You can e-mail it, yes? I always have my laptop with me. Or fax it. Or use Federal Express, no? Now, where will I be?" He rustled busily; Emily could hear his pleasure at being such a busy man as he self-importantly mentioned places and dates. He listed several cities, then said, "And after that, I'll be in London for a few weeks. A little vacation after the performance, eh? In a civilized city! Ah, London!"

She disliked his manner, artsy-fartsy, Poppa would have said. She wanted to cut through it, cut him down to New England size. But why shouldn't he feel pleased with his life? Twenty years stuck in the Soviet Union, a country that was a prison; they wouldn't let him leave, who knows why, too precious? To unreliable? And now, he flew across the world, performed everwhere, made Western dollars and pounds and francs and marks, real money. He had become known in the West only recently. Maybe he would be visiting London for the first time. Maybe she should not be so judgmental. She should not be short with him, not cut him down as a showoff, *BE NICE, EMILY*, for a change. She tried. They hung up.

Emily sat on the bench by the stairs in the hall. Her head was bowed; she could barely breathe. If it happened, if he followed through—such a flibberty-gibbet man, you couldn't be sure—if he did, that would be her beginning. At seventy, she would finally be introduced to the world.

Success is counted sweetest
By those who ne'er succeed.
To comprehend a nectar
Requires sorest need.
Not one of all the purple Host
Who took the flag today

Can tell the definition so Clear
of Victory—
As he defeated—dying—
On whose forbidden Ear
The distant strains of triumph
Burst agonized and Clear.

When for years she'd been telling herself it didn't matter, that

I'm Nobody—Who are you?
Are you—Nobody too?
Then there's a pair of us?
Don't tell! they'd advertise—you know!

How dreary—to be—Somebody!
How public—like a Frog—
To tell one's name—the livelong June—
To an admiring Bog!

She was overflowing; gratitude poured from her soul at the thought that people who knew music would listen to hers, would criticize it, for good or ill. Her name would be known to the musical literati. She sat like a statue covered with flowing marble, a painted mantle; clouds of music rolled off her body.

She raised her head. She wanted to share this with Maddy, but Maddy was in New York with Parrish. She'd call her there but would wait until tonight; afternoons, Maddy was always in the hospital. On impulse, she picked up the phone and dialed Connecticut. The clinic receptionist answered.

"Oh, I thought Clea . . . is Clea Rossi-Oldfield available?"

"Just a minute. Who's calling?" a woman asked peremptorily.

What poor manners, Emily thought. "Her aunt. Emily."

"Oh, Aunt Emily! The composer? She's just on the other line, sweetie, hold on a sec."

What a nice woman, Emily thought with a smile.

"Aunt Em?"

"Clea. I'm sorry to disturb you at work."

"Are you all right? Everything okay? I heard about Parrish . . ."

"No, I'm fine. It's good news. This man—this Russian—well, I guess he's Ukrainian . . . he wants to perform my work with the Cleveland Orchestra!"

Clea shrieked. She kept yelling. Everyone within earshot must have dropped everything, as she told them the news. Emily laughed, listening to the chaos. Clea came back on the line, bubbling, adding to the noisy nonsense. Emily let herself weep a bit, just dampening her cheeks, let herself enjoy it before she checked her tears, as she had to, reminding herself that Sikorsky had a reputation to make and was gambling on her doing it for him. But wasn't it great that he was willing to try her out, that he, a Ukrainian man, was open to an American woman, something that couldn't have happened thirty years before, even twenty? Maybe even ten. Who knows?

I was lucky I lived to be old, she thought. Like Louise Nevelson, Louise Bourgeois, Alice Neel. A woman who lives long enough may finally be told she has done worthwhile work. If she lives past her sexual years. Is menopausal. Only then.

She walked to the kitchen and put water in the kettle for tea. Push those feelings aside, push the past away, give up the bitterness about the long, long wait and all the mortifications. She sat in poppa's rocker waiting for the kettle to shriek, hands clasped as tightly as if she were in church. Dread roiled her stomach, terror pulsed in all her capillaries, her temples beat, her fingers tingled. She had wanted this too long, too hard; would success kill her?—or worse, Clea or Martine? She would not let herself dwell on negative things like her awareness that Sikorsky needed someone who would enhance his reputation, and that a man would more assuredly do this with more certainty than she. That he might at any moment find someone more likely to gain him prestige than Emily Oldfield: What did she have going for her, anyway, except maybe her old family name? What, except her mind, her heart, her life? No, don't think that way. Try to seize the joy and let go of the anger and dread. Try to enjoy the moment, to believe that it had come, your time, at last. Try to remember what your beloved Emily wrote to her beloved Sue:

To be alive—is Power—
Existence—in itself—
Without a further function—
Omnipotence—Enough—

To be alive—and Will!
'Tis able as a God—
The Maker—of Ourselves—be what—
Such being Finitude!

A few hours later, Emily realized she was too anxious about Clea to let it rest. It's typical of my generation, she thought: I can't believe that I'll be allowed to accomplish anything in the world without losing everyone I love. All that brainwashing, from the movies, books, magazines. Nonsense, probably. But . . .

So she called Clea again and arranged to spend a weekend in Bridgeport with her. Clea was overjoyed. "I'll have you in my house! The first time!" she crowed. "Come during the week so we can show you the clinic while it's working, and then spend the weekend together."

Emily left on a Wednesday, meandering down Route 7 into Connecticut. She drove slowly, looking around. Her driving made people nervous because she looked around so much, but landscape was meant to be looked at, wasn't it? She liked to look, to see the flower born to blush unseen, the violet by a mossy stone, half hidden from the eye, believing, insisting, that the flower was born to please itself and not the world, and that the violet was as lovely hidden by its stone as in a pot set beneath the portrait of Isabella Gardner and Giotto's Christ, the only two so honored in Gardner's museum. Was that the same as a tree falling in an empty forest? She supposed so. But weren't things meant to exist in all their glory and then die, wasn't their meaning resident in that existence alone? Did things have to become part of another story to have a meaning?

Did it matter if her symphony was heard?

It seems to matter to me.

Reading the other day about quantum theory, waves and particles, which didn't exist until observed, how could that be? Was that true? Was life like that, was the violet nonexistent until the poet wrote about it? Was it necessary to celebrate the violet, the particle, the wave, to hail it? Hail life! And Adam named all the beasts, was the naming the same as calling into existence? Was the function of the poet to create reality? Was she creating sound?

She shook her head hard from side to side. She gazed around her. She was interested in odd things, the color of the leaves of a particular tree, the shape of another, a flower she did not recognize, the warehousey buildings in one part of the state, the cutesy charm of those in another. She preferred the warehouses to the cutesy places, perversely, she supposed, because they were useful. As she loved the chaos and filth of a working port but was unmoved by the prettiness of Mystic Harbor. The drive down took her hours, but that didn't matter to her.

She found Clea's house easily. She had not even gotten out of the car when Clea came tearing out the front door, crying, "You're here! Just in time for dinner, too! How long did it take you? What time did you leave?"

Emily was too embarrassed to tell her she had left early in the day, meandered, had had lunch out, had meandered some more—so she just smiled. "I had a lovely drive down."

Clea hugged her, grabbed her overnight case, put her arm about her and led her into the house. Hallie was in the front hall on the phone, but she mouthed hello and waved. Martine came running down the stairs to embrace her shyly, and when Emily could not let go of her, allowed herself to be led into the living room and seated beside her great-aunt.

"Tell me what you've been doing," that personage ordered.

"Well. I've been on the Web, doing research for a history paper. I have to write about the Vietnam War. Do you remember that? It seems incredible to me, so many soldiers killed, and so many Vietnamese, for no reason. Wasn't it? I mean, we didn't win. If we had won, what would have happened?"

"We would have kept the communists from taking over. We would have kept a puppet regime in power, one that put our interests first. Although I'm not sure we really had any interests in Vietnam. As it was, they did take over. The people got the government they wanted, instead of being colonized by outsiders."

"Are they communists like the ones in Russia?"

"Not exactly. In the beginning, the Vietcong were just people who wanted to run their own country instead of having the French do it."

"That seems understandable."

"Yes. In the beginning, we thought highly of them. I don't know what changed our mind, really."

"Was it a bad war?"

"Yes."

"Because it killed so many people? We lost more soldiers than in World War II, one article said."

"Yes. And millions and millions of Vietnamese. And it was a war in support of colonialism, which upset a lot of people. After all, our country was founded in opposition to colonialism. Our revolution was against colonial tyranny. Our history, the way we think about the United States, is a democratic system, opposed to rule from outside. But in Vietnam, we supported colonialism. A corrupt French puppet government."

"Oh." Martine was wide-eyed. "I read that people went on marches. Did you?"

"Sure did," Emily said. "To Boston Common, with thousands of others."

"I didn't know that," Clea put in.

"It was so long ago."

"In your radical days? I didn't even know you were political. I thought you were an artist . . ."

"In an ivory tower? I guess I've become that. I'm hardly political at all anymore."

"Why not?"

Emily shrugged. "I guess because it seems useless to me. The press has changed. They censor things more than they ever did before. Not that they ever told the whole story, but at least they used to cover protests. By the time of the Gulf War, there were still protests in New York, San Francisco, London . . . but the newspapers hardly mentioned them, and TV didn't cover them at all to speak of. I guess I think we're done for. We're becoming a fascist state, and we hardly say boo."

"We are?" Martine was aghast. "Fascist?"

"I think so. Ever since Reagan, the rich have become richer than ever, the poor poorer and the rich dictate everything that happens, the poor are barely thought of. It is assumed that the rich deserve their wealth because they're superior to the poor. One percent of the people in the world own 57 percent of its wealth. Isn't that the basis of fascism?" she appealed to Clea.

"I think fascism is based on a myth, you know, some myth of the folk, an ideal tradition . . ."

"When men were men and women were servants . . ."

"Yes," she laughed.

"But isn't this one based on something like that? The wonderful plantation system, the good old days when white masters were beloved by their black slaves because they took such good care of them?"

"I don't know anyone who believes that," Clea said.

"I do," Hallie said, entering. "Hello, Emily." She bent and kissed her. "My son says hello too. He's thinking of going to med school, how about that?" she asked Clea.

Clea gave her a high five.

"We're discovering Emily's radical past."

"Hardly radical. I'm a humanist. An anarchist. I have no politics, because there's no political form for anarchy. Who do you know who believes that?"

"My mother came from Mississippi," Hallie said. "She lived there until she was grown. She told me all about it. She was a teacher up here."

"I see."

"We talk politics in this house all the time. We drove Jenny crazy when she was down here. We couldn't stop talking about the campaign."

"It's a disheartening campaign, isn't it."

"Yes. Because it looks like that moron Bush will win."

"Yes. What a shame. But Gore is so busy disavowing progressive ideas. He's running in fear, cowering in the center. That gives the right an edge."

"You got it," Hallie said with disgust.

Martine was attending with interest. "Do you think there's hope?" she asked her mother.

Clea glanced at Emily. "I know how Emily feels. She's been through this for decades, and things seem to have gotten worse. But, yes, I think there's hope. Only because there has to be hope. We can't manage without it."

"Does that mean you don't really have hope?"

"There's always hope!" Hallie said passionately. "Look at South Africa! Ireland! Vietnam! Not that things are perfect in those places, I don't mean that. I do mean that people don't give up. They will not. And after enough time, they triumph. Then they can start to try to create justice."

"Until the elite finds a new way to subdue them,"

"God knows they keep trying," Hallie agreed.

"And you shouldn't give up," Emily told Martine. "I decided long ago to keep my cynical views to myself. It's unfair to burden the young with them. I shouldn't have opened my mouth. I usually don't."

"Is that why?" Clea asked in wonder.

"That's why."

Clea gazed at her aunt. "Sweet Emily," she said, "Wouldn't you like some dinner?"

"I could eat," Emily said, smiling, hearing her father's voice.

•

The women took Emily to the clinic the next day, and she pitched in just as Jenny had, working the telephones, helping with patients, helping with the babies. At the end of the day, Clea found her mopping the floor of the reception room. "You shouldn't do that, Em!" she cried, trying to grab the mop away from her.

"Don't mind at all. Haven't mopped a floor in decades. It's satisfying. I'd forgotten. It looks so different when you finish. That's the thing about women's work: It has to be done over and over, but each time it gives you satisfaction. It makes something visible happen. Unlike shuffling paper."

They were tired Thursday night, so they bought takeout from the Chinese restaurant and watched television. Still, their tiredness did not keep them from having a noisy, lively discussion of emergency rooms and hospitals after watching *ER*, deconstructing the program. Martine listened wide-eyed to these arguments, a little smile playing on her face. What an education she's getting, Emily thought.

Emily worked at the clinic again Friday, becoming quite expert in some jobs. The atmosphere there was thrilling to her because it was so unfamiliar. What was strange was not her fellows' color—music students come in all sizes and colors, in Rome and Boston as well as in Steventon—but their class.

Emily's huge family, like Maddy's, had sprawled over class lines for decades. The occasional Abenaki forbear, the slave girl who had been incorporated into the family, or the Asian professional one aunt had unaccountably married had been fully middle-class people and constituted no threat. But some cousins had been drawn to partners with no education, no drive for wealth, and no fondness for middle-class manners. These their siblings found unacceptable. No one used the word *class* to describe the differences, but that was the only word Emily knew to describe them. She remembered her aunt Dot, after a visit to her younger sister Dilly, who lived among wrecked cars and old tires in a rusting trailer, long before such things were called RVs, with a man who worked on cars and drank beer and let the cans pile up outdoors, who were a scandal among the Oldfields and the Hutchinsons, saying how sweet it had been there, with the two of them, because they had no pretensions. And later, Dot had taken a job sorting sheet music in a small plant that opened in Lindale, working with women from various immigrant communities—Portuguese, Italian, Polish. She loved them.

"You know, I hate middle-class women, Emily," she had told her young niece. "They're so self righteous, so judgmental. These women—they have compassion for each other, they know how hard life is. They don't lie the way my so-called friends do. And when they laugh—it's real."

And so Emily found it with the poor women she worked with at the clinic—women from Guinea, the Dominican Republic, and Mexico, from Mississippi and Alabama and from many generations of New England forbears. When they accepted her, she felt worthy; when they approved her work, she felt blessed; and when they laughed with her—or even at her—and laid a hand on her arm, she felt loved. She was thrilled when Ida let her take the mop forcibly from her hands so she could go home, or Lashona allowed her to finish taking stock of the medications cabinet so she could help a hysterical child, or Mildred let her help with the huge pile of Medicaid forms she had to fill out.

She had a deep sense of satisfaction that night as they ate out at a local vegetarian restaurant, where Emily happily had a pear salad with Gorgonzola, one of her favorite meals. They asked her about Sikorsky, her symphony, and modern music generally, matter for several lectures, had she been so minded. But, happy though she was at their interest, she kept things simple.

Over the weekend, Clea and Hallie took Emily and Martine to the beach, then sightseeing; they cooked corn and lobsters on the grill, and behaved as much like silly girls as they could. Martine was right at home in this climate, and even Emily got caught up in the giggling and jokes. So when she set out Monday morning, she felt as satisfied as if she had eaten banquets in several different countries during her stay, and had finished every course of every one.

By the time she got home, she was ready to put the last touches to the symphony. She waited a week, then reread the score; then she copied it and sent it off to Sikorsky. This time, she did not worry that she would lose Clea, or about her future sanity if he refused it. She was home free.

22

A few days later she returned from Bridgeport, Jenny fixed a special dinner, steak tartare made from rib steaks she had ground in the food processor. She knew Tim loved it, and had learned by watching him how to prepare it. With it she served fresh made pommes frites and creamed spinach, with raspberries and cream for dessert. She lit candles and arranged peonies in a low bowl on the table and opened a good burgundy. Tim felt like hugging himself. Jenny did not often take care of him this attentively, although he loved being catered to (as who does not? Jenny thought, smiling) and loved her for doing it, since it was all done to his standards. And after their loving encounter that morning, he felt utterly secure, all his doubts and fears of the last week erased. So when, after dinner, she said there was something she wanted to talk to him about, he was not stiff or defensive at all.

"Shoot," he said.

"You know, I loved being in the clinic Clea and Hallie run. It's really wonderful, it gives you such a great feeling, helping those people, and the women there love them, they've come to trust them, it's really great!"

He smiled, touched by her tender heart. "Would you like to give them a donation? We could spare a couple of thousand."

"Oh. That would be nice. They could certainly use it. But that's not what I was thinking." She began to spear some salad with her fork, then let it rest on the plate. "The thing I loved most was the babies. They are so adorable. You can't help falling in love with them. Everyone does, it's just natural. And in holding them, taking care of them, giving them bottles, or changing them . . . I came to realize . . ."

Tim's face began to darken.

" . . . that I really want to have one, Tim."

Silence. Tim chewed potatoes. Jenny slid her spinach into her mouth.

The silence had become heavy when Jenny said timidly, "Aren't you going to say anything?"

Tim finished his dinner, patted his mouth with his napkin, lay the linen on the table.

"You were there a week. You were enchanted. I can understand that. But that doesn't mean you have any idea how much work an infant can be. How consuming they are. Where a baby exists, there is no other life. Do you realize that? It takes up all the space, its sound completely possesses the air. Its demands come first, above anything and everything else. Above art, above food, above your own life. You have to sacrifice everything else. That's what having a baby really means."

Jenny looked at her plate. His voice, she thought, wasn't really angry. She looked up at him to check. His face was calm, but there were pink patches in his cheeks.

"Tim. Tim, I know you've been through this and I know I promised when we got married . . . But that was seven years ago and I'm older and I'm different and I can't help that. A baby's not a sacrifice if you want it. Only if you don't. And you don't. So I promise that if we have a baby, I will take complete care of it, do everything, all the work, I won't ask you to lift a finger . . ."

He lifted his napkin again and thrust it down on the table with a thump. He stood up. "That's not possible! Do you hear what I'm saying? I know what I'm talking about! There is no way, no matter what you do—forget being an artist, by the way!—there's no way that bringing a baby into this house won't disrupt everything in it, my work, my life, my peace of mind, not just yours. There is no way I won't get dragged into caring for it! And I don't want to take care of a baby! I told you that before we got married! I've already done it, and it sucks!"

He strode away from the table, walked through the kitchen, and went out the back door. She heard the door to his studio open and close. Slam.

She sat. He never even had dessert.

After a while she rose and cleared the table, storing the remains of the food, covering the raspberries and whipped cream she'd set out for dessert, wiping down the counters, polishing the dining-room table. Her face was drawn.

It was early, only a little after nine, but she went into the bedroom and prepared for bed. She wasn't really paying attention to what she was doing, moving like an automaton, going through the motions. She put on a fresh nightgown, a polished-cotton one that buttoned at the neck—it was a chilly night—and slid between the sheets. She reached for the remote, but put it back down on the bedside table and picked up a book of poems by Louise Glück. But she didn't open it. She gazed at nothing.

It was sad. That was all she could think, how sad it was. She could understand. She couldn't blame him, really. Of course he was right: A baby in the house would change everything, would leave nothing unaffected. She could see that, just from her experiences of the past few days, with the babies in the clinic. They were tiny and helpless, yet masters of the universe. When a baby was present, everything around it fell into shadow; its noise, its needs overwhelmed everything else. Helpless, what did they have to enable them survive except their voices? They screamed and stank. They moved their tiny hands and feet. They tried to focus their eyes. They were adorable. What else could they do? And he was right, no matter how assiduously she tried to care for it by herself, there would be a day when she had to leave it with him, a moment she'd ask him to hold it, an hour when she'd ask him to change it. And it wouldn't be good for their baby if he had nothing to do with it, anyway. If he ignored it totally. A baby needs to be loved by everybody in its world. Or else it feels the cold wind.

So it was just sad, there was nothing else to say. Terribly sad. She sat there feeling it, just feeling it over and over, a pain that required a certain amount of time to wear itself out. It would wear itself out, in time, that she knew. It might take time. Days. Weeks. Months. But it would.

She heard the back door open and glanced at the clock. It was eleven. Steps through the house, kitchen, dining room, living room. She'd left all the lights on. Steps approached the bedroom. Tim appeared in the doorway. He looked at her. She glanced at him. Sad. He left the doorway. Steps retraced to the kitchen. Door locked. Lights switched off as he went, returning to the bedroom. He came in and closed the door. Quietly. He went into the bathroom. She heard him pee, heard him wash, heard him brush his teeth. She didn't feel more or less. He came out with his sweater in his hand, laid it on the slipper chair, unbuttoned his shirt. He got undressed. She didn't watch him or not watch him. Sometimes he slipped into her sight. Sometimes he vanished. He pulled on his pajama bottoms. He came toward her and sat on her side of the bed. He took her hand.

"I can't keep you from having a baby if you want one," he said.

She smelled alcohol.

"No," she agreed.

"I mean, I don't want to keep you from having a baby. It's important to you, I understand that."

"Yes."

"It's just . . . I don't think you have any idea how much trouble they are."

"Probably not. But it doesn't matter to me. I can put off painting for a few years, if that's what's required. I can put everything else aside for a while. A baby is the center of a life. It gives your life meaning. It's the most important thing in life. Even Maddy says that."

"I understand." He picked up her hand and put it to his lips. "And I will try to be tolerant. I will try to be patient. I will not stand in your way."

She glanced at him then. "Are you saying? . . ."

"Yes. I'm saying yes. Have your baby."

She shook her head. "That's really sweet of you, Tim, but it wouldn't be good, it wouldn't work. You're too angry about it. Too . . . adamant against it. I don't blame you. I'm not blaming you. It's just . . . sad." A single tear tracked down her cheek.

His voice rose, "What does that mean?"

"It means you shouldn't be forced to do what you don't want to do. I wouldn't feel right imposing a baby on you against your will."

"So, what? . . ."

She looked at him full in the face. "Excuse me?"

"What are you going to do?"

"Leave you, of course. What else can I do? I'm so sorry. It's so sad. I do love you to pieces."

He sat, aghast. He let go of her hand. He stood up, went back into the bathroom. He closed the door. She heard water running. After a while he came out, towel to his face. When he put it down, she saw his eyes were red. He returned to her side of the bed, sat down. Looked at her directly.

"Don't do it, Jenny. Don't leave me. I want you to stay. With a baby or without, I want you. If it's with a baby, I will do my damnedest to be a decent father to it. Unlike the way I acted the first time, when I was monstrous. I blamed everything on Clare. Every time they screamed, I screamed too—at her. It's no wonder she left . . ."

"Oh, Tim," she shuddered. "That would be awful."

"I won't do it. I promise."

She just gazed at him.

He looked at her imploringly. "I'll go for therapy! I swear! I'll learn to be less selfish. Selfishness hasn't brought me anything but misery, anyway; time I tried something new."

She was biting her lip. She wished she could talk to Maddy. But Maddy was going to take Parrish to New York for treatment tomorrow, she was full of dread and anxiety, and this was no time to ask her for help. Maybe Alicia would help her. She would call Alicia tomorrow.

"What do you say?" Tim asked. He was stroking her cheek.

She clasped his hand. "I don't know."

"What don't you know?"

"Whether I can trust you."

He removed his hand. He glanced down at the bedspread, then up at her. "That makes two of us."

•

Unfortunately, Tim's resolution to become a better husband and father had a perverse affect on him: He found himself totally unable to do the deed that would enable him to make such a change. Jenny, who had indeed had premonitions of this eventuality, presented a deeply serious face to her mortified husband, although she was inclined, on her own, to giggle. She wasn't worried; she was sure it would pass. What did Alicia think, she asked over iced tea in the back yard.

Alicia recalled, "Some years back, when Steven was coming close to his fiftieth birthday, he fell into a depression," she said, pouring iced tea from a sweating glass pitcher. They were sitting on a patio in Alicia's garden, surrounded by sweet-smelling shrubs. It was afternoon, and hummingbirds buzzed in the bee balm and delphiniums that Alicia had planted to attract them. "Months went by and he didn't improve. I began to get angry. You know, depressed people don't act sad. If they did, you might feel sorry for them. But they don't: They act angry. They're hard to take. And at some point, I'd had it. I told him he had to shape up." Alicia paused. "That really shocked him. I don't talk to him that way."

Jenny understood completely.

"Well, after much arguing and even some weeping on his part, he came out with it. There was a woman. I don't know who she was, she must have been a patient or a colleague, who else does he meet? Anyway, I guess he had developed quite a yen for her."

"He was having an affair?" Jenny exclaimed, shocked. This didn't fit her picture of Steven somehow.

"No, but he wanted to. He was thinking about it. Anguishing about it. This was during the years when we only came up here weekends, so he was with me all the time. It would have been difficult for him then to manage an affair. But the thought of it upset him because his father was quite a philanderer: All his life, he had had a second, or even third, woman in his life. He was like a hoarder who never feels secure without an extra couple of cans of coffee on the shelf. His father's behavior made Steven's young life a misery, because it upset his mother so much. She was always in tears, and always reproachful to her husband, and the father was always angry when he was home. Their home was a battlefield, and Steven, when he was a boy, determined, vowed that he'd never act that way. So when he started to feel . . . lustful . . . he was horrified. He hemmed and hawed and fought with himself and finally made up his mind once and for all, that he would not have an affair, would never have one. But once he'd decided that, he fell into a profound depression!" Alicia laughed. "The price of virtue! And he became impotent!" She laughed again, merrily.

Jenny gazed at her, wondering why she was laughing. "What did you do?"

"When he told me? I'm sorry to say I laughed. Poor Steven: reaping the rewards of virtue!"

Jenny was speechless.

Alicia noticed her expression. "Oh, don't be upset, Jenny. I couldn't help laughing, you have to admit it's funny, and eventually Steven laughed too. And soon afterward, his depression ended. And his impotence. He was just dramatizing himself, feeling sorry for himself. Because when he told me about this, I told him I too had made a decision earlier that year not to have a love affair. And that outraged him. He didn't feel I had the right even to think about having an affair. He was horrified that it so much as entered my mind. He felt it was absolutely incumbent upon me to be faithful: I didn't have the right to temptation." She laughed again. "There was a certain shifting of our mutual gears before he could take that in. And it made his own decision less of a sacrifice. Less dramatic, too. I mean, he had to consider, what if I'd made a different decision?"

Jenny frowned and sat silent for a while. She didn't care for the vision Alicia had sketched; she hoped it wasn't what her marriage would become. "So you think it will pass?" she asked finally.

"I'm sure it will. My suggestion is, flirt a little the next time someone passable is around. You'll see."

"You'd have made a good military strategist, Alicia," Jenny said ruefully.

Jenny told Tim about her conversation with Alicia. He was horrified. "You told her I—"

"No, no, of course not, darling. I mentioned an article on impotence that had been in the paper. Said I hadn't realized it affected so many men. Said I'd never really encountered it."

"Oh." Calmed by the lie. "Do you think I should see a doctor?" he asked. "Maybe take Viagra?"

"Well," she mused, "I just have this feeling that if I told you I was back on the pill—and you believed me—you'd be fine."

He groaned, sitting cross-legged on the bed facing her, his head bent. "Do you hate me, Jenny, luv?"

"I'd like to, but I can't." She laughed, holding his head in her hands. "Do you think you'll ever get used enough to the thought of a baby that you'll go back to normal?"

A month passed and he had not, however. He went to a doctor, not a local one but someone in the city, a man he had never seen before and intended never to see again.

"I feel like Stephen Dedalus, looking for a confessor on the other side of town," he said. The doctor, hearing the story, theorized that the problem was psychological, and Viagra might not help, but prescribed it anyway. "What do you have to lose?" he said. He thought it was funny, much to Tim's chagrin.

The Viagra had no effect.

But by then, Jenny had missed her July period. "My God, Tim, maybe I'm already pregnant!"

"How could you be?"

"That day. Remember? When I got home and we were so happy to see each other. And you carried me into the bedroom? And we were so . . . before I told you I'd stopped taking my pills . . ."

"My God!" he whispered. "You mean I've been depriving myself of my greatest joy for nothing! Come here, woman!" he ordered, and grabbed at her.

"Tim!" she giggled, slithering away, but they ended up making love. This time, Tim had no problem.

She went out and bought a pregnancy kit. The test came out positive. Jenny was ecstatic. "Not only am I pregnant, but this baby was conceived in one of the best fucks we ever had! In ecstasy!"

Tim, who inclined to superstition, had to admit it seemed "meant."

"What do you mean, meant? Like by a god or something?"

"Yes. How else can you explain it?"

"Well, it seems pretty straightforward to me. I got off the pill, we made love, and I got pregnant. I'm awed at how clever my body was, leaping at it that way. As if it knew what the affect on you would be once you heard my motives."

"Ah. You think you manipulated the whole thing!"

"No." She smiled, embracing him. "I think it just happened, but that it's a brilliant expression of our passion. Yes, that's what I think."

"All right, Jenny, luv. But I'm going to take it as meant."

She thought that that was not a bad idea, given his opposition. She decided it could only help, and when she heard Tim tell one more of their friends that it was "meant," she just smiled. Despite her determination not to tell anyone until she was further along, she burst out with the news the first time she saw Alicia, Emily, and Maddy; and pretty soon everyone in Steventon knew she was pregnant.

•

September arrived golden, as always in the Berkshires, soft light slanting through pines, the air soft and musky with the sweet scent of crumbling leaves. At first it was still summer; late September and October were still gorgeous and light, but shocked by the last lingering touch of a dying mother, her hands already cold. Then harsh November arrived with its gray skies and gray branches, premonitions of the frozen months of winter, when all living things wanted to hibernate.

Emily always felt a certain excitement in September, a leftover from childhood, perhaps, the anticipation of a new school term, new experiences, new friends. But everyone felt a resurgence of energy, an end of the indolence and sweet easiness of the hot, humid days. And life was so sweet these days. Clea had returned to her; Sikorsky was going to perform her work. Her life had completed itself, suddenly, become the whole she had craved but barely dared hope for.

Maddy knew all this. Maddy and Emily had been friends for sixty-odd years and knew almost everything there was to know about each other. Between them was a deep, silent acceptance; each was central to the other, whatever other ties they had. Maddy felt that Emily was different, had a kind of untouchability. Maddy knew that Emily was not like other people whose minds were filled with people and their doings, with desires and longings. Emily's mind was full of ideas, structures, building blocks, and sensations, especially sounds. She was different, she had a kind of untouchability. Maddy summed it up as, That was how Emily was. She could not have defined the way her friend was, the way the still, silent core of her was beyond reach, even to her. It sat like a soul on a rock, contemplating the world, a little wistful at times, but mostly contented to be itself, playing with chords and progressions and rhythms and tones. When they were younger, Maddy sometimes missed being able to feel Emily. But she found the core of her friend in Emily's anguish over Clea in the years the girl had lived with her aunt. For all the romance and drama of her early life, Emily's greatest emotional crisis occurred in her middle age, centered on Clea.

Emily's time abroad, her adventures (as they seemed to Maddy), did not show at all on the outside. No one would guess, meeting her now, seeing her tall, slender body, just a little hunched with age, her hair still blond, with gray blending in pulled back into a dowdy bun, that she was revolutionary, that rebellious ideas and feelings lurked inside that mind. People were always shocked when Emily came out with some radical statement.

Maddy knew that Emily was sailing right now, basking in September light, smiling in the sun. She tried to tell her friend she knew, to swear to her that she delighted in her good fortune and was happy for her. But it was difficult for Maddy, because she herself was in such grief. She knew that Emily was trying to tell her that she was grieving with her, worrying with her, utterly aware of her anxiety about her son. Nevertheless, the two friends were as far apart as they had ever been, their two states of mind close to unbridgeable.

By September, Parrish was very ill. After three months of treatment with toxic chemicals, his white-cell count was low and he was feverish. He went home after his September course of chemotherapy but had been almost immediately summoned back to the hospital because of fever. For weeks after that, he was in the hospital; finally, the fever would drop and he would be sent home, then the fever would rise again. In October he returned to the hospital, lucky enough to get one of Sloan-Kettering's small private rooms, and lay there silent and uncomplaining, while his family tiptoed around him.

Maddy was with him, sitting in a corner, reading; once she looked up and thought, Thirty years ago I'd have been knitting or crocheting. Funny, it doesn't even occur to me to do it now. I no longer have to be useful all the time.

Charley stayed mostly in Steventon. They all—Parrish and Jean, Maddy and Charley, and sometimes one of the older children would go down to New York the day before Parrish was to be admitted again. But once Parrish was settled in his room, Charley and Jean and the children returned to Steventon, where the children could maintain some semblance of their normal lives. Jean needed Charley, and he spent much time at her house, running errands, driving the children to their sports meets or the dentist. Now that Parrish was sick, sitting still was impossible.

Parrish had guests regularly: Emily drove down with them in September and stayed with Maddy at Alicia's for a few days. She came to the hospital and played gin rummy with Parrish when he felt well enough. His sister Lily and her husband Parsons stopped in several evenings, and Alicia came with Steven one night. Even Parrish's oldest son, Charles, with whom he had a rocky relationship, showed up in October and stayed for several days, bedding down at Lily's. But Parrish got upset when his brothers flew in from the West Coast, Thomas from Los Angeles and Benjamin from Arizona. Their appearance startled him into knowledge, and he fell into a depression. He told himself it was not written in stone that this was his final month or week or day or whatever the fuck it was, it just reflected what his mother and his doctors thought. But added to how he felt, it constituted a pretty strong argument.

Anyway, he didn't especially enjoy visitors. He was feeling poorly, and he was not social at the best of times. He dozed, he watched television. He wanted his mind to float without catching on anything. He did not want words, which might convey import, because there was only one import hovering out there for him now. He wasn't ready to die. He was too young. Besides, he hadn't really had his life. Of course, that was his own fault . . .

He did not like thinking back on it; he'd wasted so much of it. If there was a god, he should know there were things Parrish still needed to do: make amends somehow with Charles, with his father and mother, and with Susan. She hadn't come, of course, nor did he want her there. He felt only guilt toward her, so she wasn't his favorite person. And he wasn't thrilled with the way he looked these days, gaunt, hairless, pale. Vanity, vanity. Right to the grave.

Apologies, apologies. Did any man face death with anything else hanging over him? It was hellish that he owed so many people apologies. He'd made some when he was first in AA, but that was years ago. He hadn't stopped being rotten though. He'd had some blessings in life: good parents who'd stuck by him. They'd stuck by him when he put them through hell, and even when they abandoned him, told him he had to do it on his own, they'd let him know they were pulling for him. And once he'd gotten sober, they'd helped him pick himself up, start over. He'd found Jean, she was a good wife, he'd had more kids, they were cute as hell and he'd treated them a little better than he had Charles. He just wasn't cut out to be a father, funny, when he had such a nice father himself. He'd like to make it up to Charles somehow. To this day he couldn't treat him well. Something about the kid just roused the devil in him, made him furious. Made him yell. Couldn't seem to help it. All he had to do was look at the kid and he saw red. He wasn't like that with other people—only Charles. He'd liked teaching and his students. He liked people. It was just something about Charles.

People had told him to fight the cancer, fight it, guy, they said. But how did you do that? Stay positive, do what the doctors ordered. He'd told Maddy he would fight. But she'd said, "No, sweetheart, don't fight. That takes too much energy. Let yourself roll with it, let your body embrace the cancer and transform it into something positive. Love your body, all of it." She had this funny idea about loving the cancer to death, sort of. He didn't get it, it didn't make sense to him. How could you transform cancer into a positive?

Anyway, how could you love your body? Disgusting pit of lust and evacuations. He had always, as far back as he could remember, loathed his body, its needs, its endless crying fucking needs, its emanations, its smells and excreta. Alcohol blotted it out; drunk he was an angel, soaring with song and dreams. His mother was a smart woman, everybody said so, but she knew nothing about him. Never had. She had no idea how much he loved her, wanted her to love him back. He couldn't seem to please her whatever he did. His father, on the other hand, well, he was a pussy cat, but useless. Didn't have a clue. And his brothers and sister were completely different from him. He was so lonely, he'd always been alone. He was a changeling, a baby inserted into a cradle in a stranger's house, a cuckoo, god knows where he came from originally. He had yet to meet his own kind. Maybe afterward. Maybe in some life to come they'd come strolling up to him, welcome him, hello, brother, you finally found us. They'd have wings and when they spoke it would be music. They'd have marble pillars instead of bodies, and the only thing they'd smell of was lilacs like the ones on the lawn beyond his mother and father's house. A wall of them, smelling like heaven.

He had lain there with the poison dripping into his vein, not feeling it but sensing that he was lying in a toxic dump, knowing that it wasn't helping, that the tumor just went on growing. He didn't understand why the doctors continued when the tumor just went on its merry way. It paid no more attention to the poison than Superman would pay to a hurled hammer. It was a supertumor. Hah. Just like him to have a supertumor. The doctors scratched their heads. The truth was, they didn't know anything, nothing at all. One of them admitted as much to him, which one was that, Connolly? Roth? But they persisted, fools in their folly. He doubted they'd find wisdom.

And now, with his fever, they had something else to think about. A new set of doctors, infectious-disease specialists, guys he'd never seen before. The other ones had disappeared. Never even came to see him. He was so sick. They didn't care. He was hot. The room shimmered. He couldn't eat. Maddy had made him homemade chicken soup, but it made him sick just to smell it. The only thing he could keep down was ice-cold water. Or aloe vera poured over ice. That calmed his poor mouth, full of open sores.

Maddy came over and looked down at him. Her face was expressionless, but there was something in her eyes . . . He looked back at her, saying nothing. Their eyes connected. Maybe for a moment there, just a moment, she saw him, understood. He tried to smile up at her, held her hand, tried to be someone she would like. But when she let go and walked away, he knew he hadn't succeeded. He just couldn't get through to her.

23

When the tears started to rise up and threatened to spill over, Maddy let go of Parrish's hand, walked away from him and left the room. She didn't want to embarrass him with her tears, make him have to deal with her grief. That would be unfair. He had to deal with his own, after all: She could see he was grieving the loss of his own life. She wished she could get him to see how much she loved him; how unbearable it felt to her to see him so sick and thin and white, like a little boy lying there looking up at her begging her to take the pain away. He'd never had much ability to deal with pain; a scratch or a cut, even when he was tiny, bothered him so much more than the others. With the others, a kiss, a cookie, or for more serious hurts, an ice cream, was all it took to distract them, cheer them right up, send them running back outdoors yelling to get back in the game. But not Parrish. He'd cling to her, and sometimes, she knew, she got impatient, she had so much to do in those days, she didn't have time to carry a little boy around in her arms, she had preserves to put up, a vegetable garden to weed, clothes to sew, a house to clean . . .

Now, pangs kept attacking her heart, blows on a cymbal, one for every time she'd put him aside, set him down on his feet and told him to be a big boy, told him to stop whining, scolded him for throwing the cookie down and stamping on it. That was pretty funny, now that she thought of it. Not at the time, though. She'd failed him then and was failing him now, that was her experience of motherhood, one long failure, even though she was trying especially hard because it seemed imperative that he die feeling loved. But how? You can't make someone feel loved if they don't. Grief overcame her and she headed for the public toilet, ran inside and locked the door and gave vent to it, let herself sob, much good that would do; oh Parrish, what can I do for you? If I could die for you, I would. How can it be that children die before their parents? That was proof, if more were needed, that there was no god. That alone.

•

Had the whole fuckin' family decided to come down? What the fuck was that supposed to mean? He wasn't up to asking. He just lay passive: Let them do what they wanted.

Jean came over and took Parrish's hand. He smiled at her. He knew she needed him to smile at her. She tried to smile back, but her face was full of tears. She probably loved him. He thought she did. He never could feel it, though, not really. He thought he had when they were first together. They stayed together because they had the kids, a house, a mortgage, and she needed his salary: Little as it was, it was more than she could earn. High school teachers weren't well paid. You made a life and you lived it but after a while you didn't know why you were living it, it was just habit, just bewilderment. What else can you do? She loved the kids, he could see that, she was a good mother, and he liked that about her. And she was kind to him. He tried to be kind to her, but once in a while he would look at her and see her breasts, huge lumps of fat on her chest, she was nothing but lumps of fat, big breasts, big butt she had, her boobs had always been big, that's what had drawn him in the beginning, but now after three kids and some weight gain, they were huge, drippy mammaries, big hunks of fat, like her rear end, and the emanations, oh, he couldn't bear to think about it. Revulsion made him turn his face and excuse himself, close his eyes. Maybe she'd think he was tired.

Jean tried to give him heart with her look, but she kept weeping like a damned fool, she couldn't stop. He looked so vulnerable lying there, like a scared kid, big eyes and white face, the real Parrish, the one he didn't know she knew, funny, wasn't it, the one she'd fallen in love with. Forlorn, that was what he was, always had been, her heart had gone straight out to him, she had wanted to hold him, make him know he was safe, let him feel safe. Sometimes she thought she'd succeeded, but other times he pulled away from her just as if she was his mother, someone who had let him down, someone he couldn't trust. But when he let her comfort him, then she loved him again in the old way, the way she had at the beginning.

Hard to keep that up over so many years. Here they were, three kids later, seventeen years they'd been married, they hadn't had a bad life except for once in a while when his temper exploded, usually on the kids, always on Charles when he visited (she'd come to hate Charles visiting, he must have hated it too poor kid, he'd stopped coming years ago, but sometimes he'd let it out on Parry or Amelia, never on Meg, the baby. Some baby she was, eight now, the others already adolescent, life goes by so fast, she was just a girl herself a little while ago), she didn't know how it happened that she was here, overweight, with gray in her hair, watching her husband die. It would be hard without him, she could go back to nursing but it had been years and she'd probably have to get more training, and it was so hard and now that she was heavy she wasn't sure she could do it, nurses didn't earn that much, anyway, well, neither did teachers, but since she'd been helping out at the grocery store, they'd had a little extra. It would be hard, but she knew he'd provided for them as best he could, they wouldn't lose the house, anyway, and she knew Maddy and Charley would help her out, they always had. They wouldn't abandon her. In a way, they had turned out to be the best thing about her marriage, she loved them, they'd been better to her than her own parents, and she just loved Charley, and Maddy was always such a help when she was in trouble, always available for a cup of tea and advice. Kind. Not at all like some mothers-in-law, like her sister Kate's, say.

Parrish was a pretty good husband, only sometimes he looked at her . . . she tried to ignore it, it was just a mood, she knew, he seemed to need to get away . . . but it was almost like he hated her. She had read somewhere that some men needed to distance themselves from their families sometimes. Like a cold wind coming off him, it pushed her away. Just sometimes. She tried not to take it personally—it was probably just a mood. Maybe he was upset he hadn't been something more than a schoolteacher; maybe he had had great ambitions. Jean herself thought being a schoolteacher was great, she wished she could do it. But men were different.

She knew she loved Parrish, but she couldn't help wondering if she'd miss him. She remembered after Kate and Mitch split up, and Kate, sitting in her kitchen having coffee one afternoon, told her that before they'd split, she'd often wondered if she'd miss Mitch if she could ever get free of him. Well, then she had, and a few nights later she got the answer to her question: She'd run out of milk, late, when the kids were sleeping, and she didn't want to go out to the store and leave them alone. For the first time, she wished Mitch were there.

When Charley came in, everybody else moved away to give him room, they knew how much Charley loved Parrish. But Charley was a tender touch anyway, and when he put his hand on Parrish's cheek, Parrish put his hand up and clasped his father's and let tears show on his cheeks. He wished he knew some way to tell his father how much he appreciated all of what he'd done all those years. All that picking him up out of the gutter all those times; all the times he'd cleaned up his vomit, cleaned him up when he was covered with it. All that dealing with police and police stations, flying or driving over half the East Coast, he'd really given the old man a whirl. His father kept patting him and he ran his hand over his cheeks because they were wet, and then put his hand back on Charley's and felt guilty because it was wet but left it, anyway. His father had paid all those fines, had paid for him to go back to school once he was straight, had stood by him all the years. He wondered why he wasn't like the old man, and why he had this lingering sense that his father was a . . . well, a wuss, a wimp, he'd always felt that way, especially when he was a kid, he didn't know why. When other kids bragged that their old men could beat up—oh, whoever—he never opened his mouth. He couldn't picture his old man beating up anybody. And he knew Maddy loved Charley because he would never beat up anybody. That was the trouble, wasn't it. A castrating wife. She'd castrated him too, look at him, frightened of his mother. What a picture.

He turned his head, and his father read it as a signal and lifted his hand and stepped back a little. There were tears on his father's face, and Parrish knew he was ashamed of himself for crying, as Parrish was himself. God, it was hell being a man.

Now Maddy was prodding Charles to approach his father's bedside. He stood a few inches away from Parrish, his mouth in a hard line. Maybe he was a little scared, or trying not to cry. Parrish stared at him, contempt already forming in his mind, scaredy-cat son, twenty-eight years old and still terrified of every shadow, what did he think Parrish was going to do, rise out of the bed and kill him? He tried to control himself, reminding himself that he wanted to apologize to the boy for being so hard on him all those years. He just couldn't make himself soft, though. What was it about the boy? He reached out a hand, and Charles flinched, instantly, automatically, as if he expected a blow. Parrish muttered, "For Christ's sake, Charles," and tried to touch him. Charles submitted, but stiffly, letting his father stroke his hand, but when Parrish tried to pull him closer, he resisted, and turned a little to his grandmother.

Maddy, watching the encounter, moved a little toward Charles and stroked his back, telling him with her hands that he was safe. But he did not trust his father. How many times had his father grabbed him, then punched him in the head? He waited, rigid. Parrish pulled his son's head close to his face and spoke in his ear. "I'm sorry," he said, then let the boy go. Charles staggered away from his father, retreated to the other side of the room, stood against the wall. He stayed there, staring.

•

God, Dad said he was sorry. He said he was sorry. Charles tried to feel what that meant. He thought he should feel good, but somehow he felt nothing. It felt wrong, and after accusing himself of ingratitude, he defended himself: Does he think "I'm sorry" could make up for all the years? Does he think that?

He watched as, one by one, his uncles and aunts, his half brothers and half sister went up to his father. Some of them said something to him. Some touched his arm. Some kissed him. Why were they doing this? Was his father really going to die? He didn't look like he was dying. He didn't look great, but he didn't look dead either. How did they know he was dying, if they knew it? He didn't know that. Just he had this fever, was all. You couldn't die of a fever, could you? He didn't understand what was moving them. He wasn't sure why they were there. Oh, he knew, Gramma Maddy had said he might die, they should say good-bye just in case, but he wasn't dying, he was his same old skanky self, he pulled my hand toward him as roughly as he ever did when he hit me. He was as alive as he ever was. It was Charles who felt dead.

He was staying with Gramma and Grampa at Mrs. Gilson's apartment. He was uncomfortable in that fancy place, but it was even worse at his aunt Lily's, that was even fancier. He and his mother had always lived in their little trailer with its beat-up furniture, a TV, two cars, and a computer. There was still a lot of junk around their place from Billy Burton, who'd lived with them for a few years and left all his stuff when he took off, well, when Mom threw him out. She never could tolerate another drunk once Dad was gone. He'd been meaning to clean it up but somehow he never had. One of these days, he would. It was so heavy, parts of old cars, a whole chassis, part of an old plow, old tires, rusted machinery. But maybe someday it would come in handy. That's what Billy always said.

Because Charles had plans. He was twenty-eight and worked on a road construction crew. Right now they had a job on the Mass Pike. They made good money when they worked, but half the time the weather was bad and they couldn't go out. He gave his mother most of what he earned. She'd had such a hard time, raising him alone. When Charles was little, Dad had given her money once in a blue moon; they wouldn't have survived if Grampa and Gramma hadn't given her money, too, sometimes years ago. For years, his mother had cleaned houses to earn enough to support them, and she worked so hard, she was exhausted at night. It was hard work, cleaning two whole houses every day, sometimes three, and then she would get home at eight or nine at night. But living was expensive, heating the place, it was electric heat, cost a fortune, taxes were high in the Berkshires, and just the insurance for the car, you had to have a car in the Berkshires, and gas was through the roof now. His bastard father a drunk for all those years, then when he gets it together, he marries somebody else. His mother had had a couple of guys who lived with them for a while, but they always ended up being drunks, or hitting her, or hitting him, or just leaving. She wouldn't let anyone hit him now, his mom. Too bad she hadn't been able to stop his father. Maybe she thought he had the right. He hit her too in those days.

He never went to see his father anymore, but Gramma had said he had to come now, because his father might be dying. But what difference did that make? He hadn't gone to see his father since he was eighteen and the old man stopped paying anything for him. That's why college was out for him. His father had gone to college, but he didn't bother trying to help Charles go. Mom said she'd clean on weekends if that would help, but he wouldn't let her. He'd go at night. And he did: He worked all day and then went to classes at the community college. He was going to have a better life; he was saving money to finish school. But then, last week, Gramma handed him twenty-five thousand dollars in a check, just handed it to him said it was for college. His eyes filled up remembering. He never expected anything like that. Nobody had ever taken care of him like that. He put that check in the bank. He would be able to go to school full time, just get a part-time job. His mom said Maddy had always been a good soul. She liked Maddy. Gramma. He'd finish college, and he'd teach school like his father, he knew he could do it, he wanted to teach math. He'd always been good at math.

And once he had a good job, he'd get married. He'd marry someone sweet like Pammy Smith, she was a girl who fit right in your arm. And he'd never ever hit her, or his kids, either. He'd been reading about stuff like that for years, his high school counselor gave him books one time when he came in all bruised up after a visit with his old man. He'd found more in the library. How kids of alcoholics fucked up. How kids whose fathers hit them hit their kids. He wasn't going to do that. He was going to have a decent life. He didn't want his kid standing there like he was right now, watching his father die and not giving a goddamned fuck.

•

Coming around now, what the hell, when he hadn't seen them in years, they'd both moved about as far away as you could go. Both of them these big successes and him only a schoolteacher. They made big money, Thomas a lawyer, Benjamin an accountant, he had a huge ranch out there in Arizona, not that he needed a ranch, he didn't work it, he just lived on it. Coming around to say good-bye when they didn't care whether he lived or died, well he didn't care if they did either, funny, when they were brothers, and once upon a time they'd been close, he and Thomas, anyway, Benjamin was so much younger, they'd hardly known him. But Thomas was three years older than Parrish, and Lily three years younger. Once upon a time, though, Parrish had thought Thomas was the sun and the moon and the stars and they played together every day, slept in the same room, they were more than brothers, they were soul mates. But something happened. Charley sent Thomas to prep school, he was smart in school. Parrish wasn't so smart, he didn't win a scholarship like Thomas, who went off to Amherst, wanted to be a hotshot lawyer, wouldn't even go into Dad's firm, hurt Charley, went to California to represent movie stars, life in the fast lane, that was, that's what it meant, married a woman looks like a movie star. Lily too, another smart one, but Parrish was the best looking, everyone said so, those dark blue eyes like his mother, that dark hair and dangerous edge. He might've been a movie star himself if he'd ever thought of it. No, they might be his sister and brothers, and they might be standing there looking at him with their mouths twisted and tears running down their cheeks, but they didn't care, not really, and neither did he, even if his cheeks were wet too.

•

Parrish died early in November. The family mourned. Maddy's friends gathered around her silently, as did Jean's and Parrish's. An invisible circle enclosed the Golds, a cloud cutting them off from the world. Emily looked and listened, knowing them so well, having known them for all of her seventy years, knowing all the love and rage and wishes and dashed hopes that had entwined themselves in

Parrish's cells and blood and muscle, and theirs too. She knew too, from the deaths of her own parents and siblings, that grief was lashed with guilt, with regret that things had not been better, that there had not been a perfect union. And the more guilt, the more grief. Was there ever a perfect union? a relationship of pure love? What about the mother of a newborn infant, was that pure? Was there a mother anywhere who had not, not once, not for an instant, felt, damn, why does it have to cry so much, so early, so loud, so piercingly, I wish it would vanish, just blow away . . .

Emily thought grief, soaked in salt and rue as it was, had a kind of purity. What the other Emily wrote about: the Bustle in a House the morning after death. Putting Love away we will not want to use again until eternity. As if we had a sheaf of love for each special person, a packet meant for them, with a tag and a ribbon around it, that couldn't be given to anybody else. The love reserved for that person had to stand on a shelf until eternity, gathering dust, wouldn't adhere to a new friend, not even a baby.

The Golds carried Parrish's body back to Steventon for the funeral, so the whole family could stay together, at the Gold house, which had room for that many people, and so Parrish's colleagues and friends could take part in the mourning, and say something at the service. And much was said about Parrish's devotion to his students, whom he had doted on, whom he had given extra help to, a special chance. And he was remembered by his pals, whom he had helped when they had put on new roofs, repaired their cars, pulled out trees felled by storms. Benjamin recounted amusing anecdotes from his childhood, when Parrish was his adored older brother, and Lily recalled Parrish being her protector. Thomas remembered a little tyke toddling behind him, a little pest trying to join in activities he was too young for. These memories created a texture for Parrish's life: He had been loved. Only one friend dared to mention the bad years, but he emphasized Parrish's courageous recovery from them and the loving support of his friends and parents in this effort. Maddy wept. Jean was dry-eyed. Susan looked grim.

Then people gathered their belongings and went home. The Golds—even those who weren't close to him—went home with new shadows or lines in their faces, a little sadder, a little older, a little closer to death. And Maddy and Charley remained struck dumb with grief for a long time.

There is nothing worse than to have your child die before you. Everyone knows that.

Charley turned to activity. He spent several days a week at Jean's house, devoted to helping her out. He brought her huge bags of groceries and dropped off sweaters and pajamas Maddy had ordered for her and the children from a catalogue. He extended his line of products; he spent more time in his garage office, and he let himself smoke one or maybe two more cigarettes a day. How could it hurt now? Now that the worst had happened. So what if he got lung cancer? Parrish was already dead of it.

But Maddy languished. Throughout the next months, her friends sought ways to distract her. They took her on expeditions, on a shopping trip to Pittsfield, to lunch at an inn on a lake in South End, to see an experimental theater piece in Lenox, to visit a cup garden in New York State. She appreciated the efforts, and after the first weeks, she sometimes smiled. A month and a half after Parrish's death, on a visit to the studio of the sculptor Daniel Chester French, Emily said something that made her laugh. Her three friends stood stock still for a nanosecond, then moved to embrace her.

But Maddy knew she would never recover. Losing her boy was a thing she couldn't recover from. The most you could do was go on. But if she had been inconsolable before, she was now connected, irrevocably, to Pluto, Hades, Dis. And no Persephone she. Married to death she would remain.

The friends didn't stop trying. Emily started calling about films she wanted to see, when for all the years of their friendship, Maddy had been the one who initiated their movie trips. Jenny and Alicia arranged lunches, trips to museums in northern Massachusetts; Alicia arranged a theater trip to New York for all of them, to see *Dirty Blonde*. Maddy was observed laughing at this play, several times. But the most successful diversion was created by Maddy herself, when she decided to hold Thanksgiving dinner at her house, as usual, and insisted that her friends come with their families.

She invited Jean and the three children, but for the first time, she included Susan and Charles. She wanted Emily, as always. But this year, she insisted that Jenny and Tim, and Alicia and Steven also come, with Steve and Neil and Mariette, newly returned home from France. She invited her grandniece Amy and Amy's husband, Don, and their new baby, Lanie. This project, familiar to her after fifty-odd years of cooking Thanksgiving dinners, was engrossing, required hard work, and yet was not a strain on her, partly because of its familiarity, partly because she hired Debby Dew to help with the cooking and Sean Schwartz to help serve and clean up. She'd already coped, over the years, with roasts dropped on the floor, vegetables burned, lumpy gravy, collapsed pies, crushed cakes, too little space at the table, leaving the cranberry sauce in the ice box—problems common to the event. So she could do it with half a heart and half a brain. Which, she thought, was about what she had. Her friends, seeing her becoming almost herself, relaxed.

•

She planned her usual traditional dinner, fancied up by new elements. The turkey was organic. Humph, she thought, we didn't have to pay an arm and a leg for organic turkeys years ago: They were all organic! Now the vegetables, too, were organic. There was no question that the organic vegetables, however expensive they were, tasted better than the usual ones. She had always said food used to taste better years ago, but people didn't believe her. Years ago, eggs, all of them fertilized and fresh from the barn, had a taste that couldn't be replicated now; lamb had a lovely flavor, edged with a bitterness like that of watercress, not the bland, almost fatty taste it had now. Emily told her that lamb still tasted the old way in Greece, where the sheep were a quarter the size of American sheep, which were raised with hormones.

In the living room, before dinner, she would serve cold shrimp and cocktail sauce, quesadillas (which she'd only recently learned to make), and guacamole, none of which was traditional. In her mother's day, they served a soft cheese that came in jars, actually cream cheese mixed with pimiento or chive, spread on Ritz crackers or stuffed into celery stalks. They'd have prepackaged olives, little green ones with red pimiento inside. And sometimes her mother would spread commercially sliced ham with Cheese-Whiz that was also sold in jars, and roll them up and slice them into bite-sized pieces.

But the rest would have been familiar to her—the turkey, mashed potatoes, baked sweet potatoes with brown sugar on top, creamed white onions, mashed rutabaga, green beans with pecans, giblet stuffing, cranberry sauce, gravy. Although nowadays practically no one ate gravy, she still made it because Charley would have been shattered by a Thanksgiving dinner without gravy. For dessert she made pies—apple, pumpkin, and pecan. Jean contributed a chocolate layer cake, Emily brought cookies, Charles and Susan came with champagne, Amy and Don offered red wine. Alicia and Steven brought scotch, a huge bouquet of brilliant flowers, and an enormous platter of cookies. Tim brought a bottle of port for after dinner. No one but he had ever had port before.

Familiar as the meal was, it required enough planning and labor to occupy the top part of Maddy's mind. At least that was how Emily explained it to Alicia. Emily believed that the mind was divided into two major parts: the reptile brain, which, she claimed, was deep and unchangeable, seat of all the ineradicable, vicious, greedy needs and hatreds that plagued the human race and of all the desires and dreams we also can't eradicate; and the top of the mind, which is self-conscious, and where we spent most of our time, and from which we had created civilization. If the top of the mind isn't working, we have no memory; we don't live in the reptile brain unless we have a terrible disease, like Alzheimer's, or are terribly drunk or beside ourselves, she said, so it rarely afflicts us with its poisons and nectars. But if the top part of the mind is burdened with grief and if it gets filled with something else, like Thanksgiving dinner, we can let the grief go, and experience a lightness, a relief, a distancing of pain.

Alicia was reluctant to impose her crew of six on what she felt was the already overburdened Maddy, but Maddy would not hear of them not coming.

"I need you to be there," she said. So of course, they were. Mariette came back from Paris with a person named Alfie, someone new in her life who had arrived at the Gilson's Steventon house with her unannounced. Alicia instantly began to worry about how Steven would react to the man—who had long hair and a distracted manner—and worried about it all the first day, until, lying in bed that night she realized she wasn't sure how she felt about the newcomer and was laying all her bad feelings on Steven. She worried about how Steven would receive Neil, and how Mariette would act toward her, Alicia. For if Steven had problems with his son, Alicia had them with her daughter. Not that she had ever mentioned this to anyone. Not even the women.

Who, of course, knew, if only by the infrequency with which she mentioned her daughter and the shakiness of her voice when she did.

They also knew that most women had problems with their daughters these days. Emily, who was always full of explanations, said it was because of the changes that had occurred. In the old days, she said, all women were slotted for the same fate, the only difference being the economic level on which they would live it out. Women worked or finagled or politicked to arrange the economically best marriages for their daughters that they could find, but that was the most they could do. In those days, daughters were slotted to live lives similar to their mothers' imitated their mothers' actions, and sometimes their characters. Their lives too would be devoted to raising children and serving men, looking after houses as scrub maids or supervisors, sewing basic clothing or embroidering cushions. There was little ground for competition or argument between mothers and daughters, and in farm country, at least, daughters usually remained very close to their mothers, often seeing them every day. Mothers helped daughters with new babies, daughters helped mothers tend ill husbands and brothers; they put up preserves together, quilted together, gossiped together.

But now, Emily said, daughters had a million things to choose from, all of them different from what their mothers did, even if their mothers did something besides raising children and serving men. And daughters blamed their mothers for not preparing them for the anxieties they faced, and for not understanding them when they happened. And some mothers tried to keep the daughters back on the farm with them, were jealous of their daughters' choices. Some daughters resented their mothers' simpler lives. And other things, she said, leaving the rest dangling.

•

Just before Thanksgiving, Emily heard from Sikorsky. He called to say he would be sending a contract. He wanted to play her symphony at his premiere in Cleveland, and he wanted her to come out and work with him on it; he would introduce her music to the world in March 2001.

Emily sat for a long time with the phone in from her hand. Her heart pounded steadily, hard, like a drum announcing powerful news, not at all erratically, not with excitement, but with power. Her eyes were closed as she thanked the gods she did not believe in for letting this happen while she was still alive, for not treating her as they had her great namesake, whose masterpieces had largely been left, tied together with embroidery thread, her flower blushed unseen except by a precious few. And for allowing her at the same time to have Clea in her life, to have Clea her beautiful healthy self with the beautiful healthy Martine at her side. To have her work succeed and her family intact: It was what she had always wanted, would always have asked for, but had always believed would not be permitted to a woman. Yet here she was. There was nothing more she could ask of life, and nothing more she ever would ask.

24

Thanksgiving was cold and gray, the air chilly, the scene a drab brown except for the snow left from a storm some days ago, which had turned the huge Gold lawn white all the way to the trees. People began to gather at the Golds' at three in the afternoon, parking their cars in the long driveway or off to the sides, under the trees. Jean and her children arrived first, Jean greeting Maddy with a tearful "Our first Thanksgiving without him, Mad."

She didn't have to say that, Maddy thought: Is there anyone here not thinking it? Embracing her, she pardoned her: She's not the brightest button in the box. Maybe she has no other way to express what she feels. The younger children were boisterous, and Jean sent them out to the hill behind the house with a sled. Amelia, at thirteen a sedate young woman, settled herself in a corner with a book. Jean scolded, "Girls don't sit in the corner reading, Amelia! Converse with the ladies!"

She looked up sullenly. "It's boring," she said.

"It's good manners."

"The boys watch TV!" she protested.

"That's different," Amelia said.

Maddy said tentatively, "You know, Jean, she's right, boys are always allowed to watch TV on holidays. So maybe we should let the girls do what they want, too."

"My family used to let the boys watch TV," Amelia put in, "but they never let me read!"

"Was that fair?" Maddy asked, and Jean looked perplexed. Finally, she burst out angrily, "Well, anyway, Amelia, I want you to go outside and watch the kids. They're out there sledding all by themselves. They might hurt themselves."

Amelia appealed to Maddy, who gazed at Jean, then back at Amelia. "Maybe it'll be fun," she smiled at the girl.

"Get your coat and boots back on! Go ahead!" Jean insisted. The girl moved reluctantly. She gathered her things and dragged them through the house to the back door, which she slammed as she went out. Jean affectionately kissed Charley hello, then sat beside him, an expression of self-satisfaction on her face. Did Maddy think she was going to run Jean's family just because Parrish was dead? Some nerve! "How's your business going, Charley?" Jean asked.

•

Susan and Charles arrived next. Susan was stiff and nervous, her voice high and tense. She had not been to the Golds' for Thanksgiving since Parrish left her in 1975, and she was not sure how Jean would receive her. But Jean had come to view Parrish's death simply as another example of his many abandonments of her, tacitly accepted Susan as a fellow-victim. She welcomed Susan with some warmth, pleasing Susan, who had felt keenly her exclusion from the prestigious Gold family. Her legend of her own life was that Parrish had broken her heart and ruined her life by becoming an alcoholic. The two women silently made common cause. After all, Parrish had left them both.

Observing this, Maddy thought nothing better could happen. They were similar in some way—women flying on one wing. Bright as Parrish was, he needed to feel superior to his women and had married people who were not his intellectual equals. They were good women by the old standards for goodness in women, Maddy thought—faithful, devoted mothers, hard workers. But for Maddy, stupidity was almost a crime, intolerable.

Charles furiously repudiated his mother's image of him as his father's victim, even though he shared it to some degree. He wished his mother did not see herself that way, either: It gave his father more power than he wanted him to have. But he carried no weight with her, and knew better than to say anything. He found a beer in the fridge and moved over to Charley, who had come into the kitchen to fix drinks for the newcomers. Charles asked his grandfather what he thought about the new Fords, which silenced Charley utterly. He drove a two-year-old Chrysler; he knew nothing about cars and cared less. But he would not admit this. He said nothing at all, which didn't matter to Charles, who went on about cars for fifteen minutes.

Maddy thought Charles looked more . . . together . . . than usual. He normally looked as if he were wearing the wrong clothes, as if his arms and legs did not move synchronously with his body; his eyes always seemed to be rimmed with red, his mouth to gape open. But today . . . what was it? His mouth was closed. His eyes were dry. He was wearing new boots and a nice suede jacket. Maddy gazed at him and smiled. The money she privately had given him had made a difference. Money does matter, she thought. Money was love. It didn't matter. On his arrival today, he had told her that he had registered for the spring term at the community college, going full time. "On your gift," he added, grinning.

"It's really from your father, sweetheart," she said. "But he had to do it secretly, remember."

"I know," he said and winked.

Winked!

•

Maddy's great-niece Amy and Amy's husband, Don, and their new baby, Lanie, came in next. Lanie, not so new anymore at eight months, was able to scurry across rooms on all fours with great speed, pull herself up on a coffee table, from which she would wack whatever object she found upon it. She had been drumming happily with a figurine until her father gently removed it from her, at which she shrieked. Amy looked worn out. Her hair was brown from the roots to cheek level: Below that, it was blond. "I just haven't had time to get it done," she apologized to Maddy.

"It looks good brown. It's better around your face. Maybe you should let it grow back."

"Really? It isn't streaked with gray? That's why I started dying it in the first place. I'm only twenty-six, too young to go gray!"

"I never noticed it. But people do start to get gray hair young. I had them at thirty. But they don't really show."

"Thirty! I'm only twenty-six!"

"I know. But you just had a baby, sweetie. Give your body a chance to bounce back."

"Oh. Will it?" she said tremulously. "I looked in the mirror after I got home from the hospital, and . . ." Tears filled her eyes. "I had a big belly, and my hair . . . and my nails are soft now, they keep breaking. I thought I'd never be the same again.

"Ah," Maddy said, understanding. "I know. I remember. But you will bounce back. I promise."

"Oh! Thanks, Maddy." Amy embraced her.

•

Don looked irritated, pale, martyred. He barely glanced at the baby and spoke to Amy in short, one-word bursts. Seeing this, Maddy worried about his effect on Tim. But then, Tim had been a father twice before, he knew how it was. Now that there were three of them, the men had retreated to the kitchen, where Charley presided over the bar and Don was happy to speak to Charles about the new Fords. Charley listened seemingly with great interest, but heard not a word. Amy joined Jean and Susan chatting seemingly happily in the living room, while the baby crawled around and on them. The women didn't notice the men's desertion; it was usual after all, and they were busily giving the latest news about sisters and brothers, neighbors and friends, endlessly interested in the people of their world, making silent judgments and feeling silent jealousies. They took turns lifting Lanie, setting her on their laps, petting her, soothing her, and offering her the bottle of juice her mother had brought. Charley carried in a tray of manhattans and martinis for the "ladies," as he put it, and they crowed with pleasure; such a treat, Jean said;

she hadn't had a manhattan in years, Susan said; and Amy too reached for her cocktail with a smile. Countrywomen, they did not drink often and when they did, drank beer; cocktails seemed terribly sophisticated to them. They were delighted. Maddy had her usual scotch—none of that poisonous TNT for her, she said, remembering past disasters with martinis and manhattans.

•

Alicia and Steven, with Steve, Neil, Marietta, and Alfie arrived next. Maddy was a little anxious about the Gilsons, because they were in a different class from the others, and the two groups might not mix well. Of course, they all knew each other, and knew the place of the others in Maddy's life, but Maddy feared they might not be able to talk to each other. Steven immediately and with some speed headed for the kitchen, where Maddy had told him Charley was hanging out, and sank into the monologue on Ford cars, to which he listened, as Charley did, but with a little contempt.

"Ford," he said sotto voce to Charley, "you might as well buy a German car as buy a Ford."

"Eh?"

"Ford worked with the Nazis during the war. Surreptitiously."

"Is that right?"

Steven nodded.

Charley nodded too, as if he suddenly understood something. "Yeah, I know lots of people won't buy German cars."

"Good," said Steven. "How's your mail order business?"

Charley grinned broadly and began to talk. Steven liked Charley, whose simple pleasure in things was contagious. He almost wanted to hug him as he recounted his marvelous success story. He wondered if Charley had ever played tennis.

•

Alicia and Mariette joined the women and were instantly entranced by Lanie. An infant in a room eradicates both the necessity to talk and the desire. Requiring constant attention, a baby mesmerizes everyone around. So the idle gossip was broken by bursts of laughter, sudden cries of "Isn't that adorable!" or "How sweet!" and adults rising suddenly to swoop up baby falling, teetering, with a box of matches in its hand, or a baby heading for a precious porcelain vase. After ten minutes or so of this, Mariette turned to her mother with a roll of her eyes—boring!—and Alicia smiled back with intense delight at being the recipient of her daughter's commentary. It suggested intimacy, and she had wondered if Mariette, after two years abroad, would still feel close to her. Mariette had not been a faithful correspondent, calling only occasionally and writing even more rarely. But she had come home flushed with pleasure in herself, and that, Alicia felt, was a good sign.

Her young man, Alfie, did not sit with them, but remained at the edge of the room with Steve and Neil, talking in a circle. Then they found some white wine on the dining room sideboard and sipped it, talking in low voices. Alfie had spent several years in France; Neil had visited France often and Steve several times, so they had built-in subject matter. Maddy glanced at them, grateful that they were taking care of themselves.

She knew Alicia and Mariette were bored; she hoped that Jenny's arrival would fix that. Mariette did not last long at her mother's side; she rose and departed, without any apology, heading for the three young men at the edge of the room. She joined them with a sigh and a roll of her eyes. Alfie gave her a knowing grin, a raised eyebrow. "Nappies and formula," she replied. They all laughed.

•

When Jenny and Tim arrived close to four o'clock, Lanie was the first person Tim laid eyes on. He looked around and saw no men and immediately grasped the situation. Still, he stayed to greet and compliment all the women, who were utterly charmed by such gracious manners. At five months, Jenny was beginning to show, and Maddy and the other women made a huge fuss over her. Tim left her without worry, heading for the kitchen. He had been consistently affirming of Jenny's pregnancy, and Jenny hoped he had forgotten his objections. But at the sight of the active, demanding, vocal Lanie, she began to feel a quiet dread. She was grateful for his departure.

She sat beside Alicia and began talking about Lucian Freud; she and Tim had just returned from New York, where they'd seen a gallery show of Freud's work, and she was excited by it. Alicia also knew his work, and the two of them were immediately engaged.

"He strips away all the surfaces, you know? But his vision is so ugly!"

"Like his grandfather," Jenny said.

"Yes, I guess people found Sigmund's outlook ugly too. He reduced everything to two drives. It was hard to believe him. Lucian shows lumps and bumps and warts and lines and peculiarities. Like a naturalist sketching a bird with all its coloring, its stripes and spots, its ugly little protuberances, its odd sexual organs, its cruel beak . . ."

"You're right," Jenny said thoughtfully.

"When you compare him to painters who idealized people, like David, say," Alicia put in. "He's hard to take."

"Yes. Quite a shock. But not compared to Rembrandt," Jenny added.

That stopped Alicia. "You're right."

"I think of that poem by Gerard Manley Hopkins—how does it go? 'All things counter, original, spare, strange / Whatever is fickle, freckled (who knows how?) . . .' You know?"

"Yes. But it has the line 'Glory be to God for dappled things . . .' I hardly think Lucian Freud is thinking about glory or god."

Jenny laughed. "Probably not."

The conversation abruptly stopped when Emily came in. Maddy, who had been trapped in the mindless talk of the family women, had pasted a smile on her face and sat like a frozen mold, but when Emily arrived, her smile became real and she hugged her as though Emily was a lost pet who had managed to straggle home.

"Thank god you're here," she whispered.

"Oh, I know. It's always like that. Why I hate holidays," Emily whispered back.

"But there's something interesting going on around Alicia," Maddy whispered. By now, Alicia and Jenny had risen to embrace Emily, and the four formed a circle. The relatives looked up, startled by Maddy's abandonment, but forgave it, knowing that a hostess has a duty to spread herself around. Charley peeked in, saw Emily, and immediately went to fetch her a scotch; he also got Alicia and Mariette some wine, and Jenny a seltzer. Being a man, he was licensed to remove himself, and he returned to the other mindless conversation between

Don and Charles, which was now on football teams, another subject he knew nothing about. But neither did Steven, so they had each other at least. Unfortunately, though, they had nothing else to talk about.

Emily was asking Jenny, "How's the painting coming?"

"Good. I'm happy. I more or less finished myself. I had myself sitting on a kind of ledge, my legs hanging down, like from the edge of a porch. Then I changed it, so I'm sitting cross-legged. Maddy's standing on the left, her hands on the back of your chair, Emily. Then you, sitting. Then Alicia, leaning back against the wall so she's a little shorter than she actually is. Then me, sitting cross-legged. Over my head is a painting. One of mine. A house in the country, a small house. What do you think?"

"I can see it in my mind. Yes. And patches. On the floor."

"Yes!"

"Lovely."

Jenny smiled in deep satisfaction. "Do you think so?" Wistfully. Then she lay her hand on Emily's arm. "And the symphony?"

But that, of course, was not describable.

•

A pall hung over the party because of Parrish's death. Emily waited until the pies were served before making her announcement. "People! I've got some news. Andrei Sikorsky's going to play my symphony at his premiere at Cleveland next year. In March."

"Oh, Em!" Maddy cried and got up and went to her and embraced her, burying Emily's head in her large bosom. Everyone else cried out as well.

"Just think! A famous composer from Steventon!" Don boomed, pounding the table for emphasis, and Amy assured Jean, "I always knew Em would make it."

Jenny and Tim, who (unlike Amy and Don) had actually heard Emily's music, hugged her and offered quieter salutations. Steven too offered felicitations, and Emily saw that he was deeply impressed. It was the thing she liked most about him, his profound love of music, his understanding of it. "You'll have to come to the premiere," she said, and Steven glowed. Alicia glowed too, in reflected glory, for that moment not minding being his reflection.

Charley announced that the news required champagne, and he went to the kitchen to fetch some bottles. The table sat happily through the ritual opening and pouring, then toasted their local hero.

But later, in the kitchen cleaning up, at a moment when only Emily was present, standing at the sink, Maddy said in a low voice, "I'd planned to be gone by then. But now I'll stay. I haven't stood by you all these years to abandon you now that your music is finally going to be played. I intend to be at that concert, Emily Jane. I'm going to Cleveland with you to hear your symphony."

"Gone?" Emily asked, pale-faced.

Maddy nodded.

Emily paused. "Were you intending to take steps to make yourself gone?"

Maddy hesitated. "Not immediately. I thought force of will would suffice. If not, then maybe. But the way I'm feeling . . ."

"How are you feeling?"

"So tired. Just so tired. Ever since Parrish died."

Emily, who did not trust force of will as much as Maddy did, thought a bit. "You know, Jenny's baby is due in March."

"Yes. I want to be here for that, too."

"So you'll plan on staying with us until next fall?" Straight-faced.

So of course Maddy had to laugh.

•

That night, standing at the bedroom window in her cotton nightgown, gazing at the black hump of mountain against the purple sky, Emily reviewed the day. Her heart clutched at the thought that Maddy wanted to die. Now that Emily thought of it, Maddy had been hinting at this for a long time, talking about how tired she was. Her old energy seemed to have vanished like smoke. Did she really think she could make herself die by willing it? People did believe that, but Emily doubted it. Force of will might keep us alive, but haphazardly. The will was powerful, but not subject to the top of the mind, to consciousness. That story by Thomas Mann she had read in college, she'd never forgotten it, "Mario and the Magician": Freedom exists and also the will exists but freedom of the will does not exist. Will cannot exist in a vacuum. Parrish wanted to live but didn't. But Maddy's will wanted her to live, Emily thought, or she wouldn't be here. She has to want to live, Emily thought. Has to.

Maybe the reptile brain, not accessible to the self, controlled will. It was strange, wasn't it, that part of the brain should be inaccessible to the rest of it? So you could get drunk and forget everything you did; or go into a coma and awaken and speak and have no memory of speaking. And people reach the reptile brain through meditation. Or rage. The rage of people like Slobodan Milošević, or Hitler, who blame everything on certain people. The American group, what were they called, the Aryan Nation? Or Hutus or Tutsis, whichever it was that started that terrible massacre. Or the massacres in Sierra Leone, or in Somalia, or Cambodia. Or that man who shot people from some tower in Texas: What did he think they'd done? How was what he did supposed to help? Those people believed, with their entire being, that eradicating somebody else would end all problems. That was reptile thinking, stupid and incontestable.

Yet music, too, came from the reptile brain, and poetry, and art, didn't they? When I blank out and people find me absentminded I am probably thinking with my reptile brain. It is where the first things are buried, the things that were planted in the baby, that grow into irrational loves and hates, needs and repulsions, the deepest desires, fetishes, the terrifying images that haunt us in delirium. Things that can't be changed.

Maddy says we aren't very evolved and unless we change our ways, we are doomed. As a race.

The things we do. Horrible, cruel world. Me too. Just this morning, I was preening, admit it, Emily, you were looking in the mirror and thinking how much better you'd held up than your sister Mamie, she's let herself go, two years younger than you and looks ninety—well, eighty. So lined, so bent, her hair that stony gray with no life in it. My hair still looks blond from a distance because there's enough blond in the gray. It's pretty hair. How dare you be vain at your age? And poor Mamie, she's been so sick, how can you make yourself feel good at her expense? And why is it necessary anyway?

She's never been kind to you. She always resented you.

All of them did, all but Martin. Because Poppa loved me most.

They wanted me in their lives, but only as a witness. I was supposed to stand there and tell them how wonderful they were. They weren't interested in knowing anything about me. Still, John left me the house. Could have left it to Crighton. Or Momma. Or even Mamie. Or all of us. I wonder why he did that.

Looking at Parrish in his coffin, remembering photographs of him as a baby, a toddler like Martin, stumbling on little fat legs, Maddy must have seen his big, open, clear, innocent eyes, arms reaching up to the loved Momma, the one who gave food and warmth and safety. For Maddy, that moment is now, he is still a baby, reaching his arms up to her. Even though he's in his coffin. I am still a schoolgirl, getting on the bus every morning, my braids hanging down my back, my mind always wondering, wondering, asking about everything, I felt I understood nothing. That girl is still alive in me, I am still she, I feel like her . . . I am an old woman, close to death . . .

Read the other day that some star far distant in space, millions of light years away, is sputtering, burning, ready to implode, to disintegrate. Actually, it disintegrated millions of years ago, but astronomers can see it now because light takes so long to reach us. So it's happening now, isn't it? Simultaneous with now. As I am simultaneously that questioning twelve-year-old and an answering seventy-year-old. So is Poppa still alive?

In my dreams.

Emily dreamt, regularly, about a house, a huge old house that was hers and not hers, hers to live in, but she did not control it, Momma controlled it, living in a large, dark back bedroom from which she rarely emerged. Emily wanted to fix the house up, paint it, rearrange the furniture, there was too much in some places, not enough in others. Some rooms were superfluous; there were three different kitchens, for instance. And some were nearly empty, with furniture crowded into a corner and covered with dust cloths. And sometimes she stumbled upon a gorgeous room, in the way she had stumbled, years ago, upon a building in Rome, seen it and been struck dumb, this gorgeous edifice stained black with soot. She had put off her errand and walked to the building, Michelangelo's Laurentian Library, as it turned out, a miracle on an ordinary city street, like the

Piazza Navona, which she wandered into one afternoon, from an alley where she bought a piece of fruit from a vendor's cart and then glanced up . . . and that miracle was there. There was, for instance, a library in her house, golden from sun, filled with beautiful, curved furniture high polished and serene, Victorian chairs, a heavy old desk, a settee with a curved back. And Poppa was there, working, always working; he helped her when she tried to cover up the ugly patches of raw cement in the basement, hanging large towels on a clothesline to conceal them. He handed her the clothespins, he was smiling, he loved her. And Momma too, the few times Emily would venture into her room; she was glad to be there, glad to be alive, glad Emily was her daughter. But she could never fix the house up properly—she did not have the money, the house was so big, its attic so huge, so hard to reach and dangerous to approach, but filled with precious relics of the past that Emily had never seen, surprises and richness she would love to uncover . . .

Everyone was there in this dream, her brothers and sister, their dog Benny, everyone was content, glad to be alive, together . . .

Why wasn't life like that? Because babies, let's face it, that isn't how babies were, not how we are, sweet little innocent adorable bundles of love. Not at all. Look at that Lanie. Kept ten adults hornswaggled all afternoon trying to keep her happy. The only relief came when she got tuckered out and fell asleep. What did Blake say? They leap into the dangerous world, "helpless, naked, piping loud: Like a fiend hid in a cloud." And Parrish as a baby was pretty fierce, Maddy said, adorable but a clinger, constantly whining and holding on to her. Could drive you crazy. And when he was grown, he drove them to despair, Maddy and Charley, drinking to spite them, to show them, to hurt them, to hurt himself.

He was cruel to Charles. Emily would never forget the afternoon she'd driven to his house with medicine she'd picked up for Jean, who was in bed with pneumonia. (Why hadn't Parrish fetched it? She could no longer remember. He'd given up drinking. He'd left Susan and Charles, but that day Charles was with him; Parrish was adding a room onto his house and had demanded that Charles help him. Charles was about twelve or thirteen.) It was after school hours, and

Parrish was working on the far side of the house. As she drove up and walked to the front door she could hear him yelling. He didn't hear Emily or he would have stopped. She had never in her life heard such vicious, sustained yelling at a youngster. Parrish called his son stupid and useless and a son of a fucking bitch, a hopeless idiot, when in hell would he learn to use his head, stupid fuck. He must have smacked the boy, because she heard Charles cry out.

She rang the front doorbell and left the package on the front step, walked quickly back to her car, and backed out of the driveway. Since that day, she had understood Charles's unfriendly taciturnity, the wary look around his eyes, his untrusting glance.

Yet Parrish had been loved. Who could understand? And the chances were that Parrish loved Charles.

My mother probably loved me.

She probably loved Father, too.

No hope for the human race. Cruelty as built in as the beak in the bird, the claws on the cat's paw. In all of us. Me and Momma. Father and Momma. I adored Martin yet I left him.

I wanted my own life. She smiled. That was a thing she was pleased she had done. Momma didn't want her to do it, fought her viciously. But Emily won. Maddy didn't even try to get free of her family. So eager to please her mother, who was more difficult than mine but gave Maddy love. Love is the strongest weapon; it can imprison a person utterly. And withholding love is a master strategy: It keeps your kids panting, eager, begging . . .

Family love. Such a mixed bag. Why the women were so important to each other. A curtain against the wind: It didn't stop but could soften it, a cushion on a rock, a soothing drink in a desert. They all knew what life was like. They'd all been ground down by it, crushed, smashed, stabbed. Yet they'd survived and knew how to survive. They did what they could to ameliorate things, offering friendly love, not as absolute or intimate as the parent's, not sexual, less demanding, but a love that could heal. We embrace the hurt one in a way that lets her know she is seen, her hurt and hurting, and accept her hurt and hurting, and how it must feel to her. They try to do that for their men too. But Emily thought that men were resistant to healing; they slunk off alone to nurse their wounds, feeling unmanned, feeling that letting the women soothe them would unman them further. Wouldn't allow themselves to be seen, wouldn't allow themselves to know that they were seen. Well, what did she know. Charley certainly felt Maddy's love. Maybe Steven and Tim did, too. Maybe.

That's what love is. Not the nonsense pushed in the movies, lust and pleasure. Desire fulfilled was great when it happened, but it wasn't lasting. That didn't make it unimportant, it just wasn't enough. And you couldn't make it happen, couldn't force it or learn it. You could learn to love, though, could teach others to love. The women had taught themselves and been taught by each other: They had learned how to cherish each other. Maddy was the first, the woman who was never cherished—or at least, never felt it—started it by cherishing Emily. So bighearted, no matter how she talked about her shriveled heart. She cherished Emily, and then when Alicia came, they both cherished Alicia, and then Jenny when she joined them. Clea and Hallie knew to cherish too, themselves and the women they helped in their clinic. Cherishing is circular. Like that circle Alicia talked about, the black movement for abolition inspiring and leading to the American women's movement, imitated and added to by the British women's movement, imitated by Gandhi in the Indian *satyagraha* movement, and again by Martin Luther King Jr. in the American civil rights movement, which ended by bestowing its benefits on the women's movement through the legislation it generated. A brilliant and miraculous process. Seeing and valuing, that was cherishing. It made life bearable, and in the end it became its meaning, because the only meaning life offers is the experience of it, the living itself, how it feels, how the years have felt, what the mind and heart and body have done and known and felt.

Maddy would be all right, Emily told herself. She was not going to die yet. She would die someday, and they would mourn her and celebrate her life by dancing, just the way she danced, her large ungainly body hurling itself, its inner fire driven against the barricade of air, as if she would fly, out of sheer exuberance, sheer joy in the moment, in the doing. But not right away, please. Not for a long time. Let me go first.

25

On March 25, 2001, Lady Day, the first day of their year, Maddy and Charley, Alicia and Steven, Jenny and Tim, Clea, Hallie, and Martine, sat with Emily in Severance Hall in Cleveland, waiting for Andrei Sikorsky to enter the auditorium. They were stiff and silent, almost holding their breath until he appeared, then applauding wildly with the rest of the audience as he walked to the podium. They held their breath again as the applause stopped and he raised his baton. And then a thin flute announced the theme, the oboe joined it, trumpets and horns gradually entered, slowly becoming forte, then fortissimo, and the symphony began. The hall attended raptly: There was no rustling, no coughing. There was a gasp as the first movement ended, and a few hands clapped. To console Emily for this, Maddy grabbed her hand from one side, and Alicia took the other, and the second movement began the same way: a flute, an oboe, but this time, violins, and with another theme.

Emily was not entirely happy. Sikorsky let the brasses get too harsh in the first movement and took the modulation in the second much too slowly. Also, he rushed the finale. He made it sound martial almost, triumphant, when it merely offered joy. As Emily thought of it.

But the audience seemed to like it. Emily knew that that did not guarantee that the musicians would, even if the orchestra members stood at the end and clapped ceaselessly. Sikorsky then beckoned until Emily stood and walked to the stage and mounted the steps and the hall stood and gave her an ovation. But that was common these days, she told herself, it meant nothing; still, there were tears in her eyes, she clasped Sikorsky's hand warmly, he kissed her hand, then her cheek, who knows, maybe it really was good, who could tell, there was no way of telling for a hundred years at least, so she might as well enjoy it, mightn't she? Here she was, all done up à la Clea, with a new haircut, (bobbed hair! after all these years! no more nightly brushing!) and a smart black pantsuit Clea had found for her in New York. Besides, it would never happen again, a premiere was once in a lifetime, and this was hers. She let herself smile at the audience; she beamed, and they loved that and clapped harder.

Then it was over. There was a party following the concert, given by a wealthy patron of the orchestra. They all went, the Steventon crowd, keeping an eye on Emily but not crowding her. Tim was thrilled to meet Richard Stoltzman, the great clarinetist, who was a guest; all of them were delighted to meet the musicians, the conductor, the Cleveland patrons, but pleased most of all to be together, with their beloved Emily, at her moment of acclaim.

"God knows she waited long enough," Maddy muttered.

"She didn't mind the wait," Clea said. "She loves the process."

Jenny looked at Clea. "Yes," she said. Jenny was now enormous in her pregnancy and was having trouble moving around. She could barely stand, sit or lie.

"How are you doing?" Clea asked.

"Well, you know how it is in the last month. Miserable. I'm so huge and front heavy I almost topple over. But I've been warning this kid for weeks that he can't come out until later in the month—I was not going to miss this concert," she laughed.

"Suppose he decides to come out there?" Tim had asked anxiously.

"There are doctors in Cleveland, aren't there?"

But Tim couldn't rest, and he had arranged through the orchestra manager to have a gynecologist on call in the concert hall with them, with an ambulance standing outside. Famous artists could get away with things like that. Of course, it cost a fortune, but Tim didn't care. But the baby held his peace.

•

The baby—they knew he was a boy—held his peace for another week, as if he were in training to be a good baby, until his mother was back home, lying miserably on her back on the bed, pillows propped against both sides to help hold her belly up. Tim was watching *Nightline* in bed when she suddenly sat up and grunted. He grabbed the stopwatch to time her contractions, then agreed it was time, and wrapped her up and helped her to the Volvo (she wanted to go in her car) and drove her to the hospital, where in less than an hour she produced an eight-pound-three-ounce boy with a full head of blond hair. Maddy, Emily, and Alicia were there within twenty minutes of Tim's call, waiting outside the delivery room when Jenny was wheeled out, the baby lying in her arms, tears dampening her beaming face and Tim walking beside her, pale and weary, but smiling broadly.

The women cooed over the baby, cooed over Jenny.

"Your life is now changed forever," Maddy said.

"A new life!" Emily breathed. "A brand-new life! A whole new life!"

"Beautiful," Alicia gasped. "You're all beautiful."

The baby was red-faced and didn't seem able to see; his tiny hands clutched spasmodically, his fingers lifting as if he were exercising them. His feet kicked out in little bursts.

"That's what he's been doing inside me!" Jenny exclaimed. "He's had me black and blue!"

The nurses wheeled the exhausted Jenny to her room, her entourage following, all talking at once in low voices, which became silent when they reached the room, where three women lay sleeping; this hospital did not have private rooms. It was two in the morning, and Jenny needed to sleep. The women, and then Tim, bent and kissed her good-bye, then tiptoed out to the hallway.

"You high?" Maddy asked Tim. "I'm so high I know I won't sleep. Want to come back for a drink?"

"I am high," he said. "But it's late. Charley must be asleep."

"Yes. We'll go to Emily's. No one to disturb there."

"Great!"

"You coming, Lish?"

"Of course." Alicia grinned.

So they all went back to Emily's house, leaving Jenny behind with the new love of her life sleeping peacefully in a crib beside her bed, the helpless one who would in the course of the next days seize her heart with eagle talons that would never release it, in as absolute a love as exists on earth. Which would make Tim jealous. Understandably: There was no cure for this. Much as Jenny loved Tim, she would always love the child more. She would give her life for the child—at once, if necessary, or in bits and pieces over the years. This is how lives get changed.

Emily opened champagne—empty though her fridge usually was, she always had champagne cooling. And crackers and cheese and pears, which was all she could drum up, but which they ate with gusto, the four of them crowing and laughing and offering ridiculous names for the baby, and generally acting so silly that Tim comprehended for the first time why Jenny loved her friends so much. They were as much fun as his bohemian friends used to be, he decided, on much less alcohol. Emily put music on the CD player and Alicia and Maddy danced, then Tim did the kazatsky, ending up on his ass in the middle of the room, all of them laughing until tears streamed down their faces.

•

In May, Clea called Emily, gravely upset. A change, she said, an unwanted change, was occurring. Could she come up and talk it over with Em? This time, Emily did not plan lamb stew: Enough was enough. She bought a chicken roasted on a spit by Pam Willis at the local grocery, and picked up roasted potatoes and vegetables from the gourmet counter at the supermarket and bought a key lime pie at

Pietro the caterer's. There was a grinding in her chest. Clea wouldn't tell her what was wrong over the phone, but she sounded distressed. She swore no one was ill and said that the problem did not involve Martine.

When Clea arrived around six on Friday, she looked awful, dark rings under her eyes, her face strained, drawn, and pale. Emily did not rush her. Clea managed a smile, hugged her aunt, carried her bag up to her old room, and came back down ready to enjoy her gin and tonic. She began to explain immediately.

"Hallie's been offered a fabulous job. Two hundred K a year, big-name hospital and a chance to work on sickle-cell anemia. It's her specialty, has always been. But of course she would have to give up the clinic.

"There's a job there for me, too, in hospital administration. Almost as much money. We'd have to live in Manhattan, though. Martine goes to private school anyway—it's necessary, in Bridgeport—but this would mean a very different kind of private school, you know, a fancy place. Like Dalton or Brearley. I don't know what to do."

"Should I take it that Hallie wants this job?"

"Yes. I could probably stop her if I made a big enough stink. She loves me enough that she'd turn it down if I gave her an ultimatum. But you know she'd never forgive herself. Or me. She comes from ambitious parents. They were educated people, they had high hopes for their children. And she was a brilliant student, scholarships, all that. This is her chance. And her mother and her aunts are still alive, they all live near each other in St. Albans, on Long Island, in a real community. Her mother is comfortable, but she has these aunts who live on Social Security. With this new job, she'd be able to help them, which she can't do with the meager salaries we pay ourselves at the clinic. And it's a chance to work on this disease, this thing that has plagued her all her life—two of her uncles died of it, and one of her grandparents. It's in her family, her genes. It plagues the black community, you know . . ."

"Of course. It's understandable, anyway. Most people would want to earn more money, have high prestige, do work that's challenging intellectually. Not that what you're doing now isn't challenging too, in a different way."

"Yes. It makes sense."

"And you?"

"Well, I'm really a mess. Because I don't know if I want to go with her. And I don't know whether my doubts are . . . fair. I don't know whether I'm pissed at her for thinking about leaving the clinic, it's been our life . . . or if I really don't want this new life, you know, fast, high paid, Manhattan, high pressure. Or whether I would want it if I weren't terrified of it. Or terrified for Martine. I don't know my own feelings!"

Emily smiled. "Nothing unusual about that."

Clea smiled weakly. "You mean I often don't know my real feelings?"

"No, I mean all of us, well, many of us, I really mean myself, often don't know our feelings. You may or may not, I don't know. I haven't seen enough of you over the last few years. But I've been like that all my life. I never know what I feel until it comes out of my mouth. I still don't know if I didn't want to marry because I didn't want a wife's life, being a servant, or because I feared I'd fall under a man's thumb. Or was it just that I was devoted entirely to music? Whatever I've done or haven't done, I haven't known why. I've felt compelled to do what I've done, but never been sure why."

Clea thought about that for a while. Finally, she said, "What I never understood about you is why you came back here."

"To Steventon?"

"Yes."

"And what do you think?"

"I think it was because of Maddy."

Emily gawped.

"I've been reading these letters Emily Dickinson wrote to Susan Dickinson, you know, her sister-in-law? They keep making me think of you and Maddy . . ."

"You think I've been in love with Maddy all these years?"

"Could be, no?" Then Clea laughed. "Given my orientation, it's kind of natural for me to think that."

"I do love Maddy. But it's never felt exactly the same as the love I've felt for . . . men. But the kind of love that . . . you know, the feeling that a person comes first in your life . . . I don't know if I feel that for Maddy. I felt it for my father—but that was so long ago—and your father, once, and you. And now Martine. I guess Maddy's the most enduring love of my life, though. Although I was never 'in love' with her . . ."

"So why do you think you came back?"

"Like you, when you left New York years ago and opened the clinic, I was tired of the competition and pressure of Boston—which isn't as bad as New York but is a hell of a lot worse than the Browning School. I really wanted to concentrate on writing music, and that was hard to do in Boston because I had to do so much teaching and administrative work. Committees, meetings . . . and I was constantly angry in Boston, because I knew that if I'd been a man, they'd have been more supportive of my creative work . . . And I was looking for a way out of the relationship I was in. And my mother was blackmailing me—threatening to sell the house if I didn't come back. I wanted to save it for you or whoever would want it—you know, I have a lot of nieces and nephews sprinkled around the country. Maybe I just wanted to hide. And maybe I did want to go back to where I had a perfect friend."

"Yes."

"Or maybe I thought here I could create something I had no name for, but have indeed found here: a woman's culture. A world made by women, where a woman can live in their own world in harmony."

Clea burst out, "I think that's sort of why I got involved with Hallie. I think that was what we both wanted. It makes life such fun. And that's exactly what I'm afraid we'd lose in New York."

"You've lived in New York, you know what it's like."

"Yes. I loved it then, but I was younger. I don't know that it's a place where I want to raise Martine. What little remains of her raising. She'll be going to college in a few years . . ." Her voice trailed off.

"You could create a women's world in New York."

"Maybe. But there's something else . . ."

"You want a refill?"

"Umm. I'll get them."

"We'll both get them. That'll be quicker."

They walked to the kitchen, poured drinks, and walked back, talking all the while.

"Something else?"

"I'm thinking of getting more training in medical ethics. I feel some enormous changes are coming, and I want to have a voice in them."

"Like what?"

"All kinds of things. Stem-cell research. Genetic experiments. No matter what the right says, these things are coming. They can help too many people, they may have almost miraculous possibilities. There's no way they're not going to happen, probably within ten years. And human cloning. And selective breeding. What used to be called eugenics will come back under some other name, a terribly perilous business, so close to Big Brotherism, to totalitarian control . . . I'd like to be informed enough to be part of the debate when all this happens. And it will. Soon."

Emily paused. "Really!"

But Clea was somewhere else. "On the other hand, I love the clinic. I mean, I really love it. I love our patients. I feel a part of their lives. It's so satisfying. I can't imagine doing anything that would make me happier. So I don't know . . ."

"Maybe you can find someone to take it over."

"Doubtful. There's no money in it."

"Some people only want money. Others only want not to have money. Could you keep up the clinic without Hallie? Would you be happy?"

Clea's eyes filled. "I wouldn't be happy anywhere without Hallie."

"But if you went with her . . ."

Clea shook her head. "It won't be the same. She won't be the Hallie I know. She'll be a different Hallie. Maybe I won't love her as much . . ." Clea's gaze drifted away from Emily's.

"And what about Martine? What does she want?"

"She'd like to stay where she is. You know how kids are, they hate change. But I can see New York excites her. She'd probably love living there. And she'd get a better education, no question. And have friends who are more sophisticated . . . smarter, probably." She fell silent.

"Hungry?"

"Yeah! What's for dinner?"

"Willis's chicken."

"Great!" Clea laughed. "Always liked that almost as much as your lamb stew. Or McDonald's."

Laughing, they started for the kitchen.

"You don't have to decide immediately," Emily said.

"No," Clea agreed doubtfully.

•

Jenny and Tim had named the baby David Hugh, after Jenny's father and Tim's father, since Tim already had a Junior. He was going to be a big person, they surmised, as he exploded in size month by month; he was a little slow in other ways, though—sitting up, gaining hand-eye coordination. They suspected he was going to be noisy too: From a few days after his birth and for the next six weeks, he spent from four o'clock until eight, every day, screaming. People called it colic. Whatever it was, there was no cure. Nothing helped, not a bottle, not a changed diaper, not being carried around and jounced up and down, sung to, or caressed. He cried. And cried. And cried.

Jenny saw Tim's patience tried to the limit, and forgave him when he stormed out to his studio. He was careful not to slam the door behind him, though (slammed doors made the baby quaver and cry out in terror). But he also shared the two o'clock feedings, changing him, walking him; he didn't even mention spit-up on his shirt collars, or pee on his lap. Not wanting to break the spell, she did not thank him—nor, in principle, did she think she should—but one day in June as he prepared to change David's diaper, she burst out in delight, "You want to do it! You're not doing it to help me! It's not that you don't want to be involved! You do!"

He stopped dead in the middle of the kitchen, holding a clean paper diaper in his hand. "Actually, I never was a father before. Not really. You know?"

She smiled. She moved to him with a glide, as if she were on a rolling walkway, just glided into him and hit him hard with her body and stayed there, pressed against him, her head leaning hard into his chest. He clasped her, murmuring, "Jenny," and she raised her face to him. "I love you," she said. "More than I ever thought I could love anyone."

"Is this the effect of David?"

"Could be." She laughed, releasing him.

"The little beast spreads love, shit, and pee wherever he goes," Tim continued.

She laughed. "And spit-up."

"And screaming," he sighed.

"It will pass."

"But when, oh lord, but when?"

"I know. Soon, I hope."

They stood, nuzzling, in silence. Then he asked "So, when are you going to go back to painting?"

"Well, not right away. It's impossible now. But I have a plan."

"How did I know that?"

"You know how hard I worked while I was pregnant."

"I was noticing. I wondered if you were planning a show."

She gave him a look. "Smart-ass."

"So, when and where?"

"Well, I don't know where. But soon. Maybe in six months."

"Wow, Jenny! How many canvases do you have?"

"Fifteen. Well, twelve. Will you look at them and see what you think? Twelve I'm sure of. Fifteen maybe. The three others . . . well, they're not as good. And the centerpiece will be *The Women*, the big painting of my friends . . ."

"Have you finished that?"

"Almost. I kept putting it aside, doing other things, small things. Fruit and vegetables—sacred food. The shops in Winchester—you know, shop fronts in different lights. A couple of barns in different lights. The waterfall behind the house. The mountain opposite Emily's house. Five of those."

"Your Mont St. Victoire?"

"No. Not at all. Totally different. My mountain is just a shape. I'm not copying him, Tim . . ." She was pink and irritated.

"I was kidding, kid."

•

Several New York galleries proved to be interested in Jenny's work—well, of course they'd express interest, she thought, when the great Tim Halliday is the one who brought in the slides—but none could schedule a show before the following year. So (not wanting to show in Tim's gallery, which offered to "fit her in") Jenny made arrangements with a New York dealer for 2002, but found a gallery in a small compound of antique shops in Winchester that wanted her for a show in June.

It happened that Alicia's book, which she had finished shortly before Parrish died, would also be published in June and the two women decided to have a joint "opening" to celebrate Jenny's artwork and Alicia's publication. The gallery was a large, bright white space with large windows and natural-wood trim and floor. Jenny's paintings occupied the entire space, with *The Women* having place of honor in the center of the longest wall. Maddy's grandnephew Lewis had installed a sound system in the gallery, and Jenny put on an advance CD of Emily's *Eros* Trio and one of her symphony, played by the Cleveland Orchestra with Sikorsky directing, which would soon be released. Alicia's books were piled up on a central counter, and they stood, jacket facing out, on every low space. The jacket front featured a painting by Jenny of a local back road with an old stone house surrounded by trees, and a photograph of Alicia taken by Mariette on the back.

The party was large: People from the local art world crowded next to people from the local book world, people from Steventon next to people from New York. All of Alicia's people were there—Steven, Steve, Neil, Mariette, and Alfie. Clea, Hallie, and Martine had come up from New York; and even Jenny's father came with his wife—he who hadn't even attended Jenny's graduation from college. Marcus and Ippolyte were not there: Tim felt it best to invite them to the show in New York. But some of his friends from the New York art world showed up. Maddy's family thronged the place, twenty-odd of them at one count. Even Lily and Parsons had come up from the city.

The painting of the women was, they all agreed, gorgeous. The figures had blocky forms. Maddy, the tallest and largest, a rectangular block of deep red, stood along the left-hand margin facing right toward the others, as if she were guarding them. Emily, a block of a brilliant blue, sat in a high-backed chair in front of her, facing right and with her head bent, studying a sheet of music in her lap. Alicia, in her emerald gown, leaned back against the wall behind them all, her hair a wild halo around her head, her eyes piercing the viewers'. And Jenny sat at a lower level, cross-legged at the far right, wearing yellow pants and a white T-shirt, sketching. Above her head hung a small painting of a house, a large house like Emily's or Maddy's, big enough to hold a huge family. The figures were not looking at each other, but Jenny had managed, by intermingling their shadows, and by brushstrokes and background patches of color, to unify them into an interconnected group, a force field, an expression of human will.

People wandered the gallery, admiring the paintings. Quite a few bought paintings, and several wanted to buy *The Women*, but Jenny would not sell it. Everyone picked up the history—which Alicia had called *Women of Steventon: 1630–1880*—to glance through it, and many bought it. Acquaintances were full of praise.

Alicia, standing with Maddy, regarded the throngs idly walking about. Steven was in a corner, talking to Neil. He had discovered that Neil was a music lover, an amateur cellist, and trained in musicology. Steven had a knowledgeable person who talked about music the same way he did for the first time in his life.

Alicia said, in a low voice, to Maddy, "I never really understood that I was afraid of Steven until the day I got my check—the advance on the book—because suddenly I wasn't afraid anymore. Isn't that strange?"

Maddy smiled. "Fairly common, I'd say."

"Oh!" She looked pained. "But why was I afraid of him in the first place?"

Maddy groaned. "Ask me an easier question."

"Don't tell me you understand. You can't have been like that.

You were never cowardly like me."

"I don't know if it's cowardly. But I was . . . not really intimidated by Charley . . . but I felt inferior to him when I married him. He'd been to college, to law school, I had only finished high school. He was the one who earned the money. I was dependent on him. How can you not be a little—well, feel a little—as if he's the boss."

"Not you, Maddy, surely!" Alicia gasped.

"You didn't know me fifty-odd years ago, sweetie."

"No."

"But it doesn't work. Marriages in which men are the boss never work. They may last but they are never happy. I don't know why that is. Maybe because the woman is given the responsibility for taking care of everything. And if the man recognizes that, and lets the woman take over, there's a great chance for a happy marriage. Happy for both partners."

Alicia laughed. "I can't picture Steven making me the boss in our marriage—or my being boss."

"But you are."

"What?"

"Of course you are. Yours is the will in the family."

Alicia gazed at Maddy in shock.

"Ask your kids if you don't believe me. You know, women never understand how much power they wield."

Alicia took a gulp of wine. Have to think about this.

Afterward, everyone went back to Emily's house. She had hired a caterer, and Maddy helped her plan a party for her friends and their friends. This project was Emily's final attempt to keep Maddy interested in living. Her tiredness of a year ago had vanished. She was excited by Emily's new career, by Alicia's new book, by Charles's engagement to Pam Smith, and by a new being among them, who at the moment sat in a stroller being wheeled by his father, pointing to and exclaiming loudly about Mommy's paintings, long familiar to him, hanging on these unfamiliar walls. He was now lying in his portable crib on the floor of an upstairs bedroom of Emily's house, sucking his thumb. He was the first baby to occupy that room in over sixty years.

"About time," Emily said the next day at breakfast. "It's about time there was a baby in this house again."

"I have to tell you, Martine wants this house," Clea told her aunt.

"Martine is fifteen years old."

"She's already picked out a life for herself. Which includes Oldfield house."

"Well, isn't that nice!" Emily smiled. "Especially if she still feels that way in ten or twenty years."

Clea grimaced. "Yeah. If . . ."

"Oh, who knows at twenty what they're going to want at forty? Or sixty? I always used to think it was crazy to promise to love someone until you die, when people got married at twenty—or even younger. How could you predict?"

"Well, in the old days, chances were you'd be dead by thirty. Certainly by forty. It wasn't as much of a promise then."

"I suppose. I used to have a kind of dream. When you first came to live with me. I imagined you getting married and having a child and living in Oldfield house with me and your husband and your family, and the house being full again."

"Umm. I think there's a better chance the house will be full again with paying guests, if it's ever full again at all."

"A bed and breakfast?" Emily sighed.

"Does it really matter?"

Emily stopped, put down the coffee pot. "Maybe not."

"Life is so different now. It's the moment that matters now, not the line, the tradition, whatever. That was important when survival was tricky. But now, physical survival is expected. It's emotional survival we worry about." Clea laughed. "We're all such a bunch of nutheads."

"Life is different now, Clea, you're right. And different things matter now. But continuity matters to me. You matter to me. Partly because you're you, partly because you're Martin's daughter, and he was my brother . . ."

"Yes, I suppose."

"But the house? I don't think it matters very much. Not the way it used to. Anyway, it's gotten so expensive to keep up, a good-sized family couldn't afford to live in it unless they were millionaires. Maddy says that's the cruelest irony."

"We could probably afford to keep it now. Hallie and me. With what we earn together."

"But your apartment is so big! You must have enough expenses!"

"We do. But we're rolling in money, Em, I swear it. We hardly know what to do with it. Well, we still help finance the clinic. Avella and Emilia, who run it now, love us. We keep them going. And we go back to visit every once in a while. Of course, we've lost touch with our patients. Sad."

"But you like what you're doing now?"

"We love it. Like you said. A different kind of challenge. A different kind of happiness. A different kind of misery."

"That's the greatest thing about how things have changed: that you can try different things in the same life—you're not doomed to repeat one thing endlessly the way our parents did. My father . . . I sometimes wish he'd just left us and gone to live with . . . Jean Harlow, or whatever her real name was. I never told you about her. She was a widow who raised bulls. I wish my mother could have gotten a job running the army, or the navy, or the marine corps . . ." she laughed. "People . . . men . . . women too can try new things. Have more experiences. More life."

"More life. I like that idea."

"Me too," Emily said. "Did I tell you the Amsterdam Concertgebouw has commissioned a *large work* from me? Kind unspecified. Anything I want, but a large work."

"Yay! How fabulous!" Clea jumped up and down. "More life, Emmie! More life!"

Afterword
The Writer as Thinker

The most important influences on my way of thinking and feeling have been my reading of English and foreign literatures, philosophy, psychology, art history, sociology, and anthropology, and my experience as a wife and mother. My life, when married and divorced, and the lives of my friends, the lives of my children, all seem to me rich with implication.

—Marilyn French

Marilyn French was born Marilyn Edwards to a family of Polish origin on November 21, 1929 in New York City. As a child she read voraciously and played the piano, hoping to someday become a composer. But she also wrote from a very early age, even launching a neighborhood newspaper in which the grimmer local truths were eclipsed in favor of what was surely an early form of fiction.[1] Indeed, French perceived when quite young a certain gap between the world of fiction and real life, which she already associated with her mother's sadder stories. Although serious about music and very interested in philosophy, French decided to study English at university since only literature promised to fuse the varied experiences of life together into one discipline. She worked her way through Hofstra College (now University) in Hempstead, Long Island, obtaining a BA in 1951, having married Robert M. French Jr. the previous year. They had two children. She supported him through law school, writing seriously from 1957 but publishing very little. In 1964 she obtained her MA at Hofstra where she then taught English from 1964 to 1968. In 1967 she divorced her husband and undertook doctoral studies at Harvard University, Cambridge, Massachusetts where she received her PhD in 1972. She was an artist in residence at the Aspen Institute for Humanistic Study in 1972, and taught at the College of the Holy Cross in Worcester, Massachusetts until 1976, after which she served as Mellon Fellow at Harvard from 1976 to 1977. Her PhD thesis was published at this time as *The Book as World: James Joyce's Ulysses* (1976), followed immediately by her first novel *The Women's Room* (1977).

Marilyn French's own life experience served as the basis for *The Women's Room*. The success of this novel allowed her to leave teaching and write full-time. A prolific writer, she is the author of five novels, several sociological and historical works, a personal memoir, two books of literary criticism and a great number of articles, book reviews, essays, and introductions (see complete bibliography at the end of this afterword). Although still best known for her popular first novel, now a classic of second-wave feminist literature, several of her books are widely read in the United States as well as abroad and also studied in women's studies courses. Indeed, Marilyn French is among the very few feminist writers who have succeeded in publishing important books in several categories of fiction and nonfiction. Whether in literature, literary criticism, sociology, or history, French has made significant contributions to many of the debates of her time. Her flexibility as a writer coupled with the fact that as an engaged feminist she approaches her craft in a particular way, defying genre boundaries and literary conventions, have made it difficult for publishers and critics to categorize her.[2] Her fiction, for example, illuminates the hardships and hardiness of women which she has documented in such sociological works as *Beyond Power: On Women, Men and Morals* (1985) or *The War Against Women* (1992) and her literary criticism is infused with the political and philosophical values which characterize and unify her work as a whole.

The Nonfiction

The Book as World. James Joyce's Ulysses (1976), for instance, is a study of the narrative styles of the various chapters of Joyce's novel and of the moral vision French discerns behind the text. Well-received by critics at the time, it remains a valuable reference for students of the modernist writer today. Similarly, Shakespearean critics still consider her 1980 publication *Shakespeare's Division of Experience*, one of the first feminist studies of the bard's work, insightful in its treatment of several of his plays, most notably *Macbeth*.

French has written also on the life and work of many women writers and about issues relevant to feminist aesthetics.[3] In various essays, French describes the stereotypes and narrow literary conventions which have confined their practice. She suggests, for example, that the long neglect of Edith Wharton had its origins in her ignoring repressive social codes which forbade writing about female desire. In a 1987 essay, French studies the discrepancies between the lives of such "muzzled" women writers as George Sand, George Eliot, Edith Wharton, Willa Cather, and Virginia Woolf, asking why even "women's fiction has not reflected the fullness of life some women writers themselves achieved" ("Muzzled Women," 219). Both the narrow views of critics and self-censorship are to blame, she notes: "It is still risky to create a heroine who is angry, especially at men, and difficult to make sympathetic a mother who doesn't absolutely put her children first; it may be impossible outside romance to depict women with power-in-the-world as admirable figures living rich lives. . . . It is probably still impossible to endow a heroine with both a sex life and authority" ("Muzzled Women," 227).

Elsewhere in essays published in the 1980s, French describes Margaret Atwood, Christa Wolf, and Esther Broner as continuing in the "humanization" of female characterization, as they explore "the realm of the necessary" and stretch literary convention "so it can hold a female as well as a male voice" ("Introduction to Esther Broner's *Her Mothers*" 1985, x).[4] These women and many others form a "great chain," stretching from Cleopatra to the women writers presented in *Almost Touching the Skies: Women's Coming of Age Stories* (2000), a volume celebrating The Feminist Press's thirtieth anniversary.[5] This chain of women "runs through human history. It is the chain of women who . . . have worked and struggled and written in an attempt to heal the world's sickness" (xxvi). For French sees literature not only as reflecting the society from which it emanates; it has a social function too and can influence its readers and society as a whole.[6] Her literary criticism and literature bear witness to this approach.[7] For French, art and life form an interconnected whole, anchored in the present but looking forward: "I believe feminist art can make us better, just as I think a feminist world would make us better" ("Is There a Feminist Aesthetic?" 76). Feminist writing has always represented a means to arrive at her vision of a feminist world.

Throughout her career, Marilyn French has written sociological and historical essays and books that explore the origins of patriarchy and misogyny and analyze their manifestations, in order to imagine a feminist world. The first, *Beyond Power: On Women, Men and Morals* (1985), began as a project in 1979 in a context of fear of a nuclear holocaust and the possibility of totalitarian regimes. Similarly, the rise of the religious right that accompanied the presidencies of Reagan and Bush, and the implications for women in particular, motivated French to write *The War Against Women* (1992). The three volumes of the monumental *From Eve to Dawn: A History of Women* (2002–2003), on the other hand, made manifest a life-long project. The three works—a total of five volumes—document the reality of women's condition past and present and provide the material backdrop against which French's fiction can be read. *Beyond Power*, for example, analyzes the victory of male values over female ones and the gradual establishment of institutions reflecting the characteristic mind-body split; the importance given both to the faculty of reason and to the idea that life consists of a struggle against nature. She proposes a return to an earlier feminist order based on the mother-child pair. By returning reproduction of the human race to the central place it deserves to occupy, by inventing new forms of masculinity, and by replacing a quest for power with a quest for pleasure, she suggests the possibility of a feminist revolution and a "feminized" society.[8] In the final volume of *From Eve to Dawn* (2003), French's focus on the importance of rearing children allows her to envision cooperation with conservative "feminists," walking on common ground to build a larger, more all-inclusive feminist movement.

Fiction

In *The Women's Room*, French describes the lives of American middle-class suburban white women in the 1950s, when traditional notions of gender constricted their behavior, limited their choices and movements, and provoked many forms of malaise. Mira's story can be read as composed of two distinct parts—her life prior to and during her marriage to Norm; then as a divorced graduate student in Cambridge. French also sees similarities between the generations of women—in the 1950s—for younger female students also feel as out of place on a masculine campus as the bloodied Kotex napkin suggests when it appears in Kyla's dream in a corner of the room where she is to take oral exams for her doctorate. In the novel, most importantly, a strong sense of female solidarity characterizes the relationships between women, a solidarity born first as responses to cries for help, then of the awareness that each woman's individual suffering is indeed collective. Together they form an oppressed group.

Readers loved the book, passing copies from friend to friend, and sales rose to 7 million copies. It was translated into over twenty languages and sold over 21 million copies worldwide. The novel was made into a television movie, and *The Women's Room* became a household word, symbolic of the women's movement. It became the principal novel "that changed lives," serving as consciousness-raising text for innumerable women.[9]

Three novels followed *The Women's Room*. In *The Bleeding Heart* (1980), French explores the tenuous heterosexual relationship of a middle-aged American woman and man in London. The lovers, Dolores and Victor, spend the year in a polemical tug of war in which they both unveil their views on male-female relations and their painful personal experiences. In *Her Mother's Daughter* (1987) French explores the mother-daughter bond in a possibly autobiographical rendering of three female generations. She dramatizes the ways by which mothers transmit their suffering to their daughters, generation after generation. Here, French also takes note of social class and ethnic origins in relation to women's lives. In *Our Father* (1994), French takes on the issues of incest and the solidarity of sisters. She brings four very different sisters, born of different mothers, to the patriarchal house, following their father's hospitalization. Realizing that they share the secret of humiliation and abuse by the patriarch Stephen Upton, their familial link grows into a bond over time and becomes unbreakable. Collective action, here in the form of a trial, brings change.

Illness and Writing

In 1992, Marilyn French was diagnosed with cancer and began a series of medical procedures that were to prove as life-threatening as the disease itself. Two books came out of the ordeal: a novel and a memoir. French wrote the first, *My Summer with George* (1996), in order to maintain her sanity, and it is indeed testimony to the author's indomitable will to live. In it, French returns to the heterosexual plot, imagining an older, successful romance writer living in New York, courted rather haphazardly by a mature Southern journalist in the city for his work. She also explores issues of female aging and desire.[10]

The memoir, *A Season in Hell* (1998), whose title is borrowed from French poet Arthur Rimbaud's *Une saison en enfer* (1873), recounts her battle with cancer, emphasizing the suffering induced by the treatments as much as by the disease.[11] While the book indicts the inhumanity of much of the medical establishment, it also pays tribute to the familial and female support networks that helped her to heal. For the author survived thanks to the "coven" of women who supported her, in addition to her grown children. She survived also because of her will and her writing. Marilyn French literally wrote herself well in a context of female solidarity and familial support.

Continuity and Change: *In the Name of Friendship*

Centered, poised, and confident, French could have called this novel "The Women's Room Two." *In the Name of Friendship* offers understanding and compassion, a smiling embrace across the Berkshires, from New York to California and beyond, across generations and gendered barriers. For the four chief characters in the novel, mind and body, spirit and emotion fuse, and for readers who search for feminist messages in fiction, the novel offers one: clearly, at the beginning of the twenty-first century, more than forty years after the start of the women's movement, at least privileged women can choose to experience "more life."

Like French's other works, the text may be seen as part of the consciousness-raising tradition from which it springs. Like *The Women's Room* and French's other novels, in this one individual suffering—whether women's or men's—is in fact shared, and profound change must occur for all to heal. But in *In the Name of Friendship*, far more than before, French treats men's suffering with as much compassion as women's, making clear that our social progress must be linked across age and gender.

The opening chapter places the reader in a specifically female time and space. Indeed, in an echo to Julia Kristeva's essay "Woman's Time," French rewrites the Western calendar, redefining the New Year as March 25 in a symbolic return to an earlier pagan timetable based on the movements of the planets and the Earth's seasons.[12] Four friends in the novel celebrate four special days, timed to correspond roughly with the solstices and equinoxes, and to honor four distinctive women: Mary (understood in ante-Christian terms as a modern avatar of an ancient fertility goddess or Earth mother), Emily Dickinson, Emma Goldman, and Eleanor of Aquitaine. French here signifies a temporal recentering of the female, in a return to remote rituals honoring female fertility. As she has made clear elsewhere, French believes that reproduction and the raising of children are most important human activities, requiring a recentering in society.[13] Similarly, using another female symbol, French organizes the narrative as a circle, moving from Lady Day 2000 to the same date a year later, and from the celebration of one woman's creative achievement to another's. The opening of the novel occurs appropriately at the beginning of a new millennium, which may see a new social order, a feminist era or "women's time." French also alludes to new ideas of physicists about the simultaneity of past and present. Emily, for example, imagines that the death of a star, while actually occurring millions of years ago, occurs as well in the present where the astronomer observes it across the distant reaches of space. The effect is of a compression of time, or a bending, where past meets present and relives. I will return to this idea later in a discussion of generational change and the transmission of history. I should note, of course, that, despite the uses of pre-Christian, circular or "bent" time, linear temporality also exists as the narrative moves forward from the inception of each woman's creative project to its achievement, implying a harmonious mix of male and female rhythms, in line with French's thinking.

The space in which the four women meet is similarly symbolic. They are at Jenny's, but not in the large, very modern house conceived by her artist husband Tim Halliwell: They are in the "bourgeois" screened porch she demanded he add on to it. In clear opposition to the cold, hard lines of the purely aesthetic male domain, the porch is welcoming and comfortable, providing warmth even in the cool spring.[14] It looks out onto a waterfall, not a passive limpid pool, but a crashing powerful flow, suggestive of the creative potential within each of the four women, and reflective of the four empowered women they celebrate. Jenny and her friends are at ease here, and the space is conducive to the kinds of conversation and sharing that Marilyn French underlines as vital for the health of humanity. She gives importance to this space even as she de-centers male space: Tim's studio is located in a separate barn on the property, and Charley's office occupies the garage. While Tim placed Jenny's studio close to the couple's domestic space, thereby perhaps suggesting that her work as artist is secondary to her life as wife, and while he hid her "removable" porch at the back of the house, French neutralizes his possibly misogynous intentions by making Jenny's spaces the center of the narrative. In fact, on a more general level, French's preoccupation with houses, particularly women's houses like those of Emily and Maddy, can be read as an appropriation of the Father's house. Emily, the spinster rebel in the novel, occupies her family's traditional home, which she will pass on to her female descendant Martine; Maddy maintains her family residence and manages the finances, but also sells the homes of others for profit. This female or feminist occupation of the patriarchal refuge recalls *Our Father* (1994) in which the four sisters confiscate their progenitor's space. Similarly, French's choice of names for towns in the novel reinforces the notion of a female geography and historical continuity: Steventon, where the women live, is the name of the English town where Jane Austen was born and Winchester a town she also frequented.[15]

In the Name of Friendship shares many of the preoccupations and stylistic elements of Marilyn French's previous novels and so represents continuity with the rest of her work. It is, of course, focused on female experience in the widest and deepest sense: woman in relation to significant others, in relation to her body and sexuality, in relation to work and creative experience, and in relation to society as a whole. The novel is very much concerned with the experience of mothering and the mother-daughter relationship. As in earlier novels, marriage is equated with imprisonment and a life of servitude. Self-sacrifice is expected of women, as are sexual "purity" prior to marriage and marital fidelity. And yet the narrative begins with musings on female desire, as each friend confesses her degree of youthful sexual experimentation. The recurrent references to Edith Wharton's *Summer* place the text in a particular light, especially when considering the conservative cultural context in which Wharton's novel was written. Notions of female desire and sexual freedom haunt the book, which ends with a call for "More life, Emmie! More life!" Nevertheless, French balances the novel precariously between a certain notion of biological determinism and a rejection of it, as she did in *Her Mother's Daughter* (1988). For women's capacity to bear children continues to pose the problem of anatomy as destiny, and French seems to maintain the tension that we both are and are not subject to our bodies.[16] Control over one's own body remains central to feminist demands and in this novel it is perhaps Clea who best expresses this notion, in relation to her affair with Harley Kellog. Women's traditional submission as a class draws the same analogy as in *The Women's Room*, of a victimization similar to that of the Jewish people during the Holocaust with its subsequent shame.[17]

The novel is similar to *The Women's Room* and *Her Mother's Daughter* in its portrait of relations between women of different generations and experience. This element, rare in fiction, becomes central in this novel and is linked to the importance of history and its transmission. Each of the four quite distinct female characters, whose ages range from thirty-something to 76 has a voice in the text, recalling *Our Father*. In fact, the use of several narrators, one of which is dominant and so perhaps closer to the author's own voice, was a device used and appreciated by readers in *The Women's Room* as well.[18] Here Emily may incarnate the composer French had hoped to become.

The relations between these fictional women and the reader may be intimate, for a reader may identify with one or several of the female characters, may know their experience first-hand, may empathize. Although the narrator does not here directly address the reader as in *The Women's Room*, their proximity is a given.[19] The style thus imitates informal conversation, easy dialogue among women friends, as in previous novels. Talk is not always grammatical and is often punctuated with the emotion of the speaker, laughter or tears, anger or tenderness. At Jenny's home as the novel opens, the women agree on the beauty of their surroundings with "little sighs and cries, faintly uttered yesses, contented smiles, creating a music of acceptance." French uses punctuation subjectively in order to reproduce an effect of spontaneous oral communication. When the women gather in Alicia's kitchen after Emily's successful May concert, French imagines crisscrossing conversations, which come to a sudden halt at the arrival of their musician friend. They spontaneously form a circle of praise to honor her. On the surface their banter may seem superficial, but the plot moves forward with these exchanges, as they learn about Emily's estrangement from Clea and the young woman's current life. Similarly, the excitement generated by Steven's acceptance of Steve, by Emily's reconciliation with Clea, and Clea's relationship with Hallie appears in the text as a series of exclamations, rhetorical and tag questions. Throughout the text, French reproduces the rhythms and sounds of their chatter with such words as "buzzing," "crowed," "whooped," and "brayed"—all animal-like references.

As in French's earlier novels, the narrative's overall progression is towards individual empowerment attained through the dialectical interaction of self and other, and of the self in relation to the group of diverse women friends. Jenny's sense of dread and inexplicable fatigue, her sense of not belonging or of being watched can be understood in relation to Tim, who is older, successful, and who supports her financially. As she resolves her dilemma over whether to have a child, she gains in self-assuredness and is able to confront Tim and negotiate a solution with him. Similarly, the support of friends aids Alicia in addressing the issue of Steven's estrangement from their homosexual son. Both Alicia and Emily, suffering from what Sandra Gilbert and Susan Gubar named "the anxiety of authorship," find their friends' encouragement invaluable.[20]

The essential function of friends in this text, of course, recalls the author's cancer memoir, *A Season in Hell* (1998), in which a "coven" of women accompanied the writer through her own healing process. It also recalls the vital support networks Mira could count on in *The Women's Room* as well as the caring sisterhood of *Our Father*. This evolution towards greater self-empowerment occurs as well in relation to women's creativity, for each requires social recognition of her work in order to validate it. Despite this continuity, *In the Name of Friendship* represents a significant change in French's view, as if her feminist prism had slightly refocused its angle of vision to revise certain ideological components.

In contrast to the rather two-dimensional men of *The Women's Room*, the men of this novel appear fully human.[21] Less traditionally masculine, they are allowed to feel, to fail, and to cry. French's compassionate portrayal of at least four male characters communicates a sense that they are "understood" and "loved." Charley, for example, may seem weak and ineffectual, indeed his son Parrish sees him as such, but Maddy understands how he was pressed into becoming a lawyer, a soldier, a husband, and father in order to fulfill social expectations.

One may read French's text as an indictment of traditional masculinity as well as femininity. Taught to compete, to deny their emotions, forced to join the system and even to kill, men may live lives of "quiet desperation." Tim's misogynous artist friends are poignant counterpoints to the other male characters. But their caricatured behavior in the novel functions as a catalyst for significant change: Jenny is shocked by their treatment of her and confronts Tim with rage. The resolution of the couple's conflict is not immediate, but what resolution is? French realistically portrays the negotiations necessary for a couple to resolve a problem. In fact, the description of the process of change which occurs in the behavior of Tim and Steven is new in French's fictional world. Tim moves towards accepting Jenny's desire for a child and even looks forward to being a father, and Steven accepts criticism of his own behavior at work or at a party and learns to embrace his son's homosexuality. Further, Parrish, albeit on his deathbed, realizes his errors as a father and husband and attempts to make amends to his son. Compared with the earlier evolved male of *Her Mother's Daughter*, Toni, here the changes seem to stick. There is no apparent regression. French's portrayal of men as both more human and capable of change signals her belief in the human capacity for change.

In addition, I might note that the dynamics of change between the sexes is a dialectical one. Male misbehavior incites women to make changes and women encourage men to make other changes. Thus, the heterosexual couples imagined by French in this novel function better than in any previous fiction, undoubtedly because she imagines the possibilities of new masculine behavior. Emily tells Clea, for example, that young men today, raised by feminists, love their children *like mothers*, and Maddy's uncle Philip, to take another example, learns to appreciate and love his great-grandchildren in his old age, to have "fun" with them, a new concept.

Different also from earlier novels, here French reflects on generational change, a leitmotif that opens the narrative and reappears continually throughout. She is thinking of the generations that have followed her own: those of her children and grandchildren. She suggests that "Women today have it better than we ever did," whether in relation to sexuality, housework, men, or motherhood. These experiences are indeed different for each generation; Hence, the lessons learned by one do not necessarily hold true for the one that follows. Whereas second-wave feminists, for example, rejected imposed and restrictive maternity, French creates Clea, a young woman, mothering in new ways and according to a more autonomous lifestyle. Thus, French replaces a certain knee-jerk reaction against becoming a mother early in life with contingency. Similarly, while second-wavers applauded the selfless generosity of women who devoted their time and energy to helping other women in need, young feminists in the novel like Hallie and Clea reclaim the right to receive appropriate compensation for work done. In French's novel, it is acceptable for Clea and Hallie to move to New York and live comfortably, just as it is for Emily to pursue her musical vocation, refusing to marry or bear children. French thus revises the notion of self sacrifice, and the idea that life is "something to be endured while doing your duty," so long associated with traditional femininity. Instead, she proposes that life is "something to feel and know, to experience and enjoy." Along with the concept of contingency she offers pleasure as a guiding principle for life. And yet, although laudable in a context of American puritanism, I think it is important to note that the pursuit of pleasure is really only applicable in a society of affluence, and, of course, French is quite aware of the world outside the boundaries of the novel. The author knows that, while younger generations of men and women have changed and have more choices, these possibilities ring hollow when extended outside the privileged. American middle class. Still, the text communicates an authentic optimism for the future and a contagious creative energy.

Although different generations of women in this novel may experience sexuality or motherhood in very different ways, French underlines the importance of transmitting history or the experiences of mothers and grandmothers, from one generation to another.[22] French's protagonists worry that future generations will not be able to read literature of the past two centuries since they cannot, for example, comprehend the importance of conserving a woman's virginity prior to marriage. Because young women have had access to contraception and abortion for two generations now, they may not be able to comprehend their grandmother's fear of pregnancy. French situates the major generational shift in the radical cultural metamorphosis brought on by the Vietnam War, noting how from this point onward authorities were no longer viewed as always honest or infallible. From this point on, distrust spread, infecting even the relations between parents and their children. In this novel, these changes affect fathers and sons as the younger men reject war, traditional gender arrangements, and many American values. French fills the pages of her text with lessons on the past, literary and political, bending time in the novel to bring history to the present where one may better understand and learn from it. As in the earlier essay, *Beyond Power* (1985), French notes that the United States may be sliding into a fascist state; explains her ideal of anarchy; posits the nonexistence of God; and deplores censorship of political dissent in the American media. To further underline the vital role of history, she depicts a historian at work in the character of Alicia, researching the diaries and letters of Steventon's female ancestors.

The final feature which distinguishes this novel from Marilyn French's preceding texts is the foregrounding of female artistic activity. Whether in painting, writing, or music, the creative pursuits of these fictional women become central to their lives and to the text itself. Foremost is, of course, Emily's music, and Marilyn French draws on her own musical knowledge in the sketching of her portrait and includes a bit of her own music as well. The character is also appropriately named after Emily Dickinson who never married. French defines her character's sensibility through musical scores in the text itself, the notes replacing letters, musical phrases replacing verbal ones. Emily thinks in terms of music. Interested in the immaterial, and the invisible, she is intuitive and highly sensitive. We share in the creative process as she composes, takes notes, revises, and rewrites. Interestingly, one of her projects is an opera that revises the tragic story of Sylvia Plath and Ted Hughes, since she imagines them each singing their own theme in first a different, then in the same key. Ultimately, she "publishes" her symphony, with accompanying fears, doubts, and glowing pride.

Similarly, Alicia, despite uncertainty as to her own worth as a researcher, intellectual, and writer, comes into her own as a writer. The proof of her capacities is in her book, a significant contribution to local women's history. A financial advance from her publisher gives her a degree of financial independence, straightens her back, provides her with private work space, and equalizes her relationship with her husband. French evokes here Virginia Woolf's *A Room of*

One's Own, which underlined the importance of material conditions for a woman writer.[23]

Jenny also grows as an artist, struggling at first with various male masters, from Picasso to De Kooning, as well as her own husband, deciding what she can and cannot borrow, defining her practice within but also against the tradition. Her painting of the female quartet of friends portrays each as unique and yet unified by the design. Jenny's opening at the gallery celebrates her talent and the friendships.

•

The novel was originally published in Holland in the Dutch language as *In naam van de vriendschap* (Amsterdam: Meulenhoff, 2002). This decision seems to have been the result of changes in the publishing industry in the United States and of Marilyn French's popularity in the Netherlands.[24] On the one hand, the repressive political climate in the United States and the relative absence of women editors who knew her work evidently made it difficult for her to publish the novel in her own country. On the other hand, the Dutch have always appreciated her work. *In naam van de vriendschap* was a bestseller, making the top ten lists for several weeks, and it sold well enough to justify three reprints in the three years that followed its initial publication.[25]

Cassandra-like, Marilyn French has throughout her career in her various writings called for change and then called for it again. In her eyes, literary conventions and what the reading public is ready to accept do not sufficiently reflect feminist principles. In French's introduction to the 1993 edition of The Women's Room the author offers a mixed interpretation of the republication of her groundbreaking novel:

> Its acceptance in 1977 by mainly male publishers in twenty-odd countries suggested that the world was open to change. . . . Its re-publication in 1993 is also deeply gratifying, yet it suggests that the world has not changed that much, for the book still reflects many women's reality. Real success for the author of *The Women's Room* would be a world in which the novel was incomprehensible because women and men had found a way to live together in felicity. That day remains

> distant and until it arrives, writers must persist in breaking down conventions to show the reality of women's lives, their various characters and their diverse experience, until it undoes centuries of false thinking about women (French 1993, xiv).

Change may be slow to come, but Marilyn French remains optimistic, hopeful that through women writing, conventions in literature and life will be change for the better. In *In the Name of Friendship* Marilyn French once again describes the realities of some women's changed lives, once more asking that all women share, as Clea urges aunt Emily, "More life, Emmie! More life!"

Stephanie Genty
February 2006
Evry, France

Acknowledgements

I wish to thank Floortje Damming of the Institut Néerlandais in Paris for her help in locating materials in Dutch as well as Klasien Boulloud for her help in translating these materials. Special thanks to Marilyn French for her faith in me and to Anjoli Roy and Florence Howe for their assistance in the preparation of this afterword.

Notes

The Marilyn French quotation that opens this afterword was taken from Gale Research Company, *Contemporary Authors*, Vols. 69–72 (Detroit, Mich.: Gale Research, 1978), 249.

1. The biographical information is based on several sources: Vineta Colby, *World Authors, 1975–1980* (New York, NY: Wilson, 1985), 253–256; Gale Research Company, *Contemporary Authors*, Vols. 69–72 (Detroit, Mich.: Gale Research, 1978), *Contemporary Authors* New Revision Series, Vols. 3 (1981), 31 (1990) (Detroit, Mich.: Gale Research); Gale Research Company, *Contemporary Literary Criticism*, Vols. 10 (1979), 18 (1981), 60 (1990) and 177 (2004) (Detroit, Mich.: Gale Research); *The Feminist Companion to Literature* in English, edited by Virginia Blain, Patricia Clements, and Isobel Grundy (London: Batsford, 1990), 398–9.

2. In an interview in June 2005, French talked about how publishers have found her difficult to categorize since she does not limit her writing to one genre. Instead of reading her various works as facets of a coherent and holistic feminist vision, critics have sometimes used traditional criteria and missed their significance.

3. See for example French's "Women in Language," in *Soundings* 59, no. 3 (Fall 1976), 329–44, which appeared in the wake of the groundbreaking study by Robin Lakoff, *Language and Woman's Place* (New York, NY: Harper, 1975) and treats some of the same points but based on French's own research; or her introduction to Edith Wharton's *Summer* (New York, NY: Berkeley, Calif., 1981, 1917) or *The House of Mirth* (London: Associated University Press, 1981), among others.

4. In her review of Margaret Atwood's *Life Before Man* (London: J. Cape, 1980), French applauds the Canadian author's criticism of the destruction of nature and human life as well as her vision of a more humane life. She qualifies Christa Wolf as "the poet of starvation," whether for food, love, or truth—hungers which spring from a form of spiritual deprivation. French is also sensitive to Woolf's portrayal of "the difficulty of becoming oneself in a world that demands conformity . . . of living with others when one is unlike them and refuses to hide that . . ." ("Spouses and Lovers"). In her introductions to the novels of Esther Broner, French stresses the importance of "the realm of the necessary" and notes that feminists have been attempting to fill this gap in our culture (1975, 1978).

These points recall her analysis of *Ulysses* (1946) and *Finnegans Wake* (1939), in which French interpreted Joyce's concentration on the concrete, the body in particular, rendering his work more fully "human." See in particular "Joyce and Language" (1982) and "Silences: Where Joyce's Language Stops" (1992) in which French surveys the author's four major works. According to French, Joyce moved toward a worldview that was both anarchic and even feminist in many respects, anarchy being understood as a lack of dominance or hierarchy. French writes: "The multiple perspectives in Joyce's work point emphatically to anarchic form; and Joyce's silences, his large omissions, point emphatically to the absence of the traditional Father—that is, of a principle of transcendent meaning, male superiority and hierarchy. Joyce appears to be insisting on a world view that is anarchic, non-patriarchal" (*The Book as World* 1992, 48). To support her argument, French points out that, in both *Ulysses* and *Finnegans Wake*, Joyce mocks traditional definitions of Man and redefines him by rooting the human in the body. The functions and needs of the body come to the fore in these two texts and are intransigent.

5. See French's "Star of Stage, Screen and Sexism," a review of *Cleopatra: Histories, Dreams and Distorsions* by Lucy Hughes-Hallet (1990), as well as her introduction to *Almost Touching the Skies: Women's Coming of Age Stories*, edited by Florence Howe and Jean Casella (New York, NY: Feminist Press, 2000) and finally "The Great Chain" (1991).

6. In her address to the seventh George Sand conference held at Hofstra University in 1986, she said, "I believe that all literature is political, even literature that does not touch apparent political issues, and that style and form as well as content reflect political thinking—that they are all connected, inextricable even" ("The Great Chain" 991, xxvii).

7. In her article "Is There a Feminist Aesthetic?" (1990, reprinted 1993), Marilyn French outlined the "feminist aesthetics" which inform her writing. They include a "feminist perspective" and an endorsement of female experience. The former implies a narrative point of view that "penetrates, demystifies or challenges patriarchal ideologies." Partly French reverses patriarchal views, implying that women are at least equal to men, that transcendence is illusory, the pursuit of power a doomed enterprise, that the human is made up of body and emotion as well as mind and spirit, and that we are all part of a community, connected to others as well as to nature (70). She proposes that writers move beyond thinking that has divided human experience into two unequal gender categories: "It is essential for the healing of a sick world that this division be mended" (72). Accessibility is also important, which is why French consistently chooses a language and style that aim at comprehensibility, whether in fiction or nonfiction: "I see the reader as an equal, who will out of friendship try as hard to understand the narrator's reality as she to express it. I believe that a healthy literature, one that attempts to create a healthy culture, is inclusive—of everyone—implicitly or explicitly" (75).

8. Such a program recalls, of course, the writings of Nancy Chodorow, Carol Gilligan, and Sara Ruddick, among other contemporaries of French. See, for example, Nancy Chodorow, *The Reproduction of Mothering: Psychoanalysis and the Sociology of Gender* (Berkeley, Calif.: University of California Press, 1978), Carol Gilligan, *In a Different Voice. Psychological Theory and Women's Development* (Cambridge, Mass.: Harvard University Press, 1982), and Sara Ruddick, *Maternal Thinking: Toward a Politics of Peace* (Boston, Mass.: Beacon Press, 1989).

9. Contemporary novels which had a similar impact on readers were Joan Didion's *Play It as It Lays* (Harmondsworth, England: Penguin, 1973), Rita Mae Brown's *Rubyfruit Jungle* (Plainfield, Verm.: Daughters Inc., 1973), Erica Jong's *Fear of Flying* (New York, NY: Holt, 1973), Marge Piercy's *Small Changes* (New York, NY: Fawcett, 1974) and *Woman on the Edge of Time* (New York: Fawcett, 1976), and Lisa Alther's *Kinflicks* (Harmondsworth, England: Penguin, 1977).

10. My *Summer with George* may be compared to Doris Lessing's *Love, Again* published in the same year. Indeed, as Roberta Rubenstein demonstrates in her article "Feminism, Eros and Coming of Age," *Frontiers* 22:2 (June 2001): 1–19, reprinted in *Contemporary Literary Criticism*, Vol. 177, edited by Janet Witlee (Detroit: Gale Research, 2004: 151–161), both writers depict an independent older woman's struggle with Eros and Thanatos. Referring to Simone de Beauvoir as well as a number of writings by second-wave feminist theorists, Ruben-

stein notes that growing old is more problematic for women than for men, since it is associated with decline rather than "maturity" or "ripening." Betty Friedan, in *The Fountain of Age* (New York: Simon and Schuster, 1993), likened it to a time-advanced version of "the problem that has no name" since, once again, there are no scripts available for women to draw inspiration from. French and Lessing both provide such scripts, while they also acknowledge the realities of "longing and loss and the terrible knowledge of the impossibility of satisfaction" (*My Summer With George* 1996, 242).

11. See Arthur Rimbaud's *Une saison en enfer* (Paris: Gallimard, 1873; 1999). *A Season in Hell* was widely reviewed in literary and medical journals, among them Mary Margaret McCabe, "Laughing In Its Face," *Times Literary Supplement* (6 November 1998), 28; Kathleen Woodward, "In Sickness and Health," *Women's Review of Books* 16:4 (January 1999): 2–4, *Los Angeles Times Book Review* (27 September 1998), 11; *British Medical Journal* 318:7179 (30 January 1999), 336; and Leslie Chess Feller, *New York Times Book Review* (18 October 1998), 28.

12. In her discussion of "female subjectivity," necessarily simplified here, Kristeva underlines the concepts of repetition and eternity. While the first implies cycles, gestation, and the recurrence of a biological rhythm, which conforms to that of nature, the second denotes a monumental temporality, all-encompassing and infinite, which is maternal in character. See Julia Kristeva, "Women's Time," in *Feminist Theory: A Critique of Ideology*, edited by Nanner O. Keohane and Michelle Zimbalist Rosaldo (Brighton, England: Harvester, 1982).

13. Marilyn French bases these elements of her novel on such texts as Riane Eisler's *The Chalice and the Blade* (San Francisco: Harper Collins, 1987), and Marija Gimbutas' *The Gods and Goddesses of Old Europe* (Berkeley: University of California Press, 1974), among others which served French in her work, *Beyond Power*, chapter 1 on Matricentry, for example.

14. In this novel, French once again opposes "feminine" and "masculine" aesthetics, and characteristically links art with its social and moral implications. Even in *The Women's Room*, the Harvard group mused on the organization of the ideal community and its circular, chaotically-ordered architecture. See Val's description of Spanish villages in chapter 10 of Part V. The character Dolores in French's *The Bleeding Heart* also considers the arrogance of masculine imagination in literature and architecture. See the first section of Chapter 8 for her views on Versailles. In *Her Mother's Daughter* Anastasia reflects on the evolution of her vision as a photographer from male ("shooting grandiose structures") to female ("the private, the daily, the small acts that make up the texture of life"). See Chapter XIV in Part 3.

15. Marilyn French provided me with this information. Personal communication (e-mail message dated 3 December 2005).

16. Early on in the novel, in Chapter 4, French has Steven's psychiatrist colleague Marisa exclaim, "You claim for yourself a superiority based merely on

your anatomy which, whatever Freud wrote, is not destiny now if it ever was!" Maddy, on the other hand, in chapter 6, has the following thoughts on motherhood when she learns she is pregnant with her fourth child: "She told him (Charley) and resigned herself to never having a life of her own, to following her mother and her mother before her in an infinite line of self-sacrificing, hard-working women whose destinies were indeed their anatomies." The tension is further underlined by French's position that having children is the most important of human activities. Throughout the novel, however, French stresses the fact that women today have more choices. The resolution of the tension lies, among other things, in a more equitable sharing of childrearing and housework.

17. Neva expresses the shame of belonging to a people of victims, and daughter Alicia makes the link with her own very "feminine" helplessness, in chapter 9. In *The Women's Room*, Mira equates her hatred of men with her hatred of Nazis, equating woman with Jewish victims: "Like a Jew released from Dachau, I watch the handsome young Nazi soldier fall writhing to the ground with a bullet in his stomach and I look briefly and walk on. . . . Forever and forever I will hate Nazis even if you can prove to me that they too were victims" (290). French has repeatedly compared patriarchy to the Nazi regime and men to Nazi soldiers in other novels. Other contemporary women writers have used the same analogy, just as they have used parallels with African Americans. See for example *Long Division* by Anne Richardson Roiphe (New York: Simon & Schuster, 1972). Finally, it is worth noting that Betty Friedan in *The Feminine Mystique* (New York: Norton, 1963; 1986) had also used the comparison. Her twelfth chapter is entitled "Progressive Dehumanization: The Comfortable Concentration Camp," which refers to the situation of suburban American women in the 1950s.

18. French enters the minds of male characters too, as she has previously. Here, most notably, the thoughts of Parrish are transcribed as he lies dying of cancer. See chapters 22 and 23.

19. Readers will recall the narrator's interpolations in *The Women's Room*, such as the following concerning her shallow male characters: "You think I am making him up. You think, Aha! A symbolic figure in what turns out to be after all an invented story. Alack, alas. I wish he were. Then he would be my failure, not life's" (283). Or "You think I hate men. I guess I do, although some of my best friends. . . . I don't like this position. I mistrust generalized hatred" (289).

20. See Sandra Gilbert and Susan Gubar's *Madwoman in the Attic. The Woman Writer and the Nineteenth–Century Literary Imagination* (New Haven: Yale University Press, 1979). In the first two chapters the authors discuss literary paternity, authorship, and authority, demonstrating that the woman writer, convinced she had no precursors and constricted by current definitions of appropriate feminine behavior, was plagued by "a radical fear that because she can never become a "precursor" the act of writing will isolate or destroy her."

21. Personally, I would argue that French has always sought to portray men as she observes them in society, as caricatures of conventional masculinity, brought up according to restrictive notions of the masculine gender, often suffering from the imposed behavior, despite the fact that they benefited overall from the patriarchy. See for example Victor of *The Bleeding Heart* or Toni of *Her Mother's Daughter*. Critics, on the other hand, derided her portrayal of men in *The Women's Room* and no subsequent novel has really been able to shake the critics' first impression.

22. Marilyn French noted in a personal communication that "the many references to Emily Dickinson, her poems, and mention of her birthday, reinforce this theme of continuity among women over generations. Along with the reference to Eleanor (of Aquitaine). . . . So the large theme, hovering behind the action is a centuries old passing on of certain values and traditions by women" (e-mail dated 3 December 2005).

23. See Virginia Woolf's *A Room of One's Own* (London: Grafton Books, 1929; 1977).

24. Personal communication, Interview, New York, 19 June 2005.

25. See Tomas Ross, "Top 10 Verschenen. *In naam van de vriendschap* van Marilyn French, *De Pjotr Story* van Aat Ceelen . . ." *Elsevier* 58: 38 (21 September 2002): 110–111. In the *NRC Handelsbad* weekend edition of 14–15 September 2002: 59, the novel appears in fifth position.

Bibliography of Marilyn French

Compiled by Stephanie Genty

Fiction

The Women's Room. 1977. New York: Harcourt, 1978.

The Bleeding Heart. 1980. London: Abacus, 1987.

Her Mother's Daughter. 1987. London: Pan, 1988.

Our Father. London: Hamish Hamilton, 1994.

My Summer with George. London: Penguin Books, 1996.

Nonfiction

Memoirs

A Season in Hell. A Memoir. New York: Alfred A. Knopf, 1998.

Sociological and Historical Essays

Beyond Power. On Women, Men and Morals. 1985. London: Abacus, 1988.

Women in India. New York: UN Publications, 1990.

The War Against Women. London: Hamish Hamilton, 1992.

From Eve to Dawn. A History of Women. Volumes 1–2: Origins. Toronto: McArthur & Co., 2002.

From Eve to Dawn. A History of Women. Volume 3: Infernos and Paradises. Toronto: McArthur & Co., 2003.

Introductions

The House of Mirth by Edith Wharton. New York: Berkeley Books, 1981.

Summer by Edith Wharton. New York: Jove Books, 1981.

Her Mothers by Esther Broner. 1975. Bloomington: Indiana UP, 1985: ix–xv.

The Women's Room. 1977. New York: Ballantine, 1993: vii–xiv.

A Weave of Women by Esther Broner. 1978. Bloomington: Indiana UP, 1985: ix–xv.

The Search for Signs of Intelligent Life in the Universe by Jane Wagner. New York: Harper and Row, 1986.

Almost Touching the Skies. Women's Coming of Age Stories. Eds. Florence Howe and Jean Casella. New York: The Feminist Press, 2000: xi–xviii.

Articles

"Macbeth at My Lai: A Study of the Value Structure of Shakespeare's *Macbeth.*" *Soundings* 58 (1975): 54–68.

"The Voices of the Sirens in Joyce's *Ulysses.*" *The Journal of Narrative Technique* 7:1 (Winter 1977): 1–10.

"Missing Pieces in Joyce's *Dubliners.*" *Twentieth Century Literature* 24 (1978): 443–72.

"Joyce and Language." *The James Joyce Quarterly* 19:3 (Spring 1982): 239–56.

"Women in Joyce's Dublin." Proceedings of Ninth International James Joyce Symposium, Frankfurt, 1984. *James Joyce: The Augmented Ninth.* Ed. Bernard Benstock. Syracuse: Syracuse UP, 1988: 267–72.

"The Great Chain." Special Address presented at Seventh George Sand Conference, 16–18 October 1986, Hofstra University, Hempstead, New York. In *The World of George Sand.* Eds. Datlof, Nathalie, Jeanne Fuchs, and David A. Powell. New York: Greenwood, 1991: xxi–xxvi. (*Contributions in Women's Studies*, No. 122).

"Muzzled Women." *College Literature* 14:3 (Fall 1987): 219–29.

"Is There A Feminist Aesthetic?" *Hypatia* 5:2 (Summer 1990). Reprinted in *Aesthetics in Feminist Perspective*. Eds. Hilde Hein et Carolyn Korsmeyer. Bloomington: Indiana UP, 1993: 68–76.

"Silences: Where Joyce's Language Stops." *The Languages of Joyce: Selected Papers from the 11th International James Joyce Symposium, Venice 12–18 June 1988*. Eds. Rose Maria Bollettieri Bosinelli, C. Marengo Vaglio, and Chr. van Boheemen. Philadelphia: John Benjamins, 1992: 41–53.

"On Danis Rose's Edition of *Ulysses*." *James Joyce Quarterly*. 35: 4 and 36: 1 (1998): 830–834.

Literary Criticism

Books

Shakespeare's Division of Experience. New York: Summit, 1981.

The Book As World. James Joyce's Ulysses. 1976. London: Abacus, 1982.

Book Reviews

"Spouses and Lovers." Review of *Life Before Man* by Margaret Atwood. *The New York Times Book Review* 3 February 1980: 1+.

"Heinrich von Kleist Could Not Last." Review of *No Place On Earth* by Christa Wolf. *The New York Times Book Review* 10 October 1982: 11+.

"More Than the Sum of Her Sex Life." Review of *George Sand: A Brave Man; The Most Womanly Woman* by Donna Dickenson and of *Marianne* by George Sand. *The New York Times Book Review* 17 July 1988: 3.

"This Is How It Is for Us!." Review of *Russian Women Studies. Essays On Sexism in Soviet Culture* by Tatyana Mamonova. *The New York Times Book Review* 24 September 1989: 18.

"Star of Stage, Screen and Sexism." Review of *Cleopatra: Histories, Dreams and Distorsions* by Lucy Hughes–Hallet. *The Women's Review of Books*. November 1990: 16–7.

Other Articles and Letters

"Women in Language." *Soundings* 59 (1976): 329–44.

"The Fearful and the Innocent." *Horizon* 21: 1 (January 1978): 30.

"Symposium: I Would Like To Have Written . . ." Famous authors reveal which books they would most like to have written. *The New York Times Book Review* 6 December 1981: 7+.

"The Book That I'm Writing." Nine prominent authors report on their work in progress. *The New York Times Book Review* 12 June 1983: 12–13.

"Advance To Go, Collect $200: A Tract For Our Times." *Southern Humanities Review* 18:2 (Spring 1984): 151–63.

"Personal and Political." Letter. *The New York Times Book Review* 1 April 1984: 25+.

"Are Women Naturally Dominant?." Letter. *The New Times Book Review* 16 September 1984: 39.

"A Writer's Symposium: Writing in an Era of Feminism." Writers answer a questionnaire. *American Book Review* 6:5–6 (1984): 3–4.

"The Emancipation of Betty Friedan." In *Fifty Who Made The Difference*. New York: Villard Books, 1984: 437–446.

"Women and Power." Reply to Lawrence Stone's critique of *Beyond Power. The New Times Book Review* 21 July 1985: 25.

"Self-Respect: A Female Perspective." *The Humanist* 46 (November/December 1986): 18–23.

"Symposium." Contemporary American Fiction. Pt. 1. *Michigan Quarterly Review* 26:4 (Fall 1987): 732–5.

"Men, Women and Armageddon." Letter. *The New York Times Book Review* September 1990: 42.

"A Choice We Never Chose." *The Women's Review of Books* July 1991: 31–2.

"The Masculine Mystique." *Literary Review* 36 (Fall 1992): 17–27.

"Where Do We Stand on Pornography?." *Ms.* January–February 1994: 32–41.

"Treason, Abortion and Women's Rights." *Free Inquiry. The International Secular Humanist Magazine*. 18: 3 (1998): 10.

"Fifties: Endless Summer." *Ladies Home Journal* 117: 5 (May 2000): 124.

"Woman's Fate." *Free Inquiry. The International Secular Humanist Magazine*. 20: 4 (2000): 32–34.

Works Under a Pseudonym

Solwoska, Mara. "Death by Water." *The Ohio Review* 16: 3 (Spring 1975): 80–93.

The Feminist Press at the City University of New York is a nonprofit literary and educational institution dedicated to publishing work by and about women. Our existence is grounded in the knowledge that women's writing has often been absent or underrepresented on bookstore and library shelves and in educational curricula—and that such absences contribute, in turn, to the exclusion of women from the literary canon, from the historical record, and from the public discourse.

The Feminist Press was founded in 1970. In its early decades, the Feminist Press launched the contemporary rediscovery of "lost" American women writers, and went on to diversify its list by publishing significant works by American women writers of color. More recently, the Press's publishing program has focused on international women writers, who remain far less likely to be translated than male writers, and on nonfiction works that explore issues affecting the lives of women around the world.

Founded in an activist spirit, the Feminist Press is currently undertaking initiatives that will bring its books and educational resources to under-served populations, including community colleges, public high schools and middle schools, literacy and ESL programs, and prison education programs. As we move forward into the twenty-first century, we continue to expand our work to respond to women's silences wherever they are found.

For a complete catalog of the Press's 250 books, please refer to our web site: www.feministpress.org.